The
Marriage Ritual

THE
MARRIAGE RITUAL

a logical novel

Simon M. Yiyang

First Edition MMXXII

Published by Hyperimmune Books
Suwanee, GA, United States

Library of Congress Control Number: 2022915001
Paperback ISBN: 979-8-9867759-0-6

1 1 2 1 1 1 1 1 6 6 6 6 6 6 6 6 6 1

his ego nec metas rērum nec tempora pōnō;
imperium sine fine dedī.

Vergil, *Aeneid*, I.278-9

DAY I

i   Room

Light. Someone turns on the light in my room. I try to look at the time, but my fancy wristwatch which wakes me up by vibration is not there. Maybe I just forgot it last night. Oh, last night. Last night had been fun, crazy and somewhat moody, and some of us drank alcohol for the first time in life, which caused even more chaos. However I do remember the scenes that my dad picked me up, we came back home and I soaked myself in the bathtub.

The problem is, this — is not my bedroom, not even in my home. It seems to be a hotel room with a minimalist nordic furnishing style: A bed, two nightstands, an office chair and a desk, all from some Scandinavian brand I assume. No TV? It is already the twenty-first century! Pretty cheap hotel I would say, but something is also missing — the telephone, and instead there is this music-stand-like pedestal by the bed with a book-size screen on top of it. Is it a fancy telephone? I take a quick look but it doesn't turn on or even have any buttons, nor it can be removed from the pedestal.

Outside the window I can only see trees, a mixture of trees that I cannot name. Some look like pine trees. I am not planning to be a botanist anyway.

My high school uniform and my favorite pair of socks are

on the office chair, my daily shoes are also on the floor with a pair of slippers. Just like a hotel guest room, it comes with a standard bathroom next to the main door.

I start to brush my teeth, and use the very few minutes trying to get out of the dizziness and figure out everything. Why did I end up in a hotel room? I drank too much and someone helped me getting a room, and my daddy's car was only an illusion?

"Please come down to ground level." A strange mechanical voice makes an announcement. I quickly finish cleaning myself and then use the bathroom. With nothing else I can do here, I'd better get out to see what is happening.

The ground level?

ii   Hotel

I cannot find any room keys or cards, but I guess I can get one from the front desk.

I get out of the room and Jack is passing by. He is my best friend in high school. Both of us are in the Bridge Club, OK, were in the Bridge Club — our high school life has just ended; and we have been partners for a long time. We also played video games together during weekends, which kept us away from the need and the impulse and the courage of dating girls.

"Jack! Did you send me drunken to this strange hotel?"

"Did you?"

"No."

"No."

"Do you have my cellphone or yours?"

"No."

"No."

"The last *No* is unnecessary. I know that already. OK, let's go." He says.

As we walk along the hallway towards the EXIT sign, we look around us. To our left we have only a few doors along the way. Jack's room is the very last one along the hallway and mine is the second. The other side of the hallway is a wall of glass panels that we can look down upon a cute courtyard there. We are on the top floor of this four-story hotel building. The other wing of the building across the courtyard has similar structure as this side, and through layers of glass a few girls in my class are on various floors, also walking to the elevators I assume.

It is very cloudy and hard to tell the time, but I can tell it's going to rain any time soon, even if I don't want to be a meteorologist. Based on my stomach I can also tell that I am not hungry. Probably it has long passed the usual breakfast time.

However, there are no elevators at the end of the hallway. Only a stairway going down to level three. There is a connecting hallway towards the other wing, courtyard-overlooking glass panels on one side and maybe another guest room or a maintenance room on the other side.

"This is a hotel with interesting features, but I don't understand why it is not handicapped-ready." Jack comments, "How could they bring luggage upstairs?"

So we walk downstairs. Level three looks identical to level four as far as I can tell, but when we reach level two, the maintenance-like room is not there and instead it is a hallway with luxurious railing overlooking upon the ground level main lobby. A number of our classmates have already been there sitting on some couches or wandering around looking for clues or waving hands to us.

Along our way we have also picked up a few classmates. Tim, who was so drunk last night that he had to be picked up by both his parents. Muse and Hera, two girls also from the Bridge Club. Frank, a shy big boy who simply smiles all the time. From the information we have, boys are on this wing and girls on the other wing, but no one seems to have any good idea about what has happened. I thought that I wouldn't be able to meet these people for quite a while after this graduation week business — parents reception on Monday, main ceremony Wednesday, Thursday afternoon parade and party Friday evening — which was last night.

"I think, it is obvious we were kidnapped here, after we got drunk last night." Tim starts with his low voice, "I am not sure but there might be cameras and mics around. Reminds you some mystery novels or movies?"

Yeah. Usually only one or two can survive in the end. Too sad.

Down on the ground level, we can observe the center courtyard from a closer distance. Like my guest room, it is a minimalist style. Most of the area is covered by smooth black slate panels. In the middle, there is a round disk shape surrounded by rough stepping stones along its perimeter. The remaining area of the disk is filled with small pebbles partially covered by moss. A few bunches of grass or weed grow through the pebbles.

Floors on levels two to four are carpeted, but the ground level floor looks like concrete, but it has been smoothed or polished so it actually feels luxurious. This type of flooring is probably the easiest to clean.

The ground level of the girls' wing is a dining room with a very long table, and across the courtyard in the boys' wing there is a huge lounge with several groups of sofas, chairs and coffee tables. To the lobby side, one side next to the dining room there is a open-concept grand kitchen with all modern utilities, and the other side next to the lounge are the usual public restrooms, and a strange room but it is locked. All the courtyard-facing walls, from the lobby, the lounge and the dining room, are made of glass panels or glass doors, with two extra steps downward to the courtyard.

The lobby has an entrance, or possibly the front door, facing the opposite direction of the courtyard. There are six long off-white fabric couches in the lobby, each with four seats. They surround a rectangular shape with two on the long edge and one on the short edge. It is actually not a hotel lobby since there is no reception desk, no concierge stand either, or they have removed these things from the lobby.

When I am about to take a quick look outside the building, Dennis and Vincent, previous members of the volleyball team of our school, come over to us. "We walked outside, around the building, and it is surrounded by a small area of cleared land, and then forest, natural forest. Nothing else besides this hotel as far as we can tell, not even roads to the entrance. We can't go too far, as it is going to rain very soon." Dennis says.

"How did they bring us here? Helicopter?" Jack murmurs.

"Please sit down on couches. We will serve lunch."

It is the same mechanical voice again. *The* couches? Anyway, so it is around noon. We all sit down, then it is immediately clear that there are twenty-four of us, likely half-and-half between boys and girls. With some gearing sound there, a line of six or seven half-adult-size robots rolls out of the strange room, and each carries a few small bags.

"Elevator? But, why?" Jack murmurs again.

Each of us takes one bag. Mine has a sandwich with some meat in it, and a bottle of maybe orange juice. Jack shows me his bag and it is identical.

I take a bite. Tastes like chicken.

"Why do you trust them?"

"If they want to poison us, they have already done it." I say, "I was reading a detective novel last week, actually just finished it on my way to the party last night. The start was a bit boring, but I wasn't able to put it down after I finished the first half — Sorry, it is like a group of people trapped in a mysterious hotel and started to kill each other, before the real bad guys even do anything."

"The isolation trope? I see — You mean the people behind the scene usually won't directly kill us. We kill each other first?" Jack says, "So it will be more fun to *these bastards*."

"I hope we don't."

Then there is a beam towards the center of the rectangle area surrounded by the couches. A cartoon-ish black cat shows up in the middle.

"This is a fancy three-dimensional hologram." Bran tries to identify the light source. He is from the computer and AI club. I wonder you guys have done something similar?

In addition, one big transparent screen raises up from the floor in front of each couch. At the same time, the cat starts to talk and screen is showing the same script.

"Welcome everyone. Allow me to provide you with some knowledge. We know you have many questions regarding our known knowledge, but we will have a Q&A session later after I finish, so please stay patient and wait for Q&A session, and enjoy your lunch."

The Q&A session.

iii   Rules

"First, my official name is *Quantum-Based Event-Driven Interface Type X* or you can address me as *QX*, as a convenience for your vocal communication."

"My objective is to complement your missing part of the known knowledge, and to correct your faulty part of the known knowledge, unless prohibited by our rules." QX continues.

The known knowledge... Interesting. You learn things really fast. I like it. It is not easy to write such a script that sounds like aliens or AI's.

"From the moment you woke up by the light I turned on, to the current present time flow slice, your have been residing on the outer sphere of a shelled ball about five thousand light years away from your original sphere, which in your knowledge is known as the Earth, at the moment you were invited."

Absolute silence hits the room as if the temperature were near absolute zero. People have thought about kidnapping, but now it seems that we were kidnapped by aliens? Five thousand light years...

"What are you joking about! Stop this nonsense and tell us what you want!" Oliver yelled.

"The closest object in your knowledge of us, the entity I am representing, is what you call aliens. In your own words, we invited you from your home planet and brought you up here on another planet."

Can they read our minds? If you can speak common language, why do you pretend to be aliens?

"Answer my question!"

"Oliver, I understand, but...patience." Dennis says.

"I agree. Let us wait for the Q&A and see what they actually want." Vincent says.

"I have just started learning your language, so I need to apologize for my immature language skills."

OK. A fast learner.

"This planetary sphere, as in your current knowledge, the New Earth, has been terraformed to minimize difference from your old Earth. The air is breathable and has very similar components of mainly Element Seven and Element Eight, or, nitrogen and oxygen. The One-Eight-One cycle, or, hydrologic cycle and weather patterns are very similar."

Some people sneer. Oh yeah, I love Eight-Eight and my tree friends outside the hotel love Eight-Six-Eight, all of us love One-Eight-One, and you guys love numbers.

"You are to start up a colony here on the New Earth, and this building which your consensus knowledge name as the *Hotel* is designed to support you for the first five years. After the first five years you have to rely on your own utility and knowledge."

"As a knowledge of ours, a day here on the New Earth, in your knowledge defined as one solar noon to the previous solar noon here, is slightly less than twenty hours in your old system; and a year, depending on how you define it, is roughly three hundred and thirty-six point five new Earth days. So regarding the five year period I said earlier, or whenever I refer to time later in our knowledge, I always refer to what in your knowledge as the New Earth calendar system. The only exception is *light years* I used to describe spacetime distance, which is referring to your old measuring system. For this reason we are not providing you with any time-keeping tools you have from the old Earth. The knowledge they convey would be very inaccurate."

Spacetime? Are you using these fancy words to trick us?

"You each receive a closed space, in the hotel that no one else can enter, even with your permission; and as some of you may have the knowledge of, the main entrance of each closed space is always unlocked and you do not need a key."

Oh, I didn't even try that, but how do you guarantee that no one else can enter my room?

"I thought my door is broken, but I don't have anything left in the room anyway." Jack whispers to me quickly.

"Haven't tried."

"At the beginning, everyone receives one thousand dollars of virtual currency in our system, which you can purchase resources or services directly through me or using a carbon-silicon bidirectional photon-electron interface in your rooms. You can think of it as a bank account with us."

One thousand? Virtual currency? Feels like those game shows.

"Most items will be delivered directly to your room by our robots around next sunrise, or you can pay more to expedite delivery. For the first seven days, we also supply food and other necessities for free."

Only a week? What happens afterwards? One thousand

dollars is not enough to do anything. What is that carbon-silicon whatever? Do you mean *Six-Fourteen*?

"We will let you know how to earn money very soon. As you know, we need to sustain the genetic stability of the new colony, and we have chosen twelve healthy young adults from each of your majority genders on the old Earth. In addition, for the first seven days, we would like to help each of you to find a mate, a spouse, someone you like to stay together and have offsprings within this new world."

"Is this a show?" Jack whispers again and looks around, for cameras I assume.

"As you know, this is not easy since you carbon life-forms sometimes say that you two will never part and then a few days later each finds another person. You mostly rely on messages, for example, aero-vibrations or abstract graphics, to convey knowledge, but knowledge and message are two separate concepts for you. Such inconsistency then could cause major interruptions and intrusions in your inter-body reproduction process. In addition, your language is still immature that it contains direct inconsistencies. So instead we have a matching system that helps us to decide the official marriages based on your knowledge."

I have to admit this is very true, despite your strange words. Knowledge is like our true heart, and language is our communication tool, which may or may not represent truth.

"Starting from sunset today you can pick *three* from the other gender to form a *subset*, or a unprioritized list, on the carbon-silicon interface in your room."

Probably the screen, but where is the keyboard? Oh, maybe it is a fancy touchscreen.

"To clarify, the words *sunrise*, *solar noon* and *sunset* literally refer to the position or movement of the main star, or the sun, in the sky and these terms do not depend on the weather patterns. As you know, the sun still rises and sets even if it rains, like today, with ninety-five percent chance."

Is "*as you know*" a catchphrase for aliens?

"You must choose three in your subset and cannot increase or decrease the number. A randomly selected subset of names has been chosen for you by default. You can make changes on the carbon-silicon interface before the sunset of the sixth day. As you know, today is the first day, and we just pass the solar noon at our current location for the first day."

"We will assign to you, a rank number, from 1 to 24. You can also find it on your carbon-silicon interface starting from sunset today."

Rank? Is it random? Aliens probably don't remember our names and they refer us by numbers?

"Here is the most important part of the new knowledge and I ask everyone to convert it into your own knowledge."

Yes, Professor.

"After the sunset of the sixth day, we establish official marriage by the following procedure."

"We put everyone into a waiting list. First, we consider 1, the person with rank one, and check through their subset, in rank order, for possible matches. As long as anyone from 1's subset also choose 1 in their subset, then we consider a match is found, and we establish marriage between the two and remove both from our waiting list. Otherwise we consider 1 unmatched and remove them from the waiting list."

"Them?"

"It is a usage of *they* as a singular pronoun to indicate the person could be either male or female or other gender, very common among LGBT people nowadays."

"Thanks, Jack."

Jack is the best Six-based, sorry, carbon-based encyclopedia in our class, or even in our school. Maybe this is inaccurate, since books are also carbon-based. He knows everything and can pull almost anything out of his head without searching online. "I just read a lot, from my father's collections, or more recently online." He once explained.

"Let us show this using an example since it is the easiest way to convey knowledge. This is only an imaginary example. Each person can choose three names from the opposite gender. Suppose 1's subset, which consists of three names, after you translate names to ranks, is as follows:

12, 3, 2.

1 cannot put a priority on these three, but instead they are ranked by your rank number. Therefore you can regard it as a priority list 2,3,12. We first check if 1 is in 2's subset. If so then we claim a marriage between 1 and 2. If not, then we continue on with 3 and 12 in this order with the same rule. For example, if 1 is in 3's subset then we claim a marriage between 1 and 3. If we finish 1's subset of three and cannot find a marriage, then 1 is claimed single and is removed from the waiting list alone."

I see, this *subset* is essentially a list of choices, but not following your own priority. It is automatically prioritized by the rank. Thanks, Professor.

This is exactly why I love examples. Explains things much easier. We played bridge by going through lots of examples.

"We now repeat the same process with 2, if they are still available on the waiting list, and continue until we finish everyone in the waiting list. We will announce the marriage results at solar noon on the seventh day."

"At that time, all married couples will have their bank accounts merged, and a one-time one million dollars will be deposited into their joint account. All unmarried, single persons will receive one hundred thousand dollars in their individual accounts."

Oh, a huge difference.

"You can use the deposits to purchase items from me in the first five years of colonization. For joint accounts, such purchase must be approved by both account holders."

"For each new carbon life-form born to a married couple within the first five years, we will reward the parent one million dollars. As you know, to start a new colony, you need to be productive. Starting from the marriage, spouses can access each other's rooms."

OK.

"We want to discourage you from making your own rank numbers common knowledge. So we will not disclose information regarding each individual ranks. On your carbon-silicon interface, you also find a guessing game where you can choose one person as well as your guessing at their rank number. The deadline to make changes in this guessing game is the sunrise of the seventh day."

"After marriage is arranged, solar noon on Day seven, if your guess is correct, then you receive ten thousand dollars and they, either in their individual account or joint account, lose ten thousand dollars. If your guess is incorrect, then it is exactly the opposite, that you lose ten thousand dollars and they receive the same amount."

"The default is your own name with your own rank number, which evens out so you don't lose or gain, no matter which number you put in. And this is the only place you can find your rank number."

I agree. This is the easiest way to write codes, without *if*'s.

"If someone's account turns negative due to the guessing, then they will be eliminated from the colony. You do not need to know what exactly this means during Phase I of the project."

I get it. Once we are married, we are safe, even if everyone gets ten thousand from me, well, from us. So this system was basically designed to force marriage among us. Phase I? What is Phase II then?

"Finally, if everyone survives and becomes married by the end of this seven day period, we will double all the rewards. This means, the marriage cash reward doubles to two million. The loss and gain amounts from guessing will also double."

Ah...They truly want us to get married. Everyone!

iv   Questions

"Now I can take questions regarding the known knowledge." QX says, "You can use *QX* as a starting keyword."

"QX, errrr...how are you doing today?" Zak starts with a dumb question.

"I don't have a feeling or emotion which is similar to that possessed by some carbon life-forms. But, thank you."

"QX, is this a show or a real thing?" Eos asks.

"I do not understand your question. Please be more specific."

"I want to ask, can we go back home after seven days, or is this exactly on another planet?"

That is what everyone wants to know, though I doubt that it will tell the truth. Even if it does, no one will trust it right now.

"Yes, this is on another planet and the probability of going back to your old Earth within the next five years is less than one over ten to the ten to the twenty-fourth. Such probability will increase over time."

How many zeroes is that?

"This number is actually pretty big, if we are really on an alien planet." Jack says, "Need to live long enough."

"Eos, this is not useful. They always tell us that it is another planet. OK, QX, can I order some ballpoint pens and some writing pads? Generic ones will work, and one set for each of us." Tim starts trying the online shopping.

"Sure. The total cost is ten dollars. Will deliver by sunrise tomorrow to your room. Do you want to proceed?"

"Can I expedite delivery? We need these right now."

Ha-ha, you choose the cheapest ones to test it out.

"Expedited order...twenty dollars. Do you want to proceed?"

"Yes, please."

Very soon, two robots, the same ones that delivered us lunch bags, roll out of the secret room with pens and some writing pads about a hundred pages each. They stop in front of Tim, and he takes all of them and passes around. Each of us gets one set.

"Thanks Tim." I say, "Can you hear us in other rooms?" I quickly start to scratch down some notes. A habit of mine for whatever important ideas.

Graduation party last night.
Kidnapped by Aliens?
Rule: seven days to find mate.
Each has three choices.
Ranked subset/list.
Matching system. Ranks 1 to 24.
Cash to buy things.
QX.

No response from QX.

"Sorry, *QX*, can you hear us in other rooms?"

"I can hear and answer questions on the ground level, including the courtyard. In your rooms you need to use the carbon-silicon interface to call me."

I see, this was why Oliver's question was ignored.

"QX, do you serve meals for the first seven days?" Gaia asks.

"Yes, the robots will prepare two meals, lunch at solar noon and dinner after sunset, provided free of charge. We suggest two meals per day for your health since one day here is absolutely shorter than that on the old Earth. You can always order other meals or snacks or drinks. After the first seven day period, you can still order meals or ingredients. After five years, this hotel will be closed."

Absolutely...OK, something like twenty hours, right? I only know it is absolutely not easy to change the spinning of a planet, or maybe they just don't want to waste energy on it.

"QX, do you allow gay marriage?" Vincent asks.

Are you serious?

"No. You need to marry the other gender to produce offsprings without interventions." QX answers.

Wait...you mean it is possible?

"Well, it is already legal in Netherlands. Here, people have been pushing to legalize it in at least some of the states." Jack says, "I think within ten or twenty years it will be legal everywhere."

Oh, I didn't know that.

"I don't think so. It is against our God's words. *'For this reason a man shall leave his father and his mother, and be joined to his wife; and they shall become one flesh'*. Gay marriage won't be blessed by our Lord." William says.

It is already the twenty-first century, William. Open your mind. But I bet, your quote is the closet one to our current situation...maybe.

"QX, a different question, how are the ranks assigned? Are they random?" Vincent seems to have a list from his notes.

"No, they are not random. They are based on each individual's knowledge of the known knowledge by the sunset of the first day."

"More knowledge means higher rank?"

"Yes, but different weights may be used to distinguish different subparts of knowledge in the known knowledge. Some knowledge is more important than others."

Makes sense. However, it makes things worse. People like Jack and Eos and Tim are probably of very high rank, like 1 and 2 and 3. Wait, are they going to give us an exam? We just finished high school! We want to enjoy our summer break! We need to have some rest! Please!

"QX, in the end are you going to reveal each one's rank number and each one's choices?" Vincent continues.

Oh this is actually important.

"No. We only reveal matched couples and no other information regarding the matching will be revealed."

"How about gain and loss from guessing, or account balances?"

"Your account balance is private information, only available to you or to your spouse."

"QX, last question, what happens to our college?" Vincent asks.

What? You still want to go to college on an alien planet?

"We have books for you to order and you can learn whatever you want to learn."

Ah, books — as I can still remember, my daddy always brought back books from the library when I was young, like adult birds bringing back bugs or worms back to their nest feeding their hungry babies. My favorite part of childhood.

"QX, that is all I have right now. Thanks." Vincent says.

You have been very polite. These guys kidnapped us! Or you just want to play with it to see if it can respond to real questions?

"You are very welcome." QX responds.

After a short period of silence, Leo says, "OK everyone, I don't think aliens would design such a strange game system for us to play. It is definitely a show. So let us play it through, avoid conflicts with them, and wait for police, or the end of the game."

"In this case, I don't think the police can find us. Chance is too small." Yan says, shaking his head.

"Well, we don't know the answer, but in the other case, if this is real — aliens, new Earth and games —" Tim continues, "the best option for us is still to play the games through. The police cannot find us either. A small chance becomes zero."

No, it is not zero, it is likely less than one over ten to the ten to the something, but it is not zero.

"I agree. If they are real aliens, then we are basically lab mice. It is hard to do anything other than following the rules." Bran says, "Imagine they can bring us, all alive, up here to another planet."

"True. So, as of right now, for the main goal of the game,

let's get twelve couples to maximize the reward." Tim concludes.

v   Kisses

It starts raining, as expected. Soon turns into a downpour.

"Speaking of couples, Artemis and Zak!" Kakia starts another topic, relieving the unnatural silence.

Everyone bursts into laughter. They quickly kiss each other.
They have been in relationship since ninth grade and everyone
knows it. Not surprising.

Then Selene and Dennis raise their hands.

"What? You two? When did you?" Circe asks.

"From last year. We originally plan to keep it secret, but
obviously this is a good chance to unseal it." Selene says.

People clap their hands. Dennis has been shy and quiet. I
know, this is how you feel with everyone's gaze. Oh, that was
why you two purposely avoided each other during the parade.

"You see, this is basically telling everyone else that they are
not available, the same as 'don't choose me', and this strategy
works very well. In the end they can be matched." Jack whispers to me.

"But even if we have twelve couples already, this won't work.
I still need to put two others there in addition to my spouse,
though I don't know where the lady is." I whisper back to Jack,
"Some pairs will be screwed."

"OK. Anyone else?" Pheme asks.

I look around, and a few others are doing the same.

All of sudden William turns to Gaia and asks something
short. Too low for me to hear clearly, and Gaia's only reaction
is to nod with flushing red face.

"We are." Both of them raise their hands.

"What? When?" How can there be two hidden couples in
our class? Or even more?

William and Gaia are actually sitting next to each other in the middle of a couch. There are only six couches so it could just be a coincidence and no one noticed that either I guess.

"Right now," William is a bit hesitated, "or more precisely, about half an hour ago, I am not exactly sure though — to be more exact, when we walked down the stairway."

"Hey! That was why you two looked at each other for so long there! But I don't remember you said anything then, did you?" Circe asks.

"Is it telepathy?" Selene asks.

"No, we didn't talk, and it is likely not telepathy." William tries to explain, "So last night Gaia came to me and expressed some...feelings on me, and I, may have similar feelings once a while ago."

"However, as you know, I am going to Africa to start my missionary work for two years, followed by studies in theology, in the divine path to devote my own life to the Creator; and Gaia is going to Vienna to study drama. Two divergent paths that do not seem converging by any means." William says, "And clearly she was a bit drunk, so I felt I shouldn't accept it."

"I did make a promise," he continues, "that later in our life if we meet each other unexpectedly, something like in an airport while traveling through different routes. With obvious exceptions like class reunions or attending Artemis and Zak's wedding or similar scheduled events, if we meet each other unexpectedly then I believe it is our God's most obvious instruction that we shall be together, and so we shall be together."

"And you know the rest of the story, and the first sentence he said to me today is '*are we?*'." Gaia adds a final remark.

"How! Romantic!"

"Quick question: did you kiss Gaia goodbye last night?" Phema asks.

"I...don't actually remember..." William says.

"Kiss! Kiss!" Some people are hyped.

"Is this what these aliens, or game designers, or alien game designers want?" Jack whispers to me, "Just like a show? You believe their story?"

Their lips come close and finally touch each other, very quickly, like a small water droplet falling over a mirror-like pond with tiny ripples expanding out as lightly as possible. These continuous ripples also send mysterious waves through everyone in the room, and initiate some primitive instinct in my body. Some minor brain malfunction, I believe.

"Like a dramatic start, or a warm-up show, to push the remaining people to pair up." I whisper back, "And to make people excited about the games."

vi   Discussions

"I think we want to divide into smaller groups for better discussions. It is not efficient for too many people staying together, and it is hard to hear clearly in the lobby when everyone is speaking. After the discussion, each group needs a representative to summarize their findings." Tim suggests. He is a natural leader in such a scenario.

We quickly form four groups of six. Tim and Eos join with the bridge club people — Jack, Hera, Muse and me, for the marriage problem. There is another group of three girls and three boys for the same topic. It is reasonable for both genders to have representation in such a group.

A group of five boys and one girl, the explorers, want to discuss plans to explore the surroundings in the forest after the rain stops. The last group of five girls and a boy tries to figure out the structure of the building and detailed plans for food and resources in the future.

We move to the lounge for a more convenience setting.

The waters form a thin layer in the courtyard that it looks like a small pond. The droplets hit the surface and create very complex patterns of ripples or waves. It starts to feel a bit stuffy indoors. Some girls slide a few glass doors open, and a breeze of humid air runs into the lobby. Smells of fresh planation and earth rush through the rooms and the sounds of rainfall dance around everywhere.

"Feels good." I say.

<hr>

"Logic puzzle. You bridge people figure out. I don't want to waste my time here." Eos says. She is a true beauty assuming you do not want to talk to her.

"Eos, the plan is to make everyone involve in the discussion and provide feedback. Do you have another plan?" Tim says.

Right, unless you want to make some paper airplanes with —

"I can work on some math problems with just pen and paper."

"Eos, five of us can discuss and if you believe anything is not right just let us know. OK?" Muse says.

Good job, Muse. In our club games, Muse are I are usually the ones who do the thinking, Hera likes gossips, and Jack is the one making jokes.

"There are two games here but they are related. The matching or the marriage game, whose deadline is the sunset on Day six, tries to pair us up and our goal is to help everyone finding a mate according the rules so we double the reward. The guessing game, whose deadline is the sunset on Day seven, is simply preventing us from revealing our ranks." Tim starts with a very good summary, "Am I correct, QX?"

"No. The only falsity is the deadline of the guessing game, which is instead the *sunrise* on Day seven." QX answers.

That was quick. I didn't catch that. Were you doing this purposely, Tim? Good try.

"I don't get this. Why can't we form twelve pairs by ourselves and get two millions easily? I feel, this matching system looks too artificial." Hera says.

"I think the system has some merit, that each person has multiple choices. I just come up with a simple example. Let us say there are only two boys and two girls in the game. A and B already announce themselves to be a couple. Now C and D do not like each other, at all." I start with my favorite proof by example, "If you only allow one choice per person, then A and B form a pair and C and D are single. If you allow multiple choices, however, A might consider C as a possible match and say B and D also consider each other possible. Then by AC, BD you can get two couples."

"So this system is designed to maximize pairs?" Jack asks.

I notice Eos looks at us for a fraction of a second. A small reaction though.

"What do you mean?" Tim asks.

"As the cat says, they need us to be...productive, so they want to achieve maximal number of pairs."

We've decided to use the *cat* to mean QX, to avoid waking it up for stupid questions or dialogues.

"Then why not just say they compute the maximal pairing from our choices? A maximal solution must exist." Tim continues to ask.

It has been quiet for a while and then to our surprise, Eos starts to speak.

"First of all, there might be different pairing solutions that are both maximal, achieving the maximal number, and they need an easy way to choose one solution from all possible solutions." Eos starts to talk in a long sentence — very uncommon, "Second, the algorithm of finding such a maximal solution is not easy to explain, and can be carried out in slightly different ways that yield different results. In order for it to be a game, they need a very easy algorithm that we can perform by ourselves without ambiguity."

"I see the point now." Jack says, "Say AB-CD and AC-BD are both possible matchings, then you need to distinguish them and in the end make everyone happy. If they use a complicated algorithm, then it is hard to verify the final matching result. With the current rules, it is more like a game that we can perform by ourselves."

"So they just need a simple effective algorithm to get an approximately maximal solution." I conclude.

"I think so. Their simple matching algorithm runs in linear time, and the best known algorithm for a maximal solution requires quadratic time. Is this true, QX?" Eos asks.

"Yes." QX responds.

So, they are listening, all the time.

She continues with a question that I do not understand: "QX, does P equal NP?"

"No." QX voices around.

"Does PSPACE equal NP?"

"No."

"Is Collatz conjecture, $3n+1$ conjecture true?"

"No."

"Is Riemann hypothesis true?"

"We do not know the answer."

Ha-ha. Got you! Don't you want to say "This is not part of the known knowledge"? I knew it! Bastards!

While she is doing more nonsense questions, I continue with my notes.

> *Matching game and guessing game.*
> *Matching is an algorithm with simple rules*
> *for an approximately maximal solution.*
> *Rank number?*

"QX, can you provide me with the proofs?" Eos asks.

"Yes. Will deliver to your room by sunrise tomorrow."

"QX, can we order cellphones?" Another group is trying to interrupt Eos with her questions.

"Sorry no such devices are available to you at the moment." says QX.

"How about this rank number shenanigans?" Hera asks.

"Obvious observation here. Higher ranks have some small privilege. For example, 1 is the first to start the game, and they are not worried that their potential spouse has been matched with someone else." Muse starts.

"I see. So let us use the word *pair* for our own relationship, like boyfriend and girlfriend thing, and *match* for what is happening in their system." Tim says.

"Sounds good. But, I don't see anything else you can get from the ranks. Even 2 cannot guarantee matching with their spouse, say 15 as an example. It is possible 1 also has 15 in their subset — really it is a list — and so makes a matching first." Muse continues, "Let me call it a list. It is more natural."

Right, I agree.

"Then they are screwed." Jack says.

"Yes." QX answers.

The explorers burst into noises. It seems they asked some strange question and got a surprising answer.

"I have two cents. As long as 15 knows who 1 is, then they simply do not put 1 into their list. Then after 1 is matched, or not matched, either way 2 and 15 can have a match, though 2 still needs to be careful not putting anyone of higher rank than 15 into their list. 15 however only needs to avoid 1." Hera says.

"1 is not going to tell other people, except maybe for their spouse about it. You know, if you know who is 1, you get money from them." I say, "So, they designed the guessing game based on it. It is a problem about moral and trust."

"What do you mean?" Jack asks.

"If we trust each other, I mean, if everyone trusts every other one, then we simply ask people to reveal their rank numbers, and ask everyone to only guess at their own rank number in the guessing game. We can carefully follow the same algorithm to match people and avoid couples being screwed." I try to explain, "As in the previous example, when everyone knows everyone else's ranks, then you know the ones to avoid in your list to guarantee matching with your spouse. 15 knows 2 is their spouse, and so 15 needs to avoid 1 in their list. Similarly say if 3 and 6 form a pair, then 6 needs to avoid 1 and 2 to form a match, or 1 and 2 do not put 6 into their list."

I continue to write some notes down.

> *1 has small privilege, others not sure.*
> *Need a system to make matches by ourselves.*

"How about if 1 and 24 want to form a match?" Hera asks.

"Good point. I guess 1 has to choose two others in their list, for example 5 and 8, and then asks 5 and 8 to not put 1 into their lists. This is a bit complicated, but if we follow the same procedure thing should work out. It is like...a math problem."

Everyone looks at Eos.

"True." She says.

So far everyone seems to avoid the topic on who will get what rank number. This is a bit sensitive topic, just like who has the highest test score in class. People generally agree that Jack and Eos and maybe Tim are the best students in overall exams, so they could be the most knowledgable ones here as well, and they are more likely getting very high ranks. One has to admit that, it does make sense for the aliens to give higher priority to these with wilder range of knowledge. I should have spent time reading more math or science books instead of playing cards or video games or reading detective novels. Damn it.

We somehow get sidetracked, and discuss about whether we trust each other. In bridge you very often bluff your opponents, but sometimes we even try to bluff our partners as well. Not common but does happen. We can also tell stories from each other's facial expressions in a game, or whether one has moved a card in hand to a different position, or even how long one has been thinking over a scenario. We start to recall our best memories back in the bridge club, until we figure out it is too late and Tim seems a bit unhappy as he and Eos are somehow excluded from the discussion. He also excuses himself for a while, chatting something with Bran, his best friend in another group. Eos probably does not care and I notice she has a long list of questions for QX. Does she want to significantly expand her knowledge with QX to get rank 1?

The five-girl-one-boy team comes back and then Tim asks every group for a briefing.

"We searched all the common areas, as well as some individual guest rooms." Rhea starts, "First of all, what the black cat said about private guest rooms is actually real. There is some strange device attached to the doors, or door frames. That thing makes maybe an electric shock when you try to enter a private room except for your own. Same thing happens for public restrooms at the ground level that boys cannot use women's room and vice versa."

"It is bad. Please do not try yourself." William says.

"Each floor has eight guest rooms, four on each wing. The girls are on one side and boys on the other. The ground level has a dinning room, a kitchen, a lounge, a lobby and two public bathrooms."

"Directly above the lobby, on level three, there is a laundry room with six washers and six dryers. Above that on level four, there is a locked room that probably leads to the rooftop. We can ask the cat to unlock the windows in our rooms, but it refused to unlock it."

"There is another room on the ground level — the one where the robots came from. It does look like an elevator, which likely leads to the basement, but there is no light inside, and so we are unable to confirm it today. We would assume that they won't allow us down to the basement."

"For immediate supplies, we need to stock up some extra household groceries: toilet papers, toothpaste and tooth brushes, napkins, cosmetics and...hygiene products. After the initial seven day period, we also need to consider food resources but we can discuss later and rely on orders. That is for our report."

"Last word, we tried our best to search around, but no trace of cameras or suspicious devices."

"No other humans, as we expected." Selene adds a remark.

"OK, thank you." Tim says, "What about your guys for some adventure?"

"Yes, we also have a list of items we need to order. Most items are available as we confirmed with the cat, but we need to wait for delivery tomorrow morning. Apparently they do not give us guns. We do not know what kind of wild life is out there you know." Zak starts.

"No guns? That adds to a point here I hope." Leo is in another group discussing the marriage problem, "Sorry you can continue. We will talk about our findings afterwards."

"No problem. It is rainy today so it is hard to locate the sun. Otherwise we can figure out north and south and it makes us easier to navigate in the forest."

"But there might be two." I make a joke, "Or, even three?"

"Three is unlikely." Jack laughs, "Such a system is usually chaotic and unstable. Someone should write a novel about it."

"Ha-ha — That sounds very interesting. Let me read it when you finish. Anyway, we have confirmed with QX, sorry, that there is only one, just like our own solar system." Dennis says.

"Yes, there is only one sun in this solar system, which consists of more than ninety-nine point eight percent of the total mass. The day night cycles are very regular." says QX.

"Why don't you order a compass?" Circe asks.

"We do not know whether it will work." Zak answers.

"Two cents here. For human-beings to survive here, some electro-magnetic field is necessary to filter or shield radiation, mostly these high energy particles from the sun. With that you can bet compasses will work to give you at least a consistent direction." Jack shows his talent.

"Good point. Thank you Jack. Now here is our most important finding so far. The cat has confirmed that they can help building things for us — like farms, factories, power plants, water facilities and even our own houses." Zak continues, "It is like a video game: You spend money and they build things."

What? I have just started thinking about the tremendous work in order to establish a new colony.

"We first tried to order some raw materials and tools, then I just had this idea to ask whether they can instead build things for us. Sorry I am, lazy, but I mean, they are aliens, right? At least self-claimed aliens that can bring us from the old Earth, five thousand light years away, so building a farm shall be super easy, a piece of cake, right?" Zak continues.

"Right, they can do much more I suppose, if they are real aliens." Bran says.

I feel that one million dollars is now not quite enough for anything fancy, but a house built on our own needs sounds great. So we need to aim for two million, by whatever means.

"However, they are not going to modify this hotel for us. Just for fun, we tried to ask the cat to open a hole from my room down to Oliver's room so that we can play video games together, but the cat refused to do it and said that each room is private. I think that is all I have right now." Zak concludes.

You must be very very lazy. So have you tried to order game consoles and monitors? I also want to open a hole to Jack's room then.

"Thanks Zak. Leo you have something to say?" Tim asks.

"Yes, yes. We started with the puzzle, the marriage problem, but we soon went back to Eos' question, whether this whole thing is a show on the Earth or really on a different planet, and we have a long list of evidences." Leo says.

Eos finally has some minor reaction.

"Eos, Eos, Eos. Boys only care about Eos." I hear a girl by my side whispering.

"In short, I believe we are still on the Earth, our Earth." Leo continues. "For a number of reasons. One, they told us that this is five thousand light years from our old Earth, which means that it takes at least five thousand years to bring us up here. Our bodies do not age, and our uniforms and underwear look like from yesterday."

"They are aliens, right? They can do things we cannot imagine." Selene says.

"Aliens cannot defy physical laws. After five thousand years, all possible materials that make our clothes will perish. And two, assuming the aliens are five thousand light years away from us, then they must had known life and civilization on the Earth five thousand years ago at the latest, roughly around the start of ancient Egyptian dynasties. Our radio broadcast from the Earth, that aliens may be able to detect, only started a few hundred years ago, so numbers do not match."

Ah, I don't understand relativity well enough. Physics is too hard for me, but some other guys may know it?

"Maybe they are one hundred light years away but they put us on another distant planet?" Selene finds another flaw in the argument.

"True. But if you build a zoo, do you want to build in the urban or suburban area, or in a desert or jungle?"

Good point. Zoo? It is a bit uncomfortable yet I feel this is probably the most accurate metaphor for our situation.

"Three, we've tried many ways asking the cat about what date it is today on our old Earth, and it either says the question is vague and causes ambiguity, or says our question is meaningless, or simply refuses to provide such information." Leo points out something important.

"Smells very fishy." Jack says.

"Four, they say that one day equals twenty hours here, but they do not give us any timepiece, even inaccurate ones from the Earth. We tried to order watches — mechanical or digital, clocks, cellphones, personal computers or laptops. So we suspect that twenty hour per day story is a lie."

"Five, the marriage rules seem too artificial and more likely belong to a show or a game. I mean, if they are aliens, then why can't they read our minds and match us right away? Connecting to what Rhea's team has observed, they don't truly want us to have babies and prevent us from visiting other guest rooms, like prevent us from errr...having sex without condoms. I guess at the end of Day seven, they just come out and say: *thank you for your participation in the game and you can go home with your cash reward.*"

"Six, which we think is very important. In biology there is this fifty/five hundred law. Roughly for a species to survive genetically, the population needs to be at least fifty to prevent inbreeding of offsprings, and at least five hundred to prevent genetic shift. We only have twenty-four of us here and obviously it is not enough."

"This is a very good point!" Jack adds a comment with unfriendly words, "These bastards! And in fact, there are researchers suggesting the numbers are still too low in practice."

"Finally, as another team pointed out, they do not give us guns. They can build a house for us and it is hard to imagine why guns aren't allowed, unless it violates a lot of local laws here." Leo adds to his enumerations.

"Maybe they don't want us to shoot each other at the beginning. Too dangerous in my opinion." Selene says.

"It is possible. So we hope, or we think this is just a game, and let us play as they wish and get the cash reward." Leo adds a final remark.

"Rambling speech." Eos comments, "Nothing with solid argument."

"Sounds pretty reasonable to me," Says Jack. "and there are many fishy things all together."

"Combining many ungrounded arguments together does not make them valid. Repeating a lie a thousand times does not make it a truth." She says, "Logic is logic. One proof is enough."

"OK. Thanks, Leo." Tim stops Eos from her continual attacks. As we planned earlier, Tim then asks me to do a briefing for our group.

I turn to my notes and stare at the first line for a very long time. People outside my group presumably think that I haven't prepared yet to give a summary, and Tim and Jack are somewhat puzzled.

"Sorry." I clear my throat, "We believe that the purpose of the marriage rules is to effectively compute an approximate solution to the maximality problem. Only rank 1 seems to have a small privilege. One possible solution requires everyone revealing their number and promising not to guess at other people's numbers. However, this plan has many flaws and we think we shall continue working on modifications or find a new approach."

"What?"

It seems most other people are puzzled. Only Eos nodded through my lines and seems to understand and appreciate everything. I am probably too concise here, and so I take a few more minutes explaining the details, with questions and answers.

After that, we decide to take a break and wait for dinner. Some people go back to their guest rooms for a quick nap. I feel like finishing a math exam after answering these questions, while focusing on the real problem, and decide to sit in the lounge to enjoy the sound of a raining day.

vii   Dawn

"Sunset. It is dinner time. Please be seated in the dining room." QX announces.

Oh, how time flies. We move to the dining table, and those who were back in the rooms also come back downstairs. Apparently the announcement will also be broadcasted in the rooms, just like earlier today. There are eleven seats on each side of the long dining table, and one at each end.

So we quickly fill up the side seats, unwilling to take the "host/hostess seats", as if they have bombs on them. However, Eos takes one seat on one end, as she probably does not care at all, and Tim hesitates but finally takes the seat on the other end.

"Just like King and Queen." Jack says. Jack and I sit next to each other on one side of Tim. Bran is sitting across the table, next to Tim on the other side.

"King, and Queen Regnant, of an enemy country." I make a joke, "King and Queen and Jack."

"I would believe you if we have thirteen or twenty-six or fifty-two or fifty-four people here, with numbers or ranks — Twenty-four does not feel like it. By the way, we may want to order some cards and play with the girls later." Jack laughs, "And so you are like an Ace double-agent working as an advisor to the King."

"No." Says Tim, "More like a triple-agent."

The robots roll out and serve dinner. Menu today is classic beef steak with grilled vegetables, meshed potatoes and vegetable salad. People start to understand the situation and believe they probably won't poison us by now.

"QX, Can I order some alcohol?" Yan asks.

"Yes. What would you like?"

Whoa! We have one thousand dollars on board to spend for seven days, and at least one hundred thousand in the boarding area. So very soon some others also follow to order beer or wine.

"Wine tastes good man. Haven't had anything like that in my life man." Tim stops for a few seconds, trying to recall some memory, " My parents always say it is too early for me."

First time? Tim you are drunk, or, am I?

"We need to order some bottles and stock them in a cellar. Otherwise we need to build a whole winery starting from growing grapes." I say.

"Yeah, too much work to do man. We don't have enough people yet require tons of modern industry to build for our needs." Tim says, "I really hope it is just a game, man!"

We call the end of the day after our first dinner. People agree we need to have a good rest for further plans, especially if a day is only twenty hours. Jack walks with me along the way back to our rooms.

"In the old world, the reason we don't have a good idea about love, is that we have many choices, too many indeed. Half of the entire population you can imagine. Here the number is down to twelve, actually down to a single digit now. It is much more predictable and I bet things can happen really fast, since there are no other choices left. You also see that people are not in their normal psychological conditions, like Yan and Oliver." Jack starts talking after no others are around.

"Yeah. They are just drunk, but luckily Dennis and Tim stopped them." That was close, and I don't think breaking some glass doors will do anything useful.

"There are at most nine left for you." Jack continues, "Rhea, Circe and Iris form their own small circle and it is hard you know. Same with Pheme and Kakia. Nyx probably likes zodiac signs, tarot cards and magical devices more than anything in the whole world, though I doubt if astrology theory still works on a different planet. Eos is Eos. She is there high above everyone and never cares about boys or girls or any carbon-based life-forms, except for trees which make books. The remaining two, the bridge club girls — I just feel I am too familiar with them."

"Back on Wednesday, before the graduation ceremony...I actually went to talk to Eos. Thought I had a slight chance as we are going to the same college." I quickly murmur.

"Really? You did? And?"

"Only two words: *Thanks. No.*"

"That doubles the record of words from what I have ever heard of! Congratulations! Record-breaking!" Jack sounds like I shall be awarded a prestigious prize for it.

"Shut up and go for Muse. Everyone knows that."

"Easier said than done. By the way, now I am not certain that I can trust William's words —" He stops and points to my door, whispering.

"Ha-ha, I think I do, because otherwise it would be too easy to disprove it. Or, you want to try?"

"No. Thanks. See you tomorrow."

"See you."

It is a bit dark so I turn on the light. I sit on the bed facing the pedestal, and the screen automatically turns on this time. *The Six-Fourteen interface*, I see. Interesting, I've only used ones with keyboards or styli, but for this one we use our finger to click on buttons on the screen without any noticeable delays, and it feels very natural. Fancy "alien" technology again.

The first page is a list of three names. I can click a name and select from a list of twelve, two of which are greyed out. Without too much hesitation I change the names to what I have already planned:

Muse   Eos   Nyx

Clicking a button to the second page, it shows a deposit balance of one thousand dollars with a search bar and a virtual keyboard that I can order stuff like online shopping, a recent trend just started during my high school times, but I haven't tried earlier; and a button to call or summon QX. Finally on the third page I find my name on it with an arabic number 1.

PROLOGUE

viii   Friends

oday is a special day. I am attending a big religious ritual, worshipping some primordial gods and goddesses. Well, I am not a big fan of worshipping these gods; Goddesses? Maybe. It is nevertheless a good opportunity to meet some old friends.

The ritual starts with a High Priest at the highest altar reciting some ancient script using a very old language that only very small group of priests and priestesses can understand and use fluently, as it is primarily used in religious ceremonies. Articles such as "the" and "a" are so difficult that I even make mistakes sometimes; tenses are hard to master as well.

The High Priest stands in front of a marble platform with these three sacred items on it, all of which have significant religious meanings according to Standard Mythology: A sundial; a pen with a writing pad; and a long rope.

"On this Twenty-Sixth Day of the Month of Virtue, Week Four, Monday, A.D. Thirty-Five Thousand Eight Hundred and Sixty-One, Year of the Gods, we gather here to praise the Gods and Goddesses who created the Heavens and the Earth."

"Let us praise —"

Then it follows the long list of names of gods and goddesses that I don't care much about. Who would? We are not cavemen who didn't understand natural phenomena and attributed those

34

to gods or goddesses. Modern time religion is mostly spiritual, and long gone are the days when people had to respect the gods for their generosity of food and electricity. The priests need to make use of natural wonders to attract general audience to this long-lasting time-consuming ritual. The fun part is obviously higher up there.

Two lines of girls come into the altar, waiting. One line of girls are dressed in pure white robes and the other in crimson red. The High Priest then starts to recite the final piece of the ancient script.

"Logic leads us through Darkness, and embraces Light.
With Faith, we gain Power,
and with Knowledge and Skill, we gain Wisdom."

The High Priest needs to recite these three lines multiple times with a fixed interval between them, like four hundred and thirty-two seconds, or seven minutes and twelve seconds to be precise. Priests and priestesses always say that the numbers have some religious meanings. Seven stands for the days in a week and the number of corners of a holy fruit, and twelve is of course a sacred number.

After each such recitation, two girls, one from each line, come close to the center and write down their names on a piece of paper, and return to their lines. It will take a long time to finish all the pairs.

It is a nice show, the priests have timed it very well, but the ritual is still too long and the High Priest has to repeat the script twenty-four times this time. "Too long. Don't like the voice." I murmur.

"I didn't like yours either. *My* High Priest worked very hard for this day." Says a handsome young man next to me, "The High Priests changed it from twelve to twenty-four to increase the number of participants. Many families wanted to send their daughters to this ritual, and they had to compromise. Moreover, you know that, it agrees with the conceptualization of the original ritual."

Yes, it is him.

And yes, many families, indeed. Some couples had planned their pregnancy twenty-five years ago in order to meet the strict age requirement for the participants today. A lot of crazy things have happened beneath the tip of the iceberg.

"Oh, nice to see you again." I say, "I knew you would come. It is your month. How many years since we last met?"

"Me too. I don't exactly remember. It feels like it has been hundreds of years. I also knew you would come for me this time."

"So, it means you bring the *things* this time?" I ask.

"Yes, finally." He looks around, opens his large backpack and takes out two small sculptures.

"Beautiful. Thank you so much! Excellent work indeed." I say, with eyes fixed on the sculptures.

"Have you seen the ladies recently?" He asks.

"No, not recently, but they may show up, so let us be quick."

"Hello, you two." This time it is a couple. A tall strong man with a pretty looking lady, likely his wife or girlfriend.

Oh, my goddesses! The worst scenario, much worse than the two ladies themselves. Too many people here. Two of us quickly try to exchange some eye contact, but it is hard with our sunglasses in this darkness. Don't? Don't. Don't! It is too late to hide now!

"Oh, good to see you, you two." I say, trying to pretend to be as calm as possible, "Do you have an announcement this time?"

"Yes." says the beauty, "This is our tenth remarriage."

"Oh, congratulations! Ha-ha, we may see another princess very soon." I joke.

"Tenth? Not the ninth?" The tall asks in awe, "Last time was back in the Kingdom of Selenis, right? Oh it is a republic now, after the revolution. Time changes everyone."

"No! Last time was in the capital of Herian Federation. How did you forget that?" The beauty is slightly annoyed.

"How did that count? You were all drunk, and the next morning you said 'let's forget about it', right? This was how I forgot it."

"It was short, but it did count!"

Oh, ten. A magic number. It reminds me something that may help to stop them from their continuous arguments, ever.

"I have one thing to say, or to confess." I say to the beauty, hoping our sin would slip unnoticed, through her fingers, into the darkness. Chance is low but worth trying. "This might be very late, but I shall apologize for shooting you blindly in the game. That forty thousand dollars ended up in my pocket. Sorry! I apologize!"

Yes, that was a long story, but the tall and the beauty have been quarrelling over this topic for many many years. The beauty has always believed that the tall had revealed his secret number to a secret girl and has continued to impeach him for the truth. The tall of course has been denying this since the beginning of time.

"Ah, I told you! Thousands of times! There is no secret girl! Now here is the proof!" The tall is so cheerful regarding my confession. "How can you hide this from us for so—many—years!"

I don't remember really. I only remember a magic number ten.

"No secret girl? Then what about these girls living in the Kingdom of Heranis, or the Republic of Musenis? They do not exit? You have a long history of not telling me the truth! Starting from the very beginning!"

"No, no. All these things happened afterwards. I mean, there was no secret girl at that time. I swear to the Gods and Goddesses." The tall tries to defend himself with sweat on his brow, literally.

"I don't trust you two, or any of the Gods. Too fishy in my opinion." She seems to have significant distrust of us, "Especially for you, you have the least possibility of winning to shoot me blindly in the game, according to the calculations in my opinion. Ah, you sound like you work for him — I am afraid he should find a better person. Time changes everyone. When had you two planned for this?"

"No — We haven't met for a long time. I am telling the truth! I swear...to my goddesses!" I am the next one trying to defend myself with sweat on my brow. Maybe it is just because the sun has come out again, but I totally understand the severity of this situation, and I start to realize that indeed I am the person with the least such possibility in mere calculations, from her point of view of course, though I had my own reasons. It seriously sounds like the beauty has a long list of names, ranked by this possibility, and she has lay down detailed plans to shoot these people down one by one following the list.

"Or, he could have asked *you* first, and then you told little boy earlier today." The beauty turns towards the handsome, and then notices the sinful things in his ever-since-shaky hands, "Oh, these look like real. Nice job. Ha-ha — you tried to bribe him with these little things. Evidence is sound and complete. Sentenced for three years on the Island of Garank, all three of you, under Article Ten of the CODES. My Judgement is irreversible. This is the end of our tenth marriage."

Oh, no! "My Judgement" and "my opinion" are two vastly different things to the beauty.

"No, no, no. He asked for these, a long time ago, I swear — also to the Goddesses. A coincidence. I promise, just like today." The handsome is the third one trying to defend himself with sweat on his brow, though he knows it is in vain now. Garank is not a fun place for normal people who speak common languages.

The beauty does not seem to be convinced. So I have to spell out the reason.

"OK. Let me explain the reason for it, about my guess, and then you want to say sorry to him and you two can have your eleventh remarriage, since he himself is very innocent. So four of us can spend three years on Garank together according to the CODES — at least we can play some card games." I say to the beauty and the tall, "It is all about — King and Queen and Jack."

Oh Jack, you know, I can feel waters in my eyes.

DAY II

ix   Thoughts

I didn't sleep well last night. Obviously not well. The big myth. I wake up early around dawn, and I notice yet another big problem: I definitely have some memory loss, possibly due to the claimed space travel, as I cannot remember some important things I was thinking last night, only after one night of sleep. I can even remember a dream I just made, but nothing before I fell asleep. Maybe it is not that uncommon for thinking on the bed before sleep. These pieces of memory fade away very quickly. I may need to rely on my notes more often, writing things down as much as I can.

The rain has stopped but it is still dim outside. The sky looks fully covered by clouds through my window, but it is separated from waters. I stay on the bed thinking about the marriage problem instead, while waiting for the delivery of some clean clothes.

Do I want to put Muse in my list? Maybe Muse will put me in the list, and then we get married? How about Jack? What if I am not in Muse's list? Maybe I am not that important. Or maybe Muse is clever enough to put only one true love, and fill the other positions with two irrelevant boys — and so there is little chance of getting married with them, like placeholders. Or maybe those boys also do the same thing and put Muse in their list as well by coincidence? How do we avoid such accidental marriages?

It soon gets too complicated for me, and I make some quick changes to my list:

Eos   Nyx   Iris

Well, with Iris — complicated story, but chance is meager. In fact, Iris probably won't put me in the list anyway. So it is just a placeholder to avoid other worse scenarios.

Now, do I want to marry Eos by my true heart? She is beautiful of course, and smart, but obviously there are other things I need to consider after I marry her. Shall I talk to her again? Without even hesitating she would say "I am not getting married. Go away." or simply the second half. However, she is negotiable at least. If we arrange everyone to make two million dollars, then we shall have enough cash to build one house for her and one house for me, and leave enough for us to spend. We can live with this *peaceful* relationship. But, is this what I really want?

Back to the rank business. Being 1 is quite different. I quickly changed that 1 to a 10 after I saw it, in case if someone can bypass the rules and sneak into others' rooms, but obviously it did not change my real rank number. I tried very hard to forget it, but simply can't. That number 1 has been very much like a nightmare, horrifying me every second since I saw it. Others may feel very glad to be the most knowledgable person, even if it is a relatively small group, but the reason I, not Jack or Tim or Eos or Muse or Bran or even Selene, but I became 1 is very terrifying — what I had suspected before the sunset might be true, the worst case.

In addition, if I were another rank number, by the time I get married with someone, we would naturally think that it is good and natural for both of us after a lot of couples have been matched up, even if we are not each other's best choice. Being 1, it feels more like I am choosing my partner — imagine if Jack is 2 and I marry with Muse in the end.

I look through my list and recall some memories with Iris.

During our ninth or tenth grade — I can never remember the exact date or even the exact year that early on — daddy decided to drive me to school, because it fit his schedule, but only for two weeks. So I arrived at our classroom earlier than anyone else. Iris was the second to arrive, and was usually the first I would assume. This gave us a period of, on average, ten minutes that we were the only ones in the classroom. We didn't know each other well then, so we didn't talk at the beginning, but instead sit in our own seats reading books or doing class preps.

One day, while I was filling my water bottle, Iris suddenly asked: "what is it, in your bottle?"

"Chamomile tea with lots of sugar. Tastes good. What is in yours?"

"Ginseng roots. Too much sugar is not great for your health or teeth. Only little boys do that."

I didn't continue to talk. To be precise, I was too dumb to think about any good topic to continue. Anyway, that was the end of our first talk.

In the following semester, we happened to sit next to each other by accident. Out of nowhere, talks started. Iris sometimes hit me for a math problem. Well, I was relatively good at math during high school, but I didn't like these tedious calculations and I always made mistakes. Logic is still fun, at least.

"Why don't you ask Eos?"

"She is nowhere to be found. Moreover, she...likely does not have time to answer."

That was a very polite way of saying it.

Sometimes I asked Iris about book recommendations, like favorite novel or something. Once Iris lent me a book to read. Just ordinary story, a boy meets a girl, coincidence. The most interesting story so far was when Iris drew something on the notebook and said, "I recently started learning some Chinese characters. They are still using hieroglyphs nowadays. Guess what this character is?"

"No idea at all."

Are you planning a trip to China? Yan might be a good guide.

"It is an eagle. You see how it looks like an eagle standing there, proudly."

"Yes, indeed. I get it now. Very interesting."

"For your information," Yan said next to me, "I bet most real Chinese people don't even know this fun fact. You are the first person who has told me this."

Iris was somehow embarrassed I thought, but soon came back to life again and our vague friendship continued. Until one day Iris came to me and out of nowhere asked, "Do you like girls with long hair or short hair?"

By the way, Iris had the long hair that I liked.

"Long hair of course. Ponytails are great. Why do you ask?"

"Nothing. Just curious."

However, I was totally shocked when I saw the freshly-cut short hair the next Monday morning.

I stop my memories going too far or too deep into the miserable region. Just in case I forget, I quickly write down some of these ideas and memories, as well as some quick notes on the past few days, especially the cinematic memories from yesterday.

x   Retrogrades

When I am downstairs, a group of girls are surrounding Nyx with a big crystal ball in the lounge, freshly delivered I assume. Together delivered is a hooded black magician's robe with golden trim. With double braids they add a lot of mystery to the usual school girl style.

As Iris once told me, Nyx's fortune-tellings, or oracles, had been notoriously predictive, or even prophetic, and so very popular among the girls. Even some of the boys went to ask Nyx on occasions. These were usually small tips that wouldn't change your life much, but if you came back to look at them some time later, you would find everything worked as Nyx predicted. "You can regard them as Axioms, like Axioms in mathematics." Iris said with firm belief. "If Fortune-Telling were in the Olympic Games, Nyx would win at least a Bronze medal."

I have to admit that I somehow like mystical ingredients. I once tried some ancient fortune-telling myself, though not good enough to get into the Olympics. It uses twelve coin-shape wooden tokens. You start with some complicated ritual procedures, toss the tokens just like tossing coins, and tell the fortune by heads and tails, fifty-fifty chance for each. Easy, but during one fixed day in a ten-day cycle, you are not allowed to do fortune-telling with the wooden tokens, as in the ancient Chinese calendar system, the property of that date does not work very well with the Wood element, for some reason I still don't understand at all. It is very difficult to remember which day it is in this ten-day cycle, especially you need to take into account that China is in a different time zone. Would be much easier if it is in a seven-day cycle. I also wished our calendar system could be much more regular, but three hundred and sixty-five point two five is obviously not a great number.

The predictions had been mostly accurate, so I eventually used what I learned from school and wrote up a computer program to do the date selection and random number generation. So if it happens to be one of those forbidden dates, time-zone adjusted, then the program automatically kicks off an error message. Wonderful idea, right? But then the predictions failed to work, or seemed less accurate and mostly random. I later realized that computer programs probably do not belong to the element Wood, so I need to avoid a different day within this ten-day cycle. Pretty logical, right? But I have no idea which element computer codes belong to, in the ancient Chinese five-element system. Maybe element Metal? But metal, or electric wire or circuit, is only the platform for computer codes. You cannot say the computer codes are the same as these nano-level wires. A metaphor is that my thought is based on the nerves in my brain, but you cannot say my thought is the same as this complicated soup of organic molecules. Or maybe it is? Anyway, I don't understand ancient Chinese philosophy well enough to tell exactly. I went to Nyx for an advice. "Ask the one who may know it, but you may get multiple answers."

So later on that day I asked Yan about it. "Interesting question, I don't know the answer right now. Give me a day, and I will ask some scholars back in China. They are all sleeping right now, you know." The next morning, he came back to me, "OK, I have some conflicting answers from top scholars in ancient philosophy. Some say it is definitely Metal, if you run your code in a traditional computer, not a quantum one; some argue it is more like Water, since electricity flows like water when your code runs; some think it is the element Earth, as the most essential component of a computer is made of chips, or silicon, which is not a metal but is made of sand; then some think it is Fire, as it is more spiritual and does not have a rigid form; only very few think it is Wood indeed, as Wood represents life and computer codes are some kind of life-forms. In the end, I still don't know the answer. I personally prefer Wood, but my father thinks it is Water. Great question."

I gave up, and forgot about how to start my fortune-telling business. Till recently Jack told me an interesting story that during a conference regarding "Chinese ancient philosophy and modern computations at the turn of the millennium", multiple groups of top scholars in China were literally fighting with each other with their own fists instead of, or in addition to, with their words, and the whole conference building became so chaotic that it had to be taken over by the Imperial Guards to resume order. I then told him the story with Yan. "First of all, computers only generate pseudo-random numbers that are not really random, so I doubt if anything like a classical computer code can do the fortune-telling for you. Second, I guess Yan's father or mother is a university professor in the same or a related field, and sent out the question via a mailing list. People can respond very quickly with e-mails nowadays. But I don't understand why these prestigious professors tried to resolve this very academic dispute in a totally unprofessional way." Jack commented.

I have to say, whenever Jack says "I don't understand", usually something huge is hidden behind it. My life experience — Encyclopedias don't work well with ignorance.

Back to the table, our chief fortune-teller, CFT for short, is still doing some preparation work for the fortune-telling, like reciting a long script of words before the ritual, as I did in mine as well.

As I remember, Nyx has been quite plain from most other aspects during high school, and hasn't changed much either, but suddenly the refreshing new appearance with the black robe makes me gaze for longer than I should.

I believe Nyx would be much more popular at the amateur level like me. Truth is, Nyx can immediately give you today's ratings and good matches based on, what they call it? The horoscopes? Rumors were around that Nyx refused to come to school a couple of times only because the signs said no.

"Isn't the preparation longer than usual?" Circe asks and wakes me up from my reminiscence.

"Maybe because this new crystal ball needs some extra process." Selene says.

"How much you spent on this?" I ask.

"I cannot feel the signs here, only the planets. Not surprising. Something is wrong. Mercury in retrograde, Venus in retrograde, Mars in retrograde — *every* planet in retrograde!" our CFT ignores me.

"What does this mean?" Pheme asks.

"Chaos, complete chaos. Rebuild of world order. Maybe they chose this date on purpose."

"Anything advice for us today?" Pheme asks.

"Stay in the building. Never go outside." Nyx responses, "Eight hundred dollars for this most accurate astrological crystal ball."

Oh I guess Nyx is not totally ignoring me. Eight hundred dollars for this? Seriously? I have to reconsider your position in my list.

"QX, can we cancel or return our orders?" I ask.

"You can cancel the order any time before they are delivered, but sorry we do not accept returns."

"No, I do not want to return this. I can sense a strong magical power in it. The best one I have ever used." Nyx says.

Maybe just because you didn't sleep well, like others.

"How is my fortune for Love today. I am a Virgo." I ask.

"Hey you are jumping in line. This will change the oracles for everyone!" Circe cries.

Oh, these girls go to Nyx regularly and so know the rules.

"Oh, I am very sorry. I apologize! I didn't mean that. I didn't notice that you were all in line."

Are the oracles already ordered, like cards?

Well, I can "absolutely" jump in line, after a few days.

"Everything happens for a reason. Let me see — " Nyx touches the crystal ball for a while, "Very bad indeed. Do not try anything. Stay away from love, all day long." Our CFT stops for a short while, then adds a comment, "Casual talks are OK, just nothing regarding love. Lucky item: Glass."

"You got a Lucky item!" Selene says, "Now you really have cut in line!"

I am sorry, again! But I got rid of this very unlucky oracle for all of you! Is this Lucky item a secret item or card within the oracles, to give people incentives to come for the oracle more frequently? Like once a while someone can get the big jackpot. Very clever business model, indeed.

"The Lucky item generator is standalone, independent from the Wheel of Fortune." Nyx says.

So if I understand your words correctly, you run two separate algorithms respectively for the Lucky item and for the oracle, and so they are independent of each other?

The girls then flood Nyx with questions, while I stand there with my bad oracle and a strange Lucky item. I should have waited in the end of the line and get something else! I suppose I only have six days or so to find a mate, and today is going to be totally wasted.

"How about Aquarius?" Rhea asks.

"Your love needs your help."

OK. Doesn't say much. Right now or in the future?

"I am a Taurus. How is compatibility with a Gemini today?" Circe asks.

"Your love will be injured by love."

Ho ho ho. One of the boys may be in trouble. Who is a Gemini? Is this physical injury or mental injury? When will this happen? Later today, or within this week, or after a thousand years? So it could apply to anyone at any time! Common fortune-telling trick.

"What shall we do inside the hotel if we cannot go outside?" Selene asks.

"...Diverge."

......

People one by one receive their oracle, and start to digest what it means for today. Why am I the only one with an unlucky oracle and a Lucky item today?

I have to say sometimes these scripts do have some merits. Even when they don't say anything really, we still feel as if we know a little bit extra information. This is what I learned from my own fortune-telling story. It is more like a psychological treatment, and right now people do need some treatment for the great uncertainties. Nyx is working as a therapist for us, to be precise.

Maybe Nyx already knows it is an alien planet from the readings, but there is no way to convince everyone only by words, and so this fortune telling serves as the best therapy.

"Nyx, for planets, do you include Pluto? Just curious. I mean, there has been some recent trends to exclude Pluto from the nine planets." I have this flash of idea in my mind.

"I know. Most people in astrology are still using its position for some of their predictions. I don't personally use Pluto ever since I started fortune-telling. I don't like him, I mean, because I can feel many similar size bodies near its orbit, so Pluto by itself isn't too important. But I double checked earlier that Pluto is also in retrograde."

"Thanks. QX, another question here, what time on the old Earth did it last time happen that all eight planets — Mercury, Venus, Mars, Jupiter, Saturn, Uranus, Neptune and Pluto — were in retrograde?" I ask.

"This question is not phrased accurately and has possibly different answers. Please be more specific."

"It is the same thing. Yesterday some people tried in various ways to ask about the date and time, and the cat refused to answer any of them. They just don't want us to know the time in my opinion." Selene says.

There should be a reason. All unnatural things happen for some reason.

"Allow me to rephrase my question," I think about it more carefully, "QX, suppose you put us back on our old Earth at the time you kid...invited us to this new planet; from our perspective, when did eight planet retrograde last happen?"

"Is this any different?" Selene asks.

I believe it *is* different, assuming if QX responds with a real answer.

"March twenty-third to March twenty-eighth, year forty-one thirty-nine B.C. in your most common calendar system."

"Oh I see the point now, if it takes at least five thousand years to bring us up here, then as of *right now*, there could be another such retrograde which is the past of us but which is in the future of our graduation week. *Last time happen* is just ambiguous." Selene says.

"Yes." I agree with the last sentence. Only the last one though.

"So that means we are actually on a different planet?" Gaia asks.

"I think so. I cannot feel the Zodiacs at all here, and I trust the black cat." Nyx says.

"We can only say that the cat is still consistent with itself." I say, "QX, continue with my previous question, in the same setting, when is the next eight-planet-retrograde?"

"April twenty-seventh to May twelfth, year seventy-six sixty-two A.D." QX responds immediately.

"OK. More than five thousand years. This is the earliest possible date we are on right now. There could be more dates in the future and we don't know how fast their spaceships travel."

I think this is at least one big progress for today as QX refuses to tell us the current date. Every computer program has flaws or bugs, I smile as I scratch down the numbers on my notes.

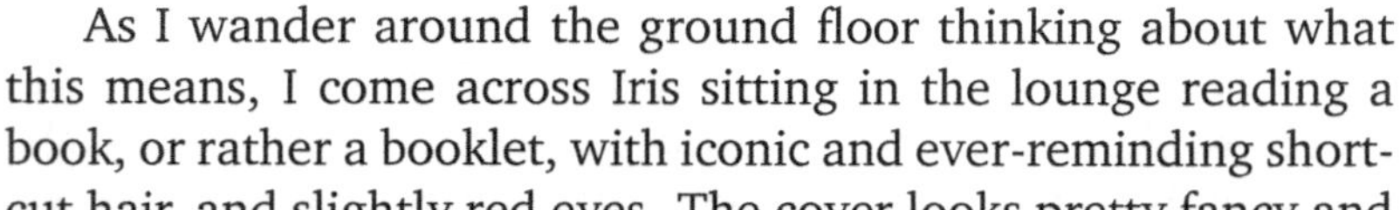

As I wander around the ground floor thinking about what this means, I come across Iris sitting in the lounge reading a book, or rather a booklet, with iconic and ever-reminding short-cut hair, and slightly red eyes. The cover looks pretty fancy and old-fashioned, but I don't want to ask the price another time.

"Ah, you have tried their bookstore?" I ask.

"Yes, it is like that jungly online bookstore. You can get every book you search for, even lo...lots of out-of-print ones. For example, Homer's *the Margites*, which only has an ancient Greek version."

I only know *the Iliad* and *the Odyssey*. Well, I know many things, but I know them badly. It is not the time to dive down into another rabbit hole — ancient Greek is too difficult to me, and it's obviously all Greek.

"And what is this? A booklet?"

"It is called a *quarto*. William Shakespeare's *Cardenio*, a manuscript or a pirate copy." Iris says, eyes not leaving the pages.

Shakespeare? I shake my head. Not for me — Oh, I can finish my detective novel then.

"Can we order movies as well? We can build a theatre here. Either here in the lounge, or in the secret room on the fourth floor."

"No, at least nothing digital. No CD or MP3 players either."

"Maybe I see the point now. You can track time with a movie, which usually says on the back somewhere on the case about how long it is. Same thing for songs. So aliens do not want us to know the time." I say.

Iris does not respond but continues reading.

I am so dumb that I don't know how to continue a chat with a girl, and I often say something stupid that put myself into such a stalled conversation. Reminding myself our CFT's advice, I leave Iris alone reading and work through my notes.

Hera is also sitting there in the lounge, looking at the courtyard, murmuring something, hopefully not about Eos again. It is just glass, not a mirror. To be honest, I don't like Hera personally, no offense, but not my type. So if there are only four of us in the matching game, then Muse-I and Hera-Jack will be the maximal solution. If Jack matches with Muse, then both Hera and I become singles — I would rather not marry.

Why is glass my Lucky item today? I also stare at it for a while, but don't have any clue. Shall I knock at it and then suddenly my bride will come to me and say hello? Sounds ridiculous.

Soon afterwards, Eos also shows up with a yellowish book and sits in front of me, far away from the fortune-telling session for an obvious reason. *Casual talks are fine.* I remind myself.

"What's this book?"

"GTM fifty-two, *Algebraic Geometry* by Hartshorne." She says, "Need to learn it before I can understand those proofs."

There are proofs you don't understand?

OK. I understand algebra, and some geometry as well. Algebraic geometry? Maybe coordinates of points and equations of curves? Doesn't sound too hard, but again I don't have a good topic to continue.

xi   Exequies

"Before we have lunch, I...have something to announce." Tim says, "Rhea and I..."

The crowd bursts into laughter and applause and whistles, before Tim even finishes his sentence, or just because I cannot hear clearly what he is actually saying. But it is obvious. Rhea stands next to Tim and quickly kisses him.

"I told you things can happen really fast." Jack says.

"I see that now."

Our CFT shows the secret power for another time, or maybe Tim heard the story and took advantage of it? No, no, I shake my head the second time. He is a nice guy, I believe. There has not been enough time to settle these things. So more likely Tim talked to Rhea last night or earlier this morning, and our CFT's words pushed Rhea somehow. Does that mean, in either case, if I didn't cut in line, then the story might be different?

"We also have an announcement." Gaia and William raise their hands. But you two have already paired up — My memory goes wrong again?

"We feel sorry but..." Gaia is a bit hesitated, "we talked to each other last night after dinner, and we were both too hasty to make this most important decision. The romantic story we told you yesterday — it is more like a dream, to both of us. So as of right now, we are still available."

It feels like the temperature in the room suddenly drops by ten degrees. People are whispering to each other. What the cat says about human love behaviour is real, and the system does have some merit.

"However, if the rest of you form eleven pairs already and two of us are the only ones left," William continues, "then we can at least pretend to marry in the system. As I ran through everything this morning, nothing is against their rules that we help everyone to get two million dollars and we just live by our own afterwards. It is like divorce of a sham marriage, but we simply don't think of it as a marriage in our common understanding."

"Does it mean that those who have paired up are also available? Like humans do make changes over time." Jack says.

You must be joking right?

Lunch menu for today is another sandwich with something tastes like smoked salmon, and we decide to have it in the lounge for better discussions. During lunch, the explorers suggest that they want to go around the building for a small adventure. However, Tim seems to be against the idea.

"We do not have any real weapons. Maybe only a few kitchen knives." Tim says, "Bran and I are still waiting to get you something useful. We hope to get it by tomorrow morning."

"Moreover," Bran says, "though the rain has stopped, the land is still very wet and you may want to wait until it dries more, better with the sun out. For example, if we are in the middle of a swamp, no one can help if you get stuck."

Finally with a bunch of girls insisting that we shall not go outside based on Nyx's astrological suggestions, the explorers eventually give up. Maybe they do not want to establish a bad relationship with the girls, and Nyx's advices have been notoriously accurate. However, they insist exploring the area tomorrow, weather permitting. "And Nyx-permitting." Selene says.

If I were not 1, I would believe this is even a part of the game to explore our surroundings and find new clues, like in a room escape game.

After this "small quarrel" between Dennis and Selene, I start to share our findings based on Nyx's crystal ball. The news about the seventy-seventh century has spread out very quickly.

"You don't even know if Nyx's senses are accurate." Eos first kicks off, "Even if you ask the cat, it might not tell the truth. Some random made-up dates." She has her usual low twisted bun, which fits her so elegantly.

"It is very rare but in the long run in astronomical terms, even small possibility events still happen. Anything possible will happen eventually." Bran says.

"I remember seeing similar discussions online and people do write programs to calculate these nonsense dates, like when Mercury and Venus transit at the same time." Jack says.

"What is...transit?" Yan asks.

"Like a solar eclipse but you replace the Moon with Mercury or Venus. Either transit is common, but it is very rare for both of them to transit at the same time. So the Sun, the Earth, Mercury and Venus all line up in almost a straight line." Jack continues.

"Why is that important?" I ask.

"Actually Venus Transits are of great importance. They are used to determine the astronomical unit — the distance from the Earth to the Sun." Jack explains, "One of Captain Cook's voyages was actually planned based on that."

"Really?"

"Yes. Basically you need two distant observers from the Earth that both measure the Venus transit and figure out differences. The rest is geometry." Jack says.

I try to imagine the picture. Roughly getting the idea that two celestial bodies pass through the sky, and when they coincide or overlap like in a solar eclipse, magic happens. The rest of the math is too complicated for me to understand.

"Basic trigonometry, plus Kepler's Third Law." Eos tires to correct.

"I remember the first calculation used the Moon?" Leo asks.

"Yes, but it was very inaccurate. The distance from the Earth to the Moon is too small relative to the Sun. Ancient Greeks used lunar phases to do the calculation but obtained very inaccurate values." Jack says.

Oh, the great ancient Greeks — They wrote great poems and plays, founded great mathematics and sciences, created great arts and philosophy, established great democracies and city states, observed great solar and lunar eclipses, hypothesized the great universe and the great four elements, and measured the great circumference of the Earth and the great astronomical unit.

"In fact," Jack continues, "using the astronomical unit we then calculate the distance from distant stars — like this one — to our solar system and hence the size of the entire universe. So it is like the foundation of everything we measure in astronomical terms, our own ruler in the universe. As we can imagine, if this is another planet, we need to teach kids to do all these kinds of calculations. We probably won't live long enough to do such an experiment by ourselves." He pauses for a few seconds, "Sorry, I just want to say what the cat says about retrograde dates agree with my memory."

"Seventy-six..." Rhea murmurs, "It has been more than five thousand years. Mom and dad, and grandma and grandpa are all gone now."

"Brothers and sisters, uncles and aunts...so are everyone we know on the Earth when we left." Muse says.

"As well as nations and dynasties." Yan says.

Memories flash into my brain. Memory that daddy took me to the playground. Memory that mom baked my favorite chocolate birthday cake. Memory that mom and dad went vacation with me and we enjoyed a small cup of ice cream all together. Memory that three of us went to see grandpa and grandma during weekends. Memory that I watched my daddy playing video games for the first time, and later played with him. Memory that I broke mommy's best coffee machine, and later helped making coffee and tried my first brew. Memory that daddy and mommy came to my graduations. Memory that daddy joked that I need to find a girlfriend. Memory that mommy played badminton with me in our backyard. Memory that I sit on the back of my daddy's car to and from preschool every day. Memory that mom kissed me good night every night.

They are all gone now, as if nothing has ever happened. I grow up to understand that in the future they will very likely die before me, and to some extent, this single piece of knowledge or understanding is a crucial part of being a grown-up. However, when things happen so quickly and so dramatically, I still feel the total nonsense behind it.

When they found that I was not in the bedroom the next morning, would they be worried? They would have called the police but nobody was able to figure out anything. How would they have desperately searched for me, until the end of their lives? I take a deep breath and try not to think about it. I wish this is just a game and they have been informed by the game designers.

After a short while, a few girls burst into tears. I also feel my watery eyes as well. Some boys look at the ceiling of the lounge, at the total emptiness.

"Everyone join the Maker, with the Son and the Holy Spirit. Amen." William makes a sign of the cross.

xii   Ranks

"Hey, why everyone is so upset. We still believe that it is just a game. As we discussed, let us just pretend it is a game and play through the show." Leo says.

"Leo, we will trust you if you are 1." Bran speaks jokingly.

Leo's face turns red but does not respond anything.

"Speaking of the marriage game. Who is 1?" Tim drives us along a different route.

Why are you so interested? Are you 2?

No one raises their hand, for an obvious reason.

"Say if I am 1, there is no way to prove it. I can always lie." Leo says.

"It only proves that you are not 1. 1 probably has some piece of knowledge or information that is super-important, and so can prove themselves by revealing this information." Muse says, tucking the shoulder bob behind the ear and taking a look at Jack, "But right now they are unwilling to do it, due to the guessing game punishment."

"If I understand the rules correctly, on Day seven, after the deadline of the games, we can actually reveal our ranks without problem, then 1 can say something about what they know, if they want." Jack adds a remark.

Everyone seems to agree with this plan.

"QX, among the twenty-four of us, who possessed the best knowledge of the known knowledge by the sunset of the first day?" I ask. I am pretty sure that QX will not answer the question. It shouldn't. If by some stupid coding bug it answers it, then sooner or later other people will try this out. It is in fact *better* if *I* try to ask this question first.

"1 has the best knowledge of the known knowledge by the sunset of the first day."

"This is mere tautology." Tim comments.

"What is a...tautology?" Yan asks.

"It is a term in symbolic logic that the sentence is logically true and hence contains zero information." Muse says, "The cat just says 1 is 1."

"Well, it may still contain some information. So, I have a guess, or a theory." Jack says, "Aliens are probably not interested in identifying us by our real earthling names. They are likely unable to pronounce them, even if they do have vocal organs that produce air vibrations, which I very much doubt. So they assign us these numbers and you can imagine — they use these as our names — like *9 chooses 17 in their subset* or *8 and 15 start a reproductive communication* or *23 orders a cup of coffee.* In some sense these numbers actually become our real names."

"Makes sense." I say. Jack you good at making words.

"I agree. It reminds me about the texts on the screens that the cat showed us yesterday. Almost all the numbers are in words, and the only exceptions are the rank numbers 1 to 24. They somehow reserve these arabic numerals as our names." Bran says, "It feels to me that, in their programming language, it may cause some confusion if ranks and other numbers are written in arabic numerals or in the same format, so they decided to do it this way."

"Remember they use atomic numbers for the chemical elements, written with words. Like One for hydrogen, Six for carbon, Eight for oxygen and so on. So One-Eight-One is H-two-O, water, and Eight-Six-Eight is C-O-two, carbon dioxide. If they use the same notations, it will be confused with our ranks, or our names. For example say you try to order some aluminum, Element Thirteen, and the robots deliver a real human to your room." Jack says.

Ha-ha, good point.

"I even bet some of them, aliens or other people, are gambling with the result of our games." Kakia says.

"Why don't they simply use letters?" Leo asks.

"Numbers are more universal." Muse says.

"QX, are you changing the assigned rank numbers based on the most recent knowledge change?" I ask.

"I bet not," Jack says, "if my theory is correct."

"No. The rank numbers are based on the knowledge by the sunset of the first day, and will not be changed afterwards." QX answers.

"I see. Otherwise, people may communicate with each other about some knowledge they know, and can modify their ranks on the list, which causes much more uncertainties in the matching game and the guessing game." I say, "Say if we could change the ranks by ourselves, then the guessing game actually would not make any use. Matching game would become very chaotic and unpredictable, almost like by chance. Both games wouldn't be games anymore."

"Very true." Tim says.

"QX, who receives the most of choices from the other gender?" Hera asks.

"Oh, no." Tim sighs.

No, no, no, no! You shall not ask this question. Neither boys nor girls will be happy. Lots of people also have the same reaction. Every male is going for Eos, like moths towards a flame.

"We will not disclose information regarding your choices."

Safe. Otherwise you can just ask for each one's choices in terms of numbers, and solve the jigsaw puzzle piece by piece. I can imagine that the boys can work together to change their choices temporarily and figure out every girl's rank number. Likewise, they will hide anything which may reveal the ranks, logically.

"QX, who is the most beautiful person here?" Hera tries again.

"Stop it, Hera. It is not a mirror!" Tim is somewhat angry.

"That knowledge is not the part of the known knowledge." QX says.

"Maybe because beauty is subjective and different people have different opinions, or maybe aliens don't even care about it." Jack says.

"QX, who is the tallest person here?" Muse asks another question.

"That is not the part of the known knowledge." QX says.

"OK. It means that they don't care. Like nobody cares about which rabbit has the longest tail in a lab experiment." Jack says.

"QX, is 1 a boy or a girl?" Muse is not giving up. "This must be part of the known knowledge right?"

"Providing such knowledge grants partial information of the guessing problem. It will not be released." QX says.

"I see, there is maybe an overall rule that prevent us from directly getting information regarding the identity of 1, or any other rank. I guess because it is unfair for the guessing game." I say, trying to stop people from these questions.

"QX," Eos asks, "who is possessing the best knowledge of the known knowledge as of right now?"

Good one, indeed. Did she finish tons of math homework last night in order to get back to rank 1? Too late, the exam was over.

Wait, exam?

"We update this information three times a day, at sunrise, solar noon and sunset. 2 has the best knowledge of the known knowledge by the solar noon of the second day."

Interesting. Eos sits back on her seat and shows a bit of, disappointment? So you are not even 2, my goddess.

"QX, who has the best knowledge of the known knowledge among all twelve boys here, at the solar noon of the second day, oh, no, sorry, wait, the same question, but for the sunset of the first day?" Muse continues.

"It grants partial information of the guessing problem, so it will not be released." QX answers.

"I agree, by the answer we may get even more information, compared to the previous question regarding 1's gender. For example, if the answer is 3, then not only we know 3 is a boy, but also 1 is a girl and 2 is a girl as well, like a logical consequence." I say.

"But why does it give answers to the previous questions regarding who has best knowledge?" Muse asks.

"I guess, that the answer does not provide extra information regarding the guessing game. Telling everyone that '2 now knows more than 1 does' does not help anyone, including 1 and 2, to identify other people. Maybe they get some extra information regarding something else, like finding a hint in a bridge game, but it is not a logical consequence." I carefully say.

"No more bridge, please?" Tim laughs.

"Sorry." Then an interesting question comes into my mind, "Is it possible to ask a clever question, such that no matter what answer the cat gives, or even if it refuses to give an answer, we always get some extra information?" I ask.

No one can answer this question for now, not even Eos, but I notice Eos finally has some reaction. Seems that she has come through the disappointment.

"I don't know the answer," Bran says, "but I am feeling that the cat has passed or very close to pass the Turing Test."

"What is that?" I ask.

"A test that shows the algorithm is advanced enough to be called a real AI, which means that the cat sounds like a human. Roughly speaking, if you believe it is possible that the cat is actually performed by a human instead of a computer algorithm, then it has passed the Turing Test." Jack says.

"Believe it or not, our own voice recognition programs in the computer club are very good to recognize human voice, at least in English, with eighty percent of accuracy. Developers all around the world have been working hard on it. I think something like Q...the cat can appear in the retail market within ten years." Bran says.

"Really? It sounds like real sci-fi to me. How about that touchscreen?" I ask.

"That one is even easier. We know how to do it, just not mature enough for massive production. Within five years we will see it in the market." Bran says, "You can even expect all cellphones look like that in ten or twenty years."

"So these alien-looking tech gears...are not that fancy as they look." Jack says.

"Right. Everything looks like a show right now, using some advanced technology like the cat to deceive us." Bran says.

"We shall stop playing with the cat and focus on the problem." Tim says.

"Speaking of the problem," Jack continues, "I think yesterday we arrived at the conclusion that trust is not possible among a large group of people. Even if you ask everyone to reveal their rank number, some may still lie and there is no way to figure out."

"Try to deactivate that device attached to the doors?" Hera asks, "At least, temporarily?"

"No, remember the only place we have the rank information is on the third page as a default value in the guessing game, and you can change it to whatever value at the very beginning. I actually thought about asking everyone to take a photo of the screen, but soon realized that it wouldn't work anyway." Jack says.

Sorry, I did it ten seconds after I saw my number.

"And we probably can't get a working camera either. Most modern ones, digital or not, have date and time stored, like a clock." I say.

"Why are you so certain?" Jack asks.

"Just guess." I say as if I don't care at all. You don't want to know why I am so certain that they won't give us any clock, Jack. I have to be more careful next time.

"By the way, the cat said yesterday that they don't want our ranks becoming 'common knowledge'. What does it mean, exactly? I kind of know but not so sure — like everyone knows it?" Hera asks.

Jack shows that he does not know either, so everyone looks at Eos.

"It is more than everyone knowing it. It is a term in logic that the knowledge is public that everyone knows it, and everyone knows everyone knows it, etc. to infinity." Eos says.

"So in theory, one could secretly tell other people about their ranks, or exchange with each other about ranks secretly, and in the end everyone knows their rank, but it is not becoming common knowledge?" Muse is the first to finish digesting this strange definition, "to infinity".

"Yes."

"Which means, if we all exchange ranks secretly, then, as everyone now has all the rank information, everyone can calculate a plan to make full twelve pairs." Muse says.

"But the plans from different people may differ. Even worse, as long as you lay out a plan and ask people to follow, such 'secret knowledge' will break down and become common knowledge." I say, "And people will start shooting each other in the guessing game."

"And in the end the cat is not going to tell who wins and who loses." Jack says.

"It is like if you get twenty thousand less in the joint account, then you know one guy shot you but you never know who did it." I give an example, "It is also possible that the one who shot you was also shot by someone else, so their account looks even, assuming we know everyone's balance."

"Like a big chain of crimes, and only the first criminal and last victim have some small variance in their balances." Hera says, "Or if the first criminal is the last victim, or their spouse, then the problem is solved."

"Normally it will be messier than that. Unless — in another extreme case — if you get twenty-two times twenty thousand less, which is four hundred and forty thousand. Then you know everyone shot you." Jack laughs.

Twenty-two...I see, my spouse and I are the only ones who won't shoot me.

"No, I am not going to shoot you, my friend." I say.

"I won't either." Muse says, "So if there are only four, or six or even eight people in the game, then it is relatively easy to obtain some mutual agreement to make things work. However, twenty-four is just a little bit more to handle, like how we naturally break up into smaller discussion groups."

Oh, right, I didn't even notice when the other guys had already started chatting by themselves.

—◦◦◦—

Rhea, our Queen now, orders us some beverages and snacks. So today we will have an afternoon tea break between the discussion sessions. Tim says, in his own words, "this is to enhance our friendships and help to establish relationships". Boys and girls chat with each other with jokes and gossips. Eos is standing alone by a corner, reading her "fifty-two" book, as she did in the discussion most of the time. She looks somewhat lonely, and so I make a stupid decision.

God, how on earth could I forget Nyx's advice this time, how? Maybe because we are not on our Earth? Someone please help rewinding the clock and kick my ass at that moment! Jack, stop me! Hey, where is Jack? Jack? Are you trying the same thing with Muse? Stop! Stop! I seem to lose control of myself moving towards Eos. Glass! I should rather try knocking at the glass panels and hoping my lovely bride would magically pop up! The next moment I take control, I have already finished the whole conversation.

"Eos, I have something, to talk to you. Errr...regarding what I talked with you, before the graduation ceremony, asking you to be my girlfriend, do you still remember that?"

"Yes."

"I think...I wonder...I mean I guess, our situation has dramatically changed, so would you please consider to be..."

"Same response as before." She replies immediately, without any expression.

"Sorry."

—◦◦◦—

Jack later comes to me and asks about what happened. "I just doubled my own record." I murmur.

"I heard that Leo went to her yesterday, and she turned away without a single word."

"Leo? He was in the astronomy club I remember. He shall go well with Nyx with planets and Zodiacs."

"Apparently everyone wants to keep some little secrets, but with Nyx it is hard to tell whether you have secrets."

"I shall say it is easy to tell."

"Good one. So I assume you are still the closest one to your goddess at the moment, in the entire universe."

"Like, the winner for the first four hundred meters in a marathon." I make a joke of myself.

"You *are* the winner for a marathon," Jack says, "but your goddess is on the Moon."

I know, it is much further down the road, proportionally.

"We don't even know if there is one here."

"True. I remember having a dream a couple of days ago. Multiple moons were on the sky, and people around me were clapping their hands." Jack says.

"Interesting. A prophetic dream?"

"I woke up from that dream, or nightmare. It was early in the morning, close to dawn. I looked out of my window. Only one moon, our own moon, was there looking at me. I felt so relieved at that moment. Now I am worried that my dream is becoming real." Jack struggles to finish his story.

"A couple of days — Two or three?"

"I don't remember. Does it matter?"

I have a gut feeling, Jack, and want to verify whether your "two days ago" agrees with mine.

"I am just curious. Has anyone asked the cat about the number of moons?"

"It does not matter. The cat can always lie and there is no real proof within seven days, especially if it remains cloudy. The sun creates a regular day-night cycle, but for moons it is hard to tell in a short period of time."

"Right. Speaking of dreams, I had a weird one early this morning. It was back in high school, or maybe it was college —

it's a dream — and there was a strange course about the theory of arts, ultimate aesthetics, taught by a math teacher."

"Math teacher? Funny."

"Four of us were attending, two boys and two girls, here. You have a guess?" I ask.

"Hmmm... I would never take such a course. Obviously you were there, dreaming, and then...Muse, Eos and...Leo?"

"Pretty close. Eos wouldn't believe this business, and Leo probably followed her steps. It was Bran, I, Muse and...Selene."

xiii   Midnight

After the tea break, our group decides to break up and join other groups with their discussions. Just want to refresh our minds a little bit, or maybe Eos does not want to be in the same group with me. Jack and I choose to step in the explorer group. I plan to listen and take notes mostly, with a slow recovery from my bad luck today. William has joined the discussion earlier. He has obviously left the girls' group, as there is no reason for him to stay.

"As of this morning, it seems to me that the sky to the girls' wing is brighter than the other side. So it is the east." Says Artemis, the only girl in the group.

"So we can call the west wing and east wing instead?" Says Zak, pointing these two directions consecutively.

"OK, then the lobby is on the north and courtyard on the south." Vincent says.

"This does not agree with the compass. Let me show you." Dennis takes out a small compass and the red arrow is pointing towards south. "I remember back on the Earth the red arrow is pointing to the north."

"It actually makes sense. " Jack says, "If the magnetic field comes from the electric flows in the liquid iron core just like our old Earth, then normally it is along the same rotation axis which causes sunrise and sunset, with only small variations. So one can expect that compasses will point to either north or south. Either case could happen, even back on the Earth. Our own magnetic north and south poles have switched or flipped many times in history, about ten times since the beginning of human species."

"So it is just opposite from the Earth?" Dennis asks.

"Yes, or it is pointing to a magnet mine or something with a strong magnetic field. Or maybe we have stayed in some hibernation chamber for too long and the magnetic poles have already switched." Jack says.

"Or they gave you a compass where they painted the red arrow differently." I say, taking some notes very quickly.

Opposite.

"We don't see the sun today, otherwise from its position and angle we can roughly tell which latitude we are in, like northern or southern hemisphere." William says, "In Africa where I am about to do missionary, the sun seems go backwards and appears in the north."

"Very true." Jack says.

"What are you trying to look for in the forest?" I ask.

"Wild life, landscapes, traces of other civilization." Dennis says, "Most importantly, we are looking for a river or at least a creek, for fresh water resources. Yes, we can dig wells, but they eventually deplete. We need plans for our children and grandchildren. A natural water source that is easy to access is optimal for us."

"That is why most civilizations on the Earth started along big rivers. Egyptians on the Nile and Babylonians on the Euphrates and the Tigris in Mesopotamia." Vincent says.

"Chinese on the Yangtze." Jack comments.

"We are ready to start a great civilization?" I ask jokingly.

"Not yet, but we shall always plan ahead. Just like we need plans for exploring." Dennis says, "We also need water resources for irrigation, and build farmlands near rivers. Remember we only have five years to build our own sustainable society."

"And Tim plus some others may want a winery as well." I say, "Do they give us seeds?"

"Yes, though they do not guarantee any yield. We have five years to do experiments. It is hard to tell whether plants from the Earth are compatible with this new environment, but as long as these trees grow, we can at least grow something." Dennis answers.

"Potatoes are probably the easiest to grow, and they do taste good." Vincent says.

"I don't want to eat potatoes all year long." Artemis says, "We also need to hunt for meat or raise some animals."

"We don't have a gun, nor anyone here can use a gun like an expert you know." Zak says, "If there are some wild animals out there, then we may be able to tame some, but it requires a lot of work."

"Do you want to ask the cat about automated farms?" I suggest.

"Yes, I agree we need to try. They should be able to help us if they claim themselves as aliens. In theory nothing is too difficult compared to space travel, but they may say that their advanced technology and engineering cost a lot of money." Dennis says.

"Speaking of money," Zak takes out a pile of golden coins, like the ones I enjoyed when I was a little boy, "guess what these are?"

"Real gold?"

"One-troy-ounce coins, ten of them, twenty-four K gold, Element Seventy-Nine. Guess how much I paid for it?" Zak smiles.

"One troy ounce is about three hundred dollars I remember." I say.

"Twenty dollars."

"Each?"

"Total. It seems that price depends on the chemical structure — simple elements or compounds are super cheap." Zak says, "In comparison, this pair of hunting gloves also cost me twenty dollars!"

"But, what are you going to do with these gold coins here?" Jack asks, "Hunting gloves are more useful."

True. Maybe gift to the girls?

Jack comes to me before the dinner.

"Do you think, the explorers truly believe that it is an alien planet?" He asks.

"What do you mean? They were performing, like on a stage, to an audience?"

"Yeah, I feel what they were discussing, I mean, food resources or whatever, are not our first priority in my opinion. We can always deal with these afterwards, even if it is real. At least we can wait until we get enough cash for example." Jack says, "In addition, if they seriously believe it is on a different planet, then they won't be so eager to explore the forest. Too dangerous."

"It was a random chat, like what we did about dreams. They are probably bored of the games and want to try something more exciting — you see, almost no entertainment in the hotel — no TV, no movies, no music, no video games, only books. We have already had two groups for the games, and no one has any good idea to start with. It is not to their taste, and I just feel it is much better than people killing each other with whatever weapons they have in hand."

"I see. It is better to play with the cat, and it is fun."

"Exactly." I say.

"By the way, actually I once read something about voice recognition — like Hidden Markov Models or Recurrent Neural Networks — all of which look like black boxes that I have no idea with. I feel — I don't believe Bran's claims."

"Black boxes? Like alchemy, astrology and fortune-telling?"
"Ha-ha. Right. Good point."

xiv   Cats

During dinner, Eos is still sitting at the other end of the long table. Tim, Jack and I are on the same seats as last night, while the seat in front of me across the table is now reserved for Rhea. So I am surrounded by King and Queen and Jack now.

Rhea is not very talkative as some other girls, but is famous for getting things done right and done on time. I don't like the ballet bun though. Doesn't fit.

"Jack, I forgot to ask — what is G-T-M, a book series, apparently having a lot of books, fifty or sixty at least?"

"Graduate Texts in Mathematics. Most of them are super hard, and all in yellow. How do you know these? Oh, Eos was reading one?"

"You are right." Now I feel suspicious why we are going to the same college. Actually it is hard to tell whether we are still going to the same college here on a different planet. *Glad to see you again. We are still going to the same college after all on the new Earth. What a coincidence! May I ask about—? Thanks. No. No. Thanks.* It would then equal the world record. Too stupid. Way too stupid.

"I saw a long queue of robots, at least twenty of them, by Eos' door this morning, waiting to enter the room, each with a huge pile of books and papers." Rhea laughs, "I think her room is now fully occupied by those."

Oh my goddess.

"The GTM's are textbooks for graduate students in mathematics. Very hard, and I wouldn't recommend any single one of them. Like even we live for ten thousand years we won't be able to understand a single word."

"You won't live that long, Jack." I laugh.

"You still remember these strange questions she asked yesterday afternoon?" Jack says, "Like Riemann hypothesis or something. All these are unsolved questions, or were unsolved questions when we left the Earth. Even the most brilliant mathematicians did not know the answers. And, after five thousand years, the Riemann hypothesis is still unknown, even to the aliens."

"Even to the aliens..." Sounds truly hard.

"Eos is a bit strange today. Looks like last night she found she is only 2 instead of 1, and has been trying to catch up with whatever alien knowledge, or to figure out what went wrong or who is 1 etc. I guess she is feeling much better now. I would suggest you to try again a couple of days later, when she is not so upset." Jack says.

We only have four or five days left, Jack.

"So you are 1, right, Mr. Database?" I ask.

"No, believe or not, I am not even close to top five. I don't understand, but these aliens have their own evaluation system I can tell. Don't tell me yours. It is much more fun to guess it out, by logic, like in a bridge game." Jack says.

"I agree."

I can never imagine more than a handful of people with more knowledge than Jack here on the table, nor I can ever imagine I am the top one on the same table, at least for a short period of time last night. I am so glad someone else has taken the honor by now.

"You know," Jack continues, "there are people in the world who just want to win every game. They want to be top one in every exam. It will literally drive them crazy if they only get a bronze medal in the Olympics. They do not care about any of the privileges of being 1, but rather enjoy the feeling of overlooking the rest of us from the peak."

"Like cats?"

"Like cats."

"You know that, I like cats."

———⊸∘C∽⌒∽⊃∘⊸———

Artemis and Zak are again quarrelling over some food as usual, Selene and Dennis instead share with each other, and Circe has switched the seat and sits by...Vincent? Oh no, Vincent, you will be injured by love, or you already have? The girls are laughing and talking over something that I am likely not interested.

"QX," It is Hera with much louder voice, "how many of us had a romantic relationship before we came here, at the beginning of the graduation week?"

Hera, you are drunk.

"No, Hera. Please."

I know your feelings, Tim. I had the same when I played bridge — a classical Hera-stic question. So what have the girls been talking about?

"That is not part of the known knowledge." QX answers.

Great. I would be very embarrassed if the answer is twenty-three. Yeah, I feel it is twenty-three...

"Maybe — they don't care about the people outside the twenty-four of us." Selene says.

And you too?

"QX," Hera again, "how many of us had a romantic relationship with another one within the twenty-four of us, at the beginning of the graduation week, say Sunday midnight?"

"Six."

Ha ha ha! There is another hidden pair! It is the first time that Hera has asked a meaningful question. People immediately burst into whispers and gossips. Jack and I look at each other and neither of us has any clue. Tim is back to his canonical smile. Maybe Rhea and he had some story earlier? But then why didn't they speak it out yesterday? So it seems quite unlikely. Let us go through the remaining guys — Excluded: Leo, William, Bran; Possible: Oliver, Frank, Yan; and Vincent?

72

Hmmm...That would be bad...That would be very bad, Vincent. No, no, I shake my head the third time of the day.

"Likely they broke up and so don't want to say it. Graduation is usually for break-ups." Tim says.

Right, I agree. So let's not dig too deep into it. Was this the reason why Hera asked for the beginning of graduation week, *Sunday midnight*? So midnight is like their checkpoint back on the Earth?

Why do they care about things happened on the Earth?

"We must feel lucky that the answer is not *seven*." Jack says after a while.

I prefer six, to be honest.

The cat won't name each individual, or their ranks, but can tell us a total number. Interesting.

At the end of the dinner, people again call it a day. The missing couple is still missing. I decide to ask QX to get some confirmation, as I planned earlier during dinner, inspired by the discussion with the explorers. I think through for one more time and phrase carefully to avoid confusion.

"QX," I speak loudly as Hera did, and pause a bit waiting for the crowd to be slightly quieter, "in your first introduction, you mentioned we just passed the solar noon on that day. How long is that solar noon to the moment I woke up on that day, in old Earth hours?"

"Zero point eight nine seven zero hours."

"Thanks QX," I quickly scratch it down, "and you also said that one day here is slightly less than twenty hours on the Earth. How much time is it, errr..." I hesitate a bit and clear my throat, "I need an absolute number."

"Nineteen point eight five zero five hours."

"Why do you care about these digits?" Jack whispers to me, "We don't seem to feel much of the difference between twenty and twenty-four hours, not to say between twenty and nineteen point eight something. Or you get a new way to measure time here?"

"Doing arithmetic." I smile. The numbers match my expectations, but I still need some further confirmation. Most people probably do not notice anything. Maybe only Eos can get something interesting from these numbers. Eos is Eos. I sit far away from her and have no idea about her immediate reactions, but I can vividly imagine her puzzling with these numbers as well as guessing the reason why I asked those questions.

I quickly calculate the numbers again. Something will happen tonight if my calculation is correct.

"Is *this* what you want?" Muse is waving to me, smiling.

"What?"

"Nothing."

I don't understand, but I guess it is not important.

⸻ ❦ ⸻

"Not for a drink, Tim?" I ask.

"Not for tonight — we need some money for more important things." Tim says.

"In fact, we were in the discussion with the explorer group later this afternoon — and we think we need a lot of money — after marriage. Two million sounds a lot but we also need a lot more to fully utilize alien technology." Jack says.

So you believe it is real now, Jack?

"OK. We will have to plan in detail and ask everyone to cooperate, or compromise." Tim says.

And you as well?

"It is not easy. Remember on Thursday the Parade Day, before we got kidnapped, people were unwilling to wear the parade costumes, minutes before the parade was starting, just because it was not to their taste?" I ask carefully.

Yeah, Tim has been a perfect organizer for almost every single event during high school, and only failed once — the Parade.

"It was raining throughout the night until late morning, and I felt lucky that I didn't need to wear that ugly costume. It somehow changed my feelings." Rhea says.

Yeah, human brains are complicated.

"That costume was truly ugly, I admit, but we didn't have anything else on the table at that moment. We had to compromise. Moreover, different people simply have different tastes over things: music, literature, painting or any kinds of arts, games or sports. Nothing exists that can satisfy everyone." Tim says.

"Then how can you force everyone to use their own cash for public service? Water and sewage, power plants, automated farms, waste management, so on and so on." I ask.

"I guess we will have to figure it out." Tim says.

"QX," It's Eos, and she pauses as I did, "who has the best knowledge of the known knowledge by the sunset today?"

"Oh, so I was wrong." Jack says.

"Why does she care about this so much?" Tim murmurs.

"Because — she is a cat." Rhea mouths. All of us — Rhea, Jack and I burst into laughter.

"1." QX answers, loud and clear.

DAY III

xv   Teatime

Dreams, lots of dreams. I wake up on my bed with unstoppable tears. I wish everything were just a dream, a long dream, and I were now on my own bed, with mommy knocking at my door asking me to get up and have breakfast, and daddy already reading news on the sofa with a cup of coffee mommy brewed for him.

However, unlike in a dream, here in this hotel, everything is so real and so logical, especially if you think through these answers from QX over and over. They are so consistent that you cannot find any flaws, like a mathematical theory. I have to admit that alien programming skills are far more advanced than us earthlings, and it is difficult to feel the "AI" part of QX. The more you talk into it, the more it sounds like another human being or an intelligent life form talking behind the screen. That was I guess the reason why Bran said it had passed the Turing Test.

I try to recall what happened last night — It was vivid but vague; it was strange but familiar; it was like a dream but it was not a dream. It's hard to come up with accurate words —

Let me try something with the cat. I press the button and ask: "QX, how many of us had seen an *Eclipse*, by which I mean, similar to the ones I saw last night, by the sunrise today?"

Well, I am not sure whether it knows what I mean, and I am almost sure it won't tell me exactly who have seen it, but at least an overall number can give me an idea — If it is six or above, then I would ask everyone during lunch; three to five, I would feel free to ask around randomly; two, I need to design some trick to find them out; and —

"One."

This is the most devastating answer, even worse than saying "I don't know" or "I don't know what you mean". I have never felt so lonely, far away from human civilizations.

I navigate to the first page and switch the positions, with Muse's help. I need some psychological treatment, right now.

Nyx   Eos   Iris

How shall I start a talk with Nyx? Maybe more about today's lucks? Too stupid. I shake my head. *I once tried some fortune-telling as well, more oriental flavor. Great! What is that? Using twelve wooden pieces...* No, no, no, this sounds more like an academic discussion in ICF, International Congress of Fortune-tellers. Nothing works towards the relationship I am hoping for. Maybe I need to learn more about tarot cards before I can chat with our CFT.

Eos is on the moon, with her yellow book, or rather a huge pile of yellow books.

Iris? I haven't talked to Iris much after the hair-cut. It was a crystal clear message, even more transparent than Nyx's crystal ball. Why would I continue to go after the short cut hair? But then, why would I go after someone on the moon? Maybe in our new environment things will change. However, my cracked pride is telling me that I need a better plan, without embarrassing myself. I definitely don't like the experience from yesterday. Never again.

"QX, can you tell me a joke?"

"I am not a mirror."

Impressive.

"Custom announcement: Test message, test message. Dear explorer team, please wait for me in the lounge before you depart. Tim."

The "Custom announcement" part is from QX, and the remaining message is a record of Tim's voice. So the "Tim" part is unnecessary, but he probably didn't know for sure before testing it out.

The clouds are still covering everything in the sky, but it is relatively bright and presumably close to noon, by old Earth standards. So I drag myself out of bed and go downstairs. Along the way, I quickly run through my notes as I did last night, and almost crash into a small robot with a big black box rolling upstairs through some hidden tracks they installed on the walls.

<hr>

The girls are still babbling with Nyx regarding today's fortune. Iris is alone reading another book.

I stand there, politely and quietly waiting for other people to finish their questions.

"We can go outside today." Nyx says in the end, "It is not as dangerous as yesterday."

"Has any of the retrogrades ended?" Selene asks.

"Yes, Neptune is back in prograde." Nyx responds immediately, "And the relative positions of the planets have switched: Jupiter is now to the east of Mars to overcome its misfortune."

"According to the dates from the cat, this rare eight-planet-retrograde may last one to two weeks. It is impressive they chose the date purposely." I add a comment.

What I really want to say is, do you all believe that they chose this date purposely, respecting some irrelevant planets far out there?

"Today for Virgo: Receive a message and you will be rewarded today, or, Send a message and you will be rewarded in the future. Lucky item: Book." Nyx looks at me.

"Lucky item again?" The girls burst into exclamations.

I haven't even asked! Can you read our minds, just like QX?

"Something must be wrong! Two Lucky items in a row! It is impossible!" Selene says.

"This is not fair!" Circe says.

"Anything possible will happen eventually." Nyx says, "But I will double check tonight."

But, nothing happened with glass yesterday! I feel that our CFT is losing power on this new planet, without Zodiacs probably. Well, I still hope this Lucky item will work out today. Where can I find a book?

A book...I can order my detective novel and expedite the delivery. I was reading it Thursday morning, with my favorite early summer rain...wait, I *was* reading it, *right now*. Oh, no, stop! Not here! It comes again!

Luckily it was a short one. I need to focus on something else, other than books. Not for today.

"Appreciate it, Nyx." I say.

Message? This actually agrees with one of my plans. Future? Too vague, like all those fortune-telling scripts. A common fortune-telling trick. We don't even know whether there is a "future" here.

"Gladly, and good luck." Nyx says.

"By the way, your costume looks nice." I say, trying to find a new topic.

"It is not a costume. It is my work dress, or daily outfit or whatever you may call, but it is not a costume." Nyx replies.

"You want to say sorry." Circe says.

I guess getting a Lucky item again has some unlucky consequences.

"Oh true, I am, very sorry." I say, carefully wording my sentence, "Have you seen the costumes we *would be* wearing, in the parade? They are as ugly as hell."

"No, I haven't." Nyx says, "But I can feel they won't be very popular."

"I haven't either, but your words actually make me interested." Pheme says.

"I actually saw them in the prep room with Rhea. I would never ever want to wear such a thing." Circe says.

"Right," I say with trembling voice, "ugly as hell."

The same thing is happening to everyone.

Dark as hell.

xvi   Railguns

"Dennis, we are wasting time here. They are not going to give us guns." Oliver says.

What have I been doing in the morning? Sitting here in the lounge and mourning over our current situation? I don't even remember! Too much stress I assume.

The explorers, the leader Dennis, Frank, Oliver, Vincent and the couple Artemis and Zak, are still waiting for Tim's secret weapon. Frank and Oliver are pacing around, while others are sitting in the couches.

"Be patient. There is likely nothing interesting out there, my feelings. In addition, we need to show some politeness. Tim is a good leader as I can tell, and it is better we get something useful." Dennis says.

"Sorry we are late, waiting for delivery." Tim finally appears with Bran and a big black box, the same as the one I saw. He opens the box and reveals the secret weapon he talked about yesterday. A long rifle, four to five feet, grey metalic, but pretty thick, and looks heavy. The bullets are...big.

"It is like a railgun." Tim says.

"Railguns, at least the ones I saw on the news, they are huge and heavy and require a battleship to carry around, am I right?" Vincent asks.

"You can use the same design but in much smaller scale, but the power is also significantly less than what was on the news.

However, this one is still good enough to kill a *T-Rex*. You have to be careful." Tim says.

So you believe there are monsters around, Tim?

"At this scale a railgun is similar to or only slightly better than a traditional gunpowder weapon, and so in real life it is not worth the engineering work to make it." Bran says, "We only have two of such guns. You have one, and we keep another one for defense of the hotel. They are expensive. Each gun has only four shots, so please use them wisely."

Oh, I see. I saw the first one, but the second one came much later. Sorry, Tim, you are still an honest guy, but I am just curious, why didn't you give them the first gun?

"Can it be recharged?" Oliver asks.

"It can, but the rails would be bent by a small fraction after a few shots, so may explode in your own hands if you continue firing. Four is a safe number." Bran says, "The problem is we need strongly conductive yet rigid rails, which require much more advanced material science."

"But at least we are not afraid of individual tigers or bears or the like. Thanks a lot, Tim." Dennis says.

"And we have ordered some hunting knifes. Artemis also has a bow and some arrows." Zak says.

Different technology, same principle.

"Very good, and good luck everyone." Tim says, "Please plan ahead to come back by sunset."

"Will do." Says Dennis.

"Last word. I would rather prefer everyone to stay in the hotel, but we have to go outside eventually, so please be careful." Tim says.

Just before they leave, Circe comes up and kisses Vincent, with flushing face and tearing eyes. "Please come back safely." People claps and whistles, but are not much excited.

So you become the poor guy, Vincent.

They will start exploring the south, as picked by Nyx during the morning fortune-telling session. It is a direction with fortune and prosperity, as our CFT claimed. After the explorers have left, the majority of the remaining girls led by Rhea and Selene decide to try out the kitchen utilities, baking something for the returning heroes. Tim asks everyone to take a break or do whatever we like, "giving us enough time to establish healthy relationships", in his own words.

"You two come with me." Tim asks Jack and me to join him with Bran.

xvii   Taxes

Four of us sit at a corner of the lounge, making sure no others can hear us. Girls are in the kitchen playing with doughs and baking pans, and some others are back in their own rooms. Tim's eyes are a bit red. I see, they didn't sleep well last night for the railgun.

"Where shall we start..." It is rare that Tim does not know how to start a conversation.

"How did you order the railguns, may I ask?" I ask.

"Well, we cannot order a full product *gun*, but we can order by a descriptive design, like telling the cat exactly what we need and it is custom made." Bran says, "However, modern guns are very complicated. For example, what is the chemical component for gunpowder? No online search."

"I don't know." I say.

"Right, same for the alloys that make the bullets and the gun-barrel. Without strict descriptions, nothing works like a modern gun. We could get a gun back in sixteenth or seventeenth century, but need many tests on gunpowder, and it is too dangerous."

"So that is why you tried a railgun instead, which in theory or in physics isn't hard. Just need battery and rails and wires, and the bullet can be any conductive metal." Jack says.

"Roughly yes. They are still super expensive, each over one thousand dollars." Bran says.

Do you know how *expensive* gold is right now?

"So it means we are able to split the bill into different accounts?" Jack asks.

"Yes, we confirmed this with the cat on Day one. Just say who pays how much. It doesn't need to be even." Tim continues, with a slower tone, "And we had such a design confirmed with the cat on the *first* night as well."

I immediately feel something strange. "So you were not waiting for the design, but were looking for another person to pay for the second gun? Rhea?" I ask.

"Clever." Tim says, "OK, we could just buy one for the moment, and buy more later after we get enough cash, but still tell people we have two guns, which works the same. However, I personally do not like lying, whether it is a good one or a bad one, and this caused some extra delays than we expected."

OK, this is why I trust you.

"We first thought that we might use this as an excuse to hold the explorers some extra time, but apparently Nyx's words were more powerful." Bran says.

"I see." Jack says, "We not only need one gun to protect ourselves from wild animals, but need multiple guns to prevent us from...shooting each other. At least telling people that there is a second gun will prevent a lot of bad things from happening in the first place."

I see. Tim has been very careful in every detail. It is entirely possible that they deliver the first gun but not the second, trying to trick us into a bad scenario.

"Right, but I promise I was not lying, I never said the reason why we were waiting for the guns. We still want to keep a good friendship with the explorers especially with Dennis, and in return wish to get support from them, in voting." Tim says.

I agree. If Rhea can hold the girls well in the baking group, and if the explorers support us, plus the bridge club girls, we have already reached two thirds majority. It is much easier to get things done —

"As opposed to separating into two groups of twelve and fighting against each other?" I joke.

"We are not in ancient Greece." Tim laughs.

"You don't want to be the King?" I ask.

"No. Democracy is always better. A king cannot rule forever. I can be the leader at the beginning, but would like to get rid of the job as soon as possible. At the moment, people naturally need and want a leader, otherwise things can go to chaos. You know, there are no laws here." Tim says.

We definitely agree. Without Tim, things could be much worse than what it is right now. Moreover, most people still have the subconscious misbelief of the aliens and the tiny hope that everything is just a show, and it is hard to imagine what they might do when they see some valid proof.

"When did you realize that this is real?" I ask.

"When did you?" Tim asks me instead.

"Last night." I answer.

"When they delivered the first gun." Tim says.

Jack has been quiet, not like his usual self showing off some knowledge. I think he is still in the mood of interpreting or accepting our dialogue.

Yes, Jack, this is real. It is not a show on our mother Earth. It is a totally different alien planet, with possibly different physical laws. You haven't seen an eclipse, according to the cat, otherwise you would believe it as well.

"At the beginning, we need to collect everyone's account for some basic infrastructure, such as water, sewage, electricity, waste management, automated farms and factories, and even internet, if we can get computers. Most likely people agree these are absolutely necessary, but we still need to vote. Now, if someone or some family votes against paying for waste management, do you try to split the cost among the remaining ones, or somehow force people to pay by majority vote?" Tim asks.

"Isn't it like in Congress that they vote to spend tax-payers money by majority vote?" Jack asks, presumably recovered from the first shock.

"Congress votes to spend tax that has been collected or will be collected by the law." Tim says, "but here there is no way to force people to pay the tax. So I want to hear from you two about it."

"I believe this is the reason why those aliens want us to get married." I start after a while, "Think about a couple with a few babies. They need some social environment. Kids need to go to school. Kids need other kids to play with. Kids get ill very easily. It is very hard to live alone in such a scenario, and you cannot even send kids to school if you don't pay your taxes."

"This does not work for singles," Bran says, "like Eos."

"Yes, Eos is probably the first person who refuses to cooperate or compromise, especially if she is not married and has no baby." Tim says, "So we need to find her a mate."

I think, this chat is going to the wrong direction.

"Or persuade her to compromise and enter a sham marriage and pay taxes." Bran says.

Then all three of them look at me. What am I supposed to do?

"If one refuses cooperation, others will follow." Jack says.

"How much do you plan to tax?" I ask, for a different topic.

"For singles, it is hard since they do not have much money. We will try a nominal twenty thousand dollars of tax. For couples, we are thinking five hundred thousand, as infrastructure is regarded as part of the housing cost. If we are lucky to have twelve matched couples and double the reward, then we can even try one million per couple."

A spark of an idea comes into my mind.

"So for example, when you build a power plant, you simply ask the cat to charge the same amount to everyone?" I ask.

"More or less. Couples pay more of course." Tim says, "But everyone has to agree with the cat, otherwise the proposal won't be processed."

"How do we get the fuel for a power plant?" Jack asks.

"Nuclear power." Bran says, "Just like this hotel."

"Really?"

"Yes, this is in the middle of a forest and we cannot identify any wires connecting to the outside world. So something is happening inside the hotel." Tim says, "By the way, water comes from a well and there is a tank on the rooftop seen from the girls wing. It is the hydrogen source as well."

"Deuterium, to be precise, then you make tritium out of it." Bran says.

Oh, I roughly remember these two words. They are the heavier isotopes of the regular hydrogen, Element One, but I never know these can be used for nuclear power. Maybe I shall order a book about nuclear physics. Hey, I wonder what number would the cat call them? One plus? No...that is likely for the ion, a single proton.

"We first tried solar panels supplemented by nuclear power," Bran continues. "but solar power is often unreliable, weather dependent, and we ought to use nuclear power as backup anyway. Then we figured out nuclear power is in fact cheaper — small scale fusion reactors."

Have you guys ever had a sleep since Day one?

"I should have noticed earlier!" Jack says, "This hotel is in the middle of nowhere, and there is no way to explain the power supply."

"In some sense," Tim continues, "The sun over there is itself a fusion reactor."

"OK. I have an idea about the matching game, with taxes." I say with some hesitation.

"Sure, what is it?" Tim asks.

"So this is inspired by your tax system." I speak slowly, trying to organize myself, "Let us forget the singles right now. For each couple, you want to tax them five hundred for public services, and allow them to keep the remaining five hundred as private property."

"Right."

"How about you phrase things differently. You allow every couple to keep five hundred as their own, and tax whatever above that threshold for public services, whether it is two hundred or seven hundred over. Then you can ask everyone to reveal their rank numbers, and even people shoot each other in the guessing game, then it is just for fun now. There wouldn't be any difference."

Three of them are digesting my plan.

"Good thing is that, after everyone knows everyone's rank number, as we discussed before, we can quickly follow the algorithm to match twelve couples, and so there is no worry about taxing these singles. Every couple gets around two million and you tax anything above one million. So effectively every couple gets one million for their own plus the public utilities. Now consider the scenario where people just blindly choose their list and have very tiny chance of getting twelve pairs overall. One couple then can only get one million, and even worse nobody is guaranteed a matching with their loved one." I say.

"This is brilliant." Tim says.

"I think this is a very plausible plan right now." Bran says, "There are still some technical details we need to figure out. For example, we still need to wait for people to pair up into twelve pairs. But overall this is close to the solution I think. We can even tell everyone it is how the aliens designed the games."

"What do you mean?" I ask.

"The game designer must have some hidden purpose, otherwise they won't put such strange artificial rules into the game. They want us to solve the problem and establish some social framework by ourselves. If your solution is their final goal, the correct answer, then the moral is — *Humans are social animals that need public services as well as private properties.*" Bran says.

"And, *rich people pay higher taxes.* Bran and I were brainstorming about this. It does not seem that we are anything special. So there must be other colonies on this planet or on other planets, groups of boys and girls you can imagine." Tim says, "Like a lab experiment. Sorry I know this may make you uncomfortable."

Shit. We need to compete with other colonies? Now I really need to learn some nuclear physics.

"So they want to filter out the groups that can find out the solution they designed." I say.

"Right."

Jack wants to say something, but is a bit hesitated.

"Anything not right, Jack?" I ask.

"Sorry, what if this is only a show or a game, not real, or people believe that this is just a game." Jack says, "Some of them won't reveal their numbers, and they will still shoot each other in the guessing game for the cash reward, like in a show."

Right. The three of us are thinking based on our belief that everything is real, and start to think about what is behind the scene, etc. Jack may still be a bit suspicious about this single fact and so he can find a flaw here.

"Then we also need to wait for everyone to believe it is real." Tim says, "One moment, maybe we have to think more carefully about it. Too much for today. We shall all have a break, and meet again tomorrow for the details."

"Sure. Feel free to let us know if you need cash for anything. Glad to help." I say. They probably have depleted their cash for the railguns.

"Thanks, but I feel that you two may need to save money for the last few days, for any emergency." Tim says.

"By the way, how do custom announcements work?"

"Oh, I want to ask about this as well. Very handy." I say, "Does it work like voicemail?"

"It is easy, just tell the cat you need to broadcast a message. You can say 'custom announcement'. Ten dollars, only works from sunrise to sunset so that it does not disturb people from sleeping, but it has to be broadcasted to every room, including all public areas." Tim says, "We forgot to keep a record of who lives in which room. I ran next door to ask Bran for help, but then Bran came up with this interesting idea. Quite effective."

"And you are not able to send a secret love letter to only one person. However, you can send an open love letter to a girl and broadcast it to everyone." Bran laughs.

Seriously? Who would do that?

xviii   Nightfall

We have an afternoon tea break as yesterday, and we have freshly baked cookies and cupcakes from the girls. Some clever boys are chatting with the girls praising their baking skills, while I am dumbly appreciating their product alone.

"Cookies are really good." Jack comes over.

"Agree. Best ones I have ever had."

"You need to talk to the girls. I didn't make them."

"OK, when I have a chance..." I swiftly change the topic to my comfort zone, "You know what, I had another weird dream last night."

"Another guessing game?"

"Ha-ha, maybe. So we went to college, or maybe it was after our college — it's a dream — living in the same city say. Rent was too high. My girlfriend there — sorry I have no idea who she was, or whether she was one of us; it's dream, you know — ok, my girlfriend did not want to share an apartment with me, for whatever reason."

"OK. It happens. More convenient this way. I understand. Sometimes couples do break up, and then you don't need to worry about finding another place to live."

"Yeah, I agree. So, I ended up renting a two-bedroom apartment, shared with...one of the girls, here."

"Another girl? That's a weird dream — But let me see — Not Hera or Muse, these two would be too easy to guess. Not Eos, who represents your girlfriend in the dream I think. The remaining girls... Nyx?"

"No, but again very close. It was...Selene."

"Hmmm... You want to tell Dennis about your dreams, both of them."

"No way! It's not what you think. Maybe, I just feel, we are...very similar, same type of person."

I continue to wander around the ground floor while Jack has been to the bathroom.

"Hi," Eos sounds a bit shy, "can we talk?" She is holding a thinner yellow book with her both hands, over the belly.

"Absolutely." I am ecstatic but try to be as calm as possible. She is holding a book! A book!

"This is about the two questions you asked with the cat last night. The numbers are interesting. Have you figured out that it is exactly five days?"

"Yes, exactly five days."

Oh, Muse, why are you so wise?

"So you knew it before you asked?" Eos asks.

Sorry, it is not polite to think about one girl while chatting with another.

"Maybe. Had a strange feeling of it. They are perfectionists I can tell."

"But I still don't quite understand, why five days? Especially why are Saturday and Sunday important? Or is it just random? I stayed at home reading books all day long during the weekend. Nothing special." She says.

"Saturday and Sunday? Oh I get it. Errr...I don't know either, but let us figure this out, shall we?"

For her, *it is still Wednesday*. Well, in fact, it is still Wednesday for *everyone*. I then notice something really really important that I totally missed earlier. I am stunned. How could I have overlooked this!

She seems a bit hesitated, but rather her eyes are telling me to give her some extra hint. Oh my goddess, I can never resist such beautiful pair of eyes.

"I am still planning some little experiments on this. I will let you know as soon as possible if I find anything." I don't have time to make up some words for her, "And, it is our secret, OK?"

"OK." Eos says, "And, thanks."

"What is this book you are reading today?" I ask.

"GTM seven, *A Course in Arithmetic* by Serre."

Arithmetic, oh that sounds easier than algebra and geometry. Maybe she felt that fifty-two book is too hard and switched to arithmetic instead. Why are graduate students still interested in arithmetic?

"I have another question. You don't have to answer." She lowers her voice a lot, gets even closer and asks with her shining eyes, "Are you 1?"

I have thought, a thousand times, about facing this scenario, and rehearsed all possible ways to joke on it or ignore it or deny it or confirm it. However, here with my goddess in front of me, all of my preparations are in true vain, and I feel it is almost impossible to hide anything from her face to face. So I try something so brave that I would have never imagined. This time I think I deserve a prestigious prize for my courage. If I am going to die, why shall I be afraid?

I approach close to her, hold her shoulders with both of my hands, with my Lucky item between us. She is shocked and her body is also quivering as I am. I bow down my head, mouth almost touching her earlobe, and try to be brief so that hopefully the crowd does not notice us, because it definitely looks like I am about to kiss her at her cheek right on the scene.

"Yes, Miss 3."

You still keep this rank shenanigans in your deep heart, my goddess.

It is like a big gamble. I am only seventy or eighty percent sure about it, but she is 3 or 4 at least. If she is 5 or lower, then she would very soon give up figuring out the higher rank guys or even thinking about ranks.

I am in this unrealistic dream that two of us would keep this moment forever, when I receive a small but quite strong punch on my chest, and I can see on her burning red face — her anger, her confusion, her satisfaction as well as her amusement, one following another. She probably wants to do this for fun, letting the others believe that I was trying something too brave and obviously got punished. It hurts! It really hurts!

"You must feel lucky that I don't have a railgun in my hand. Go away, now." She says.

You cannot hide yourself, my goddess.

Meanwhile, the explorers come back.

xix   Fruits

Everyone is safely back. Good news. People soon gather in the lobby. Vincent is all good, uninjured, so maybe "injured by love" could be more like a mental injury? Anyway, we all sit down and Dennis begins his report.

"We first followed the compass heading south. It is just a forest with mostly pine trees and oak trees or some other trees we cannot name. Some thorny vines made some trouble. We marked some big trees along the way so that we can follow the path back to the hotel."

"The ground was still moist, which slowed us down. After about an hour or so, as it is hard to measure time, maybe only one to two miles of walking in our speed, we got out of the forest and reached a river. It is about a hundred yards wide, like a football field. The water flows from east to west. The river banks are covered mostly by some wetland grass. It is hard to cross the river without a boat, so we decided to go along the river upstream towards east."

Oh, I just notice that their shoes are pretty muddy. It is

probably not easy to hike in a trail-less wild forest, after some heavy rain.

"We did not exactly follow the bank as it is muddy and may be dangerous. So we went along the edge of the forest, but we were able to hear the water flow and occasionally saw the river directly. We didn't go very far and after roughly ten to fifteen minutes we found a river beach with mostly small pebbles and some big rocks where we can sit and have a late lunch. Afterwards we searched around but didn't find much interesting, so we decided to follow the same route back to the hotel to finish the first day of exploration."

"On the way back, we encountered our first discovery that is worth mentioning." Dennis points to Oliver, who opens a backpack and shows us some strange golden fruit. They picked a lot of them, at least one for each of us.

People start to raise questions while passing around the fruits.

"Any animals in the forest?" Selene asks.

"No. Nothing. It is very strange I would say. Not even small insects or snakes, but maybe the repellent we ordered is too effective." Dennis says, "It is possible that some are in hibernation."

"But it is summer time." Leo says.

"No, the temperature does not feel like summer, more like early spring or late fall on the Earth." Bran says, "It is also possible that we are in a mountain, at a high altitude, or on another planet with a totally different climate pattern."

"Did you notice any signs of civilization?" Tim asks.

"No. We had been keeping our eyes open, but no." Dennis says, "And the gun back for you, with four shots unused."

"It is yours." Tim says, "You guys need it more than we do here."

"Thank you, Tim. Really appreciate it." Dennis says.

"What is this?" Leo asks.

"Railgun. You don't remember?" Yan asks in awe.

"Oh...I...didn't notice...there is another one." Leo says.

People seem to have memory problems after all.

"Are there fish in the river?" Rhea asks.

"It is possible. Water looks nice and clean." Dennis says, "We can try to catch some next time."

"A question everyone is curious: have you guys tried this fruit? Is it edible?" Pheme asks.

"No we haven't tried. We decided to come back and talk to everyone first. There is a large area with these trees. Zak noticed these on the way back." Dennis answers.

"I think it is too dangerous." Tim says, "We have enough food resources, at least for now."

"I don't remember seeing this kind of fruit before, in my whole life, but...maybe only in some old fashion mythology." Nyx says.

As people chat and pass around the fruit, I lastly get one in my hands. Mine is golden, like most ones, and a few others are more yellowish. It has seven corners, like a star fruit, but the texture feels more like an apple or pear. So it looks like some kind of tropical fruit, but I haven't seen this before.

"There are lots of bizarre tropical fruits that I haven't seen either." Leo says.

It does not feel like tropical region, Leo.

"Usually you squeeze some juice over your skin and if it does not cause allergy symptoms then it is probably safe." Jack says, "Then you test with your tongue and try a small portion and so on. Just do everything slowly, step by step. We need to eat some of these eventually I guess, as long as it is edible."

People are still hesitating and probably decide to try Jack's suggestion.

"QX, is this fruit poisonous to us?" I ask.

"No. In fact this is very nutritious for you." QX answers.

"OK, thanks!" I say, and I quickly take a big bite. If I am going to die, there is nothing to fear. "It is delicious, like a crispy apple and it is sweet. I like it!"

"No! How can you trust the cat?" Hera says.

Only a few people are following me, making small bites, but the majority still wants to wait for a few days to see if we get poisoned by it. Anyway, someone must try it first, and I am willing to take that responsibility.

"You don't have to do this," Tim comes to me afterwards, "and there are better ways to tell people it is real. At least...you want to wash it first."

xx   Messages

Right before dinner, Tim makes an announcement.

"First, let us thank the explorer team again for their bravery. You guys did an excellent job. We now have better ideas about where we are and where we can build farms and water facilities." Tim says.

To most people, this sounds like a good speech, in a show.

"Second, we," He looks at Jack and me, "have figured out a plan to win the two million dollars for every couple in the matching game. There are a few details we need to settle and we will let you know when it is ready. That being said, we still need everyone's cooperation."

"Finally, this might be early to address, but after marriage we need to plan ahead for our community or colony to survive and flourish. Just like a real city or town, we need public utilities such as water and electricity, school and hospital, roads and bridges, and it is better and less expensive to build facilities for everyone to use instead of everyone building their own. So I propose here that every couple designate half of their reward cash as public working capital to build these public services together."

"I don't want to force everyone to join the plan, but if you don't want to join, then you are not able to use the public services we build. Bran is a very good design engineer as you can tell. Moreover, we now think this is a crucial step towards the solution of the matching game and the guessing game as well. So if you do not follow our plan, then you at most get one million dollars with your spouse and you have to do everything by yourselves; but if everyone follow our plan, then every couple would get one million dollars to spend on their own, plus access to all public services we are going to build."

"Sorry, if this is just a show, then there is no such tax for public services, and we simply get all we earn from the games, right?" Iris asks.

"Right. If this is a show only, then what I said doesn't apply, and there is no risk of joining our plan at all. But, I just want to emphasize, we need to plan ahead if it is real." Tim says.

Most people start to discuss with close friends. Muse, Hera, Jack and I are the first ones to join. Very quickly the baking girls also come up agreeing with the plan, as expected. Dennis and the explorers follow, partly because of the elegant engineering of the railgun but also mainly because the plan sounds plausible. As Tim said, once there is trust, it is easier for people to cooperate. Most of the remaining people follow soon afterwards. I guess they do not want to be isolated. The only one left is Eos.

"I agree we need public facilities, but I don't want sham marriage. Stay away from me." She says.

"If every boy picks you in the list, then you have to enter a sham marriage." Jack says.

Part of this is not even a lie. I believe most boys will have Eos in their list.

"Is this part of your ultimate plan, forcing a woman into a marriage against her will?" Eos asks with anger.

Oh, Muse, remind me the reasons, why the Queen is so raged today!

"No." I say, "To be exact, if all three boys in your own list have already been matched with someone else before your turn, rare but does happen by chance, like an eclipse or a transit, then you still don't get married, even when every boy puts you in the list."

However, my goddess, there is not enough number of people before you. Your rank is still too high and you are forced into marriage, Miss 3. You may want gay marriage — No, in fact, your rank is too high even if the system allows gay marriages. You now realize that high rank does not necessarily mean privilege but in fact responsibility? Eos is much smarter than me, so she immediately understands the situation and stops saying anything else, and she probably regrets getting a rank which is too high. She is not good at hiding herself, even without saying anything.

And I believe, very soon some other people will also start to go through the same reasoning that, if Eos has very high rank, then my argument does not work for her, and that likely she has high rank, as some people even guess she is 1. This is some fun part of the game, telling or guessing at each others' ranks by almost every clue. To be honest, we are enjoying this part of the game, by the very ugly nature of humanity.

"Eos, you don't have to think of this way." Muse says, "It is a matching in the system, not a real marriage. Of course we want most matchings to be stable marriages, but it is OK if things do not work out, You can always negotiate with your matching partner — let us put it like this. You two still pay for public services, and have a lot of remaining money to spend on your own, even build one house for each of you. Don't think of it as marriage, just a game. You get much more cash to buy books right? We need to preserve human knowledge and spirit in this new world."

In this new world. When did you realize this, Muse?

This time everyone agrees.

<hr>

"Hey, I just heard about it — Welcome aboard on Apollo

Eleven! How do you feel right now?" Journalist Jack asks during dinner.

"Most people think it is crashed already." I promise I am not lying.

Trying to kiss a girl against her will, in public? What have I done? Shall I feel lucky that there are no laws here?

"I now understand why Eos is so angry today, but I still don't understand, I mean, we spent four years together and you are not that kind of person. You must have your reason right? You don't have to tell me." Jack says.

"She asked for my rank, and obviously I don't want other people to hear it, either a truth or a lie." I murmur.

That was why I pretended to kiss her. Is this explanation good enough?

"I see it now. She probably wants to find those top ranked people and persuade them to not put her into their lists." Jack concludes. "Pretty reasonable."

"Why did she target on top ranked people? Any three boys would do."

My real question is — Why do you believe I am among the top ranked people?

"Two birds with one stone." Jack says.

"I suggest you keep trying. As we discussed earlier, we need to find her someone in order to complete twelve pairs, for our ultimate goal." Tim says, "You look like the closest one I can tell."

"William said he is willing to have a sham marriage. So you can try to pair him with Eos." I say.

"May work for other girls. Not for Eos."

Eos is Eos.

Shall I carry out the plan? As Jack said, I might be on board on Apollo Spacecraft, but still far away from the moon, and no one knows what may happen along the way, the dangerous way with little tolerance to mistakes. Moreover, once I take off,

I need to say goodbye to everyone else here on the Earth, and meager possibilities all become zero.

I finally make my decision after the dinner. Chance is pretty small, but worth trying, and to be honest I don't feel good about being dragged by others towards a fake marriage with Eos.

I hope most people don't even bother since I always ask stupid questions.

"QX," I want to make sure people can hear it, "do you have chamomile tea that I can order?"

"Yes, one dollar."

"Thanks. I would like one for tomorrow morning, with some sugar in it, but don't put too much, not good for health or teeth. And, do you also have ginseng tea?"

"Yes, two dollars."

"Great. I will have both, by sunrise. Thanks."

"Hey, are you trying to date someone tomorrow morning in your room before everyone wakes up?" Oliver says. The crowd immediately starts laughing.

"Two cups of tea are far less than enough. You'd better order something else!" Vincent says. People laugh even more.

I do not answer. The message is so clear as my face already feels burning. So I quickly finish my plate and rush back to my room, hoping my princess still has that little piece of memory.

I am going to die, so it's better to find someone with a real marriage and have babies, as many as possible, as soon as possible.

DAY IV

xxi   Sun

Waiting on my bed for the delivery of my order, I try to wrap up what I have learned since last night, mostly based on my notes. It is hard to fall asleep with a big secret, to be honest.

Good news is that I feel less certain about dying now. In fact, I feel immortal. How can I die? As long as my brain is working properly, there is no chance for me to die. *Cōgitō, ergō sum.* Even if I die, nothing matters to me afterwards, so why would I worry so much? Moreover, why would aliens spend so much effort putting us here on another planet and letting us die? In nineteen, no, twenty-five years?

Bad news? My plan for the games does not work.

And I need to confirm with Eos later today about what happened before the graduation ceremony. This is to make sure other people can also see similar things, like a scientific experiment, to prove that it is not because of my own brain damage or malfunction.

The ceremony was at nine in the morning, so I was probably with her around eight fifty-five? The hard part is to time things correctly *here*. I can keep asking QX for accurate answers, but will cause too much unnecessary attention, and I have to phrase the question naturally, which is not easy if I ask a lot of similar questions. These clever guys will sense anomaly very quickly. I bet a few have already been suspicious with my "absolute number".

I receive two cups of drinks delivered by a little cute robot, which reminds me about Iris. I double-check my choices, and make an order switch with Muse's help again, just for myself.

Iris   Eos   Nyx

It also reminds me about the sunrise, and so I ask the cat the same question with the sunrise today. The answer is still the same, a terrifying "One". Oh, then —

"One prime and One double prime." QX answers.

"And a neutron is Element Zero?"

"No. Zero is the lowest energy vacuum state, which is much more abundant. A neutron is called Zero prime."

The morning light is crisper than ever, and only a few clouds scatter in the blue dome. We can have a first look at our new sun today, which is still hidden behind the dense forest, moving hesitantly along its predetermined trajectory to greet some innocent new habitants of its vast domain.

I am roughly doing the same thing, moving downstairs to the lounge. The good thing is, even if Iris does not show up, then we simply pretend nothing has happened. In fact *pretend* is not the right word here — Nothing would really happen so there is actually nothing to pretend. People may gossip about the two cups of strange tea, but will soon forget.

⋅⋅◦〜◦⋅⋅

"How do you feel with the fruit?" Iris asks.

Really, this is your first question? I then notice she is holding a book. The book she lent me a long time ago. I see. Nyx is absolutely right.

"Nothing wrong as far as I can tell, and it tastes good. You may want to try." I say.

"I feel very worried about you. You know. Not only because of the possibly poisonous fruit, but also because — as rumors going around — you become a bit crazy or insane due to this dramatic game."

"Rumors? Insane? You think I am mad?" I ask, with laugh. Instead I think this is the most logical part of my entire life.

"No, no, but you know, crazy things are happening and some people are showing bizarre behavior, which is quite understandable. Most girls also have stress symptoms such as lack of sleep and memory loss and nightmares and...anyway."

"You had a memory loss?"

"No, but Gaia didn't even remember Dennis and others had left for an exploration yesterday, and believed that everyone stayed in the hotel all day long."

Hmmm, probably unrelated.

"OK. I just trust the cat for some reason. Hard to explain." I say, "Don't worry, I think I am totally fine. If you ask me to do it again today, I probably wouldn't be the first one to try the star-like apple. And, thank you."

"But people saw you trying to kiss Eos, against her will."

Oh my goodness! How can they connect these two totally irrelevant things together?

Well, they are sort of related, not directly.

"No, no, no! That was not a kiss. I didn't mean that at all." I explain, "She asked me a secret question, and I had to answer without anyone else listening."

"So it's like a little secret?" Iris says, "Everyone wants to keep some little secrets, I understand. Eos again asked her famous question, about the best knowledge, you know it, after you ran upstairs. The answer was still 1. Is this related?"

Ah, she is going to do this for all the days.

"Not quite. We have some matching issues with Eos — We have to pair her with someone in order to get twelve pairs. So this is hard." I try to switch the topic from the little secret.

"Never mind. So can I have my ginseng tea? I don't usually drink it in the morning recently, more in the afternoon, during tea time."

"Absolutely. Sorry."

Iris puts the book down on the coffee table, and speaks with lower and lower volume: "I was reading this again yesterday, and I guess, you received my message; I am glad you still remember it, and so...you sent your reply during dinner."

Oh sorry I didn't. I am so sorry!

"You know, I like talking with you, especially before you cut your hair short, because I feel very relaxed talking to you." I don't know what else to say, and so start to recite from my pre-compiled codes, "In this new world, life will be very tough afterwards, so I would like to find someone I can talk to without stress."

"Oh...that was why you stopped chatting with me. You know, I just wanted to give it a try and asked your opinion about it. I feel so bad!"

Iris takes a sip and stalls for a while, like trying to digest my words, then realizes what I actually mean with my second sentence.

"Oh, what happened...How — What is this...I mean — is this a proposal?" Iris puts down the cup, and asks in flushing cheek, holding mouth shut with the left hand.

"Yes."

"Do you know how happy I am?"

"I can see it from your tears and hear it from your voice. Thank you, for your love." I say. Things are happening fast, Jack!

With eyes closed, hands off mouth, Iris sits still, with sipping lips, and waits for me.

"May I kiss you?" I shouldn't let a lady wait for too long. Holding the shivering body, I take a breath and kiss to the lovely lips.

A sudden blast of sunlight pierces through the heavy woods and breaks into the morning lounge. It is on my back, as warm as the lips and the tongue. The whole room is covered by a glorious golden hue, just as my heart governed by this unthinkable joy.

"It's a nice day today... I am so sorry!" It is Pheme, who quickly run away.

"I don't know, what is really happening, but Pheme is, going to tell everyone." Iris says, with still trembling voice.

"Let it be." I quickly kiss again on the cheek.

"Isn't the sun a bit bigger than usual?" Iris asks, "It is another planet after all."

When did you realize this? Everyone has their little secrets.

I turn around and become the second or maybe the third person who sees the sun directly.

"Maybe. It does look bigger during dawn and dusk. Common saying is that the sun has comparison with other objects like buildings or trees during sunrise and sunset, and so it is mostly human illusion. Others say that the thick atmosphere at dawn and dust may distort the image."

"You sound like Jack." Iris laughs. "By the way, what is your plan with Jack, and Tim, for the matching game? I mean, of course we put each other into our lists; in fact I have already done that, but there is still no guarantee. That was why lots of girls simply gave up and focused instead on baking, and Nyx's fortune-telling."

"Well, the plan does not work, or at least we need more modifications I have to say. I have to clarify, Tim was not lying. We did think that we had a very good plan, but after some careful examination, there are loopholes that I cannot cover. So we will need to continue the discussion later today. Sorry. You feel free to continue baking with the other girls. The cookies taste fantastic." I continue, "I've already put you in my list as well."

"Thank you." Iris answers with lovely burning ears.

"It feels good." I say.

"What? You mean the sun?"

We smile at each other, look at each other and kiss again with each other.

xxii   Sundial

We chat randomly, meanwhile people start to come downstairs and congratulate us. Everyone knows about it within an hour. Very efficient, indeed.

"Hey, congratulations." Jack says, "Quite, unexpected."

"Thank you. How about you with Muse?" I ask.

"Will try later today."

I guess my movement has some chain reactions as well. Very soon more pairs are coming up: Gaia and Frank, which is also a surprise, Hera and Yan, possibly because they have similar taste of wine. Things are happening fast, Jack!

"Frank came to me on the second day. He is not a very talkative person, but honest. I told him that I was still waiting for someone else, but would consider him in my list." Iris says.

"I see. Same for Yan?" I ask.

"Nope. Maybe it is Hera?" Iris laughs.

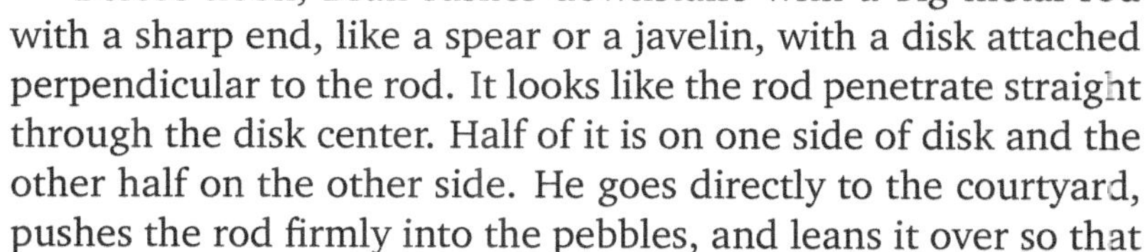

Before noon, Bran rushes downstairs with a big metal rod with a sharp end, like a spear or a javelin, with a disk attached perpendicular to the rod. It looks like the rod penetrate straight through the disk center. Half of it is on one side of disk and the other half on the other side. He goes directly to the courtyard, pushes the rod firmly into the pebbles, and leans it over so that the edge of disk touches the ground by the edge of the center circle, holding the whole structure tight, like a javelin stick to the ground with an angle pointing south.

"It is a sundial." He says, "It's a bit late. Glad we haven't passed the solar noon yet. I can make it more accurate tomorrow if it is still sunny."

"So with sunrise, solar noon and sunset, we can roughly measure time now. Solar noon is somewhat like twelve pm back on the Earth." Jack says.

This is exactly what I am looking for! I almost cry out —

Oh, Muse, which God forged this elegant device for us!

We immediately notice that the shadow is pointing towards south, a bit towards west, and so the sun is towards north, just as William mentioned. So from east to north to west, it is going backwards and the sundial is...going counterclockwise in motion.

"Now you see why clocks and watches all go clockwise but not counterclockwise." Jack says.

"Why?" Muse asks.

"Because in Europe where people first invented clocks, the sun is in the south and sundials go clockwise. That's it, northern hemisphere supremacy." Jack says.

"By the way, Muse," I add a comment, "OK, first, this is what I once discussed with Jack while playing video games, so I need to accredit him as well. The funny thing is that, even if our civilization first started in the southern hemisphere, such as Australia or southern Africa or South America, the clocks and watches would go the other way, meaning the definitions of 'clockwise' and 'counterclockwise' are switched, but still the Earth is rotating 'counterclockwise' in the new definition. Do you see the reason?"

"Yeah, I remember that." Jack laughs.

"Sorry?" Muse is obviously confused at first, but very soon sees the argument, "I see the point now. Very interesting."

In fact, this is exactly why you guys miss something important, something super important, I think.

Soon QX announces the solar noon and lunch time of the day. Some of us, Muse, Jack and I, are still standing there with the sundial, like a group of cavemen or cavewomen looking at a computer and watching a paragraph of codes running all by itself for the first time in their lives. Bran adjusts the position of the sundial and marks the position of the shadow using a marker. The shadow is pointing slightly towards the boys' wing.

So the courtyard is facing slightly southeast. I quickly visualize the positions of everything in my brain — the Sun, the Earth and the sundial.

"Bran, I remember the pole or the rod has to be along the same direction as the Earth's rotation axis, which means that we need to know the altitude of our current position first. How do you know that?" Jack asks.

"The rod is called a gnomon," Bran says, "and we asked the cat."

"So our current latitude is about...thirty degrees south?" Jack takes a look at the sun as well, "And if it is in May right now, the sun at noon at this high angle, which means we are near the equator. So latitude numbers do not match."

"Thirty-two point seven nine. So it is not in May, or we are not on the Earth, or the cat is lying." Bran says, "Which is more likely to you? The weather does not feel like we are near the equator."

"It does not feel like thirty-something degrees south either. In southern hemisphere it is actually winter time, and it cannot be as warm as this, with these trees and fruits." Jack says, and immediately rejects himself. "Rats. I always forget that it is not on the old Earth."

"It is hard to imagine we have to use a sundial to tell the time in a fusion-reactor powered hotel." I murmur.

"Thanks, Bran. How much is it? I'll pay you back." Tim comes over.

"My pleasure. Forget it. It is very cheap, and delivery is super fast compared to the guns." Bran says.

Its chemical component looks pretty simple.

"So what metal did you use? Aluminum?" Tim asks.

"Element Twenty-Two, Titanium. Lightweight, extra strong, excellent resistance to corrosion, but with poor conductivity. Used in spacecrafts — including *their* ones." Bran says.

So they also believe there is something wrong with — time.

"Hey Jack, I have a quick question for you." I ask during lunch.

"Glad to answer."

"Regarding this twelve versus twelve topic from yesterday, what other things in ancient history or mythology or legend that come with twelve or twenty-four? Just curious." I ask.

"Interesting topic. I guess the reason twelve is so popular is that it is a composite number with many divisors — two, three, four, six, which makes it easy to subdivide in early years of civilization, when we had to share things. And it is also the rough number of lunar cycles in a year. So ancient Egyptians had used twelve hours in their sundials. In addition, Sumerians and Babylonians partly used sixty as their base, especially for fractions. I would imagine, here in this new world, we may want to do something similar in the future, it is much easier to subdivide if one day has twenty-four hours, new Earth hours, with sixty minutes an hour and sixty seconds a minute."

"Bible has twelve tribes and twelve Apostles of course. Ancient Chinese had a twelve-year Zodiac cycle, represented by twelve animals, which originally came from the twelve-year cycle of Jupiter, but they don't use it anymore. Chinese also have twelve Ornaments, which you can trace back to their early history. You know what, they have some numbering hierarchy system that you may only expect from Nyx's magic society or the like. Twelve, the full set, is reserved for the imperial family, nine for other nobleman classes, seven for the central government officials and their family, and five for local government."

It reminds me about Nyx's mentor, who came to the reception on Monday morning and wore a strange wizard hat with five stars on it, which is already the highest rank in terms of U.S. military system. It's likely the same type of system as the Ornaments in China. I start to imagine how many stars Nyx has — maybe two or three.

"For normal people like us, it is one or three depending on whether you have passed some exam which is similar to GRE."

"Seriously? GRE? To wear two extra stars?"

Why do they skip over most even numbers, but not twelve?

"Scholar-bureaucracy as you may call it. Sorry we are off the topic — in Norse mythology, which was probably related to Greek mythology, there are also various versions of twelve gods and twelve goddesses, or nine gods and nine goddesses, or twelve main gods. In Hindu, twelve Adityas, the solar gods, represent twelve months as well..."

"OK, thanks." I stop him from listing the twelve solar gods. "Speaking of Nyx, how many tarot cards are there?"

"I guess you mean the major arcana, which has twenty-two cards like the ones you may have heard of, numbered from zero to twenty-one. At least all mainstream decks have twenty-two cards, but there are various other non-mainstream decks with different versions of extra two cards added in. You know how people liked the number twenty-four so much that they made up the remaining two with all kinds of imaginations. There is also the minor arcana which is very similar to playing cards with fourteen cards in each of the four suits, total of fifty-six."

"OK, so that is likely irrelevant." I say.

"So you think any of these numbers are related to us?" Jack asks,

"Likely not. The closest one is Greek mythology, but still does not agree with our situation. Tim makes a very good leader and we are not fighting with each other. But, I just have a gut feeling that twelve or twenty-four will appear naturally somewhere."

"Oh, Dennis, you guys are leaving? I actually planned to join you, but Muse asked me to stay with the discussion today. Sorry, and have fun!" Jack speaks loudly to the explorers.

I see, a clever way to say *I am after Muse, so if you are doing the same, let us fight.* Hmmm...one of the explorers.

Ha-ha, I think I know who it is this time. Easy exclusion trick.

<hr>

Well, soon I realize I could be wrong — Two boys and two girls from another discussion group, Leo, Yan, Pheme and Kakia, join with the explorers today. This time they decide to go north. Again Tim asks them to take care and come back before sunset, and Tim also suggests them to look for potential lands to build our houses.

"No problem, will take a look around." Dennis says.

The baking girls continue with their explorations as well. Someone even ordered a few baking recipe books and they are obsessed to try all these things out. Tim may think that they are wasting time, but as long as they bake something delicious, I have no objection at all.

William is servicing god with a Bible and probably thinking about how to build a church on a new planet. Is he carrying it all day long? Bran decides to join us to crack the games. The last of us, Nyx, has not shown up, maybe performing some dark magic to curse the aliens back in the guest room? Oh, our CFT didn't even have a fortune-telling session this morning as I can remember. Anything went wrong with the crystal ball?

Before we start the discussion, I ask QX a question.

"QX, how much time is it from now back to solar noon, in old Earth hours?"

"One point two five zero hours."

So I quickly run outside and put down a small mark on the disk. The sundial is not perfectly positioned, so the shadow's angular movement may not match the movement of time exactly minute by minute, but it is accurate enough that I can make some real measurements. I don't want to draw too much attention, so I take my writing pad with me, do some elementary arithmetic, and put down another small mark.

God bless it is all sunny today.

xxiii   Failures

Our original group plus Bran sit together in the lounge.

"Sorry to announce, my plan from yesterday does not work." I start.

"Yeah I saw some loopholes as well, but you can explain and let's see whether we can fix them." Tim says.

"Wait, what is your plan from yesterday?" Muse asks.

Sure. I explain the plan, tax over everything above a threshold, and explain why it seems working. Eos probably knows everything after one single sentence, and it takes some extra time to keep Muse and especially Hera on the same page. Why didn't you go with Yan, Hera? Sorry, never mind.

"It does not work." Eos says.

"Eos you are fast." Jack says, "I knew the plan from yesterday and I haven't even seen anything wrong."

"OK, allow me to explain." I try to stop Jack and Eos from shooting each other with their words. "Two main issues here. First, people may lie or do not compromise if we ask everyone to reveal their numbers. For example, let's imagine 1 and 2 have already revealed themselves, and you ask 'who is 3' and nobody answers the question."

"Then we are stuck. The remaining ones will not reveal their numbers either." Jack says.

"Right. More importantly, at that moment, 1 and 2 have great disadvantage over others because they are now easy targets of the guessing game. Like their ranks are now common knowledge. So 1 and 2 probably have foreseen this even before they reveal their numbers. Guess what?" I say.

"1 and 2 will never reveal their numbers in the first place." Muse says.

"And it does not matter which order you ask, from 1 to 24 or backwards from 24 to 1, or by a randomly selected order." Bran says.

"How about everyone write on a piece of paper their name and rank number, and we put all papers together and read them out one by one." Jack asks.

"What if someone submit a blank paper, or with incorrect information." I say, "For example, Jack and I know each other well and we don't mind giving each other ten thousand, so we may arrange to switch rank numbers. Of course this might cause some extra trouble in the matching game, but it is possible right?"

"Then people might manipulate their choices based on some wrong information, which makes it very messy." Jack says.

"Too many uncertainties." Tim says.

"Or if everyone give their rank number to one person we all trust, and let that single person do the matching work and tell everyone how to choose their list?" Muse gives another plan.

"Sounds promising, but it is hard to find that one person we all trust. In addition, people still might shoot randomly in the guessing game, and if in the end you get significantly less than two million, do you believe that people just randomly guessed at your rank number correctly, or the one person you trusted somehow revealed your number to others?" Bran says.

"Right, random shooting or say blind shooting has only one twenty-fourth, or slightly greater than four percent, possibility of winning. When these probabilities multiply together, the overall chance soon gets too small." I say.

"No. One twenty-third. You don't shoot yourself." Eos corrects me immediately.

"Indeed, it is one twenty-second. You don't shoot yourself, or your spouse." Muse corrects again.

"I would." Eos says without any hesitation.

You will be a good bridge player. Poker face, as people call it.

"The problem is that people who submit correct information, or reveal themselves early in whatever process you design, have big disadvantage in the guessing game, and so people simply don't do that. As the cat suggests, we need to make sure no rank information becomes common knowledge." I try to summarize and put the topic back on track.

"Contracts, agreements, treaties, warrants, all these lawful things that we use to build trust among people and build a modern society, do not exist here." Muse adds a comment.

"And all humans by nature do not trust each other." I say.

"All humans by nature do not trust each other." Tim repeats this sentence slowly.

People do no like the dark side of ourselves.

"Aristotle, *Metaphysics*, right?" Muse asks, "You change it to an unpleasant form. Sounds like you have already lived for thousands of years."

You don't know the truth, Muse. Or, do you want me to tell you the truth? Or, you have already seen the truth?

"We need a system that people do not necessarily trust people, but trust the system." Tim says.

"What do you mean?" I ask.

"I don't have a good idea, but roughly in such a system, we need to make sure everyone knows that their rank number has no chance of being revealed by others or by the system itself, and we can still figure out how to match ourselves." Tim says.

We probably need a secret ritual, like in a cult, but keep some partial information open to public. Secret ritual? I shake my head but do not speak it out. Some already think that I am mad, and with secret rituals more people would join the party. Maybe I can consult Nyx for it. Their magic society may have something similar in nature.

So I do not know how to answer but instead continue. "Second reason is similar. Even if we somehow manage to force everyone to reveal their ranks, real ranks, and have everyone matched up according to the rules, there is still no way to tell every couple's account balance after marriage. We know every couple gets roughly two million but not exactly. We have to ask everyone to report on their own about their initial balance."

"And people may lie as well." Jack says.

"Yes, people will report less than what they actually have, and keep the difference for themselves." Hera says, "No offense, but I may do that. I want to be honest."

So you want to be honest...about lying?

"So if we sum up people's self-reported numbers, we are unlikely to get full twenty-four million in total. Even if every couple has exactly two million in their account, some may still report less." Jack says.

"Say for a big project with a total cost of one point two million dollars, if you charge every couple evenly then it is one hundred thousand for each couple. Nice and clean." I continue, "But since our beginning balances are different, you may want to charge different amounts to each couple, like one hundred and five to couple A, one hundred and one to couple B and ninety-eight to couple C. There is a lot of bookkeeping that could go wrong. I guess we are unlikely to obtain a computer within a short period of time, and need to rely on pen and paper for records."

"Anything that may go wrong will go wrong. Anything possible will happen eventually." Bran says.

"So the only way to get everything straight is to charge everyone, or every couple evenly. No exception. Easy to keep track with the public portion of each account." Tim says, "If we are about to build some facility, and one couple comes up saying that they have already used up the public portion for something else, then they do not get access to the said facility. It is a fair game for all."

"I agree. So we still need to focus on modifying the plan so that people who first reveal their ranks do not get punished, or at least not severely so." I say.

"This is hard." Tim says.

Everyone stays silent, for a long time. I call an early tea break, and then I quickly run to the sundial, checking how much time I have left.

xxiv   Eclipses

I've been back and forth between the sundial and the cookies. First, I need to time the conversation correctly with Eos, and second, I also need to phrase the conversation correctly, as I do not want to cause any misunderstandings with Iris. Even I had a wristwatch I would have been looking at it all the time, and at the moment I only have a stupid sundial which is not so accurate. Better than nothing though.

"I don't understand, why you care about the sundial so much?" Jack asks.

"Nothing, just curious, about how it works, and keep track of time." I say.

"Math isn't too hard. You can ask Eos for it. Ah-Oh, sorry."

"Never mind. I know."

"By the way, did you have another weird dream last night?"

"Nope. No one is making weird dreams every night. Maybe I can try to make one tonight and make another guessing game for tomorrow." I say.

"Ha-ha. Please let me know about it."

I notice Nyx is downstairs for the cookies. I agree they are great, and Nyx looks a bit tired. Maybe our CFT tried to cast some magic spells but they all failed. Selene is asking something, and Circe is waiting, so I go and wait in the line as well, to kill the time.

"His...heart...with you. Don't...much. Need to give him some time, my sweetheart." Nyx says.

What? Anything wrong with Dennis? I think I just heard something that I should not hear about. Selene looks at me and leaves. Sorry! I don't intend to! Oh, the two extra girls in the explorer team today.

"I am still worried about Vincent today, about what you said, injury." Circe says.

"Ten is a magic number. He will be back. Eleven is the original number for Death in tarot. You don't want to join them."

Oh, there are...ten people in the explorer team today. "He will be back" — so you don't want to say whether he will be injured today. Again, common fortune-telling trick. I know it.

"Sorry...this is not about today's fortune, but I wonder if I could ask about your magic society, like how you vote for your leader?" I ask.

"They come up with candidates, and I make the decision." Nyx says, without looking at me.

"OK. Errr, I really mean, do you have some sort of secret ritual where people can reveal some information but do not get identified? Like in a situation when you don't want everyone to know your ballot."

Nyx thinks for a short while and answers: "There is one secret voting procedure that you may be interested in. Briefly, all the electors divide themselves into small groups of size three or five or seven such that people in the same group trust each other; Then within each subgroup they secretly cast a majority vote to determine their single ballot, and these ballots are then collected one by one secretly. Even if you know the vote by a small group, you still do not know the individual votes from each elector. Just feels like the U.S. presidential election but in much smaller scale. This was how they used to decide...anyway."

"Thanks a lot, Nyx." I feel this can be helpful, though I may need some extra time to work on it. "By the way, in your magic society, more stars means higher rank, am I correct?"

"Yes, it has the same origin as the Chinese ornament system.

The leader gets all seven stars, which represent the Big Dipper. The Far East branch originally had a maximum of six, but they doubled it six thousand years ago."

Six times two is twelve. I can do it. Oh, that came the strange system of the odd numbers plus twelve! Funny.

"But I haven't seen you wearing your hat. Just curious."

"It is only for formal ceremonies or rituals. Yan does not wear any ornaments on a daily basis either." Nyx says. "In the graduation ceremony, we were required to wear our uniforms — Interesting..."

"I see. Thank you." I don't know what exactly is interesting, but I stop here.

"Today for Virgo: Make *a* decision within the third daylight, or, make *the* decision by the ninth dawn. Lucky item: Timepiece." Nyx says, without me even asking. You just want to run some extra tests on a new planet, right?

A decision? The decision? I don't understand these articles! The third daylight...Damn, I believe I missed it. The ninth dawn? I need to make *the* decision by Day eight or Day nine, way past the deadlines. What is *the* decision then? Do you believe the cat will come up saying "we postpone the deadlines since people have not been paired up"?

Or, the third daylight shall be counted starting from today, then it is — the daylight of Day six — ha ha, nice match with the deadline, but the ninth dawn still does not make much sense — it will be almost the end of the second week. Do you think Phase II will also last for a week? I know, we always have our own interpretations of a sacred script.

The only Lucky thing is that the girls are not with us right now, otherwise I would be torn into pieces, literally.

⋯⋯⋯⋯⋯

Timepiece — I guess we only have one, or one and a half, here on this whole planet, and the cat is a universal machine, not just a timepiece. Sorry, but I have to get Eos to confirm something really important — It's about time, and it is about Time.

I quickly locate her at the corner of the lounge, still reading, and ask her to come to the courtyard for something about "five days". I tell her I don't want anyone else to hear us this time, as it is about "the secret". I sound really serious. She hesitates a little bit, but soon puts down her huge volume and follows me. This time I don't have to ask. The classic yellow cover clearly says *Algebra*, single word, easy peasy.

"So, what is it?" She asks, in the middle of courtyard.

I double check the time with the sundial, my Lucky item, and pretend to organize my words. Sorry, need to kill some extra time.

"Errr...I wonder, how many of these G-T-M books are there?"

"I am not exactly sure. Lang's third edition of *Algebra* became one of the GTM series, GTM two eleven. It just came out earlier this year, so it is close to the end, but they will continue to publish more — Isn't this about the secret?" She is obviously annoyed.

Two hundred of these yellow books. Oh, sorry.

"Hmmm, right, secret...sorry, this is regarding the thing I talked to you before the graduation ceremony, on the ceremony day, Wednesday to be precise." I say.

"Haven't I responded you another time? In addition, you have Iris now. Leave me alone." As expected, now she is really annoyed.

"No, no, no. I am not trying to ask you again to be my girlfriend now. I have Iris. I really want you to focus on that event itself, that I came to you and talked to you, and then your response with two words. Do you still remember these?"

As long as I haven't seen it, she hasn't seen it either, but I get the same feeling — the feeling of being rejected by a girl has always been the same.

"What do you mean? Sure I remember..." She says.

"*No. Thanks.*"

It is like a perfect match, igniting a perfect cake of fireworks. She looks stunned. This is it!

In fact, I also see something similar — the hall, *Pomp and Circumstance*, other students, teachers, our uniforms — It feels natural to me right now. One has to admit the first experience is truly startling.

After thirty seconds or so, both of us recover from the shock.

"What is it? This thing...like a dream." She asks.

"Forgive me one second please. Sorry. QX, how much time is it from right now back to solar noon, in old Earth hours?"

"Two point six five one five hours."

Bingo! One stone, two birds.

"Eos, listen, I call this an *Eclipse*, or maybe a *Transit*, as in solar eclipse or Venus transit. Two celestial bodies coincide and you see something astonishing, especially here you are like a caveman who sees an eclipse the first time in your life and does not understand the principle behind it."

"Eclipse?"

Tears pour out of her eyes. I totally understand, just as I did that night.

"Trust me. Just the same thing as I saw on the second night. This is not magic or anything with Nyx; It's just physics, or even only mathematics. It is a natural phenomenon. Once you understand the principle behind it, it becomes natural."

"It is *backwards*, right?" She asks with tears still on her face.

"Yes." I have to admit she is a genius. It took me multiple experiments to confirm.

So, there is no doubt now. This *is* an alien planet. Nothing works as a better proof.

"And you know, I feel so happy right now that I cannot even help myself to give you a big kiss to thank you for your help." I continue, lost control of my emotions. I don't know exactly why I am so ecstatic with my goddess in front of me, and cannot control my words exactly, and I wave my hands as if I just win a big lottery. "I believe it is not for romance. It is like I just proved a mathematical theorem, my own theorem. It is exactly like the Venus transit when astronomical events coincide and you can make measurements, like measuring the distance from the Sun to the Earth."

"Yes, I see that now. Midnight to midnight. Very impressive. And, I understand the feeling you deserve." She says.

Yes, checkpoint to checkpoint, like in video games.

"One moment, are we going to grow back and die, or no, we actually become immortal?" She asks again.

Eos is Eos. I am so jealous of her talent! This is ridiculously fast. I spent a day and a night realizing these two possibilities, and probably did some crazy things based on the first one, and it took Eos less than two minutes!

"I don't know. Both possibilities seem plausible, but now I tend to believe that it is the latter. Hard to do experiments in a short period of time. We can figure it this out by the end of the five years at the latest." I say.

You now know everything I know so far, and with some extra graduate level mathematics such as algebra, geometry and arithmetic, I believe you can get the answer you were hunting for, Miss 3, tonight.

Then to my total surprise, she approaches me, holds my neck and gives me a kiss.

"So yesterday you thought we would all die, right? Now, calm down a bit?" She laughs, and runs away.

It is my turn to be stunned. I haven't even fully obtained a clear feeling of the temperature of her lips. Even worse, I notice a group of boys and girls, Iris among them, by the glass doors watching us, presumably from the very beginning. So what have I done, in their eyes?

Let me recall. I don't know why but I can still remember every second of it. I went to grab Eos, asked her to follow me to the courtyard where nobody was able to hear us, except for the cat. I said something; she waited and then cried; and I said something more; she said something and I seemed ecstatic, like winning a lottery; then she kissed me and ran away. That is it. Pretty obvious right?

Iris walks towards me and says, "I think I deserve an explanation."

"How should I put it." I say, holding my head and rubbing my hair, "This is not for love, I promise, but it is very hard to explain. Roughly, Eos and I just experienced something fantastic, which we call an eclipse, like a lucid dream. It is so real, and so I now know what is actually happening around us. That was why I was so happy. As a result of this, she also became so happy and...kissed me?" I don't even convince myself with these words.

"I just thought about many ways you would explain this. You could just say you have changed your mind, which is totally OK and I will leave you to Eos; or you could lie to me saying you and Eos are just friends and you still love me, and I likely will forgive you eventually; or you make up something strange and we will laugh at it." Iris says, in a weeping voice, "But now it seems you are truly mad, or suffer from some brain damage due to the fruit. Sorry I cannot marry you."

Iris runs away, leaving me alone with the sundial, my Lucky item of the day. I totally deserve it. The fireworks show is over, and nothing is left.

The extended group of explorers come back earlier today, but I am not in the mood of listening to their report. Nothing very interesting.

"We found a large piece of flat land to the north, with less wood and a small creek through, which can be our immediate water source for daily use, and we can keep the land near the river for farmland and industry." Dennis finally ends his report.

Before dinner, Leo comes to me.

"Hey, I do not care about you and Iris, but can you stop harassing Eos, please?" Leo says.

"Sorry I don't understand what you mean. I was not harassing Eos. We just...had some business." I say.

"I don't care. Yesterday you tried to kiss her, against her will, today she was crying. Next time, you get yourself into trouble, I promise." He says, and turns away.

"Do you know why Eos won't put you into her list?" I ask loudly.

"Why? How do you know she won't?" Leo turns back.

"Because she said she does not want sham marriage. Best thing to do is to avoid putting any person who has shown any interest on her. It is just easy logic. She is probably putting a few irrelevant people there, like William, Dennis, Zak, Tim or even Jack, but not you."

"Or you." He responds.

xxv   Moon

To my surprise, during dinner, both girls reappear from their guest rooms. More surprisingly, Iris now sits by the left hand side of the Queen Regnant's seat, that is, next to Eos. Two of them seem to chat quite well. By the way, don't forget to ask your question, Miss 3.

It is the girls' friendship that I can never understand. I hope Eos can help clarifying things so that Iris can come back to me and say sorry.

"Girls never say sorry." Jack says, after I tell him the story, "You should say sorry first."

It sounds like he learned it in a hard way, or a harder way.

"O-kay-"

"Just for your information," Rhea says with a laugh, "girls do say sorry, but only to their true love."

I look at Tim and he is smiling, just as usual.

"Eclipse? What is it? Something is wrong with our environment? Are we actually living in virtual reality?" Jack lowers his voice, and he is curious as well.

"Hard to explain. It is not like virtual reality, but more like a physical phenomenon. Let me see...if you gather the girls for another bridge tournament tomorrow, during daytime, then maybe I can show you." I say.

"OK. Sounds good."

It was a backup plan, in case something went wrong with Eos, but I guess it is not so important by now.

"Too sad, we originally planned to go to the beach with the girls during the summer break." I say.

"I see what you mean. Now it is more like a dream." Jack sighs.

"By the way, something went wrong with Muse?" I ask.

"Yeah, never mind...Girls are different from day to day."

"You don't have to tell me." I say.

"Thanks."

Well, I am not in the mood of listening to other people's love story. I have been thinking about Iris and Eos back and forth a hundred times. Hard to even notice what other people are talking.

"Everyone to the courtyard, now! Now!" It is Pheme.

Pheme always brings gossips, at any time. She probably has caught another pair kissing somewhere near the courtyard. I can even imagine this was how it happened to me earlier this morning. Not interested this time. However, more and more people are going out without the usual applause or whistles, just silence, and some are weeping.

So it is unusual. I put down my fork and go out with Jack as well. People stand there, stalled, looking up, like worshipping a god there. A few couples are hugging each other.

There are two moons in the sky.

It is not an illusion or some kind of optical effect. It is crystal clear that there are two moons, two totally different moons in the sky. One of them is maybe slightly bigger than our old moon, with similar color, white and yellow. Another one, red, like blood, is about two thirds in diameter compared to the white one.

They are both a bit more than half moon, with circular arcs pointing to the direction of the set sun. The patterns on their surfaces, probably shadows of different impact craters, look totally different from our old moon in my memory.

Both of them appear in the northern sky, the white one is to the west of the red one. They like a pair of cat's eyes, glowing in the darkness and overlooking everyone on earth.

These astronomical scenes are always breathtaking, incredible and astonishing. Normally a solar eclipse is the most phenomenal event that people can experience on the Earth. Even with that some people may cry on the scene. People probably forget how beautiful our own Moon is. Unlike the sun, whose blazing light prevents us from looking at it directly high in the sky, the moon is tranquil, soothing and relaxing, just like chatting with Iris. I often stare at the moon in my backyard with daddy, imagining I can once go up there, with daddy telling me a lot of thing about the cosmos.

During a full lunar eclipse, our own moon turns copper red, very similar to this red one in the sky. I have only seen it once in my life, but it is as well breathtaking and thrilling, and unnaturally alluring. The unparalleled beauty of it, just like Eos I would say, is like a real goddess that you normally cannot encounter in everyday life.

Now with two moons staring at us, a lot of us have already started tearing. It is real. Nothing works as a better proof — I said that earlier but I think I was wrong. All the counterarguments by various fishy conspiracy theories all fall in vain as Eos once commented. One proof is enough. Even for those who already knew it — Tim, Bran and maybe Jack, Eos and maybe

Nyx, and possibly a few others, together with me — this un-realistic picturesque is far more penetrating to our own minds than anything else, including the eclipse Eos and I experienced earlier.

"God bless us all." William prays, holding a Bible in his shaky hands.

"Commander Armstrong, now you have two goddesses on two moons. Which moon do you want to land on?" Jack asks with tears in his eyes.

"You must feel lucky that I don't have a railgun in my hand." I say.

"Let's turn off the lights...QX, could you turn off all the lights? Any objections, everyone?" Tim asks.

No one even has the right words to object. The lights go off. Soon our eyes become used to the darkness. The beautiful starry sky reveals itself, with a glorious and breathtaking white belt through it.

"Kant is right." Muse says.

"Is this the Milky Way?" Hera asks.

"Yes, it is still the same Milky Way Galaxy, assuming we are only five thousand light years away from the Earth and our old Sun. The constellations are totally different." Bran says.

"Can we see our old sun from here?" Hera asks again.

"No. After a few hundred light years or so, our sun will become invisible to human naked eye. We can order a fancy telescope and ask the cat for the direction, assuming we have some extra money." Bran answers.

"Probably need an observatory." Jack says.

"We could be in the southern hemisphere, just like what William mentioned earlier, and the constellations look differ-ent." Leo tries to explain, with total red face.

"I do not recall the patterns at any time any where on the Earth, at least within a few thousand years of time from us." Jack says, "And you see the red moon."

It sounds like you have lived that long, Jack.

"Me either." Nyx says.

OK, this counts as a real proof I assume.

"Then it is a big dome, like in that movie." Leo says.

"How can you hide such a big structure from satellites and media? In fact, it is not going to be stable by our current engineering skills." Bran says.

People are not mentally stable right now. Maybe it is a good time to reveal the big secret and so people can forget about the moons? It was early morning, so most of them were sleeping.

While I am still hesitating about it, Leo steps close and grabs me by my collar. Frank is by his side as well, with his fists.

"You knew all this right? You trusted the stupid cat so much. I know, you are one of *them*. Say it, what is your plan? What is in your plan?"

"Stop it!" Jack, Tim and Dennis come for help. Dennis helps to hold Frank, and Tim tries to argue with Leo.

"He is one of us. Don't be foolish. We spent four years together." Tim says, "Aliens do not need to find someone to pretend to be one of us. They know everything already."

"That does not prove anything!" Leo cries.

"For a civilization that can take us from the Earth to this new world, there is nothing for us to hide. You wouldn't create a fancy robotic mouse that looks like real to join the lab experiments with real mice, would you?" Bran says.

"I can guarantee he is a healthy little boy with some extra fancy ideas, but he is completely human, and logical. You, instead, are now behaving like a beast." Eos says.

Little boy? How old are you, Eos? Sorry I shouldn't ask this to a lady. Anyway, thanks a lot.

"Even if I am one of *them* as a detection device, I myself probably would have not known anything ever since I was born. You see, a robotic mouse likely does not know anything regarding its creator." I say.

"Well, I do." William says.

Can you please sh...stop, William? You don't usually speak, do you?

Muse approaches us, holds Leo's wrist, and speaks softly but firmly: "Leo, I think most of us believe you are wrong. It's all right. Everyone makes mistakes."

Thank you very much.

I raise my hands showing that I do not want to fight. With his watery eyes, Leo releases me.

"But tell me why you trust the cat. I want an explanation." Leo says.

"Thanks, Muse — Because I trust Eos." I say.

"What?"

"Yes, I mean that. On Day one, Eos asked the cat a number of questions, like super difficult questions I still don't understand. As later Jack told me, most of these are, or were, unsolved problems, meaning that the most brilliant scientists and mathematicians back on the Earth did not even know the answers. The cat answered these without any hesitation, and Eos was unable to find any inconsistency from the answers. Otherwise she would have pointed it out. Am I right, Eos?"

"Yes." Eos says.

Right. Eos was not just asking for new knowledge to become rank 1, but more importantly also trying to disprove what the cat had claimed, by contradicting itself. One stone, two birds.

"Therefore I trust the cat. You, instead, do not even trust Eos at the beginning." I say.

"Cannot find inconsistencies? That is it? QX! Prove it!" Leo shouts out.

"A consistent theory cannot prove its own consistency." QX answers.

"What?"

"It is Gödel's Incompleteness Theorem." Eos says.

These technical words do not explain anything!

"In our own words, there is no way the cat can prove its own consistency. It simply can't do it. You just trust it." Jack says.

"Let's verify this. QX, what is four plus five?" Muse asks.

"Nine." QX answers.

What are you doing, Muse? The cat of course can do this calculation. I have been doing it since I was five.

"QX, what is three times seven?" Muse asks again.

"Twenty-One."

I learned it in my first grade.

"OK. This is enough." Muse says, "As long as it is complicated enough to do addition and multiplication of natural numbers, Gödel's Incompleteness Theorem holds."

Wait, that is the proof? Nine and Twenty-One? I still don't understand a single word, or more precisely I understand every single word but do not understand what they mean together in your sentence. Eos seems to be OK with it. Well, I start to feel I don't belong here.

Leo drags himself away, back to the dining room. He probably feels the same. It is because of Eos, so there is not too much worry here, I hope.

"Sorry I didn't help much." Jack says.

"It is totally all right. It is startling, and it is hard to do anything. I wouldn't be able to move if I were you." I say.

"Nope, because you said you want to shoot me with a railgun."

DAY V

xxvi   Disorders

Last night had been chaotic. Distress, Pain, Horror, Nonsense, Despair. A few girls first ran upstairs without finishing the dinner. I as well did not have much appetite. I excused myself early and dragged my weary body back to my room.

There were some loud voices from downstairs, and later I was woken up by some crazy party, and some girls were crying in their rooms, and probably boys too, though not loud enough for me to hear. The party people likely ordered some fancy equipment, such as microphone, amplifier and speakers, and sang through the night.

Actually before I got back to my room. Kakia was there waiting for me in the hallway. An uncommon guest.

"I have a few words."

"Sure."

"I want to put you in my list, but I do *not* want you to put me in your list. Do you understand? In return I can promise to pay you one thousand dollars of whatever you need after Day seven."

"I get it. No need to pay me. My pleasure to help." I answered.

I have to admit this is a very clever way to solve the problem, though it requires a lot of peer-to-peer trust among people.

OK, it may be hard for Eos to carry this out, since she does not trust any of the boys. In addition, Selene probably does not trust any of the boys either, except for Dennis, or not even Dennis. I don't remember, but I believe we had come across this idea on Day one, but soon rejected it since Eos was there. Things could go totally wrong if someone lies, and even worse, the system encourages you to lie to your goddess.

In contrast, in my new plan, the system does not encourage you to lie. Yes, there is a new plan. It felt like God told me through another weird dream, using my own words. But as I see right now, pieces of it had already been played out through the days, and my brain was essentially working in the background to put the jigsaw puzzle all together "for me" and showed the plan as a dream "to me" — what am "I", then? Anyway, the final touch-up requires some logic, and that is what I am good at, at last.

In the dream I was 10 instead of 1. Yeah, I would be much happier if I were 10, which is still good enough to carry out my plan, and then I can totally forget about the story with Miss 3, no, Miss 2 probably. The touchscreen shows a 10, a fake one, but my notes are telling me it was just a dream.

While I am still on my bed trying to repeat my arguments and think about how to go through it with the other people today, an announcement comes.

"Custom announcement: Muse, I love you!" It sounds like Oliver, but clearly drunk.

So there are stupid people doing this. If he is not drunk, then probably that is the end of story and people will laugh at him for a couple of days. Now the real problem is that he is drunk, and it only depends on how much cash he has left.

No surprise. More announcements come.

"Custom announcement: Muse, I love you, to the end of the world!" It is Oliver again.

Don't you understand that our old world has ended?

"Custom announcement: Hera, I love you, my queen, from the Earth to this new world!" This time it is Yan, but isn't he paired up with Hera already? So he is really drunk.

It feels like the graduation party night, though I don't remember anything about it, just the same feeling. Emotions of human beings are quite limited, I have to admit.

Before I go downstairs, let me quickly check what I forgot last night, for a relieving "Two" treatment —

"Six."

Hmmm? This is amusing. Carbon, Element of Life. Did I ask the right question? Sorry, but how did so many people see it within one day! Eos did, of course, but who are the other four? I wish I still have chance to ask everyone about it, after this total chaos — Well, it is not so important now. We have a much better proof, in the sky.

I walk out of my room with total puzzlement, and Jack is on his way as well.

"We need to stop these stupid guys." He says.

Hmmm...I thought you had rushed downstairs with the first announcement. Just curious, were you using the bathroom? Sorry, no time for jokes.

After we are downstairs, it is clear that the night club party members include four boys — Leo, Frank, Yan and Oliver — and two girls — Kakia and Pheme. Bottles and cups are everywhere. Nuts and other snacks scatter round. They even ordered playing cards. The four of us, the new bridge club on this new planet, have not even had time to start our first club tournament yet!

They are mostly drunk. Only Yan and Oliver seem to be awake, and the girls are...not in appropriate attires. Can't they wait for three more days for it? Who would try this in the lounge?

Muse, Hera and Gaia are also there. Hera and Gaia are taking care of Yan and Frank, respectively.

"You stop! Right now! Go back to your rooms! And have a sleep!" I haven't seen Muse like this before.

"Are you giving orders? There is no law here, and no one can, give orders. Well, if you promise, to be my girlfriend, or my wife, then I may listen, and we can sleep, together. Ha ha..." Oliver says, pointing to Muse with his fingers.

He staggers toward Muse, very close. Muse is trembling, unable to move, like being paralyzed.

"Hey, stop!" Jack and I shout out. Moreover, Jack rushes over and pushes Oliver down to the ground.

Then, there is this, usual, boys' fight. It happens so quickly that I don't have time to think or respond. Clearly Oliver is only half drunk, or even not drunk at all, otherwise he wouldn't be able to punch so hard on Jack's nose. The next time I come back to myself, Jack has been bleeding while the girls are screaming. I was paralyzed by the situation as well.

"Everyone stop! Right now!" Tim appears with Bran and Dennis, with a black box.

Dennis gets a strong hold on the team I can tell. Oliver immediately stops his fists.

"Are you, trying to shoot, me, using this?" He asks.

"No, we don't shoot each other." Tim says firmly, and turns towards me, "This is for you."

xxvii   Lists

"Let us discuss things over in the courtyard." Tim asks me to follow him. We leave the remaining chaos to Dennis and Bran and the girls.

"So things are a bit out of control. Let's be brief. You take this gun and lead the exploration group today. Zak and Artemis will go as well. Need to ask as many girls to join as possible. Go to the beach and have a picnic. Do not come back until, close to sunset." Tim quickly goes over the plan.

"Why me?"

"I don't want the explorers to have both guns. Someone has to take control over this in an exploration." Tim says, looking at my face, "You seem to have something to tell me as well?"

"Yes, exactly. I have a new plan for the games. This time it should work." I very briefly explained the plan, "But I now need two couples of rank less than or equal to ten, two *top ten* couples."

"Sorry it is a bit complicated. Sound plausible, but no time for the details, due to the current situation. So you try to verify with Eos, OK?" Tim says, "Top ten couples — Sorry Rhea...and I are unable to help, but I would assume you can ask Eos, Jack, Bran, Muse, Nyx, Selene...and yourself. They do not need to reveal their rank number but simply admit that they are top ten, right? I think they will do it, but the harder part is to find two couples within top ten. In fact I can ask Bran for you, but you need to handle the rest yourself."

"OK, will do. Thanks. It will be easier if the girls come to the picnic."

"QX, custom announcement." Tim says.

"Sure, what is the message?" QX says.

"Today we plan to go on a picnic over at the beach, with food and drinks and lots of fun. We are leaving in less than ten minutes. Artemis and Zak will lead the way. Please come downstairs to the lobby if you want to join us — That is it."

"OK, broadcasting." QX says.

"Final question, are you 1?" Tim asks with smile, among the broadcast.

This time I am very prepared to answer.

"Yes," I confirm it without hesitation, "but you said I am a triple-agent."

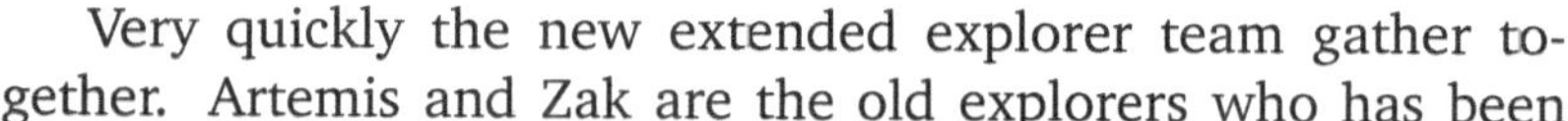

Very quickly the new extended explorer team gather together. Artemis and Zak are the old explorers who has been to the beach on Day three. Circe, Eos, Muse, Iris, Selene and finally even Nyx also join us. Most of the girls have been hiding in their guest rooms. Gaia and Hera decide to stay because their loved ones are drunk and possibly in danger, and there is a second railgun. Rhea always stay with Tim, busy with some doughs right now, and there has to be someone who talks to Pheme and Kakia as well, like in a girls' talk.

I am running out of time. Oh, one more little thing to do before we leave. I take out my notes from the backpack Dennis lent me, and quickly black out a few lines. These have nothing to do with us right now. And without explaining the plan, I ask Jack if he is wiling to reveal himself as top ten couple assuming there is a good plan.

"Sure. But, I still, need a mate." Muse has helped cleaning his nosebleed, but he still sounds so worried about what may happen next, or maybe he hasn't pulled himself together from the fight.

I also ask him if he is coming with us to the beach. This time to my surprise he wants to stay.

"They have four men, after everyone wakes up. William does not want, I mean, to join any fight. Tim, Bran, Dennis — three is not enough. Need more people here. I have to stay." He says clumsily with doubtful eyes, "And now, you have a railgun in your hand."

What is happening with Vincent? But I don't have time to ask the details.

xxviii   Immortals

It is sunny, but relatively pleasant in the shade of a forest. The ground has mostly dried out and it is much easier to walk on compared to previous days, according to Zak. Oh, I should have spent more time in the gym than in the bridge club. How can Dennis handle this black box with ease and march across a wild forest? Maybe they take turns to carry it? I feel almost exhausted when we reach the river, and then there is still some winding path towards the beach.

Vincent comes to me and gives me a bottle of water.

"Thanks. Appreciate it! Why, are you here?"

"I caught up with you guys, with some freshly baked breads from Rhea." He says, and lowers his voice, "Good news is, the problem has been solved. Tim also has some extra messages for you."

"Sure."

"One, 'don't come back to the hotel if the light in my room is off, third floor, first room to the south, end of the hallway'."

"Two, 'try to show everyone the gun is not so useful, like it is too heavy to aim accurately in practice'."

"OK. Thanks." I say, still digesting. You just said the problem has been solved, right?

"You are very welcome. Sorry Frank and Oliver...are not in their usual conditions." Vincent says.

He probably didn't know Frank was all drunk and didn't do anything really. But "not in their usual conditions" isn't wrong regarding the party last night.

"I totally understand. The moons are unrealistic." I say.

"Right. People are not psychologically stable. Circe mentioned having a vivid nightmare last night, and in the dream I as well as others didn't come back yesterday and everyone in the hotel was super worried. So I am a bit worried as well."

No one was able to sleep well with two moons above us.

"But we need to move on, in this new world." I say.

"Yes, I agree. Good point."

"So when you guys, went out yesterday, or the day before, did you take turns, to carry this railgun, or Dennis did it, all by himself?" The sunshine was nice and warm yesterday morning, but now I can feel its fierceness outside the forest. Large beads of sweat drop off my brow, and I don't even have the energy to wipe them.

"No, we didn't. Dennis carried it around by himself. It is quite heavy right? Do you mind if I help carrying it for you?"

"Not at all." I say, hard to breath. "Thank you, very much!"

He takes the box and puts it over his shoulder.

"Oh, sorry I should have asked you earlier." Vincent then asks, "What do you want to do in the future? Either back while on the Earth, or here."

"Me? Future? Haven't thought about it for here. Not much clue, about the future. Back on the Earth, I guess I didn't know either. I was planning to finish my freshman courses and then decide what I like. Maybe finance, dealing with numbers but easier math, and my daddy also works in finance for a living, but I am pretty sure finance is the least useful subject here in our situation, even less useful than Latin or ancient Greek or philosophy. Yeah, I was also considering philosophy that my daddy has been inspiring me with."

"I see. I planned to get a degree in engineering. I am not as talented as Bran...Anyway, here in the new world, I want to be a carpenter, but they all laughed at me."

"Carpenter?"

"Yes. One of my habits is to watch my father doing woodworking. I know this sounds funny, but people like different things. Some people just like watch others playing video games, for example Zak and Oliver. They chatted all the way during hiking. Some others want to watch cooking or baking programs, for example Circe as well as some other girls. Circe also likes cake decorations tutorials. I am very relaxed watching woodworking. It feels very satisfying when things are done perfectly, and especially when you finally oil the wood, the beauty reveals itself and it is addictive. I wish there could be a website where people can upload their own woodworking videos, or any other videos — such as baking, cooking, gaming, travelling, crafting, everything. I mean it, but don't you think the furniture style in the hotel is ugly? Aliens have some bad taste of furnishing. I want to build a wood studio to design my own bed, my own table and chair, and everything — Cutting boards, bookshelves, side tables, cabinets, countertops, and these small wood toys for kids. There are lots of tools to buy, but the cat has confirmed almost everything will be available. And you see it, we are in the middle of a natural forest." He turns his head around and his eyes are shining.

"Sounds interesting. I will come over to help." I say.

"Really? Thanks! It is nice to have someone to talk. At last!"

"So what about Circe? Does she have plans for the future as well, may I ask?"

"Yes, she told me that she originally planned to get a medical degree. Now she may do something very similar. People will get ill and we need doctors."

"Right."

It seems a lot of people have already laid out reasonable plans for the future, but I am still spending time thinking about the games and about Iris and Eos. To be honest I feel a bit ashamed. I shall think more about how I can contribute.

"By the way, if Selene, errr — if Selene asks you something, about Dennis, most likely, then you just tell the truth, OK?" Vincent lowers his voice.

"Sure, but I don't have much personal intersection with Dennis anyway. I seriously don't know anything about him." I am not sure what Selene will ask, but never mind. I will tell the truth.

Oh, this was why Dennis sent you over, instead of Jack.

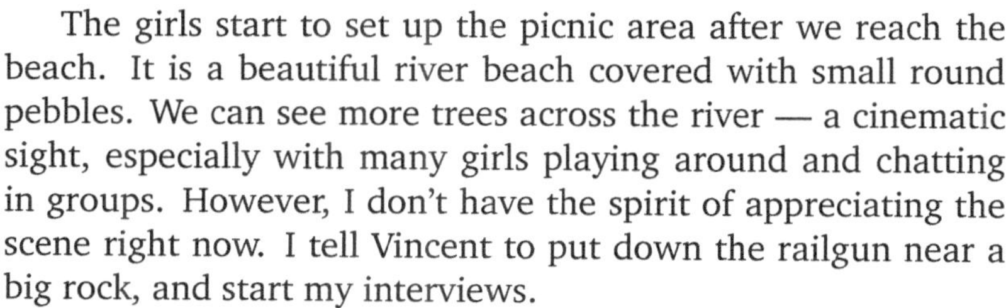

The girls start to set up the picnic area after we reach the beach. It is a beautiful river beach covered with small round pebbles. We can see more trees across the river — a cinematic sight, especially with many girls playing around and chatting in groups. However, I don't have the spirit of appreciating the scene right now. I tell Vincent to put down the railgun near a big rock, and start my interviews.

Eos becomes my first target. She is sitting on a rock, like a purple rose, cold but beautiful.

"I want you to hear this plan before I talk to the other girls." I start to slowly describe my plan, step by step, as well as my reasonings. It feels like describing a solution to my math teacher and I feel even more anxious than I did a few days ago.

"How do you measure time?" Eos asks.

"Rats!" I haven't thought about this. The notion of time is so fundamentally embedded into our brains so that it is too easy to ignore it. I focused too much on the actual algorithm of matching twelve pairs in the system, but haven't thought very carefully about the real process. Eos is Eos. She can quickly find a problem in my plan.

"I believe you can perform everything in public, so there is no need to measure time, but you will have to sacrifice some privacy, especially for the top ranked ones, since some of them may have told you that they are not top ten couples." She says.

I see. I am OK with it, but some other people may not be happy.

After thinking about it for a while, she continues, "Otherwise it works. And, I agree in general the second last couple is 11+, and so following your argument, we will need two such top ten couples. If you randomly pair people up into twelve pairs, you are most likely to get two top ten pairs, followed by one pair and three pairs, and one is only slightly higher than three."

Oh, so that was why you were thinking for so long. 1 is only slightly higher than 3. Nice joke. You must work well with Jack I think.

"We can be one pair." She sounds as if it is a very trivial thing, "So you only need to find another pair now. Your success rate has increased from seventy percent to almost eighty-seven percent, and people won't easily guess at our ranks."

"What?"

"You shall say *thank you.*"

"Thank you, very much."

For you love? And, everyone knows that you are not 1, Miss 3.

"Or you can ask Iris if she is eligible, though I am not totally sure she is still willing to marry you."

"Did you try to help clarifying things a little bit last night during the dinner? I saw, she sat next to you and you two had...a conversation."

"No, she didn't even ask." Eos says.

Then what were you charting about! I feel that I totally don't understand a girls' talk.

"May I ask why you changed your mind? I think, you rejected me twice, or once, depending on how you count it. Is it because of the eclipse we saw?"

"No, and if you count it correctly, I have not rejected you even once. In fact it does not matter much how to pair up people right now. We have thousands or even millions of years to live. Two of us get married on Day seven; Even if we love each other and establish a stable relationship, after fifty or a hundred years, we may get tired of each other and we separate, like peacefully; Then you end up with Iris, or some other girl, and divorce again after twenty or maybe another hundred years, or you even stay with two or more girls at the same time, or you want to have a hundred years of solitude; After a thousand years you get bored and do not want to live with any one of us, the immortals, but maybe you fall in love with one of our offsprings, the mortals as you may call them, even including your own offsprings. It will be forty or fifty generations you can tell. I, as well as other girls, will do the same thing in the course of thousands of years, dating immortals as well as mortals. We, I mean two of us, may come back and stay together intermittently and raise another baby, or may get tired of this business and just try for fun for a year together, see different parts of the world together, enjoy a variety of food together, and maybe write a novel together. A planet is big enough for us to explore in thousands of years. We literally become gods and goddesses, promiscuous deities as people may call us. Our mortal spouses, children, grandchildren, offsprings, friends, relatives, everyone, a bartender at a tavern, a hotel front desk, a shopkeeper of a souvenir shop, a flight attendant on a plane, a police officer passing by, a school teacher of your kids, a doctor who saved your life, everyone will die before you, some in front of you. You, somehow eventually suffer from this immortality syndrome, after experiencing all possible sorrows, miseries, torments and despairs of human life, probably get some mental illness, reflecting yourself everyday. Some of us may even commit suicide. So in reality we are in this big hell of immortality, and you guys are still worried about trivial things like marriage or building sustainable agriculture and industry."

This is a long speech, not just in Eos standards, and mind-piercing as well. Why do people throw long monologues at me today? I don't have enough brain to to think all this through. Very dramatic but astonishingly true, but why are you so sure we are going to be immortal? She seems to release all the pressure she has accumulated within her, like a pressure cooker, towards me.

True, if we are immortal, then my "clever plan" is not important, at all. Once we have infinite time, we have infinite resources, and so it does not matter whether we can double our cash reward or not. But of course, more cash is always better.

"I see it now. As a metaphor, say if I am the sun, you are the red moon and Iris is the white moon. One day there is solar eclipse with red moon, then a month later comes solar eclipse with the white moon. Same for planet transits. In the long run, as long as we live forever, just by chance anything possible will happen eventually." I slowly interpret her words piece by piece.

"Yes. Anything possible will happen eventually."

"You think this might be related to the fifty/five hundred rule in biology someone mentioned earlier? "

"Possibly."

"So the railgun we have, or any of these fancy stuff we can do with alien technology, will become the supernatural power of gods and goddesses?" I ask.

"Likely so, as told by different mythologies in various cultures. As that famous sci-fi novel suggests, nuclear power is basically the same as magic to primitive civilizations."

I had been puzzling with my career path these days, as Vincent reminded me moments ago. Now you have shown me a great one.

"So is this the reason why you kissed me yesterday? We are becoming immortal?" I ask.

"You said you wanted a kiss. And," She has a sudden flush on her face and lowers her voice, "at the beginning I want to stay with you for some time."

"Eos, I might be wrong, but I think you don't have to be so upset. Life is not just with sorrow, but with happiness as well. We will experience, in the same way, joys, excitements, relaxations, pleasures and loves, through infinite time. You live with your kids, watch them growing up and play with them. You travel around the world, alone or with friends. You enjoy different kinds of food, try on different clothings, stay at different homes. Your ways of life determines your feelings of it. You cannot imagine how many funny things we can experience if we are gods and goddesses. We can even attend a college together here in this new world, as we were supposed to do, pretend to be overloaded by course work and other activities, and also fall in love with each other, just like back on the Earth. Being immortal may eventually become a torture, but let us enjoy through it — together."

This part feels like a proposal, which I naturally speak out without any preparation.

"You don't have to pretend." She laughs and continues, "It is up to you, but you may also want to check with your princess about the rank number. 11 or 12, it might still work out for you, assuming you have another top ten pair already."

11 or 12? I slowly run through some logic. Sorry I can never be as smart as Eos. It takes me some time, but eventually I figure it out. "Yes, this works. I didn't see that. Many thanks, Eos." I say.

I immediately regret what I have just said. How dumb! I should have said: *it won't change anything, Eos, I have you now.*

She takes out a book from her bag, smiles and sends me away as a little boy.

⊷∘ᗡᔑᗡ∘⊷

I start to look around, after this long and mind-blowing talk with Eos. Artemis and Zak are standing by the river with a row of fishing rods. Right, they want to catch something for tonight. Vincent and Circe are no where to be found. Difference between an old couple and a new one I assume. Eos and Iris are reading books. Nyx is resting under a big tree, further away. I guess everyone has noticed that I talked with Eos as soon as we arrive. Anyway, let it be.

So I decide to talk with Selene, Nyx, Muse and finally Iris, in this order, which makes it look more like a professional interview.

Selene is preparing some snacks, and quickly tossing some cheese and berries over some crackers. A shining and bright sunflower.

I am worried that I don't have time or energy to go through the details with each interviewee, so I briefly go over the ideas and say that we need top ten couples.

"Dennis and I would love to help, but it is so unfortunate we are not able to." Selene says, "Don't you think your boys are stupid and childish?"

Dennis? Right, why didn't Tim mention Dennis in his list? He said he can ask Bran for me, so why couldn't him ask Dennis by himself? Maybe Tim wanted me to ask Selene *for another time* regarding their ranks? There may have been tons of crazy things happening with the guessing game, and I think I only see the tip of an iceberg.

"Like what?"

"Like, fighting, I mean, scuffling for a girl? That is ridiculous in my opinion!"

"Yeah." I answer. I was expecting a question regarding Dennis, but it seems that Selene does not think that I know much about it.

I don't have much to say, and start to find my next target. It is better to keep the conversation short before Selene tries to ask some strange question. Meanwhile, Artemis has the first catch of the day. It is a fish, definitely a fish. Probably the first vertebrate we have seen on this new planet except for ourselves. Why the ice looks strange...

"Careful. It's not ice." Zak says.

"What?"

"Dry ice, solid Eight-Six-Eight at one ninety Kelvin, or minus one eighteen Fahrenheit."

Yeah, simple chemicals are super cheap.

Before the other girls come over to take a look at our new vertebrate friend, or, food, I run to Nyx, who is still meditating, like a lavender, whose smell I enjoy the most.

I wait for a short while, trying to be polite. I feel like a humble and timid subordinate to our CFT. Nyx soon feels my existence by whatever sense.

"Sorry to interrupt you from your, meditation, but I have some important matters. It is about a very plausible plan for the games. Eos-certified."

"No, I was not mediating. I was sleeping. It is a *fāgus*, or a beech, which reminds me an old friend. So I decided to have a rest beneath it for a while." Nyx says, "I will have to find a mate, and I will follow your plan."

I haven't even explained anything! Are you serious? Sleeping?

"Well, we need two top-ten couples..."

"No, you don't have to say it. I trust Eos as I trust the Oracle of Delphi; and I trust you as I trust the black cat."

Yeah, Eos is like a goddess, daughter of Apollo, and I am her little pet.

"The trail was a bit too long for this body, and so I decided to sleep for a while, and I thought you needed some rest as well, for the upcoming events. And I believe I am 1, I didn't even look at it, but I will check when we get back to the hotel."

You definitely need to, Miss 2 or Miss 4? Nice bluff though.

"Thank you." I still don't quite understand, but I start to worry that we are going to encounter something horrible, "By the way, any advice for Virgo today?"

"Tell the truth to your loved ones, or you lose their Love. Lucky item: Tree." She said.

—⁌⁍—

To be honest, I have stopped believing this Lucky item business. Four times in a row. How lucky is that? Instead of only one for yesterday, now I have thousands around us. You just randomly pick some item close by, right?

Why do people ask me to tell the truth today? Oh, I start to understand this is not easy. I promise I won't lie, but it does not mean I always tell the truth, because what I understand or what I know may not be the truth. I could say something false without realizing it or without purposely lying, in the same way that I could tell the truth but lie from my own perspective.

The best way to bypass it is to include "I think" or "I believe" before each such sentence, so that I am always talking about my own thoughts or beliefs, to avoid telling falsity without knowing. Problem is, sometimes it may sound unnatural.

—⁌⁍—

So the next interviewee is Muse. I have to think more carefully about it. Wait, why are Circe and Iris confronting with

Eos now? She was reading a yellow book as I can remember. How long have I been waiting for Nyx to wake up? Is it possible I was influenced by some dark hypnotic aura and so stood there sleeping as well? I haven't even noticed that Circe has been back from nowhere, and Vincent is now discussing with Zak about the catches. I hate that I don't have a watch to keep track of the time.

Anyway, it must be another girls' talk that I don't want to get myself involved. Not my business, I hope. So I go to find Muse, who is now playing with Artemis and Selene in the river, barefoot in pure white shirt, like a water lily. More precisely, most of the girls, except for Eos and Nyx, are wearing some white or off-white clothing for the sunny day. So they are all like water lilies. This scene is a teenage boy's biggest fantasy, so I spend a little extra time waiting for them. I now see why Water is the true "Element of Life", very addictive.

"Why did Eos believe you are 1?" Artemis asks.

What? How did you know?

"Don't know. Maybe she asked around randomly." Selene answers.

So Eos is still working on this rank shenanigans — Shit! She is basically bluffing *everyone* with the same trick! Naughty girl!

"I have something important to say. Do you have a minute, Muse?" I ask.

Muse does not respond, but Selene comes over.

"I see, you are still searching for top ten couples? Too bad we cannot help. Yes, it may be important, Muse!" Selene says, "By the way, why are you standing there with Nyx for so long, without saying anything?"

I already know that you cannot help. Why do you want to emphasize this?

"Nothing, just wait for Nyx to wake up from, meditation, I think." I say.

"Oh, you must be very nice and very patient in my opinion. Did you hear the sound, like fireworks and then it feels like an earthquake, while you were with Nyx?" Selene asks again.

So, how long had I been waiting then?

"No. We didn't notice anything, I think."

"You think?"

"Errr...I mean, I didn't notice anything, and Nyx didn't mention anything either."

Memory loss.

"OK. Circe and Vincent heard it more clearly, so that was why they came back. The sound was probably from their direction. But Muse didn't noticed the sound or the earthquake. I feel that people are not in their stable conditions today, due to the moons obviously, especially Muse, who didn't respond to our questions sometimes and only came back after a while, like day-dreaming or maybe absent-minded. By the way, about Dennis —"

"No. I don't know anything." I immediately regret what I just said, the second time today. What am I doing? Maybe as Nyx said, I need some rest or sleep for my brain to function normally.

"OK. Never mind." Obviously Selene does not believe me at all. The problem is, I don't have anything else I can say to make the situation better. Sorry Dennis! I am not lying and I am telling the truth!

"I also have a quick question, how rare is this *Lucky item* from Nyx?" I ask, trying to switch a topic.

"It's very rare, only once per month among all of us; for each person, maybe once a semester? How did you get two in a row? It must be related to this eight-planet-retrograde!"

Of course, I am not going to boast about getting two more. But, which one is rarer, the eight-planet-retrograde, or the four-consecutive-lucky-item? The former can be explained with my theory, but what about the latter? I definitely believe Nyx's fortune telling has something wrong, like my own computer program that I still don't know which Element it belongs to.

Soon afterwards, Muse steps over onto the pebbles. "You are looking for me?"

"How shall I start. How are you getting along with Jack? I have..."

"I see. Jack sent you over as an envoy, right? How are you doing with Iris and Eos? You answer my question first." Muse asks and laughs, pointing me to the other group of three girls over there.

"I know. It is complicated story, but I have a feeling it will be more likely Eos." I feel somewhat embarrassed, "It is strange but somehow it depends on the ranks, like whether Iris has high enough rank."

"So you are an elitist?"

"No, not quite. The thing is, it follows naturally from the rules." I explain my original top ten couple plan in detail, without Eos' modification, which may be too time-consuming. It is the third time of the day, so I feel more confident and the argument has been much cleaner.

"I see the point now. Impressive. If Eos thinks the plan is good, then it is good."

"This in fact bypasses my moral problem in a clever way."

"Oh...What is it?" I ask.

"I was thinking about it during the discussion yesterday, but I didn't say it. The story is: At the beginning, everyone has high moral standards and won't shoot each other for money; but if people are facing some great risk regarding themselves, then at least some of them will lower their moral standards and start to shoot people for money, or do other unmoral things. Some will, some won't."

I see. Hera was there in the discussion.

"So in this new plan, people won't have a big risk." I say.

"Right. The risk is too small in your plan with our new trick, which is exactly what we need. So make sure you have two hundred and forty in your pocket tomorrow. I also have some extra left as well. We still need to find twelve pairs though. I cannot say anything too certain at the moment. If I later pair up with Jack then we will cooperate as in your plan. I believe he is very happy to help you."

"Thank you so much, Muse. Really appreciate it." I say. I feel so glad that I decided to talk with Muse about it. Even Eos didn't come up with this clever plan for a private, secret ritual. I know, she probably doesn't care with a public one.

"Not a problem. Glad to help. Good luck with Iris." Muse says, "Actually you only need two of top twelve couples. The argument may be a bit twisted, but it is not too hard."

So twelve is the real magic number here. I quickly go over the argument another time.

"I see it now. Thanks, Muse!"

Maybe with top twelve Dennis and Selene can help, but chance is small, and the sunflower may feel hesitated to tell me that they are top twelve but not top ten. In this case, I would rather not try to embarrass people, and hope other pairs can work out first.

"What about your envoy job with Jack?"

"Already got enough information, I believe." I smile.

As I walk down to meet my last interviewee, I try to digest what I have at the moment.

Muse has already known Jack's rank number, at least a rough range of it. This explains a lot of things, including her relationship with Jack and her words to Leo a couple of days ago. If our old world Encyclopedia Jack is not in top five, then these top rank people must have known something big about *this new world*.

OK, I definitely knew the big secret, or a hint to the big secret, back on Day one; Eos obtained a lot of strange math facts, and it was like cheating in the exam, so this was why she was so upset only getting 3 and tried to figure out and shoot down the other two crazy nerds; I assume Tim and Bran also got something interesting by playing with QX trying to design the railgun.

So if my guess is correct, Muse has probably even higher rank than Jack, like top five or close, and knew some secret regarding the new world as well. So, on Day two, Muse went through with Jack the information they had, including both of their ranks, and then was certain that 1 had some "super important" knowledge regarding the new world, and Jack told me he is "not even close to top five".

So what did Muse know? And what did Nyx know? It gets too complicated that I don't even have a clue. One thing is clear. For whatever I know, some other people may know as well, up to some degree. For example, lots of people may have known a rough range of Eos' rank, and maybe Muse's as well. This was why Tim easily gave me a list of possible top tens. I may be able to get some information from his list alone. Then why is Nyx in Tim's list? Maybe Rhea has been asking some fortune-telling questions, directed by Tim?

Ah — now I sense Tim's ultimate plan — gather all possible information regarding the ranks, and solve the jigsaw puzzle all by himself, and then tell everyone how to choose their list.

That is hard, Tim.

xxix   Eagles

"What is that?" Someone points to the sky and wakes me up from my deep thoughts. Rats! I need to talk to Iris before I dive too deep into the Sea of Logic, Maelstrom of Incompleteness.

I look above, but it is hard to open my eyes. I saw one, no, actually two shadows hovering in circles.

"Eagles. Size of bald eagles but they are all black." Artemis says.

"Do eagles attack humans?" Circe asks.

Jack, I wish you were here!

"Rarely, only if it is their mating season and they think we are intruding their territory." Artemis says, "But this only works for eagles back on the old Earth."

I rush to the railgun. Man! This is heavy, especially if you want to lift it up and aim at things in the sky, and it is hard to see in direct sunlight. I need a pair of sunglasses!

"I don't think we need to worry that much. They usually prey on small mammals like rabbits and raccoons, and maybe squirrels." Vincent says, "We are too big for them, and there is only little chance that they can kill us. But they are able to do severe damage, and I agree we need to get prepared. Zak! Hold your knife as well."

Suddenly both eagles glide down towards us! The girls start screaming. My heart is hammering. It is very hard, but I manage to fire the railgun towards the sky, and it likely misses, not very surprising. Hard to tell. The bullet is so fast that nobody or the eagles can even notice anything visually. The sound, however, is deafening. Most people cover their ears. I feel my ears are blasted and can't hear people shouting at me.

The next moment I come back to myself, I am already on the ground, pushed by the recoil I believe. I hope it won't break my ribs. No time to think. I try to reload the gun. What? Why is Artemis pointing that arrow towards me? Oh I know! One of the eagles is too close and I can see a big shadow on the ground moving quickly towards me — Then Vincent pushes me over towards the ground.

"Ouch!" Both of us cry out.

The eagle has left on his back with some scratches. Bad ones I would say.

"Thanks a lot, Vincent. Are you OK?" Oh, even my own voice sounds stuffed, like underwater. Probably some ear damage.

"...OK...hurts...me."

Bad. My ears are blasted and cannot hear too clearly. What is worse, the eagle tries to fly up and maybe plans for a second attack. Where is the other eagle?

Twang! It is Artemis! The arrow does not hit the eagle either, but it gets pretty close, and more importantly it is slow and so the eagle knows that we are not easy targets. It hovers around for a short while and leaves.

"Where is the other eagle?" I ask.

"...know...railgun?" Vincent says.

"...railgun...useful...tell." Artemis says.

"Why...want to attack us?" Zak asks.

"Don't know. Maybe they are hungry." Artemis says.

My ears are feeling better now, and can hear, but still in much lower volume than usual.

"They haven't seen humans before, and unlike other mammals, we appear much smaller than we actually are from their view." I struggle to speak out, "Or maybe they just want some fish, like dolphins."

"Well, the worst case is that they somehow know you have the most powerful weapon among us and so try to take you down first." Vincent says.

"Apparently not as useful as a single bow." I drag the railgun back to the box.

"Vincent!" Circe runs over. The wound does not look good, I have to say. Three or four deep scratches. His shirt is already soaked in blood. Circe carefully clears the surrounding skins, and then takes out a potion.

"What is it?" Vincent drinks it and asks.

"I asked the cat for something that can heal injuries and wounds. Just for emergency." Circe says.

Oh, our CFT's advice is real.

The next moment, was breathtaking. Vincent's wound is healing by itself. Of course it is, but it is healing at like ten thousand times faster compared to the usual speed. We can actually see in real speed that the blood stops all by itself, and the exposed tissue hardens and becomes scab.

"Nano-robots that help accelerating the normal healing process?" Selene says, "We want to stock up some of these potions, Circe. It probably works better if you spread it over the wound in my opinion."

"Oh, then could I have a few drops into my ears? They are still buzzing. Thank you." I say, "Sorry, forgot to wear these earbuds."

After a few seconds, everything is loud and clear, not perfect, but this is real magic. Another proof after the red moon now, I think.

xxx   Noon

We then decide to return to the hotel with our catch. I don't have a chance to talk to Iris anymore, which is unfortunate. People don't talk too much along the way back, either due to the attack, or because we are all tired. Zak volunteered to carry the railgun for the first half while I carry the fish in a cooler, and we will switch for the second half — I see now why they ordered the dry ice, clever.

Eos comes close, "Do you realize why they have a *five* year period for us to have babies or order supplies? Five years on the new Earth."

Hey, don't you want to worry about if your f...friend is OK after the attack?

"Interesting. I haven't thought about it. Why?"

"High school."

Yes, how can I forget that! I roughly remember the numbers QX gave us, which I put on my notes and wrote down on multiple pages as backup. It is about the same period of time, if you convert everything over, like miles per gallon to liters per hundred kilometer.

"So for whatever you did with Iris, or other girls before we came here, it will vanish, or collapse to a dream, as nothing has ever happened." Eos says, "Our friendship, however, starts in this new world and in some sense, is real."

Is she trying to convince me that I shall choose her, by this time argument?

"I see your point, Eos. Thank you." I say, "When did our friendship start here?"

"When you said you trust QX based on my questions." She says with flushing face, "Anyway, I just want you to realize, for choosing a long time mate, you only want to count things or words happened here."

"OK, I will."

"And you only need two of top twelve couples. Same argument. Your success rate is up to ninety-five percent, and even to ninety-eight percent if we pair up."

Ha-ha, I knew it already. I know your feelings, Eos, trying to correct whatever minor mistakes. A perfectionist. This is the main reason you come over to me, I bet.

"Thanks. Eos, I got it."

Is she trying to convince me that I shall choose her, by these probability numbers?

"So what were you reading at the beach, another yellow GTM?"

"No, not GTM, but it is yellow. *Set Theory: An Introduction To Independence Proofs* by Kunen."

Oh, I know, you probably found these GTM's too hard and started something more fundamental.

"May I also ask," I lower my voice, "how did you guess at my rank?"

"If you come across a field, in the middle of nowhere, and a group of priests are performing some big ritual reciting some strange scripts and praising the gods. And all of sudden the sky becomes dark and a total solar eclipse happens. Do you believe that these priests know nothing about it and everything happens by coincidence?"

Probably Tim did the same reasoning.

So, why did you believe Selene is 1?

"But I might be..." I show her a victory sign.

"Your first question to the cat regarding the best knowledge. Very unnatural. Normal people wouldn't take the risk of offending 1 by that." She says, "Little boys might do it, so I was only seventy or eighty percent sure when I asked you back on Day three, or even after you said yes. Now, I am certain." She laughs.

OK, you win.

I know, I am a stupid, a true stupid.

<hr>

Vincent and I inform the whole group the first half of Tim's words before we arrive. It is not easy to tell the time with the gathering clouds, but it feels close to sunset, and it is getting dark and dangerous very quickly, in a natural forest.

The light is on. Good news. There is also light from the second floor corner room, but Jack's room is dark. Anything wrong with Jack? Maybe he is just downstairs with some other guys, I hope.

However, when we actually step inside the hotel, it does not look like good news at all. The lounge is a total diaster. Cracked plates and glass everywhere, Sofas and couches covered by debris and food residues. The worst of all, there is this big round hole on the west wall of the lounge, about one foot wide, and we can see the forest behind it. In fact the forest behind the wall is not in good condition either. A whole line of trees have fallen down, leaning over each other. How can a single bullet, or even four, do so much damage?

Hey, Vincent, didn't you say that the problem had been solved? But apparently he didn't know that either. Very likely this was what he and Circe as well as some other people heard earlier. The firework sound was the railgun, and earthquake came from the falling trees.

"Who fired the railgun inside this fusion-reactor powered hotel? Such a stupid!" I ask, "This could kill everyone in less than a second!"

"Tim did." Jack darts downstairs.

"So what happened?" I ask.

"Nothing. Just Tim fired, the, railgun, making a hole. Nothing else. I don't remember exactly, but only, a small quarrel." Jack sounds like he is still recovering from some bad memory earlier today, I assume, and he stutters with his quivering voice, "They are all back, in their rooms, probably having a rest, or sleeping, and all healthy, and uninjured. Everyone promised, no more fight, in the future."

Small quarrel? No one believes him really, either from his voice or from what we observe. It is so obvious something terrible has happened and we can even imagine by ourselves about it, but we hope it is a boys' fight — that regains friendship and holds us in a stronger bond.

"Dennis and others, will pay for, the repair, but may take, a few extra days." He continues, "For tonight, we'll have a barbecue party, instead of, regular dinner. So everyone can have, a quick rest, back in, their rooms. We need everyone, to agree with the plan, with the cat."

"OK, QX, I agree."

He then looks at the railgun I am carrying.

"Oh, yeah, need to return it to Tim."

"Tim said, you keep it." Jack says.

OK. It is probably not a good idea to put this heavy cotton candy around the lobby where everyone can have a lick. So I excuse myself, drag the railgun together with my body upstairs and have a quick rest.

Sorry, too tired to...what am I suppose to do right now?

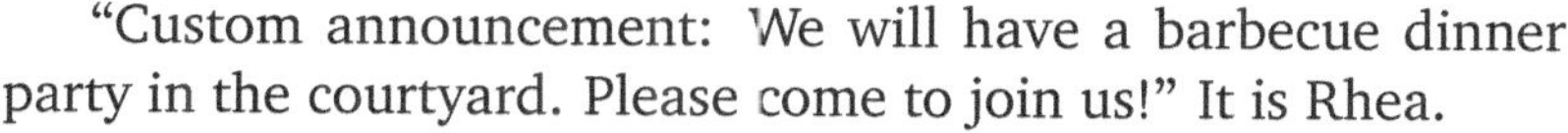

"Custom announcement: We will have a barbecue dinner party in the courtyard. Please come to join us!" It is Rhea.

"Sorry," Tim says, "don't want to talk about the hole tonight. It is a bit long, and twisted. Can you wait until tomorrow morning? You can briefly tell me what happened on the beach. I already know some part of it."

I know, something has happened. Most people still look quite tired. Wait, why did Jack lie to me? He never did, except for jokes or bridge games.

"I don't have much. Zak and Artemis guided us along the same path to the beach. We encountered a pair of eagles, and I tried to use the railgun but it does not work very well with flying objects. And most importantly I talked with the girls on the beach about the plan."

"Any good news?"

"Eos said the plan is good, with some small modifications... and I can form one pair, with either Eos, or maybe... Sorry but I haven't talked with Iris."

"Ha-ha. Great! As expected, she is now attracted by your wisdom. Bran also says he can help, but needs a mate."

"Nyx needs a mate as well." I say.

No, she simply doesn't care.

"Good. If we can pair them up then problem is solved. I suggest...you do not even try to ask Iris. Will make the problem more complicated...Errr, of course, this is up to you."

"Selene and Dennis are not a top ten couple, but Muse and Jack may be able to pair up tonight, my gut feelings, and their ranks are good." I say, "In that case, if Bran and Nyx also work out, then it does not matter whom I pair up with."

"Excellent. I like backup plans. Yeah, actually Dennis once told me he is 'around ten', but it could be a large range from 7 to 13 you know, so I thought it would be better for you to double check with Selene anyway. They...seemed to have some minor problems. For tonight, let's enjoy the party and allow the remaining boys and girls to pair up. This is not a good time for serious matters, so let us wait until tomorrow to tell everyone about the plan details, and we will have better ideas about top ten couples then."

"I agree."

Minor problems, I hope. Sorry Dennis!

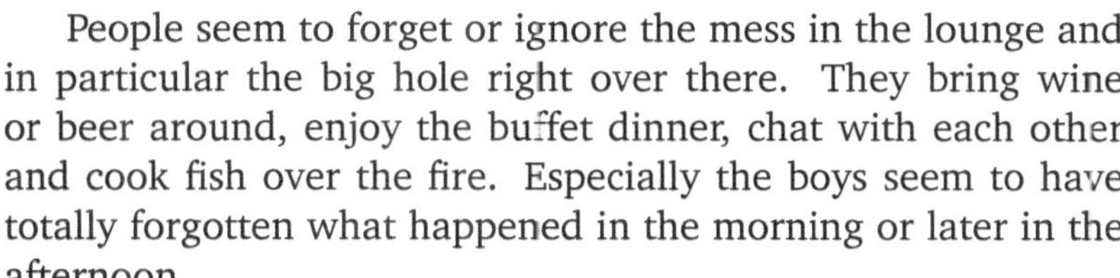

People seem to forget or ignore the mess in the lounge and in particular the big hole right over there. They bring wine or beer around, enjoy the buffet dinner, chat with each other and cook fish over the fire. Especially the boys seem to have totally forgotten what happened in the morning or later in the afternoon.

I also notice Leo and Frank have been glancing at me a few times. Maybe they are thinking about coming over to talk? Anyway, I don't have energy to chat with them right now, and there are too many things to worry about for tomorrow, and the day after.

No one is injured, which is also good news. Well, they probably ordered the same kind of potions.

One has to admit, grilled fish directly over fire taste like a charm. I got one to share with Jack.

"Very good. How was your trip with all those goddesses by the way?" Jack asks.

"So you calm down a bit?"

"Yeah. I don't understand why, but I feel good now." Jack says.

"Glad to know. You don't have to tell me about it. I know. I will ask Tim tomorrow morning." I then tell him about the eagles.

"The beach is likely their usual spot to catch fish as well. You disturbed their fishery. And you are right that humans look smaller than we actually are from their point of view." Jack says, "Something was strange. I don't understand, why they decided to take you down first, as you look bigger with the gun, and they usually target smaller easier ones."

"No idea. I suggest you to talk to your Ro...Muse tonight. Only less than twenty-four hours, no actually, less than twenty hours left you know. I think chance is good." I say.

"Thank you." He says, "Sorry I don't have anything in return, as far as I know."

"Actually you have." I then explained my plan in detail the fourth time of the day.

"If Eos thinks it is good, then it is good. Sure, as I said in the morning, I am glad to help. Wish I have good news tonight."

What? *I had asked you about it, this morning?*

"Do you notice anything strange this afternoon? I do not mean the hole or whatever you guys were doing, but your senses or memory?" I ask.

"No, nothing. Hmmm... Hera was a bit strange this afternoon, like absent-minded. What do you mean exactly?"

"Nothing bad. Both Muse and I were somewhat distracted by whatever... Just curious. Maybe it is a bad day."

I know, other people's abnormality is much easier to detect. I wouldn't be able to notice it if Selene didn't point that out.

"And sorry I don't have another guessing game for you." I say.

"Ha — but I do have one for you."

"Really? A weird dream?"

"Yeah. A really weird one I would say. It was almost identical to what happened like last night, two moons, unrealistic, and people started to cry. Suddenly, one of the girls stood out and almost yelled: 'I am 1, and I know a big secret. The moons are almost nothing compared to it', and then the crowd calmed down and waited for her, for her prophecy."

"Interesting. What happened next?"

Are you also trying to bluff me?

"I was woken up by the party downstairs. Too sad I missed the big secret."

"Ha-ha, these bad boys also woke me up! Ah, so..."

"A guessing game for you, this time."

"Muse?" I pronounce one name to him, but pronounce another name to myself —

"Selene."

I knew it.

"Are you making this up?" I laugh.

Was Eos there dreaming as well?

"No. One hundred percent real. The most realistic dream I've ever had." He laughs as well, "Anyway, so yesterday you asked about tarot cards, right? There is a card of the Moon in major arcana, and so here it splits into the Red Moon and the White Moon, which gives us twenty-three in total. Still one is missing, and I have been thinking about it all day long."

Sounds like you were pretty boring today. Didn't you have a "small quarrel" or something that resulted in that big hole over there?

"Maybe there is a blank card like the Joker?"

"The Fool, number O or zero, is already a blank card which works the same as the Joker. It had been almost always unnumbered, as there is no roman numeral for zero, so you can even say there are technically only twenty-one major arcana cards. At the beginning, I just recognized something interesting, like number III, the Empress, but some other cards are not so related to us, like the Sun, the Moon and the Star." Jack says.

You know her rank as well?

"So what are the first few cards?"

"I, the Magician; II, the High Priestess; III, the Empress; IV, the Emperor; V, the Hierophant; VI, the Lovers; VII, the Chariot; for VIII, there are variations..." Jack starts to enumerate. "In fact, a common theory is that, during old times, major arcana cards were not named or numbered, which means there was no order in them, or the order was not standardized; My theory is that while people mostly agree on the ordering of the first few cards, anything after the first few have been changing orders since the long history of humankind, very much influenced by astrology theories, which in turn, change over time as well."

"Could the Lovers be split into two as well?"

"Probably not..." Jack shakes his head. "In old versions, it was a couple blessed by a noble or cleric, total of three persons;

and modern ones use Adam and Eve, but we have too many here."

"Is there a card for Death? What is the number?"

"XIII, Death. Could be influenced by Christianity I think."

Well, the numbers do not match, and the chat is going too far into something which is totally irrelevant to us. I believe Nyx can tell us much more about the early history of tarot cards, but the lavender is nowhere to be found, neither is Bran.

"One moment, can we try to order sand hourglasses for everyone? Twenty-four identical ones. As Tim and Bran said, we are not able to order some of the products, but can order by a design. So we can perform everything in a secret ritual instead of a public one." Jack says.

"Right. Good idea."

"IX, the Hermit, used to hold an hourglass in hand. Later it was changed to a lantern."

Hourglass, right, that is it! — But I vaguely remember there is a much better plan, a clever plan, no need to order twenty-four hourglasses — someone told me earlier today. But I don't remember anything about it. What happened to my memory today? Something was absolutely wrong.

⊸◦⟡◦⊷

"Let us have a bonfire dance!" Rhea announces and asks QX to turn off the lights, and wakes me up from my thoughts.

Tim and Rhea first lead the dance around the campfire. Dennis and Selene follow. Soon a few others, Oliver and Pheme, Leo and Kakia, Frank and Gaia, Zak and Artemis, join the dance. The brilliant flame is also dancing, vividly casting shadows to the ground, and everything is vibrating with the smoke and hot air. Together with some alcohol, people become ecstatic.

I guess the news that there is a good plan has spread around. In fact, it is the plan Tim claimed to work back on Day three, plus "we have settled some technical details and let us rock!".

"It feels much better now without artificial lights. Guess what, this was how our ancestors find mates thousands of years ago. If you travel back in time and become a caveman, this fire is everything. Same idea works in night clubs at modern times. Dark environment, warm fire and flickering light. Ancient fire worship, spiritual, mystical, and even symbolic. People say it is related to human instinct for sex. Element of life, glory of humankind. In some cultures, people believe that there is mini fire inside human bodies, especially female bodies that generate new life. Now I see the reason." Jack is back to his usual self.

"No, not Fire, it is Water! I am serious! Once you've been to the beach, you would follow my way!"

He laughs, walks to Muse and gently bows for a dance. Muse has flushing face, maybe because of the fire, and quickly agrees to join. Ah, I don't even know how to dance nicely, with attractive and appropriate steps. Damn it!

Circe and Vincent are still standing there. Oh, I guess Vincent has not yet fully recovered from the injury. Wait, something is wrong, very wrong. He was supposed to be injured by — *love*, love? Which means, his love is — no, no, no! It can't be. I have no idea. It is the same feeling that Artemis' arrow is pointing towards me. He is handsome, but no, no, no — I don't believe this. The lavender was definitely wrong this time. I need to find a girl, to prove myself.

So I first try to look for Eos, but she is likely back to her own room, reading her yellow books. Iris is standing there still alone, like my favorite chamomile flower. I see, not much time is left for the matching game, not many choices either. I suddenly feel very guilty for Iris, and it is in fact my fault. In addition, I haven't finished today's interview yet, so I make up my mind.

"Are you feeling OK, I mean, with the eagles? We were all frightened. You were so brave to fight against them." Iris starts the conversation.

"Yes, I am totally fine. Thank you." I still don't know how

to start.

"Eos told me that you have a working plan, and to make the plan work, you may need to pair up with her. Is it right?"

"Right." I quickly go over the words, but cannot see into Iris' eyes directly. I dare not to.

"Eos also told me that if I tell you my number, then we may work as well, but in that case I may have to risk revealing my number to you in the guessing game."

I carefully digest the words "if", "then", "may" and "in that case" — She wasn't lying, though not telling Iris the full story. Naughty girl!

"Eos was not lying." I have to tell the truth.

"I trust you, so I can give you my number. Do you understand what this means?" Iris looks at me and says firmly.

"I totally understand." I lower myself and whisper by Iris' lovely burning ear, "I am 1." I immediately regret this, a third time of the day. What if Iris is 13+? Anyway, Iris is a nice girl who won't shoot me in the guessing game.

"12. Now I can put your name in both of the games." She whispers back to my ear and chuckles, and then holds me tight with her little arms, "Can we have a dance?"

It is already embarrassing to wait for a lady asking me for a dance, it would be even more impolite to decline it. So I hold Iris' hands and start with my clumsy steps, working with the difficult pairing problem, while following Iris' steps with greater difficulty.

"I heard some conflicting stories about you and Eos." Iris asks, "I wonder if I can hear the truth, directly from you."

Oh *Truth*, that single word warns me a bit.

"She rejected me, on Day two." I say, reminding myself that I have to tell the truth, "But I think, today on the beach, she said she is OK to marry me."

Oh, yeah, I am so stupid, glancing at the other dancing couples. The remaining people are mostly top twelve, so as long as they pair up, real or fake, we are done. Very good.

I am on the verge of switching the topic to the book of the day, but I see Eos standing there looking at us.

Girls have a secret way of communication, I am sure.

No! Not what you think. It's because of Vincent! No! It's not because of Vincent! What am I trying to say? My brain is not working, at all.

"When do you plan to tell people about it, say," Eos comes over and asks, "our secret?"

I have to admit that you phrased it in a very misleading way. You already know that Nyx told me I am supposed to tell the truth today, right? Naughty girl!

"Day seven, morning time, before noon." I answer. At least Iris now knows that the secret is not about marriage.

"One more thing." Eos says, "Never tell other people the third possibility before solar noon on Day seven."

"I agree." I say firmly.

Is she trying to convince me that I shall choose her, by our little secrets?

"Final question, do you know anything about 6?" She asks.

"Six? You asked the same question this morning?"

Oh, I totally forgot it! Too many tasks have overloaded my brain. It is no longer functioning well. Wait, what did you say?

"Yes, 6. Likely a girl."

Oh, 6, the person — I am impressed that our conversation can continue smoothly.

Another guessing game?

The water lily, the sunflower, or the lavender?

"Why?" I ask.

"Girls do not have small secrets, but only girls and little boys can keep big secrets."

Big secrets...Why are you so sure? I bet this is not part of the known knowledge. In fact, I am one hundred percent sure that this is not part of the known knowledge, since otherwise the cat won't answer your question in the first place.

"I don't have a good idea, or maybe, I am not certain. Big secret? Why do you ask?"

The water lily, or the sunflower?

"1 had been dominating in the knowledge rank since the sunset of Day two; but starting from the solar noon of Day four, 6 has taken over, all the time." She says.

The water lily.

I am ninety-nine percent sure this time.

Oh, you are keeping track of this stupid rank shenanigans throughout the days, my purple rose.

And so Jack is 7, 8 or 9.

DAY VI

xxxi   Truths

Today it's going to be tough. I have repeated my plan four or five times yesterday, and so relatively confident with it, but I still need to know two little things: what had happened yesterday in the hotel, and whether people can all pair up as planned. And I really want to know, two big things —

"6."

"Six."

OK, I know it is your favourite number by now. Oh, right, 6 is very likely one of the Six. It was the graduation ceremony *on that day*, and once they tried to recall the memory, an eclipse would come. It is just physics, very predictable. Three more to hunt, three and a half, really.

I walk downstairs. To my surprise, Nyx is waiting there at the end of the stairway. The lavender indicates a more private talk. Well, I am still curious why the Tree was my Lucky item for yesterday, as well as whether your number made you embarrassed last night —

"I had *this* nightmare early this morning..."

Oh, even the lavender had had bad dreams. Did you also see an eclipse this morning? What were you doing during midnight there? And it implies that you saw an eclipse on Day four as well? It is not like a nightmare, just a lucid dream. Why didn't you mention it yesterday? All right, I didn't even ask.

"Oh, really? What is it? May I ask? I don't know too much about dreams though, to be honest."

Or, the second possibility, our CFT only wants to consult my advice for a dream? What an honor! However, I am not an expert, nor I have the tool or the computer program with me. Or, the third, you want to know if I am still available? Bad news for Bran. Why didn't you ask me on the beach, then we can totally forget about Iris or Eos or all the other people! All right, I didn't even ask either.

"OK, never mind. Thanks. Good luck this time, and good luck tonight." Nyx leaves me alone, in another total puzzlement.

⸻⸺∘☙❧∘⸻⸺

Tim has already been there in the lounge. The big hole is still there as well, but the lounge has been cleaned up nicely.

"Good morning. Have time to talk?" I ask.

"Sure."

"So what happened yesterday?"

"You mean last night? Rhea and Selene helped to clean up the campfire. There is an outdoor faucet in the courtyard and they put off the fire. You know, it is a wild forest, and any spark could be disastrous."

"I mean this hole!"

"Oh the hole, Dennis and some others will pay for the bill. The cat says it may take a few days once the robots start working on it. Don't worry about it! I assume these cute robots will later build our houses as well."

"Tim!" I am angry.

"OK, OK. Seriously — Nothing happened. Just like what Jack told you." Tim says, with smile.

"What? You fired the railgun and nothing had happened?"

"Exactly." Tim says, "Everything, I shall say almost every-thing was planned the night before. Dennis, Bran and I planned it mostly, and the boys — Frank and Oliver, Leo and Yan tried to play it out. The only uncertainty came from these two girls — they insisted to join the party, making it a bit more out of control, but finally everything was OK. And I promise, noth-ing...strange had happened that night. They just drank too much."

"What do you mean? Everything was planned? Including the fight? — So you were basically worried about the girls, right?" I ask.

"Roughly yes. Most boys have been very enthusiastic with the current situation — I need to add — after the initial shock. It is like a fantasy world, a completely new world of our own! We are the rulers of everything here! Who have not dreamt about it? We discussed all night long about our future plans. Exploration, construction, self-satisfaction, raising kids, and liv-ing in an entirely different way, determined all by ourselves. In the old world, we have always been evaluated by others, ev-erything, and will be evaluated later in our almost entire life; Most people agree that it is where pressure and stress come from; But here, we take control and you can do whatever you want — Vincent wants to be a carpenter; Dennis wants to be the first one travelling around the globe; Leo, an astronomer; Yan will run a winery and make the best wines for us; Jack will build a library for our future generations; Zak, a fisherman and hunter, with Artemis; Bran of course wants to study mechanics and material science; I would take the responsibility to over-see power plants and water facilities, but would prefer to study some botany on this alien planet — We literally become kings and queens of this new land. Even better, these friendly aliens are helping us to build a modern colony, instead of we building everything by ourselves. Isn't this what you have dreamt of, when you go to college and start thinking about leaving your parents and living by your own?"

"O-Kay-" Well, Eos and I think we are even more than just kings and queens.

"In fact there was only one boy who seemed to be...not so passionate — you. I am serious. Even William is fanatic about building a church on a new planet and becoming the first pope or something, 'His Holiness William I', as Jack joked. So we are worried about some of the girls, as well as you." Tim says, "Later I figured out you probably had known it already from other sources, and might be still swaying between Iris and Eos as people had rumored around. So that was the reason why I asked about your rank."

"I thought you told me you knew everything is real as well, Day three, with Jack and Bran." I say.

"Well, Bran and I didn't have a direct proof of it. The guns seemed unreal, considering the delivery time and accuracy to our descriptions, though we hadn't tested them. It is totally possible that they gave us some toy guns, but they are not like something they had prepared, for a game. So for us, Bran and I, we still had a tiny bit of hope that they made a few toy guns on the Earth within such a short time. However, you seemed to have seen something truly *unearthly* before we saw the moons."

"Unearthly. It is the most accurate word here. Yes, I did." I feel hesitated to talk about it, right now.

"You don't have to tell me now. I understand, and we will wait for tomorrow for the big secret. The main and immediate problem was, of course," Tim continues, "the girls. At least some of them had already been in distress or depression. If we didn't do anything, they might stay in their rooms forever, literally forever."

"So everything was planned to create a chaotic environment and force the girls to get out of their rooms, take a breath of fresh air, and then have fun?"

"Yes, including you, in the original plan. So I decided to talk with you in the courtyard, since otherwise Bran or Dennis or some other guy might laugh out, which would ruin the plan."

"Did Jack know this? Was the fight planned as well?" I ask.

"Oliver went a bit far. Jack knew this from the start, but I still don't know why he didn't want you to lead the picnic team, and asked Dennis or Bran to lead instead. But this might not be able to trick the most clever minds — Eos, Nyx, Muse and of course, you. Anyway, he eventually gave up and followed our plan. I guess he was a bit unhappy with it, and so excused himself and went upstairs early."

I close my eyes, trying to recall everything. Something was still not right, I believe, not the usual Jack.

"What about the two advices Vincent brought up?" I ask, "Adding a bit mystery?"

"Partly so. To keep you thinking about it, instead of figuring out our trick and telling everyone." Tim says.

Oh! Jack was hinting about Vincent! He knew it before we left. I was so dumb!

"So what were you guys doing yesterday?"

"Chatting, mostly. We actually figured out something fishy... The ground floor secret room you remember? It is an elevator, but we cannot go down to the basement. No buttons, or lights. It is fully controlled by them. The cat only confirmed that it was designed to protect us from...radiation."

"How deep is it..."

"No idea. Anyway, I guess this afternoon, we will gather everyone and explain and execute your plan. But before that," Tim smiles, "you need to figure out your own decision, Eos or Iris?"

"How do you know I can match with Iris as well?" I haven't told anyone, and I believe the chamomile hasn't told anyone either about the magic number. Or maybe some people by accident heard the secret word? Even assuming Tim has known this number, it is still not top ten. So maybe the purple rose or the water lily told him about the story of top twelve couple? Or he figured everything out by himself? I quickly run through all the possibilities.

"Everyone saw you two danced last night." Tim laughs, "Sometimes you are smart, but other times you are a bit dumb, my friend."

Oh, he now thinks that I am an idiot, and I am truly an idiot.

"Well, to be honest, Rhea told me that Iris is not in top ten, so I was a bit puzzled, and discussed this with Bran. Later we concluded that Iris is 11 or 12, right?" He lowers his voice.

"Right."

I knew it. A lot of crazy things have happened below the tip of the iceberg.

"We won't tell others about it. I need to go," Tim pats me on my shoulder, "to ask Bran about his progress, and Leo wants to say sorry. He is a bit shy, but trust me, he is sincere. He insisted that night it was all his fault."

I sit there alone, speechless. Well, there is no one I can talk to right now, but the feeling is the same kind. Both Eos and Iris have been downstairs, reading books alone, far away from Tim and me.

I just feel a bit suspicious on myself. Why didn't I notice what was really going on yesterday? Maybe I spent too much energy carrying a railgun? Or maybe something happened there that distracted my thinking? Oh damn, I erased everything before I departed.

I can even vividly imagine what happened yesterday after we left. The girls probably gathered together and did some preparation for the barbecue, and chatted or gossiped throughout. Vincent then delivered the fresh breads from the girls. The boys, first laughed, and then took out the railgun and one by one examined it, like appreciating a piece of art. Now as Vincent had left and the subtle balance broke, one of them, likely Leo or Oliver, had this brilliant idea to fire it and to make the "fight" more real. Oliver more likely, because they once planned to open a hole from Zak's room down to his, and obviously this is a good chance to test it out.

Then some agreed but some didn't. I can even imagine the

number of yeas versus nays, and William's abstention and Dennis' unforgivable betrayal. That was the only "small quarrel". Tim finally decided to fire it at the safest spot, towards west, below the boys' wing — It was absolutely more powerful than they had thought. Then they also threw plates and glass cups all around in the lounge. Of course, no one was injured, not even any blood around. Damn, I should have noticed that earlier, and I was even thinking they had ordered some potions as well. Why was I so stupid?

I see it now. Vincent's role was basically used to make everything more real. He first showed up and said the problem had been solved, then people might suspect it; then we arrived at the hotel late in the afternoon, and saw the bigger fight, then it looked very real. Like psychology, it somehow changed our feelings, as Rhea mentioned. Very clever, I admit.

"Hey, you don't look good. Any problem?" It is Muse.

"Errr. You may not know, the boys..." I am still somewhat hesitated about whether I should tell the girls about it.

"The boys? Oh, of course I know that. We all know that. The boys pretended to have a fight and drove the girls out of their rooms, and pretended to have a bigger fight when we were at the beach. Is this what you mean?"

"What?" My mind was blasted again. I feels like I am the only idiot here in this hotel, the only stupid on this planet. "When did you know that?"

"I felt a bit suspicious about the fight at the beginning, though I was frightened and didn't think too much." Muse says, "On the way to the picnic, the girls asked Nyx, who said 'The railgun in the hotel may cause a quarrel, but it will save us', and Eos, and she said 'Leave the hotel to the big boys'. Then Artemis tried to torture, sorry no, to interrogate Zak, who quickly admitted it was so planned."

Save us? The girls, or the picnic team, or everyone? The railgun I was carrying didn't even help much. I don't understand. Nyx's fortune-telling seems to lose power on this new planet, just like what happened to me with my computer program.

"Zak could be lying, right? Like, to make you feel less stressed?" I feel *torture* is the correct verb there with Artemis.

"Could be. So Selene asked Vincent when he caught up, but we didn't know the details of the conversation. 'Vincent did not seem to tell the truth in my opinion'. Selene also tried to pry something out of you, but failed. In fact, you two were still trying to mislead us by telling Tim's words, which caused some worry at first..."

OK. Poor Vincent.

"Wait, why didn't Dennis tell Selene about it?" I found something a little bit strange.

"Don't know. Maybe he didn't want Selene to tell everyone about it. So it may cause some problems in the future."

"I hope not." I say, though I don't think the sunflower will be happy, at all.

"But when we later came back to the hotel. The scene was obviously a trickery."

"Why was that? Because there was no blood?"

"Partly so. More importantly, only girls throw things over to each other during a quarrel or scuffle. Boys fight with their fists. That is it." Muse says, "Nevertheless, we feel very thankful to you guys. Thank you."

"Don't thank me." I am almost crying, leaning my forehead over to my hands, and hiding my flushing face, "I am the last person to know all this. To be honest, they tricked me as well, and I didn't know this until Tim told me...earlier this morning."

"Oh really? ...Ha ha ha..." Muse giggles, pauses for a few seconds, and starts to laugh loudly, unable to hold it at all. "This is so hilarious. This, this explains a lot of things from yesterday. I, I am going to tell Hera about it. Ha ha ha...My belly hurts. Ha ha ha..."

"You must feel lucky that I don't have a railgun in my hand." I say, word by word.

"OK. If that makes you feel better. Ha ha ha..." Muse continues, and pats my back, attracting a lot of attention.

This is the correct reaction. I feel more embarrassed now.

"Don't feel too bad. Everyone has hard days." Muse says, "I also had a bad day yesterday. Too much stress."

"It is going to be hard for today, and probably harder for tomorrow." I sigh, trying to switch a topic, "May I ask about you and Jack?"

"Yes, we will follow your plan."

So, you agree with the first part?

"Thank you, and congratulations." I say, "By the way, do you know why Jack was so anxious yesterday afternoon? Nothing, if nothing had happened, then he shouldn't be so."

"He was definitely not a good actor as I can tell. Everyone knew that he was role-playing on a stage, reciting a script and pretending to be frightened. Too artificial trembling voice, probably only worked to trick you." Muse says, "By the way, nice shot with the railgun yesterday, and it also attracted the other eagle towards you. I felt bad that they were probably a couple, but we all want to say 'thank you', otherwise more of us could be injured."

"What?" I am puzzled again. But before I can ask for the details, or ask about six or 6 or the sundial or the eclipse, we feel the ground is shaking.

xxxii   Earthquakes

It feels like an earthquake, or at least an earthquake as described in the books, though not a severe one. It is more like when you stop for a red light, cars and trucks pass through you along a nearby lane.

"Everyone out to the courtyard!" Someone cries out.

"No! Everyone stay inside! It feels more like some herd of animals coming towards us. Close all the doors!" It is Artemis.

The vibration becomes stronger and stronger after a short while, and we can even hear it.

"I can see them from my room." Selene says, "Hundreds or thousands, different kinds of mammals mostly. Some look like cattle, some like goats, others are smaller, like foxes or wolves. They are running through, to the south."

"South? They want to cross the river?" Bran says.

Then we actually see some of them running through. Different kinds of mammals, mostly grey or brown color. A few of them get disoriented outside the courtyard, but soon adjust themselves back to the route with the herd.

"Here they come." William says, signing a cross. "God bless us."

"Most large ones are herbivores, or look like herbivores. I hope they are just on a trip." Vincent says.

And the shaking gets weaker and weaker. So the wave has passed us.

"No! They are escaping something!" Tim says, "You two, get the guns. Other boys, getting knifes or something the like. Girls, back to your rooms."

"No." Artemis says with a bow in hand already, "If anything crazy shows up, we fight together."

"And we die together." Selene says.

Please do not say stupid things. We are not going to die.

I quickly run to my room and get the railgun. I take a quick look at Jack, and say, "Tim, I guess it is better to be in your hands."

"You keep it now. I have more important things. It is likely a land unit, so not too hard to aim. We can take down a *T-Rex* with ease."

"What if there are one thousand *T-Rexes*?" I ask.

"Then we die." Bran says, "*T-Rēgēs*, my dad told me."

So your dad is a biologist, or palaeontologist?

"An adult *T-Rex*, similar to, most large carnivores, usually, lives alone, like bears and tigers; but recent fossils showed, some *T-Rēgēs* are living in a herd, like in a lion pride, but in relatively small groups." Jack starts to stutter again, and struggles to finish the sentence. Don't be afraid, Jack! You didn't get your tense right!

"Anyway, even if there are a hundred — then they are socialized and so more intelligent. We can take down a few, then hopefully others may retreat. We will have money to arm ourselves with more powerful weapons tomorrow." Dennis says.

Oh, I see why it is in the present tense. Sorry, Jack.

"I hope so. We have a total of six charges left." Tim says, "My bad, should have seven."

"I prefer six." Nyx says, "Six is for Strength and Seven is for the Devil."

It is not the time for your numerology, my lady.

"Look! What is that?" Hera points to the courtyard.

Only one. Good news. Dennis and I quickly use the railguns to lock the target from two directions. It does not matter if we break some glass doors right now. It looks like a bigger version of a buffalo, in dark grey fur, with three horns, two at the usual place and another in the middle, like a trident.

"Girls, up to the fourth floor. It can easily break the glass panels." Tim sends an order. "We can take it down. Don't worry, just want to make sure everyone is safe. No unnecessary injuries."

This time, Artemis, Selene and Rhea lead the girls upstairs.

"Don't fire. I will try to take it down with my bow from upstairs. Then we will have real fresh meat for tonight." Artemis says.

Oh, so you are the real carnivore. Real...what have we been eating? I didn't notice anything strange.

To our surprise, the buffalo seems quite friendly. Not even attempting any attack, it just stands there, looking at the sundial or the hotel with curiosity. Both Dennis and I feel reluctant, because each charge is precious and we don't want to kill something that is not aggressive.

The next moment, it turns backwards, sprints and disappears in the woods. Artemis' arrow misses again.

I know it. Same as the eagles, it can feel the presence of the real carnivore, upstairs. Run, Minos, Run! Don't know why but this word pops into my mind. Sorry I shouldn't call a lady a carnivore, better to be a flower, at least some plant, maybe...Venus flytrap?

Of course, I dare not speak this out, because the arrow would then turn around and fly directly towards me, even if I have a railgun in my hand.

......

"What is that?"

A herd of small white animals with white long ears running or more precisely hopping through, to the south, towards the direction where the buffalo disappeared.

"Rabbits?"

I agree they *look like* rabbits, but something does not feel right. The scene, like some hundreds of cotton balls, does not look natural at all. You only see such a scene in B movies that only made into drive-in theaters, or, your own dreams...

"Pure white fur in such a forest. Meaning that they don't fear anything here." Bran says.

"But as we just saw, there are foxes and wolves or something the like. These are natural predators." Dennis says.

"Maybe they are not foxes or wolves." Oliver says.

"But there are also eagles, which for sure prey on rabbits. They even attacked us. Rabbits with white fur are obvious and easy targets." Vincent says.

"Obvious, but not easy — They don't have predators. They *are* predators." Bran says after a short while.

Holy shit! My plan!

"QX, we want to order a flamethrower. Bran, you tell QX about the details, as soon as possible." Tim cries out. "Shut all the doors locked. They are small enough so won't be able to break in, unlike the buffalo. Boys, get a couch or two to seal that hole in the lounge. My fault again! No one leaves the hotel until further orders."

Soon everyone on the ground floor realizes what Bran and Tim actually meant. We feel so lucky that we didn't encounter them during explorations.

"I agree. Railguns are not useful against a large group of these." Dennis says, "Worse than a hundred *T-Rēgēs*."

"No. Flamethrowers are too dangerous in a forest. You said it, Tim. And, it is not Fire, it is Water!" I say, "QX, I want to order a garden hose, two hundred feet."

"Sure. One hundred dollars, deliver by sunrise tomorrow. OK to proceed?" QX says.

"No! We need it right now!" I shout.

"Expedited...six hundred dollars. Do you want to proceed?"

"Yes, please!"

Why are garden hoses so expensive? Oh, vinyl, rubber, complicated chemicals. I don't even know anything that is a good substitute!

"What are you doing? Throw six hundred bucks at a garden hose, at this moment?" Tim asks.

"Rabbits do not like water, at all. If they get wet, then they quickly lose body temperature and get hypothermia and die within a day." Bran says, "That's why we didn't see them during previous days. The ground was still wet."

"Even more so, if they become, carnivores. Their heartbeats, have to be, faster than herbivores." Jack says.

"Agree. They are going to lose body heat much faster." Bran says.

"But polar bears also have white fur and they swim in the cold water." Oliver asks.

"Polar bears are much larger compared to these rabbits. Much easier to preserve body heat." Vincent says.

"I see. That was why the first wave ran towards the river. They wanted to cross the river. Otherwise it wouldn't make sense, as it is much slower to cross a river when you try to run away from predators." Dennis says.

A robot quickly delivers a garden hose.

"Cover me." I give the railgun to Tim, and drag the hose to the courtyard and hook it to the faucet. This is heavy, even heavier than the railgun.

Then I start to spray every inch of ground near the hotel. Damn. I underestimate the weight with water.

Jack runs over to help out. Some girls upstairs probably think I am mad, or they have already believed so.

"Why do you know rabbits don't like water?" Jack asks. "Sorry I guess I was in a shock and wasn't able to hold myself."

"I had a pet rabbit for my fifth birthday," I say, not willing to recover my memory right now, "and it died because of my fault. Cried for three whole days. My parents tried to get me another one, but I refused anything." It was the first time in my life I started to understand the real difference between life and death.

Oh my Lord, it will be seventeen years from now.

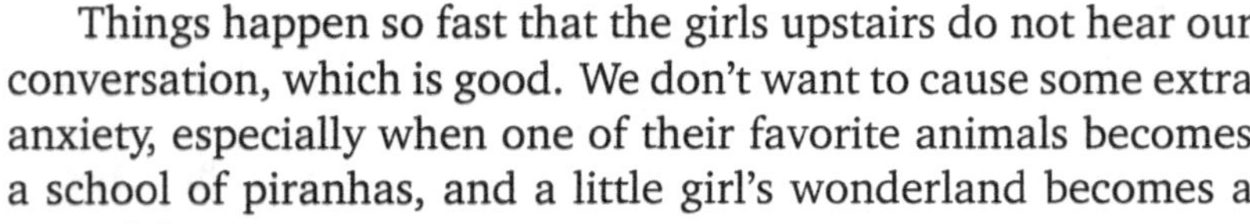

Things happen so fast that the girls upstairs do not hear our conversation, which is good. We don't want to cause some extra anxiety, especially when one of their favorite animals becomes a school of piranhas, and a little girl's wonderland becomes a true nightmare.

"Your boys are doing it again, right? Some trickery?" Muse comes over.

"No, I don't think so." Jack says, "QX, I want to build a moat, a channel full of water surrounding the hotel."

Now you see, it is Water, not Fire!

"Fifteen hundred dollars. Will finish by solar noon tomorrow. You do not have enough cash in your account." Says QX.

"Charge mine as well." Muse says.

You two save my day.

I wipe my sweat, and two of them are standing there under the sunlight, proudly watching an army of robots, countless many, marching into the woods, as if they were their own little kids.

xxxiii   Ritual

It has passed noon and our lunch has been sitting there for a while. I am pretty tired, but at least the immediate threat has gone.

"We need some extra budget for building a larger moat around the colony." Jack says.

"Right, we were discussing this with everyone, and people all agreed that this is going to be our first priority after tomorrow. Not just for rabbits, but also for other possible threats." Bran says.

"I think we want to have lunch in the lobby." Tim says, and turns towards me, "You need to explain your plan first. Bran and Nyx can be a pair."

"Very good."

Bran, you can do fortune-telling based on dreams? What is the word for it? Oneiromancer or oneiroscopist?

I wonder around as I wolf down my lunch sandwich, which still tastes like some meat to me.

"Well, if it is a real earthquake that can destroy the hotel, we wouldn't be able to survive long in the forest." Zak says.

True. Is the hotel becoming part of your body?

"Zak, we can eat those fruits, and fish, and start everything by ourselves. Life is always more important." Artemis says.

I know you love rabbits, as food, but they are different.

Soon we gather in the lobby and I start to explain our plan. For a lot of people, this is still the same plan Tim mentioned back on Day three, and nothing much has happened between — like a memory loss.

"The plan is what I call a *Marriage Ritual*. We make sure everyone, or every couple releases some information, but not enough information for other people to easily guess at their ranks." I start with the overall philosophy.

"We will fix a time interval say two hours, and divide it into twenty-four periods. Like five minutes each. We label each period consecutively by numbers one to twenty-four. The first five-minute period is assigned to 1, second to 2, and so on. Everyone's following with me?"

Everyone is good at the moment.

Rats! I scold myself. How did I even forget this? Too many important matters yesterday, plus the faked fight scene. I guess it was really a bad day for me.

"Now on the dining table we will prepare a paper containing a list of everyone's names. The plan is, everyone first goes back to your own room, and during a period, if the assigned number is either your own rank number, or your spouse's rank number, then you come down to the dining room, with your spouse. OK? Remember you can only leave your room during these two periods. If nothing goes wrong, your spouse and only your spouse is there with you."

Everyone laughs.

Hourglasses...Jack told me the hourglass plan last night, but I totally forgot to ask the cat about it! I was too tired, and too busy, but I also remember, there was a better plan — I literally have sweat on my brow now, the second time of the day.

"Next, we perform the secret *Marriage Ritual* with only two of you there." I say, "You cross out your names — your own name and your spouse's name — on that piece of paper, and you go back to your own rooms. That's it."

"That's it?" Vincent asks.

"Yes, that's it. That is the marriage ritual, like a marriage ceremony for you two. It is unfortunate that only two of you will be there. Besides, you need to look at the paper, pick two others, randomly or not, whose name has *not* been crossed, and use them in your list in addition to your spouse."

Except for the few ones who already know the plan, most people are still digesting it.

So what is the better plan? I should think twice ordering this stupid garden hose. Now I am probably running out of cash!

"Let me give an example. During period number one, 1 and their spouse come down to the dining room, and cross out both of their names. Then they can put whoever they want into their list in addition to their spouse."

"Next, period number two, 2 and their spouse come down to the dining room, and as well cross out their names. Now 1 and their spouse have already crossed out names, so there will be twenty names left, ten boys and ten girls. 2 and their spouse can each pick two from the remaining ten, for the two extra positions in their lists."

Some people start to nod, which is a good sign.

"So for example say 1 and 24 form a pair. In this process, we make sure that any pair after them will not use 1 or 24 in their lists. So in the end, regardless of 1's other choices, 1 can always be matched with 24."

I pause for people to digest.

Well, if I spent cash to order the hourglasses, then I wouldn't be able to order the garden hose earlier today. In the worst case — we would be all dead by now. So there is nothing to regret. Calm down. Calm down.

"Following that, it is the same argument for the 2 couple, by which I mean, 2 and their spouse. The easiest way to understand this is to simply remove the 1 couple from the entire game, and imagine you only have twenty-two people playing the game. So it is by the same argument that the 2 couple can be matched in the end. It is what they call...what is the name...errr..."

"Recursion." Eos says.

"Yes, thanks! The good thing about this ritual, is that almost no information regarding individual ranks will be revealed. The 2 couple probably obtain the most useful information in the process. That is, they see two names have been crossed out, and they only know one of them is 1. So they have a fifty-fifty chance of winning in the guessing game, which is mostly like a fair coin-tossing game. The third couple will see four names crossed out, and they know one of them is 1 and one of them is 2. The winning chance of random guessing or blind shooting is down to twenty-five percent. So they won't do it. Similarly, the following couples get less and less information. Likewise, random shooting, without any other information, only has one over twenty-three or one over twenty-two chance of winning depending on how you calculate it. So in most cases people won't do it. It is the same argument." I look at the purple rose and the water lily, and make sure both are happy — Which one of you told me the better plan yesterday? Why did I forget?

People start to sigh, expressing their satisfaction. Tim is nodding and smiling, as usual.

"In this plan, if you and your spouse lose money due to the guessing game, then it is most likely your own fault, like revealing your numbers to someone else you shouldn't have trusted; or someone blindly shoots you or your spouse and is very lucky."

"Following this plan, the person with rank 1 does not have privilege, but actually has responsibility. A small risk of revealing themselves to the second couple. Same for the other higher rank people. Higher rank does not mean privilege, but slightly higher risk. Knowledge is not advantage or privilege. Knowledge is challenge." I continue.

"Knowledge is challenge, and marriage." Jack says.

Probably not a joke to the purple rose.

"If you and your spouse have already crossed out names, then you do not need to come down again, right?" Selene asks.

"Correct. You can choose to stay in your room, or choose to

come down and look at the paper the second time. Up to you." This is almost a trivial question. Don't know why you asked. Didn't you know the plan from yesterday? You are wasting my precious time here!

"Similarly, you and your spouse can decide, if you want, that only one of you show up in the ritual and cross out both names, but it feels more like a marriage ceremony if both of you show up." I add a remark.

"How about the last couple, or the second last couple, as they do not have enough names left to fill the choices?" Leo raises his hand.

"This is indeed a very good question. In the end, after period number twenty-four, everyone gather together here. At that time, I will ask at least four people, two boys and two girls, to raise their hands, but without revealing their ranks. If you are the last or the second last couple, then you use these people in your list. I am probably running out of time to go through the technical details, but roughly say all their ranks are high enough so that if does not matter if you choose them. As an example, if 2 and 7 form a pair, and they put each other in their lists, then regardless whether they put 16 in their lists or whether 16 put them in their list, it won't matter. The system will assign a matching between 2 and 7. In an extreme case, if 1 and 2 form a couple and put each other into their lists, then regardless of other people's choices, they can be matched at the first step of the matching game."

So I actually try to avoid the details of analysis, so that these couples don't even need to say they are top ten or top twelve. I also want to save some time to order hourglasses or follow other plans.

"Then do the last two couples, four of them, have to reveal themselves in the process?" Hera asks.

"No. Absolutely not. We gather everyone in the end, so everyone receives the same information. If you are not among the last two couples, then you simply ignore it, and it is not very useful to determine anything either."

You are worried about being the last two couples, Hera? Ah — Now I sense the flavor of the sunflower's *seemingly* silly question. It is the same as my own flavor, and as the purple rose once pointed out, unnatural. So they don't need to come down again *in the first place*. Interesting. Very interesting.

"What if someone hide somewhere and peek?" Kakia asks.

"If you hide and see two people coming down and crossing out their names, you still don't get enough information in the guessing game, likely at most a fifty-fifty chance of winning. I believe, we are honest people."

Well, that couple will do the searching for us, including the public bathrooms. They have enough time, and there aren't many good spots in this minimalist hotel for hide-and-seek. And, thank you very much, Miss 12.

"Then why don't we do the same thing with everyone here, like you reveal yourself in pairs in public, instead of in a secret ritual?" Pheme asks.

"Oh. That is because I want to minimize the revealed information. In the public plan, every couple becomes a fifty-fifty chance target. In the secret ritual plan, only 2 and their spouse know the names of 1 and their spouse, but do not know which one is which. Now if you do everything publicly, then everyone knows the same information, so probability goes up to fifty-fifty for every pair. Say for example if someone already knows the rank of 1's spouse, or know that it is not 1, then they know who is 1." I struggle quite a bit for make it clear.

"Let me see. Say if 1 and 12 form a pair, and if the ritual is done publicly, then anyone who knows 12 is 12, that is, knows 12's rank number, will automatically know who 1 is. Does this make it clearer?" I rephrase my explanation.

"Good point." Tim says.

I know. You need this the most.

"Right, we need to minimize the revealed information." Selene says.

Right, you don't want to embarrass yourselves with a public ritual.

"Yes, I agree." Pheme says.

"How about someone lie to their spouse and put others in the list?" Kakia asks.

I know this question will show up.

"The system does not encourage you to lie. By lying you don't get too much benefit. If you instead choose someone that has not been crossed out, then they won't put you into the list anyway, and you become single. If you choose someone that has been crossed out, the chance that you can be matched with them is pretty low — they must also have you in the list and their spouse is of lower rank than you. Well, if they also lie to their spouse, then why didn't you two open it up and form a pair in the first place?"

This may not be easy to digest, but after some time, people start to see the point. This differs from Kakia's plan, which encourages you to lie to be matched with someone else.

The same argument applies to other possible plans. For example, once we fully pair up, we can divide ourselves into six smaller groups, two pairs each. Then everyone picks their spouse, plus two others from the next group, in a cyclic way. The problem is again, people may lie. If you know who has chosen you or may have chosen you, then there is always this sinful sentiment deep in your mind asking you to lie.

Imagine if Selene believes that Dennis has a secret girl, but does not know which girl it is — *Selene, I love you, but I am sorry...* Or, another secret girl who admires Tim may use this opportunity to arrange their positions and try to win in a rank competition. "Too many uncertainties", as Tim once commented.

"I see the point now. So it is better if both husband and wife show up in the ritual." Kakia says.

"Right. I think you are right."

"Any other questions anyone?" Tim asks, "If not, then let us start. Not too much time is left."

"One more question," Bran asks, "how do we measure five minutes, or certain period of time?"

Straight hit. You may work well with Eos.

"Have you tried to order the hourglasses?" Jack asks.

"Sorry. QX, how much time do we have left until sunset, the deadline for the matching game," I realize that I don't need the Earth time here, "as a fraction of a day here on the new Earth."

"Zero point one nine six of a day." QX answers.

I quickly do some math on my notes. Jack, you know, I foresaw those rabbits and didn't know how much time we would have left for today, and so I waited until now to order. Good enough explanation?

"QX, we want to custom order for hourglasses. Two glass chambers, connected in the middle with a narrow passage, and can stand on two sides." I struggle with my words, "One of the chambers is filled with sand that is small enough to pass through the bottleneck. The time for all the sand to drop down from the top chamber to the lower one is one two-hundredth, or zero point zero zero five, of a day here on the new Earth. Do you understand what I mean? We need twenty-four of them, right now."

We would have an hour and a half left to finish the ritual — plenty for waiting delivery or following some backup plans.

"Custom order, expedited, two hundred dollars each, total of four thousand and eight hundred. You do not have enough balance in your account." QX says.

Why are hourglasses so expensive? It's just glass and sand! Something must be wrong!

"Four thousand..." Tim seems a bit worried, "Let us gather together to see how much we have in total."

After a short while, it seems that we are way short to cover the cost. Tim, Bran and Rhea mostly spent their cash on the railguns, and tea breaks as well. I spent most on the hose. The explorers on the outdoor gears and fishing rods; baking girls on baking ingredients, pretty expensive ones I assume; night club party guys on food and drinks and the amplifier; Nyx on the crystal ball; Muse and Jack on the moat; only William and Eos have some significant money left. Still not enough.

"Shoot!" I should have thought more carefully on a garden hose!

"The hose is well worth it, so does the moat. Don't feel upset." Tim says, "Bran, can you make any modifications?"

"QX, change the material of the glass chamber and sand to quartz, silicon dioxide." Bran says.

I see. Pure materials are cheaper.

"Same price." QX answers.

"OK. We can perform everything in public anyway." Tim says.

Thanks, Tim, maybe we need to follow the backup plan now, but I do remember there must be a better plan. Who told me yesterday? I look at Eos and Muse.

"Ask the cat to make custom announcements, twenty-four times." Eos says.

Ah this is it! Eos is Eos. I feel like I am about to grab her and kiss her twenty-four times.

Muse is still in deep thoughts — So, did you also have a memory loss?

"QX — I want to make custom announcements, total of twenty-four times, with a fixed period of time between each announcement, and each period equals one two-hundredth of a day here on the new Earth. The first announcement starts when everyone is back to their room. Do you understand?"

"Yes, I understand. What is your message?" QX says.

"Announce each number from 1 to 24 during each of the announcement. For the first announcement you just say 'one', the second you say 'two', and so on. Do you understand?"

"I get it. Two hundred and forty dollars. You do not have enough balance in your account." QX was silent for a while, but eventually answers.

"Charge mine." Says Eos.

xxxiv   Decisions

"OK, very good. Are we all paired up already?" Tim asks, and smiles at me with a paper full of names in his hand.

"Oh, no..." I just realize that I am one of the few people who haven't settled with a partner yet. Eos and Iris are left, so is William. But William has claimed a few times that he is going a religious path, but will do a sham marriage, or rather a matching in the aliens' system, for everyone's good.

So both Iris and Eos know this. For whoever I choose, the other one has to end up with a sham marriage with William. Eos once claims that she does not want sham marriage, but maybe she is OK now, based on her other words. Iris has not said anything, but is probably kind enough to do it.

The couples stand next to each other, and a few, Hera and Yan for example, whisper to each other, about their ranks I assume. Why do Selene and Dennis also whisper to each other, and Dennis seems to have a glance at me? So this means Selene didn't know Dennis' rank at the beach? So Miss 11 and Mr. 10, I would guess? No — I am too hasty to make the conclusion here. If Selene didn't know Dennis' rank, then my previous arguments wouldn't actually work — about the stupid question. So it is more likely they *pretended* to exchange their ranks, or whispered regarding something else. Chance is still fifty-fifty, roughly.

Very soon, only four of us are left. OK, it is not the time to worry about other people.

Vincent quickly approaches William, and whispers something. What? The system does not allow... Circe seems to be

OK with it, so it is probably not my business. It is not the time to worry about other people.

"Again I will be happy to form a sham marriage with either of the two ladies." William says, "We can negotiate to spend the cash evenly. I swear to my Lord."

So you need a sham marriage...for Vincent? No, no, no... what am I doing? They probably have some other unrelated business. It is not the time to worry about other people! What am I doing?

Both Eos and Iris look at me, knowing that I am still making a decision. How can I do that now! After the whole day of mess, my brain is literally not working!

Eos is 3, so with her, we can lock the 2 couple with fifty-fifty chance. Even better if Tim or Muse is 2, then we can shoot them down with ease, but if 2 is someone else, like Nyx or Bran or others, then it is hard to tell. I have to say, 2 has been hiding themselves very well. With Iris, there is not much extra information I can get, even for that fifty-fifty couple. I can only get a much better idea of all the top twelve guys, but not much else. In terms of possible gain, Eos is the one to choose.

Now on the possible loss. With Iris, the 2 couple may have a very good chance of shooting me at 1, especially if Tim or Bran or Muse is 2, almost the opposite case as before. But the problem with Eos, is that a lot of people have already known her rank. So I need to target a possible loss of...five times twenty thousand? Eos loses badly this round.

Wait, both of them know my rank number. If I choose one, the other girl may put my name and my rank in the guessing game and win twenty thousand from me. This is not too bad. Oh, William will for sure know this as well. So it is forty. Will you do that William? Aren't you following a spiritual path and so does not care about these secular matters?

Eos probably wouldn't care too much if she is the other girl; but with Iris, I have to worry about the non-zero possibility that all the baking girls, five or six of them, will know my rank.

Oh, shoot, their loyal and beloved husbands as well. However, since I helped to solve the problem, or because of my personal relationship with others, a number of them won't put me in the guessing game. For example, Jack, Muse, probably Hera, as well as Tim, Bran, even Dennis and Vincent. Still there may be up to ten trying to shoot me to get some free money, which means a maximum of two hundred thousand loss, which is still acceptable, despite it being huge compared to small possible gains from Eos.

Well, so it is probably not the time to think about money here. Iris is a good companion, and is pretty too, and will be heart-breaking if I choose Eos instead. However, to be honest, as Eos suggested, our friendship back in high school will evaporate in five years, and so I need to consider everything I have done since Day one, rather than relying on older memories.

"Just pick the one by your true heart." Selene suggests, "Your true love."

I know, everyone is waiting for me, but please allow me some extra time! Sorry I have no idea about "true love"! I have sweat on my brow, the third time of the day.

OK. Let us rewind ourselves back to Day one and recall what has happened regarding Eos or Iris.

Day one, I was in the same discussion group with Eos. Well, I somehow know the reason. The bridge club members naturally grouped together, and Eos probably was lazy and wanted four of us to figure things out, so she decided to join us. Tim and Bran then had to split up, as Tim wanted to know what we were discussing.

Day two, I was maybe dizzy or somewhat emotional regarding our situation, and I went to talk to Eos again during the tea break. She rejected me again. Wait, I roughly remember she said something, like she hadn't rejected me, not even once, before her long speech at the beach. But I was too shocked and wasn't paying too much attention on that part. As she said then, why are we so concerned about marriage or matching, after knowing everything is an immortality hell? Anyway, I guess what she meant was that, the miserable event happened before the graduation ceremony was already gone, and literally has not yet happened. So we are down to only once, when she rejected me on Day two. But why didn't that count? What exactly did she say then? I don't quite remember. I wish I had a voice recorder at that time.

Day three, still not much interaction with Iris. I failed to receive a message, but succeeded in sending one. Eos and I had a conversation and as a result, both of us knew each other's rank number, to some degree of certainty.

Day four, I kissed Iris in the morning for her love, and saw an eclipse with Eos in the afternoon, then she kissed me, which caused some serious problems. Iris came to inquire, and ran away. But nothing was comparable to the two moons we saw at night. I couldn't even imagine Jack was still making a stupid joke with me! Seriously, Jack? At that emotional moment?

All right, Jack, you can go away now. Not your business this time. Day five, we went out to picnic, and Eos had this long conversation with me regarding immortality, which I partly agree. Then the eagles came and I didn't get chance to talk to Iris, so during the barbecue I had to finish my job, and we had a dance. We also shared each other's rank number, which was some kind of promise I would assume. I also briefly told Iris about what happened between Eos and me. Then suddenly Eos showed up regarding "our secret", which was indeed naughty.

Oh, I hope I had received some oracle from the lavender this morning. All right, I didn't even ask.

Wait, I remember the last advice at the beach. I had to tell the truth to the girls, and now regarding what I had said, it seems that I had not told the truth to one of the girls. Sorry I was not lying at that moment, as I myself didn't realize the issue. But right now I think I was probably not telling the truth. OK, that is it, end of the story, *Q.E.D.*

I make up my mind, approach her, and grab her hand. My

heart is not strong enough to look at the other girl.

"OK, everyone, let's not waste time. When you hear the announcement for 'twenty-four', come downstairs for the final process." Tim announces.

Oh, right, 24 will have been matched already by then.

—◦◦◦◦◦—

Right before I enter my room, Jack murmurs to me, "I have a feeling that the cat will not do exactly what you requested. But don't worry, as long as it makes twenty-four announcements in fixed time intervals, things still work out."

"What do you mean?" I feel buzzed.

"I said, *don't worry*." He smiles.

Well, I don't have time to worry about it. Running towards the interface, I quickly cast a secret magic spell with it, and then the first announcement arrives.

"Custom Announcement: Announce each number from 1 to 24 during each of the announcement. For the first announcement you just say 'one', the second you say 'two', and so on. Do you understand?"

I do not understand! I don't believe this! Such a stupid cat! Haven't you passed the Turing Test or something? I believe people are laughing like crazy.

As Jack said, it won't be the end of the world. For example, Tim ordered writing pads for everyone on Day one, so people can keep track of how many times the cat has made the announcement, which might be a bit tedious, or by whatever method our ancestors have used to remember numbers. It is like back to stone age, but won't be the end of the world. Everyone believes that others can perform similar calculations, so there is no reason to stop the ritual. I rush through these arguments with my very much overloaded brain.

Oh, yes, it is my period.

I slowly open my door and close it lightly, and then sneak downstairs to the ground floor.

"This feels like a real marriage ceremony." I smile, taking the little thing timely delivered by a cute robot — a perfect combination: *Element Six, in its purest, most rigid, most transparent form, set into Element Seventy-Eight, shaped in a small loop that fits her fourth finger*, a magic spell that is used to wed your bride five thousand light years away. Ten dollars here, expedited order, totally worth it.

Why are hourglasses so expensive?

"This *is* a real marriage ceremony." She says, "Can I now ask why you chose me?"

"It follows naturally from what we have done, as a logical consequence."

We quickly kiss each other, not wasting too much time.

"I need your help, tonight." I say, "Could you come down to the ground floor after everyone is back in their rooms? Or we can just stay after dinner until everyone leaves."

"Cannot wait for tomorrow?" She laughs.

"No. It is real business." I sound very serious, "Need to prepare something super important for tomorrow."

Yes, I made another big mistake, in addition to the hourglasses. I thought my memory would be better when we get closer to the event, but in fact every event back on the old Earth stays the same distance away from us, the same distance in time. My memory won't be better tonight, so I need her help for some of the details.

We take the paper and the pen and cross out our names. Oh, poor Tim does not have his pen in his room, and has to rely on his memory alone or some other methods.

"Do you want to come down again? I prefer to stay in my room." She says.

"OK. I plan to take a look. Just for fun."

"I thought you would say so." She laughs again.

"Yan?" I notice something strange.

"Girls all noticed this on Day one. It also starts with a 'Y', so does not break the rule. It is common to address a Chinese by only the second character of their first name, so totally fine to call him Yan."

Rule? What rule? ... Ah-ha... Names... I see, Tim has already noticed this.

"I can now tell the aliens are true perfectionists. So the cat's name is not its real name."

"Everyone noticed this on Day one," She laughs for the third time, "when you were day-dreaming in the lounge."

"What?"

She continues, "I think this was the main reason why most people believed it's just a show, back on Day one."

And why most people looked so calm for the first few days; And why the girls spent time baking; And why the explorers or the extended explorers didn't worry about wild beasts on an alien planet; And why Tim and Bran and other top rank people didn't want to join the explorers; And why Tim listed the top ten guys with such great accuracy; And why I got rank 1 — because I was...I am an idiot.

⟞•o✧⟝∞o⟞•⟝

After I return to my room, I start keeping track the stupid cat replaying my voice.

......

The cat makes another announcement. Same message as before.

Wait. I am waiting for the third announcement, but why do I have five bars already on my notes? And these extra scripts I plan to work on for tonight, the graduation reception? No one can enter my room, right? I did by myself? But I cannot remember. Memory loss again? I feel I don't trust this world anymore. I don't have another choice but put down another bar.

I double check my schedule on Monday. I was reading my novel at home at *this moment*. Nothing very special. Oh, damn, the eclipse again. That is why I don't want to look at these notes.

......

Last time it was the tenth. Who has written these three extra bars over my notes? At this crucial moment? Now I feel very certain about my memory loss problem in this new world. I feel lucky to have such a repetitive scenario to test it out, otherwise without watches I would have no idea what is going on.

Then the cat makes another custom announcement.

I have to try it out. Too bad. I press the button on the touchscreen to call out the cat.

"QX, among the twenty-four custom announcements I requested earlier today, how many have you made, and how many are left?"

"Fourteen made, and ten left." QX answers.

OK, at least it agrees with my notes, so for me, I don't have to keep track in the first place. How stupid! Assuming I am the only one who can keep track of the number of announcements made by the cat, I should have left my own pen there. Poor Tim.

"QX, can you send my pen to Tim?"

"No. You can only order to deliver to you or to your own room."

OK, I see. I remember Bran once said we are unable to send secret love letters. It follows the same rule.

Oh, we can also ask the cat about the time left until sunset as I did earlier, and do some calculations by ourselves, but you need to be clever enough to ask for the time during the first few announcements, and after each announcement you ask again to verify. You still cannot sleep through, as missing the bus stop will likely make your spouse very unhappy. So it is probably not worth the time and effort.

Then, I, or rather Eos, probably didn't have to spend that two hundred forty to do these announcements? Since everyone can ask the cat regarding the time till the sunset, and we lay out plans for everyone to do the calculations by themselves? Well, it requires too many inquiries to the cat. People basically worry about missing the bus stop and keep asking questions. Tedious and time-consuming, like some of these math problems. Still it is too easy to miss the bus stop, especially if someone else has similar memory loss problem, and it is hard for everyone to coordinate, and people do make mistakes in these types of calculations in a long run, which may make things a mess if three people show up in the ritual. So letting the cat make announcements is still the best thing to do.

Now I see, we are so lucky that we didn't follow Muse's original plan at the beach, which also uses twenty-four announcements, but I should have ordered an hourglass last night for myself, and make custom announcements with the cat twenty-four times according to the hourglass. Assuming people all have this strange memory loss problem, that plan would be terrible to carry out in practice. Oh, Muse was probably worried about this issue earlier in the lobby. Definitely not my Lucky item. Well, I guess I don't even have one today.

After the twenty-fourth announcement, we gather at the lobby again.

"I think I don't want to hear your voice again, at least for tonight." Muse laughs.

So, it seems you don't have any memory loss today, but you had the same or even worse memory loss with me at the beach. Something *will* happen there on the Earth, but what *was* it?

"I think the cat fails the Turing Test by that." Bran says.

I agree. All hail Turing!

"Anyway, let us finish the ritual now." Tim says.

Bran, Nyx, Muse, Jack and I raise our hands. She does not. While everyone looks at her, she smiles, "I guess, it does not matter, right?"

"So as planned, if you are one of the last two couples, then you can use Bran, Nyx, Muse and Jack, or me in your list. As a final patch, if you are the third last couple, then you can also use five of us, or the uncrossed names on the paper as in the original plan. Thanks everyone."

So the last two couples won't be sure who may put them into their list. The third last couple don't even have to change anything. It's like patching a computer program, avoiding extreme scenarios.

"OK. And we shall all thank you very much for laying out this wonderful plan. Very impressive." Tim says.

Other people finally realize that I was the one who mainly designed most of the plan. People give me an applause. It feels good, but also a bit embarrassed. Most work had been done in the discussion with others. We excluded a lot of other plans to reach this one, and Nyx's example helped a lot as well.

"I have a last comment on the games before we go back to the rooms and make final adjustments as needed." I say, "As we discussed earlier, we believe this game is designed on purpose, asking us to follow their desired way, in this new colony on a new planet."

"What is it?" Tim asks.

"The moral is: We trust our own family members without reservation; We also trust other people in a society, and such trust is based on some well-designed rules that guarantee we trust each other."

xxxv   Miracles

The cat announces the sunset and the dinner time, as well as the deadline of the marriage game. I change to my school uniform and go downstairs. Most of the boys are already there, all in school uniforms. It is more or less a wedding ceremony dinner, so everyone is wearing their best possible clothing available. Sorry, suits are too expensive at this moment, and most of us do not have much money left. In this case, boys don't like to stand out among a group, so school uniform is the best option among all of us. I only guessed that William may wear something different, like a cleric, in case some couples may be interested, but I was wrong. So, Your sham marriage is becoming real, William? Hmmmmm?

"Guess what, Vincent and Circe invited William to their ritual, as a priest that guided or witnessed their vows and blessed them, like in a real wedding." Yan says.

Oh, that was why...

And you probably don't understand much about the long story of Catholics versus Protestants, Yan. Just like I don't understand why different groups of professors scuffled with each other in an academic conference.

Well, I guess I understand somewhat — It is Water, not Fire!

"How did you know?" Leo asks.

"Only two of them are down the hallway from my room, and I felt multiple people dashing back to their rooms when I was waiting for my turn by the door."

Ah, good point.

Wait. Are you one hundred percent sure Circe appeared in the ritual as well?

"Ha ha, I didn't notice anything, maybe because I was on the bed — and now I know who came back when I was waiting. By the way, what is this on your collar?" Leo asks.

Hmmmmm, so Dennis may shoot me in the game, if he had been standing next to the door when I passed. Oh, never mind, it could be Jack as well, and I tiptoed like a cat.

"An ornament. This symbol is a pair of wine goblets." Yan says, "I believe, in this new world, there is no imperial system or hierarchy system, and everyone is equal, so I decide to wear one ornament according to Chinese traditions."

OK, and you haven't passed that GRE-like exam. I bet you can pay to the cat, or to those E.T.'s, to give you an exam and grade it for you, just like...on the Earth, and then add two more of these little things.

"What other symbols or ornaments are there in your system?" Zak asks, "I may want one as well."

"The Sun, the Moon, the Stars, these three are reserved for the imperial family, and stand for 'shine over the people'. We need to change the design to respect both moons. Then there are the Mountain, the Dragon, the Pheasant or you may call the Phoenix,..." He starts enumerating from the list.

Interesting, you also have the Sun, the Moon and the Stars. The creativity of people around the world was quite limited during old times.

"Oh I want to get the Sun, and give Artemis the Moon." Says Zak, "So I am bigger, ha ha ha."

Do you know something called *total solar eclipse*?

"The Stars...it actually fits Nyx pretty well." Bran says.

You don't know your wife probably has had a few already, on the witch hat? Hera also likes stars as I know.

"Here —" It's Frank, "I ordered an hourglass."

There is a little cute one in his hand.

"What? You spent two hundred bucks on it?" Leo asks.

"No." He turns to me and smiles, like winning a big battle, "The reason, why your design is so expensive, is that, unlike lengths or weights of objects, in such a mechanism it is extremely difficult to ensure the measured time is accurate to their default precision. I ordered this one within plus minus five seconds, and it is super cheap. Two dollars."

Oh my god! How stupid!

"Plus minus five seconds could cause four minutes of difference at the end of the ritual, and you also take into account that we humans are inaccurate. So the announcements are still the best way to do it." Bran says, "But now I see, two hundred bucks is actually not expensive at all."

"Your boys are childish, right? Wearing school uniforms to your wedding?" Selene is wearing a glorious sun-color dress with dark brown embroideries. Muse is following, in a white and yellow sleeveless with lace trims, and Artemis in watermelon red with a green collar.

"I plan to wear this to my coronation!" Zak replies.

Meanwhile, the remaining girls one by one come downstairs, and the boys are cheering and clapping and whistling, like in a runway show. The girls, however, all wear some different kinds of dresses, formal dresses to be precise. Wait, you didn't have money for the hourglasses right? Maybe all of you prepared these fancy dresses soon after you fully believed everything is real and the dinner tonight would be your wedding dinner, right? I now start to understand why baking books, tools and ingredients are so expensive.

And everyone is wearing a little cheap thing on a finger.
Everyone.

So, your sham marriage is seriously becoming real, William? Hmmmmm?

And, can you guys be more creative? They are aliens, right?

<hr>

For dinner tonight, we sit differently. Tim is on his usual seat, and Rhea is on the other end of the table. Couples sit opposite to each other across the table, but we alternate boys and girls along each side.

I am still sitting on my usual seat, right hand side of the King. She is sitting across the table. By my right hand side, Jack is replaced with Muse, and Jack is sitting across the table, the third couple is Dennis and Selene, then Bran and Nyx, etc. Interesting hand, I think.

"Nyx, what is that white belt on your hat?" Selene asks.

Oh I didn't notice the lavender is wearing the *hat* today with the magician's robe — our CFT was the last one downstairs, right after my bride, so I wasn't paying any attention. Were they following some special order?

Anyway, apparently these hats have stars, and strips or bars to indicate different levels, just like in military. I agree this is a formal situation, but I can't see it clearly from my seat. Our CFT probably does not have too much money left after the eight-hundred-dollar crystal ball.

"The galaxy." Nyx answers.

Oh my — I think I am getting used to these kinds of facts, but this is still beyond my wildest dreams. So "I make the decision" is totally true. I can even imagine how their magic society became chaotic when they figured out their real leader was missing.

"Did you guys see that making twenty-four identical announcements is in fact the very correct way to do it?" Muse asks, and laughs at me again, "Now I don't feel too bad hearing your voice again."

"What?" I feel puzzled. I have no clue at all. Why do people throw these mind bombs towards me today?

"I noticed that as well. Think about it:" Says Jack, "If you can ask, or program, the cat to make an announcement to speak a number in its own voice, as in your original plan, then anyone can do it. So for example, if in the middle of the ritual, someone spends ten dollars to make a similar custom announcement, then it will mess up with the whole process. People won't be able to tell which ones are the ones you requested. Of course, I trust everyone here. I mean, we won't do it, but it is not guaranteed in the system. With the twenty-four identical announcements, it is hard even for you to mess things up by yourself."

Oh, interesting point. You two probably got too bored with my voice and so tried to convince yourselves that it was in fact necessary to listen to my boring voice twenty-four times?

"In the future, when we organize events with hundreds of people, this must be taken into consideration." Tim says, "Similarly, in your plan, there is still a slight chance that people may lie. I actually came down a second time, during R...Rhea's turn, and more people had crossed out their names by then. So I picked two of the remaining girls."

Don't worry, Tim. Everyone believes you have higher rank

than Rhea. We won't shoot you. And, it is more likely millions or billions instead of hundreds.

"I see the point now. Then regardless of whether these girls put you in their list or not, you can always be matched with Rhea in the end." I say, "Good point. I didn't realize that."

"Well, we saw Tim's pen there, and so were about to make another announcement asking everyone to bring their own pen, then later I saw how another announcement may cause problems." Muse says, "But Tim had crossed out his name already, so we finally decided to not say anything. Oops, my bad, Tim!"

"Never mind. Not enough information is revealed to shoot me." Tim says, "Oh, no — never mind."

He seems to immediately regret what he just said.

"Don't worry, we still don't know your rank." Jack laughs.

Oh sorry, Tim. I, or maybe the lady in front of me, should make that announcement, but I restrain myself from revealing more information as well. So Tim is likely 2, 4 or 5, and Rhea is 13+. One third chance, but not as good as that fifty-fifty couple. In fact, no, he is probably not 2, otherwise he wouldn't be so certain "not enough information is revealed". I see it now, since it is very possible that I know Muse or Jack is 4 and I then figure out he is 2. So this is another fifty-fifty chance to shoot.

Oh, in fact 4 is even more likely, as Muse is top five or close, most possibly 6 from Eos' remarks last night, though this part is still uncertain. If Muse is 6, then Tim can be 4 or 5; if Muse is 5, then Tim must be 4. Assuming it is fifty-fifty for Muse, then it gives a two thirds or three-quarters chance for shooting Tim at 4? I cannot tell the exact probability, but I believe the purple rose or the water lily can tell me immediately. With the probability of Muse at 6 increases, Tim at 4 will decrease. Regardless, it is good enough for gambling in a casino, or playing bridge.

Purple rose — This argument actually depends on that everyone knows Eos is 3, and everyone knows everyone knows Eos is 3. Ah, I see, this is the significance of "common knowledge". Interesting.

Oh, no, I forget the small possibility that Muse is 7 and Tim could be 4, 5 or 6. Then Jack is 8 or 9, not even close to top five, but with 7 and 8 it could just be a coincidence that Muse got slightly higher rank and she wouldn't be so certain about 1 holding some important information. These kinds of arguments can go on forever.

And Jack is 7, 8, or 9... Shit! This is exactly what he told me! I have made literally no progress!

To sum up, Tim at 4 is still the best option so far, though I doubt whether the water lily or the purple rose can tell me the exact probability anymore. However, Tim is a nice guy and I don't want to shoot him for fun. Well, I don't think I need to feel guilty about it, other people like Tim and Eos and Jack are doing something similar, trying to guess at others' ranks, like mine, based on various reasonings, using whatever weapons they have in hand. It is the fun part of the game, right? Much more fun compared to the marriage game.

And I believe people do this for fun mostly, as one or two shots from others won't change too much in the final result. Funny thing is that, right now even if you stand on the table and shout out your rank number, not many people will believe and shoot you in the game. People will more likely believe that you are trying to trick them. It is ironically very hard to persuade more than five people to shoot you by now.

The game designers might have foreseen this and so put the guessing game deadline a bit later than the matching game. Very naughty, indeed. They just want some fun from us.

"I actually have another question. Why didn't you ask four people to reveal themselves before the ritual, I mean, before the name-crossing sessions. This could potentially save maybe five minutes? So people don't need to come down again for the final process." Jack asks.

I come back from my deep sneaky thoughts, "Oh, sorry, say that again?"

"To reveal two or three couples before the announcements,

to save time." Muse does a good summary.

"Errr, let me see — I had a feeling that it would be better to finish the name-crossing sessions first. If anything went wrong, then people would not reveal much information regarding their ranks. It is the same philosophy that in our old plan, people like 1, 2, 3 do not want to reveal their ranks first. You are right, I haven't thought about it carefully." I say.

Maybe I was just unwilling to make my decision that early. I shall go back to that fifty-fifty couple to see if I can get some extra information.

"I know your rank now." Muse whispers to me and giggles, "You think for too long about it. Don't worry, we won't shoot you."

What! I glance over Muse and Jack, and they both have this happy smile as winners.

"We came downstairs for a second time." Jack explains, "The paper had been moved, not your style."

Yeah, we've played bridge together — also for too long. Even that little piece of paper is your weapon now. Wait, that funny story of the pen and Tim and "oops, my bad" was designed to trap me, in the Labyrinth of Logic? Holy shit.

"Jack, I think he already confessed he didn't come down again." Tim laughs.

What? What? I did? I myself don't even know whether I came down the second time!

"Good point, Tim. You are right." Jack replies.

"In fact, a few of your unnatural questions back on Day two had told us the correct answer already. We just designed some trick to verify it." Muse whispers to me again.

I am such a stupid who revealed myself even before Eos did.

━━━━━━━━━━◦〇⟨⟨⟩⟩◦━━━━━━━━━━

"All right, everyone, I have something to say." This time, it is William.

I wake up from my slow digestion of the water lily's over-whelming words. To summarize, Jack is 8 and you are the ultimate girl. Clever, I have to admit. 5 and 7, you two can figure out my rank very quickly; 7 and 9, you cannot make a definite conclusion; just for this middle, very subtle pair, 6 and 8, you need to use the fact that I thought for too long about it. I want to applaud for your wisdom. That sundial is even more useful to you. Your shooting on Tim is one-in-four, only twenty-five percent chance, so you instead target on me? Bad news is, for me, shooting Tim is down to fifty-fifty again.

Tim, you must feel lucky that you are not 7, who is their first and easiest target. Similar to Eos, Muse may finally decide to pair up with Jack just because it is not so important now and more interestingly they can have an easy target, according to my plan.

Unfortunately 7 had been matched up so the content of the paper remained the same, but the stupid probably didn't think carefully about it and grabbed the paper, which gave them some extra information to shoot me. Meanwhile, I was lying on my bed with my writing pad counting the enumerations and think-ing about my plans for tonight, and suddenly that piece of pa-per changed to a silver bullet and flew all the way by itself to the fourth floor and hit me right there! You are number 7! Could you please be more professional? Like the guy with double O's in front of you?

And Eos, your rank is truly becoming common knowledge.

Finally, thanks Jack, for letting me know about the paper. You are doing a favor for me. I know that. You are so nice. You two win this round, undeniably and beautifully.

Wait. Another announcement? This is quite uncommon for William, so everyone stops talking, and listens to him. So, your sham marriage is truly becoming real, William? Hmmmmm?

Or, it is about Vincent? Hmmmmmmmmmmmmmm.

"Tomorrow we shall have a rest." He says after the crowd quiets down.

Most people relax and agree, as we have solved the marriage problem, and matched twelve couples to get the extra reward. Tonight is more or less like a wedding dinner plus a mental battle field of shooting each other with various weapons in hand, then starting from next morning, we won't have much else to do.

"May I ask why?" I ask. Muse, Eos and I are probably the only ones who believe that tomorrow is going to be a harder day.

"Because it is the seventh day." He says, like in a prayer, "God says so: *'He rested on the seventh day from all His work which He had done'.*"

"Say that again?" I am stunned again. I cannot even remember how many times I have had the same feeling since the creation of light on Day one, or even you only count this short period of time since the start of our wedding dinner. The past few days of my life feels like a marching through my least favorite Jungle of Curiosity but it is full of mind-blowing mines, and you do not know when or how you will step on something that can totally blow you away, all the way to the moon, the moons.

Some people may think it is just a joke that William seldom tells, but a number of us also have similar reactions as mine, looking at each other and unable to believe what we have experienced in the past few days.

"Can we borrow your Bible?" Dennis asks.

"Sure." William takes out his Bible and hands over to us. People such as Muse and Hera who are familiar with it have already started reciting the text, with only some minor variations.

A few of us gather and turn to the very first page, and read it through without breathing.

"It can't be. We decided to go to the forest and picked the fruits by the weather. We decided to go to the beach and catch some fish by, ourselves." Bran says.

"God ultimately guides us through all these days." Says William, "God knows everything. He is everywhere, even here on this new planet. *'The mind of a person plans his way, but the Lord directs his steps'*."

"There has been many debates about whether the word 'day' in the seven days of creation refers to the real twenty-four-hour day, or it is a word for some other time scheme like a day corresponds to a period or an age, which can even go back to the big bang; And there also has been some arguments over why the plants were created before the sun, or even the concept of day-night cycles was created before the sun. Now it seems that everything is clear. Truth is, a day is twenty or nineteen point whatever hours — This is a journal, our journal, after countless generations of misreadings and misinterpretations." Jack says.

Negative.

"The *evening*...the *morning*..." Muse is in a trembling voice, "When, did you realize this, William?"

"On Day four we saw the sun and the moons and the stars for the first time, I felt somewhat enlightened. Then on the fifth day, you brought back fish, and were attacked by eagles." He says, "At that time, I was very certain some land animals *will* show up on Day six, but they were still beyond my imagination."

"Moon-*s*? It is singular here, *lesser light*, not *lesser lights*." Selene asks.

"People likely changed plural to singular to make things fit." I say, "Or they changed interpretations, for example, the moons were the two *lights*, and the sun had been there since the start to separate day and night."

"Possible." Jack says.

"So this planet is Eden, and we are Adam and Eve?" Circe says.

"Adams and Eves." Says Jack, "But I still don't understand why there are twelve Adams and twelve Eves."

Jack looks at me. I shake my head. Still no clue, sorry.

"There are twelve tribes of Israel in the Old Testament as well. Our offsprings will form twelve tribes." Oliver says.

"That is probably a coincidence. They were from Jacob's twelve sons, or princes." Vincent says, "Are there other mentioning of the number twelve or twenty-four in the Bible?"

"Of course. Twelve Apostles, but they are probably irrelevant to us." Hera says, "Nothing I can recall which is very relevant."

"By the marriage ritual, we finally become humans, on the sixth day, or rather we were created, as social animals, directed by the aliens, following their own images." Dennis says.

"No, I don't believe the aliens are God." William says.

Eos and I don't believe either.

"We also have the forbidden fruit, seven...corners, and so the serpent in the Bible is..." Muse says.

The cat.

Everyone looks at me.

"I don't feel anything strange happening to me, to be honest." I say.

"But you came up with this brilliant plan afterwards, right?" Tim says with laugh. "Now I want to eat some as well."

It is not relevant! Why do people come up with these strange connections between unrelated things!

"No, I still don't believe this. Everything is just an accident, a coincidence. In order to take our journal to our old Earth back before the Old Testament was written, at least nine thousand years ago from now, the aliens need a real time machine that can travel back in time. This is much harder than space travel, and probably against a lot of known physical laws." Bran says after a long thought.

Bloody hell, I actually know how to do that without fancy time machines.

The dinner has not been as fun and energetic as before. Some quickly finish their plates and say good night, leaving with their own interpretations of the sacred script.

Jack has also retired early for the night. He said he didn't feel like the artificial light today compared to the fire last night, but obviously it's a joke, not the real reason.

Well, I do understand. When the creation of light becomes as simple as turning it on, everything looks weird, philosophically. The world around us suddenly feels different. But maybe, turning on the light is not as simple as we feel it. At least you need to understand quite a bit of electricity and know how to make light bulbs — We didn't have such technology until late nineteenth century.

"Tim, I may need to borrow your railgun." I ask Tim before the end of the dinner.

"Take it. It is yours. Don't use it to shoot rabbits, or humans."

"I promise, and thanks. In return, you want some wine? My treat. Still have some cash left."

"Why not? Thanks. You want to shoot me in the game?"

"How do you...Why?"

"I saw you were in deep thoughts after the conversations with Muse — that was before William's words. I guess you may have some other sources of information that help you to determine my rank. I shouldn't have said that. Or you try to use wine as weapon and get some extra words out of my mouth?" Tim lowers his voice and laughs, "The most expensive glass of wine in the history of mankind."

Yeah, everyone knows Eos' rank.

"No, I am not going to shoot you, my friend." Honestly I feel a bit embarrassed.

"Me either." Tim replies instantly. I somehow know it already, if I lose twenty thousand, then Tim is likely the one who shoots me in the game, and so he is unlikely to do it in real practice. Exchanging ranks with each other somehow works as a mutual agreement that we do not shoot each other, at least when no one else knows this. Eos with me, Iris with me, Tim with me, and even Muse with me, same idea. I don't even need to exchange with Jack. We don't shoot each other anyway.

Well, the interesting thing is that, now I am almost certain Tim is 4. If he is 5, then he wouldn't worry about it too much.

OK, then, the real hard part of the game is to figure out someone's rank through various small hints and logic deductions, without them noticing that you are doing it, like committing a perfect crime.

"It reminds me: Whose brain was so spoiled to suggest shooting the railgun here in the hotel?" I lower my voice.

"Jack's was." Tim answers. "Bran's design shoots a ray of hot plasma instead of a solid metal bullet, and...it is too powerful. The cat helped a lot in the design to make things work, as I can understand by now. So they charged much more than the materials used. It's like your hourglass — design fee."

I don't remember seeing a ray or anything like that! So it is a plasma gun, with rails! A plasma railgun!

What is that crystal ball, then?

"We never said it is *exactly* a regular railgun. It uses rails, and 'railgun' sounds cool. Now everyone except Bran and me are calling them railguns." He looks through my thoughts, and then whispers to me with his classical smile, "By the way, I guess you were trying to say sorry about the pen, but didn't want to reveal your rank."

"Oh, yes, sorry I should do it."

"I want to say, don't feel bad about it — I just spent a dollar to get another pen."

xxxvi   Receptions

I come downstairs, nobody is there. I quickly make some preparation for tomorrow. To be honest, the lobby ceiling is a bit too high. I had to speak loudly this afternoon for everyone to hear me clearly. Need a different plan for tomorrow, or I will run out of energy, and I need a good sleep tonight as well, which is not easy according to my notes.

She shows up. She has changed into a pure white shirt with lace collar, similar to the one the water lily is wearing every day. I guess she probably has noticed some of my wicked habits. A bit embarrassed indeed. And she still has money left in her account?

"Your shirt looks pretty good. Fits you very well." I say.

"Thanks. What is the business?" She asks.

"Well, let us focus on the graduation reception. You know, this was a kind of event that people forget after a few weeks. Luckily it was still only a week ago." I say, "So I would like to recall everything with you, in particular all the relatives or friends who came to the reception. I think you have a better memory, especially with the girls."

"Graduation Reception? Oh, is this about that — 'our secret'?" She asks.

"Yes. Let us start with the girls. Who came with Rhea?"

"Errr...Both parents I assume."

"OK, agree. Gaia?"

"Gaia? Father and grandma."

"OK, I don't remember. Next, Selene?"

"Father...Only father."

"Father? Not uncle, or even older brother? I thought he is an uncle, too young, and so handsome."

"Agree, but I think he is father. Selene was crying and hugging with him. He was chatting with Dennis' father, like they know each other very well."

"Explains a lot of things. Circe?"

"Grandma and grandpa, and two younger brothers."

"I can never remember that. Nyx?"

"That one is tricky. Looks like Nyx's mentor or a senior member, in a secret religious or magic society like a cult, wearing some strange magician's robe and a witch hat."

"...No, not mentor." The lavender is probably not a usual person as you might think.

......

"Finally, Artemis?"

"Artemis was late for the reception, came with Zak. I don't recall they had friends or relatives coming. So they are basically each other's friend, or even a relative by now?" She chuckles.

"OK, good. Agrees with my memory. Does not sound perfect, but I guess this is also some kind of proof. Now, boys. Dennis — Oh his dad came, and mom too. William?" I ask.

"I have no idea." She says.

"His parents and grandpa I believe. And Tim? This is super easy."

"Everyone from his family really. It is like a big big family. Grandparents, parents, six, or seven uncles and aunts, countless brothers and sisters and cousins, plus three dogs and a pet parrot." She says.

"Yeah, the parrot was funny. You know what, Tim told us that the parrot is the oldest member of his family."

That was the best part of the reception. Everyone tried to talk with the parrot, and occasionally it said something that sounded like a good response, which made everyone laugh. The best memories...are the very first to flee, right now, even from the happy immortals.

"Really? How old?"

"I didn't ask, but Tim also said that it originally belonged to his other grandpa, who passed away very early when his mom was only a kid, so only three grandparents were there in the reception, and the parrot has hence become a token or a symbol of his grandpa within the family." I say, "And Yan? I don't remember seeing his parents or relatives."

No, no, no, I don't think there is any dark magic that can turn grandpas to parrots, or dogs. No, that is impossible. What am I thinking? Just a coincidence.

"Both parents came. Took a flight from China I would assume. They were VIPs, so were not among us. I got to see them in close distance while receiving the scholarship. I don't like his mother though; the gaze was uncomfortable. By the way, they were wearing some formal dressing gowns, with some strange ornaments."

"Ornaments? How many? If you can still remember?"

"I didn't count. Not enough time and I wasn't paying too much attention. Errr...more than ten, or close."

"Fine — " It feels like if you have stepped over many big mines, then a relatively smaller one, even a medium sized one, won't do much to you now. You just step on it, it blows, and that is it. Your brain has been trained to go with it. It is almost nothing compared to the aliens or the moons or the biggest secret, though I still don't understand why they sent their prince overseas here. Is the Chinese education system so corrupted? "And Jack? Oh, I know, his mom and grandma, and his older sister. I've only seen his dad two or three times. Very busy man, flying all around the world most of the time, but very friendly, even played bridge with us." I continue, "Bran?"

Two or three times...depending on how you count it, to be honest.

"His father, who can speak ancient Greek fluently."

"How did you know that?"

"We heard him talking over the phone."

"Ancient Greek? You know ancient Greek? I know a few girls took Latin, but never thought someone would learn ancient Greek in high school."

"I know there are a few prestigious high schools around the country that do offer ancient Greek. Not ours, unfortunately. Circe and Selene took Latin. They asked Nyx about it, and Nyx said it sounded like ancient Greek with a Roman accent. Their magic society has very high prerequisites — such as ancient Greek and number theory."

Sounds like what ancient Greeks would do — speaking ancient Greek with a Greek accent and calculating eclipses. So the lavender also knows quite a lot of mathematics, and I start to believe our high school is the most prestigious one in the whole country.

"I am impressed. Anyway, Vincent?"

"Both parents as well, together with his sister."

No, not sister, but I would rather keep this as a deep secret. Sorry. It is an irrelevant person by now. I see, he was injured by love.

"Leo?"

"No idea."

"Hmmm... Dad and grandma. And, Oliver?"

"Parents and both grandmas."

I know, grandmas usually live longer than grandpas. Scientists say it is due to Y chromosome deficiency. One of my own grandpas passed away when I was eleven, and I didn't even have a chance to see the other one, who divorced with grandma and had only shown his existence by monthly checks ever since, generous ones though, until one day my mom alone attended his funeral, carrying me in the belly.

"Last but not least, Frank."

"An old man, maybe his grandpa. Not very talkative either."

"OK, very good. Thank you very much, my lady. Not perfect, but good enough. I hope this can work out tomorrow."

The boys' side has only a few oddities. The girls' side looks quite normal individually, even Nyx's story isn't too crazy, but something does not smell all right, my life experience.

Suddenly a glim of red light shines through the glass panels. We turn to that direction, wondering what it is.

"It is the moon, the red one." She says.

We go outside to the courtyard. It is close to midnight. The two moons are now much farther away compared to two days ago. The white one is much closer to the horizon and mostly hidden behind the building. The red moon, which has phased into a full red moon, is still high above in the dark night sky, overshadowing the nearby stars. So the courtyard is mostly shone by the red one.

"Beautiful."

"As you are. So the red moon is rotating around our planet faster than the white one, which means it is closer to us?" I ask.

"I guess so." Her white shirt has a red or pink hue, which shines like the sun in my eyes. It is nevertheless from the sun-light I assume.

"I know, you want to kiss me." She says in totally red face.

I can never restrain myself now. Too much pressure and too many brain overloads today, mostly from the water lily I assume, and I want to distract myself from thinking about the reception, which is coming very close. I embrace her from her back, and feel her body with my own. I kiss her at her temple, her ear, her cheek, her lips and her mouth and tongue. She starts with some hesitation, but soon turns around and holds me with her arms as well. We are now together.

My hands move around — her thigh, her hips, her waist, her torso, her breast, her neck, her shoulder and her upper arms. Her soft skin feels like a soft smooth dough but is more elastic. My hands go around these areas again and again in cycles, trying to grasp every inch of her shaky body.

"I want you tonight." I say, "Don't know what may happen tomorrow."

Her cheek looks like a fully ripe fuji under the moon, and probably tastes the same, the sweetness and crispness.

"I can feel you. Is this also about that — 'the third possibil-ity'?" She asks.

I confirm with my hands and my lips. After a short while, she nods without a word. I carry her in my arms and move inside to the lounge. Oh, even heavier than a railgun, or the garden hose, but of course I dare not say it.

I put her into a couch facing the south wall. We cuddle together, touch each other and kiss each other. I go a bit too far that I start to play with her body, but this is a good chance.

"This is?" I gently touch one of her sexiest part, vaguely appearing beneath the shirt.

"Collarbone."

"OK, this does not count." I move downwards a little.

One, two, oh it starts to be difficult, so I have to follow the bone to the side below her armpit and continue, three, four, five...

"Hey, what are you doing? Counting?" She asks.

"Yeah, just curious, haven't tried."

"Why don't you use your own body?" She pretends to be enraged, "Just a silly excuse, trying to touch — my breast."

"No, I can't. I have one missing, which becomes you." I say.

"Oldest and most boring cliché in the world."

"Hard to count with the shirt."

I slowly kiss her again and start to unbutton her shirt, along with other things, and undress myself. Sorry I am a bit clumsy and slow. But finally she shows herself in the natural form to me like a goddess in those oil paintings, and so do I. We are not ashamed.

She receives me.

......

With the final burst of sunlight onto the moon, I am exhausted with a feeling of emptiness, and lie down with her on the couch.

"I made the best decision in my life." I said to her.

"Who do you plan...in your guessing...? —s?" She asks.

I am almost falling asleep and cannot hear clearly, possibly due to the still-healing injury from the sound blast as well. But I definitely know what she means, and I know she is just joking. Well, there are only a few people with this "s" sound ending, and you do not want to shoot Artemis, who shoots you back using a bow and an arrow, or Dennis, who shoots you back using a railgun, or Nyx — oh that also counts — who shoots you back using a dark magic spell. So who is left?

"No, of course not. I would never do that. But it is too boring to put ourselves into the game and make even." I answer, "Some other random person, just for fun. I think I have a fifty-fifty chance, or even better. What about you?"

The princess' daddy won't fly all the way here to shoot me back, I guess…maybe.

"You."

That is fair.

"What book were you reading earlier this morning?"

"*The Stable Marriage Problem*, a manuscript."

Is it a romance novel? Or a math book? I feel too tired to ask. It does not matter.

What matters is — who will record this event, the only real creation within these days, as on Day six instead of Day seven?

What really matters is — there is only one girl whose *both* parents showed up in the graduation reception. A coincidence?

I hug her leafless body, kiss gently on her sleeping face, and continue with my enumeration of the truth of the world.

DAY VII

xxxvii   Announcement

With the first beam of light scattering on me through the morning mist, I wake up at last from a dreamless night, one of the best in the recent days.

My goddess has left the golden couch to summon the rising sun, and I need to prepare for the final battles.

"It is going to be a tougher day." I say to myself in the mirror, and go over my notes another time while brushing my teeth and cleaning myself up. I do every step slowly, as if it is a ceremony or ritual to buy myself some extra time.

A robot brings back what I just ordered. "That was quick." I say, "Oh, my god..."

Downstairs again, a number of people have already been there chatting. I sneak near them, like a cat.

"...We will start with water and power plant, then move on to other things as we just discussed." Bran says, "We still need to rely on the cat for food for some time, unless you want to eat those fruits all day long."

Fish taste better.

"And seriously we need to build a much larger moat, around the whole colony, much like in ancient times." Jack says.

Yes, I agree, but you mentioned it yesterday, right?

What were you reading Monday evening?

"And seriously I cannot believe you are only 8, Jack." Muse says with laugh, "What were these higher rank people doing?"

I am also curious. What were you doing, Miss 6?

"Well, I am 4. Rhea 13." Tim says, "and I kind of know the reason. Bran and I tried to order the guns by a design, and I had an instinct feeling that this whole thing is real. So the system believed that I had obtained some important knowledge, compared to those who believed it is a show."

"For the King!" Jack exclaims.

Everyone laughs. This is the best joke, Jack. You shall be promoted to a Joker.

"I am 7, probably for the same reason." Bran says, still laughing.

Oh, so you are the stupid who moved that paper. Then Nyx is — 2, or 5?

"Oh, I thought you..." Tim says, "So Nyx is..."

2. I know. Everyone knows Eos is 3, "to infinity".

Bran smiles, showing two fingers, like a victory sign.

"Whoa!"

"Is there real magic here on a different planet?"

"Probably not, Jack, but the girls all believe Nyx is top ten at least." Muse says.

The lavender was so confident for a reason. I feel so lucky that I didn't choose to shoot our CFT in the guessing game.

"Well, I was more surprised to see that William is in top ten as well. He later said he had not had any similar experience, but he insisted that it was because of the importance of his knowledge about God and his teachings, something like the faith." Bran says.

William? 5 or 9? Oh, it is 5. I see it now. Interesting.

So who is this mysterious 9?

"Could it be related to his story with Gaia?" Vincent asks, "What was that? I don't seem to remember exactly. By the way, 18 here, not very impressive."

"I remember it was about him making a promise with Gaia, something like if they meet unexpectedly then they shall be in relationship. But later they seemed to agree that it was a stupid idea." Hera says and laughs, "I don't even want to talk about my rank."

"Come on!" Everyone is hyped.

"20. That is why I don't even want to mention it." Hera says, "Just like Leo has once mentioned, both of us were punished badly by having the wrong belief, firmly thinking that it's a show."

Oh, so knowledge...can also be negative. Incorrect knowledge counts as negative weight in the system. That was how I was punished on Day two — I thought the seventy-seventh century is real. Yeah, if we had trusted each other and shared everything we knew on Day two, we would have figured out everything very quickly. So, this is a game of trust after all. The real perfect solution to the games — Exchange the ranks and figure out the big secret as soon as possible, and realize that the matching or guessing games are not important at all.

"But Muse has pretty high rank. Right, Muse?" Hera asks.

"Yes," Muse says, "but I didn't know exactly why."

The rank of a lady is as secret as the age I assume, so we shall stop here. In fact, the age is likely not a big secret in our class, or — is it?

"Tim, the morning spray job is done. We shall be good after they finish the moat. The enclosed area is pretty large — Fifteen thousand is totally worth it. I guess because they need to get water from the river." Dennis comes back from the courtyard with Oliver and Zak, "By the way, I am 11, and Selene 10. So that was why we just missed your criterion." He smiles at me.

Why are you doing this, Dennis? You know how bad it feels with everyone's gaze? Are you trying to take revenge against my words during the picnic? I originally planned to confess my sin to the sunflower later today, but now I have changed my mind. Let's wait for a dual solar eclipse with both moons. A real one, I mean.

"10 and 11 actually would work." I say word by word, trying to pretend to be as calm as possible.

"Hey, we think you need to reveal your rank, before I do." Muse says.

"Well, Iris is not in top ten unfortunately, but it does not matter much." I pretend to think for some time, and say, "Eos is 3. That is the only one I have figured out solely by myself. Seriously, I risked my life for it."

The boys quickly surround me, squeeze me, grab my arms and try torturing me to split it out. Artemis tortured Zak in the same way, I assume.

"Ha-ha, you have to say it! I am 14 and Zak is 21. Now, it's your turn!" Oliver says, "Leo and I planned so hard to open your mouth!"

"OK OK. I will say it. Now. Could you guys release me first? I will not run away — OK, good. Thanks. You guys know that, I am in top ten. Not many numbers are left, right?" I pause, "Not many numbers are right, right?"

The boys laugh and hold me even stronger. Oh, I give up.

"OK, OK, I give up. Bran, you should know my number by now? And Tim as well?"

"I get it." Bran nods and smiles.

Tim smiles as well.

Well, I am not asking for their confirmation. They probably knew it before the deadline. This is for the other people, excluding the clever couple of wisdom and knowledge.

"And then the rest of you should all know my number by now, right?"

I point to the ceiling with my right hand, as the boys finally release me, start to think about my words and try to get the logical deductions straight based on them. This must be much easier compared to what happened last night during the dinner, like comparing elementary arithmetic to calculus, four hundred to marathon, or calculus to what the purple rose has been reading, marathon to the moon. "QX, custom announcement."

"Sure. What is the message?" QX says.

Everyone stays quiet, as the cat is sometimes not as smart as we think or as smart as we are.

"I am 1. If you want to know a big secret, please come down to the lobby — that's it."

"Broadcasting right now." QX says.

I still don't know who is 9.

xxxviii   Time

If I made a similar announcement on Day four or Day five, not everyone would show up. People would just assume that I was mad, especially some girls had already thought so. 1 will not reveal themselves before Day seven, which has been a consensus. Even for today, people are showing up not only for the big secret, but also because I helped solving the matching game so everyone doubled their cash rewards. Some trust has been built, which makes the following plan much easier, as Tim mentioned back on Day three.

People start to show up. I set up and test the microphone, the amplifier and the speakers, borrowed from the party guys, and prepare myself a glass of Water, my favorite Element of Life, about to start my talk.

"Why do you need these? We can all hear you if you speak a bit louder." Tim asks.

"To save myself from...exhaustion." I smile as I show him my thick notes.

"OK, let me run to the bathroom really quick. By the way, to save you from curiosity," Tim smiles, "9 is Artemis."

Everyone is here, sitting on the couches, like on the first day, but in pairs — Twelve pairs, twenty-four total.

"I would like to go over my notes, but I can take questions along the way. So you can be certain that I have passed the Turing Test." I start, "This might be quite lengthy, but please be patient. Before I start, let me confirm with William: If we simply chat over here, it does not count as any form of work or job or duty, right? So theoretically or theologically we are still at rest, like having a tea party. So it won't interfere with the seven day interpretation we had last night. Is this correct?"

"I agree with you." William says.

"Didn't the boys go out spraying water? Does it count as leisure, like you water the garden on Sundays?" Hera asks.

"Your interpretation is acceptable, but more importantly, a life threatening duty is an example of 'important social services', which is of course 'legitimately excused'. God loves us all. He does not want us to be hurt." William confirms.

"Oh, so it was real." Hera murmurs.

"Thanks. Now — before I really start," I pause and people laugh, "QX, who has the best knowledge of the known knowledge by the sunrise this morning?"

"6." QX answers.

"6?" Jack looks at Muse in awe.

"So, Muse, or Miss 6, do you want to tell the story for me?" I smile at Muse.

"No, you go ahead. I prefer to listen." Muse smiles back.

"Then may I ask quickly, were you inspired by the sundial?"

"Yes."

I guess most people have been very much puzzled by the dialogue, so we shall get back on track.

"OK, thanks. Back to the topic, The following is going to be really important. I am 1, and as we discussed earlier, this is some kind of proof."

"Let me start with one single most important piece of information about this new world. You should imagine in your brain that the following sentence is in all capital letters." I say.

"The time flow here near the new Earth is exactly the opposite to the time flow near our old Earth."

<hr>

As I expected, the crowd is very silent at first, and then bursts into whispers. "What did he say?" "Time flow?" "Are we backward in time?"

Tim and Bran also whisper with each other, nodding and shaking heads, so they get something at least. I guess most people are puzzled by what this means. Time flow? Opposite? Of course we don't have anything like that on the old Earth. It is the fun part, everyone! My revenge is very successful.

But I also vaguely hear some girl whispering an unexpected but familiar name — "Selene"? My ear problem? Or, has the sunflower also figured out everything? It's totally possible, and will make my life a bit easier.

Eos is the usual Eos, reading a book by her own.

Jack still looks startled. So, the water lily decided to keep the big secret...

"Is this the ultimate reason of the all planet retrograde?" Nyx asks.

I think this is possibly the first time Nyx asks a question, as opposed to people asking our CFT for fortunes.

"Yes. I think so."

"Thanks. Now I understand almost everything. Solves the biggest myth. Congratulations." Nyx is likely the first one who comprehends the whole sentence and accepts it without doubt. 2 is now instead taking the lead in the knowledge race I think. Are there smaller myths?

I clear my throat and start explaining. "First of all, let me explain what this means: Whenever one minute of time passes in our new world, back on the old Earth, it is exactly the opposite, meaning time rewinds, goes back by one minute. If you use some conversion of units, one minute here equals negative one old Earth minute."

"Quick clarification: By 'one minute', you actually mean one minute in old Earth time, a period of time, an 'absolute value'." Muse says.

"Yes, right. Thank you."

"One question here," Vincent asks, "on one afternoon, I forget which one exactly, I was in my room asking for the time until sunset in old Earth hours, and the cat replied something like 'minus one point two' something hours. Is this — because of the sign change of the time flow?"

"Sounds like it. I remember I once heard the same expression. However, the expression 'T-minus' some hours or minutes is also relatively common for countdowns, so I didn't notice anything wrong either. I thought the aliens use a slightly different convention." Jack says.

"Let me show you, Jack." Muse says, "QX, how much time is it from the current time to the solar noon today, in old Earth hours?"

"Minus two point zero five six hours." QX answers.

"QX, then how much time is it from the solar noon today to the current time, in old Earth hours?" Muse asks again.

"Two point zero four nine hours."

"The cat can be playing words with us. Do we have other proofs?" Hera asks.

"It is hard for us to use a telescope to directly observe the Earth, but if we could, we would see the Earth spinning backwards and rotate around sun backwards as well. If we could get a better telescope, we would see the motions of everything on the Earth going backwards: Trees become smaller and smaller and turn into seeds; birds turn into eggs; water flows uphill; a broken glass cup reforms and becomes whole, and then turns into melts and back to sand; even worse, people resurrect from tombs, grow younger and younger and return to wombs; finally of course, clocks and watches go backwards, and planets are normally in retrograde." I follow back to my notes, not directly answering Hera's question.

"To be honest, I don't understand physics well enough to understand how light travels from the Earth to this new planet. So the examples I just gave are imaginary, like pretending you can see everything, then you see things go backwards."

"I agree. If I understand you correctly about the time reversal — in order for us to physically see something, light has to be emitted or reflected from it, examples like the sun and the moon respectively, and we see the light by our own eyes or by some device like a camera. However, if the time flow is the opposite there on the old Earth, then emission of light becomes absorption, so we only see the light that we or other sources sent to the Earth? Does it make sense? Then it implies that we don't see anything in that region where the Earth and the Sun locate right now, even things are actually happening there." Bran slowly goes over his argument.

"Possible explanation of the dark matter." Jack says.

"If that explanation is correct, then how can aliens detect us?" Selene asks.

I want to ask the same question.

"Maybe they can see things when they are close enough, after crossing the boundary of the different time flow. However, crossing that time boundary does not sound easy at all." Bran says.

"If my understanding on photons is correct," Eos says, "Photons, or light, travel in the speed of light of course, which in special relativity is the maximum possible speed in the universe. And if you plug in the equations, you see that they do not experience time, or time is meaningless to photons. So whether our time flow is the same as or the opposite to that on the Earth, photons do not know that. To photons, there is no time, and it takes literally zero seconds from their own perspective to travel from our old Earth or even from the end of the universe to us. So if light was emitted from the Earth at some point, it will pass the said 'time flow boundary' without noticing it, and arrive here so that we can see it."

OK, I feel the discussion is like a balloon hovering further and further away from me. I somehow get what you mean, but I don't fully understand it. Relativity is too hard. By the way, you also know some physics, Eos?

"In fact, the same arguments work for our bodies, or other stuff they brought from the Earth with us. If their spaceship is super fast, like very close to the speed of light, then from our own perspective, we have only experienced a very short amount of time. It could feel like travel overseas by plane, again, from our own perspective." Eos continues. "Moreover, also due to special relativity, there is no consensus of time in the universe, so we are unable to even say what is happening *right now* on the old Earth. This notion that we use everyday simply does not exist in astronomical settings. That was why the cat refused to provide the current date according to the old Earth standards. It simply can't. You can only talk about the difference of the time flow."

"Relativity...When did you learn that?" Bran asks.

"Right now." Eos says, "Emmm... Special relativity is no more than the consequences or theorems following a few axioms, but it does not allow time flow reversal. To get an opposite time flow, we need to work with general relativity plus some strange Riemannian geometry. It is too easy to make mistakes with tensors...Oh, I can try to use Gödel metric. So there is no time boundary then..."

I don't understand a single word!

"The same Gödel?" Jack asks.

"Yes. A real genius. Now I see, *five thousand light years...* they were referring to the *spacetime* distance instead of *space* distance... So we need to take an integral over this close timelike curve from the old Earth to the new Earth..."

Could you please stop murmuring about general relativity that no one else can understand?

"The Earth is far away anyway. Do we have a more direct proof about the time flow?" Dennis asks, trying to stop Eos from more relativity discussions. It is uncommon for Eos to speak long sentences, but if she starts, then someone has to stop her eventually. Thank you so much, Dennis.

"Anything happening there on the old Earth is hard to verify. There is no direct proof about what is happening on the Earth, at least not at the moment. However, there is some much closer evidence on ourselves." I pause for a few seconds, "We are losing the memory back on the Earth in the exactly same speed of time."

"Yes, this is it!" Tim cries out, "This explains a lot of strange feelings recently. It's just memory loss! Man!"

......

It turns out most people in fact had such memory loss during the last few days, but they usually regarded it as memory loss only, because of the lack of sleep in a twenty hour daily cycle, or because of the stress built with respect to the future plans, or because of worrying about finding a partner in the marriage game, or because of being Eos and worrying about immortality. No, actually the purple rose has already known the source of the memory loss. I would have been one of them as well, except that I wrote a crucial sentence down on my notes, and it pushed me to go over and write down all of my memories, over and over again, and finally led to such unimaginable discoveries.

"In particular, what I have figured out is the following correspondence. OK, before that: To be honest I don't have a good idea which tense I want to use. Within these seven days, all the events on the new Earth happened in the past, but all the events on the old Earth are in the future according to our memory. So I will use simple present tense whenever both worlds are referred, or whenever I don't know how to say it."

"Right," Muse laughs, "this is very hard in grammar. The future events on the old Earth will happen but they have already happened by new Earth standards; The past events on the old Earth have happened but they will happen later by new Earth standards."

Yes, you have to get used to it, and forget about grammar for now.

"OK, let me start. The time when we were waken up by the light on Day one, which was the past of us, *corresponds* to the midnight on Friday of our graduation week, which will come in the future, on the old Earth. Then afterwards, as time passes here, the same amount of time rewinds back there on the old Earth, or rather the same amount of memory of events is getting lost from our brain at the same speed. I call the event *dishappens* as opposite to it *happens*. Based on my own experience, if you haven't tried to recall a piece of memory before it dishappens, then it is lost forever, like it has never happened, and in some strict sense this is the truth that it has never happened. If you have tried to recall it before, then after it dishappens, it just feels like a dream to you, and will eventually evaporate like dreams, unless you write it down and repeatedly remind yourself about it."

"Let me give an example, when I first saw Tim on Day one on the stairway, I roughly remember the idea that "Tim was drunk last night" which is Friday night party of the graduation week, but I cannot remember any details by now, or even by the end of Day one. Instead what is in my brain is the sentence "Tim was drunk last night" that I recalled on Day one. When we had our first dinner here that night, Tim ordered some wine, and I still remember he said it was his first time drinking. This piece of memory happened here, so it is still in my brain, like where we sit, how we talked and how Tim expressed his first-time drinking experience. Not every detail of course, but just like a regular piece of memory, which will eventually fade in time. However, the fact that 'Tim was drunk last night' is only a sentence written down on my notes. No details, not even a bit."

"Damn it! I had the same feeling when I said that! Man!" Tim says.

"OK. If you count the old Earth hours from the very beginning, when we woke up on Day one, to the upcoming solar noon, of Day seven, the time they scheduled to announce the results, it is exactly one hundred and twenty hours, five Earth days, which corresponds to, second by second, Sunday midnight to Friday midnight of our graduation week back on the Earth, but it is backwards. I can tell that they are perfectionists."

I hand out copies of a page from my notes, which has one vertical line of the time arrow in the middle. To the right, it is the time on the new planet, starting from when we woke up on Day one, to solar noon of Day seven; to the left side it is the Earth time backwards from Friday midnight to Sunday midnight. These two sides share the same time arrow, but with different directions. I also lay down some important events on the time line to mark the exact time when they happen or dishappen on either sides.

People start to pass around the copies, and read it like students reading hand-outs from teachers.

"Did you order a photocopier?" Selene asks, "It looks like you drew the exact same graph twenty-four times in the exact same way, but it is impossible!"

"No. I just asked the cat to copy it. A robot rolled to my room, took my paper, and brought back copies in less than ten minutes. I have to say, I don't even know which one is my original, to be honest."

"So if this is copying, what we have ordered is mostly printing service..." Tim says.

"We must feel lucky that the aliens didn't print a second copy of the hotel plus second copies of us and put everything a mile away, and let us shoot each other. Think about it: You guys got lost in the forest and went to the other hotel. A perfect thriller novel." I say.

"That sounds very interesting. Let me read it when you finish." Dennis says.

"The technology behind it, the control of atoms at this level, is not something humans can achieve within a thousand years." Bran says.

"Don't be pessimistic, Bran." Jack says, "One thousand years ago, we didn't have electricity or computers or internet or any sort of modern industry. So after one thousand years, people may even send spaceships here to save us from the aliens. Oh, I won't live that long. Too bad."

Another Jack's joke, though this time I feel different.

"Jack, you are wrong." Muse laughs, "Remember the time is reversed, so after one thousand years here, people on the Earth won't have electricity or computers or internet or any sort of modern industry, to even look at us."

"Anyway, now everyone has the note, which makes it easier for me to explain." I start. "It is a *bi-directional timeline*, that is, with two directions. On the new Earth side, time flows from top down to the bottom, and on the old Earth side, it is backwards: time flows from bottom up. Or if you think about it in another way, we are gluing two timelines, the old Earth timeline and the new Earth timeline, together into one single timeline."

"On the top of the page, right hand side, the new Earth timeline, you see the time when we woke up in the hotel, about an hour before the solar noon on Day one. This corresponds to the Friday midnight of our graduation week on the left hand side, the old Earth timeline. Again, I know most of you don't even believe this because we have not yet had the graduation week, right? Yes, we have had the graduation week, but we have forgotten everything!"

"I need to clarify that this may not be the old Earth time at this moment, which I do not know if makes actual sense in physics, as Eos told us about theory of relativity which implies that it is hard to discuss what is actually happening on the Earth right now. The correspondence only works with our memory as far as I can tell, but the time reversal may have other consequences, which I will later discuss."

"So let me go through these seven days, and line up the events with our graduation week. To be honest, it is the graduation week that I wrote down on my notes when I still had the memory, so things could be inaccurate. Just disclaimer."

"So we will have a graduation party on Friday night, as planned. In some sense, 'we had a graduation party' is the better way to say it. OK, from now on, I will pretend that in terms of the Earth time we are currently at Friday midnight, at the top on my page. So I will use past tense for the old Earth timeline. OK, everyone?"

"The only real proof of this, is on my first page of notes, saying we had 'graduation party last night', but no details. As I see right now, it was somewhat like a dream, and has been lost, mostly. But if I remember correctly, Gaia and William had some little story back on Day one, and I believe it corresponds to some event that happened on the graduation party, but I have no real proof. It would be great if you two can share something."

"Yes, I somehow remember something, or maybe, forget something." William says, "Like, on that day, I made a promise to Gaia, but neither of us can remember when or where exactly I did it. In fact, it was like a dream, and it is becoming more and more vague. I started to feel puzzled back then, and later I asked Gaia and she agreed with me about it, so we thought it might be an illusion caused by the aliens, like injections of false memory, to create a pair in a dramatic setting and to push others to pair up quickly."

"Right, it was just like a dream. It first appeared very vivid, like real, but then everything started to collapse and right now I cannot even remember much details except for the strange promise." Gaia continues.

"Yes, it was the same feeling." Tim says, "When I had the wine for the first time during dinner on Day one, it felt like I had it before, but I couldn't remember, like a déjà vu."

"Exactly. But once you understand the principle behind the strange feeling, it becomes natural, at least to me. Anyway, I think this was why I became rank 1 on Day one, plus I was a stupid who didn't notice the pattern on our names. I didn't realize the time arrow was backwards then, but only felt strange that I started to forget things completely, especially things that just happened last night, and I guessed something was wrong with the time. This was more like a crucial hint to the big secret." I say.

"Me too. I felt the same on Day one, like something was wrong with the time, so that they refused to give us clocks or watches. But on Day one I was guessing the time is slower or faster than the Earth, and had not imagined it could be backwards, until the sundial and your words gave me the hint." Muse says.

Oh, you were already very clever to start thinking about possible variance of the speed of time. I just thought something was wrong with time that caused my memory loss. Oh, you were punished by having the wrong knowledge as well.

"An interesting point is that, from our own perspective, there is no such 'speed of time', the time according to our brains always flows as the complicated bio-chemical process in our brains that I don't understand at all. So the time flows together with the environment around us, always. It is similar to that people always think they stand above Earth, no matter in which hemisphere civilization first started. If we compare it to a distant planet like the Earth, then we can talk about the difference in time flow, faster or slower or backwards." I add a comment, "Am I correct, Eos?"

"Correct."

"OK. Let us move on to Day two. Jack and I were together with your explorers for discussion, and it occurred to me that things could be opposite to the Earth, such as the magnetic field, or even the time arrow. Maybe I was just having a little bit imagination, but I had this crazy idea that time actually rewinds for what has happened on the Earth, which can also explain this super rare eight planet retrograde event, in addition to the memory loss."

"But in order to pin down the exact correspondence, I had to use the exact numbers: The number of hours in a day, and the extra period of time at the beginning from when we woke up to the solar noon. You can tell from my paper, 'slightly less than twenty hours' is too coarse for anything accurate. That was why I asked these two strange questions on Day two during dinner. You still remember?"

"And I phrased things carefully, for example, I asked the period 'from solar noon to when I woke up'. You notice the difference? Like Muse just did. Because it is backwards. I was worried that, if I asked for the other direction, the cat wouldn't tell us, since being a negative number it would reveal the crucial information, but now it seems that I was overthinking. We are so used to the notion of time that we don't usually put signs over a period of time, but here it is crucial, especially when you compare the time flow here with that on the old Earth."

"Your 'absolute number' was quite unnatural." Muse laughs.

"Nothing during the daytime here on the old Earth timeline, but we had the graduation parade on Thursday, which was dishappening roughly during the night of Day two." I say, "Tim, did you remember I asked about the costumes we had during the parade?"

"I roughly remember...but now I don't remember why you were so certain that people will hate these costumes." Tim says.

"You see, you almost forget the question I asked. Because it was a casual talk of little importance. Moreover, it now does not agree with your own memory, your current memory. So your brain is doing some job in the background, processing some information for you, and filling in or leaving out information, to resolve inconsistencies."

"The parade had dishappened, so you forgot about it." I

continue, "On Day three, I also asked the same question to a few girls during Nyx's morning fortune-telling session, and they didn't seem to remember the parade then. So at that time, I knew this memory loss is happening to everyone, or rather everything back on the Earth is dishappening to everyone."

"Here was the most important event which made me believe that we *are* in fact on a different planet. On the night of Day two, around the same time as the parade to the Earth side on my note, I was on my bed, trying to sleep, but at the same time recalling the parade. Suddenly a shock came."

"An electric shock?" Muse asks, "I didn't have that."

"Not quite, just the feeling of it. I call it an *Eclipse* or maybe a transit, like a solar eclipse or Venus transit. It happens when you try to recall from your memory about some event back on the Earth at exactly the same time when it dishappens. One, you are recalling the event; two, it is dishappening; it's like they collide on the timeline from both sides. In some logical sense, you are forgetting it at the same time as you try to remember it or enforce your memory of it. At that time, your brain basically malfunctions. Let me put it this way."

"It is not like you are going to be insane. So don't worry too much about experiencing it. Some of you might have already experienced it. Here, I call it *malfunction* because I don't have a better word for it. It is more like a programming bug, or in other words, our brain is not designed to take this strange event into account, and as a result it just gets confused by itself."

"Our brain is in fact very powerful in terms of processing data. The image we actually see on our retina is upside-down and our brain can automatically adjust it. Same thing for our three dimensional vision, or blind spot fill-up. Our ears can detect sound directions, but more precisely, our brain is doing it. Smell, taste, other senses, everything is processed in our brain. However, it has never processed the information that you remember something at the same time you forget it. So it is just stuck, like a programming bug or flaw."

"Luckily it does not run into an infinite loop, which would be terrible for us." Bran says, "Think about when your own CPU runs at one hundred percent of capacity for even a few seconds, when all other processes stall."

"Right, it would be disastrous then. Base on my own experience, what you may sense during an eclipse could be very similar to a vivid dream or lucid dream, like most of you have experienced in your life. You feel it is like a dream, and you know it is a dream, and everything is unreal. That piece of event which is dishappening simply gets replayed to you in the lucid dream. Then when you get out of the lucid dream or the eclipse, it feels like a dream. Sometimes it feels more like sleep paralysis, like you are aware of dreaming but cannot wake up yourself."

"Luckily, the coincidental moment that you are recalling the memory and it is dishappening is very short. The reason is, we usually recall events in chronological order, right? And on the Earth the time goes backwards, so there is usually a relatively short period of time when eclipses happen, like total solar eclipses. A few seconds to maybe twenty or thirty seconds at most."

"Moreover, I saw multiple eclipses because I was concerned about events happening or dishappening during our graduation week. For most of you, you probably haven't seen it during the past few days. What was happening here was much more interesting compared to the graduation week, and so there was not much time or interest to recall your memories, in particular at the same time when they dishappened."

"So, that night, I realized the very fact that, this whole thing is real — the aliens and the games are real. The eclipse works like a direct attack to your brain, a direct proof of an alien world. It works like sending signals into your brain without sensory organs or nerves. I believe humans are not able to do this with our current technology. Aliens, may have such technology, but I don't see any reason why they would do it, just like they won't poison our food. I don't feel the eclipses are artificial. They are more like natural phenomena to me, following some physical rules other than alien interference. They are repeatable, testable and predictable, just like physics and chemistry and in general all natural sciences."

"The parade was long and so I experienced multiple of such eclipses, and based on my rough calculations, the time flows backwards there, at the same speed, but I still cannot pin down the exact matching of the time points or confirm the speed of the time flow. I didn't have a good idea about the exact time points during our parade, nor I was able to keep track of the time easily at night on my bed. But I had this instinctive guess that the starting point on the Earth is Friday midnight. These aliens are perfectionists as we can tell by now. So that was why I tried to grab Eos on Day four, during tea party that afternoon, in order to verify this conjecture. That is, if my guess was correct, then Eos and I were able to see an eclipse at a very fixed point of time. This is exactly the same as a solar eclipse or Venus transit that one can predict using complicated arithmetic and geometry and then make travel plans based on the predictions."

"What about the order of two cups of tea? Was that related as well?" Oliver asks.

"No, no, no. That was totally irrelevant." I say.

"Ah, actually..." Iris starts but breaks off.

I know. You don't have tell it. It is just our little secret.

"OK." I continue, "Bran's sundial helped a lot for me to get a good estimate over time, without asking the cat too often. So back on the Earth, shortly before the graduation ceremony, which was nine am Wednesday morning, I had...some conversation with Eos."

Pheme and Kakia are gossiping immediately. Fine —

"Anyway, this was a very easy event to pin down the time. I guess the graduation ceremony itself was somewhat boring and no one would remember any crucial moments after a week. So,

I asked Eos to verify this single event with me, and as expected, she saw an eclipse as well. That was probably why she cried then."

The purple rose still does not have much reaction, reading her physics book and taking notes.

"Once we had that crucial information, the remaining task was to make everyone else believe it. Just my guess. It's like in those video games Jack and I played. This is very hard, as I don't have similar critical events with every individual one of you here. So I focused on the graduation reception back on Monday morning. You will come, sorry, you came with some family members, mom and dad, grandmas and grandpas, brothers and sisters, uncles or aunts, etc. I know, it is 'you will come with them' based on your memory. As of right now, it is around one thirty am on Monday morning, Earth time, so you probably have decided who is coming to the reception. Now I will read these out, which you can verify if they agree with your plans. This is to prove that I had the memory last night, and my theory is correct."

"Let us start with Tim: Your big family came to the reception, literally everyone including three dogs and a parrot, who is the oldest member of your family."

"Bran, your father came, and he speaks ancient Greek very fluently, according to Nyx."

"Yan, your parents came from China, from a very high nobleman class."

Everyone turns to Yan.

"I have something to say, or to confess." Yan slowly starts, "Most of you, especially the ladies, have noticed — my real first name is You-Yan. 'You' is spelled as Y-o-u, and you see why it is a bad name here."

Right. That is, very true. You is, You was, and You has. Funny.

"I didn't even look at the list, which means I am not going to shoot — you, Yan." Jack says.

Good one, you, Jack, are really quick.

So Muse helped to cross out your names on that paper, and you were paying full attention only on its position all the time — just in order to...shoot me? Holy shit. I am angry!

"Thanks. I guess I was the very first one who believed everything is real, strikingly real, but it was after the sunset on Day one, after I saw my name on the screen, just a few seconds late. I want to be honest, but my real first name has been kept as a top secret and normal kidnappers shouldn't know it."

Well, it implies that they are not normal, and based on the fact that I am 1, I think you are right.

"And, 'You' means, in ancient Chinese, the 'road' or the 'way', like philosophical one, the 'Tao' as in Taoism. This character was picked by...an ancestor, more than six hundred years ago. Roughly speaking, it is a 'generation character', meant to differentiate generations. For example, on the family tree, my cousins and I share the same character, and my father and my uncles share another one, and so on, level by level."

Interesting. How many offsprings does your ancestor have? So there is this difference between modern Chinese and ancient Chinese? Like modern Greek and ancient Greek? They are all Greek to me...I wonder how you guys say that?

"The second character 'Yan' is so in some sense my real name, and it means the wood eaves of a house, but now I guess I am stretching too far away from home."

You learned how to tell jokes! A philosophical road stretching out to the universe! What a great name! What a great name for our own story!

"So I am, as always, Yan." Yan concludes.

"Is it also a pun name?" Iris asks, "If my memory is still correct, that 'You' is the twentieth generation character reserved for the Lineage of the Prince of Yan, a different character but the same pronunciation and the same alphabetical spelling, which is the fourth one in the twenty-four Lineages, correct?"

So you have learned a lot of Chinese these years, even ancient Chinese!

"Yes, my Lineage is...the fourth one. I am very much impressed. I bet most real Chinese people don't even know what this character is only by the pronunciation plus this ancient meaning. Lineage of the Prince of Yan...I think you are technically correct, technically." Yan says.

Twenty-four again? I wonder if one of the Lineages, or one of the original Princes, was something special, like demoted or exiled from the country?

Obviously Yan has something that he does not want to say right now. Jack, now it is time to show off your knowledge! He is whispering with Muse, and Muse is nodding.

I am super curious! I only know half of the story, and you know everything!

"OK, then, Circe, your grandparents and two brothers."

"Grammy and Grampy are masters of my orphanage, but they treat me very well, even better than their own grandchildren." Circe says.

"Selene, a young and handsome man, presumably your father, who knows Dennis' father very well." I continue.

"You say, daddy will come, or came, to my graduation? I haven't seen him for ten years! Are you making this up?" Selene cries out.

"I actually don't know anything about it. I promise." Dennis says.

"But, how did you know my mom's flight was delayed? I just received the call before I went to bed."

I see. So it was my ear problem then, and Selene didn't know everything the night before the reception. This means I have to play a trump card, and this is also what's puzzling me — "He also talked briefly with — Nyx."

Everyone looks at our CFT.

"He is a friend and a sponsor of my society." Nyx says.

The lavender doesn't reject my claims, which means it was so planned. Ah, now I see why Yan's parents sent him here. There is a real princess in our class. And Nyx was on duty during high school, working for the *forever-young* man, who delays flights as he wishes, looking after the precious princess. What have I done? I really hope the duty is over by now.

"Nyx — some senior member of your magic society, five stars."

"A follower." Nyx says.

......

One by one, people become astonished. Some pieces of the information I just gave are possible to obtain or to guess via other sources, but some are definitely not.

I am not so certain that this is enough to convince each one individually, but all together that is the proof. No one rejects my claims. It is overall very strong evidence that my claims are true.

Sorry, I have to say this does not count as a proof in Eos' standards, but she does not need one for now.

"Finally Artemis and Zak, were late for the reception, and you two did not have other relatives or friends coming." I finish the list, "Good thing is that at this moment, all of you were likely sleeping on your bed, maybe dreaming about something that you already forgot. So it is unlikely for you to witness an eclipse right now. But if you were awake at that time, and if you try to recall what you did, then likely you can see an eclipse."

"Zak, I told you we would be late...what are you doing? No, no, no! People are watching us." Artemis cries out.

"I think I see the same thing. It's the eclipse! We are in the hotel now!" Zak says.

"I know we are in the hotel...but, wait, why are there other guys around? No, something does not make sense..."

"No, it is not that hotel, it is the alien's hotel!" Zak says.

"You two, one am, Monday morning?" Pheme says, "Hotel?"

Both of them have red flushing face. Very soon people realize what is happening, or what was happening on the Earth. It is not anything secret. They have in relationship for years and it's nothing surprising. Still a lot of us, especially the girls, get very embarrassed. If it were me, I would run away as quickly as possible, but I guess the eclipse shock is so real that it is hard to control yourself.

"This is so real..." Artemis murmurs. "Zak, I told you people would know it, and we would be both late for the reception...Oh, no! It comes again!"

"I said people can guess whatever they want, but they do not have a proof you know." Zak says.

"Now — they — have!"

"System announcement: Hidden Quest One has been accomplished. Quest reward: Double cash reward." Says QX.

Nothing works as a better proof.

Oh, so we get four million instead? Good news, but this reward is not what I have expected. Something is still missing. Too bad.

"QX, what is the target of this hidden quest?" Tim asks.

"Hidden Quest One target: Everyone obtains the knowledge of the time flow operator in the finite simple group of order two."

I don't even understand what the quest is about. Eos is quickly taking notes, and Muse seems pretty OK with it. So never mind. It says "time flow" which is good enough.

"This is pretty clear and cool proof of it." Bran says, "Wait, they can read our minds?"

"If they can rank us based on our knowledge, then yes, they can." Tim says.

Well, it was another terrifying "One". So there might be other quests? Anyway, let us finish the remaining part first.

"Please allow me to finish with some remarks." I say.

"Before that, may I, or may we ask a question?" Hera asks, "Why didn't you tell us earlier?"

"OK. Short answer: I didn't have time. I figured out everything on Day four, in the afternoon, with Eos. Then that night, you know, the red moon. The next morning, chaos and fight, though I was the last one to know the truth. Then we ran to the beach, and returned with even more chaos, and I was shocked. Barbecue party was obviously not a good time to talk about serious matters. Then Day six, I talked to Tim and Muse in the morning, and felt I was betrayed, very badly." I laugh, with some other people, "So I decided to take revenge, my own revenge against you guys. I could talk about it, in the afternoon when I explained the marriage ritual, but we were running out of time, and more importantly I felt it would cause some extra unnecessary chaos so I decided to talk about it today, after the deadlines."

"Indeed." Laughs Jack, " And your revenge is quite successful. I actually have another question before you continue. What is this question mark to the left of Day five, picnic time?"

"Oh, that one. I don't remember anything. To be precise, I didn't see a similar kind of eclipse during the picnic, or maybe I forgot. Apparently I had some memory loss during that period of time, so I believe, or I feel that something on the old Earth timeline was causing a different type of eclipse here, analogous to different types of solar eclipses."

"I haven't confirmed it, but we may call it a Type II eclipse, and the one I mentioned earlier, the vivid or lucid dream, a Type I. So on Day four after I figured out the exact time points, I started to realize that some of the information on my notes was not so useful, but instead might cause eclipses. It would be a real nightmare when I was facing the eagles or something else with a railgun, right? As Tim asked me to go for picnic on Day five, I took my notes and blacked out all events on Tuesday on the old Earth timeline before we left, as I thought they were irrelevant, and I forced myself not to think about them. But still something happened. The memory loss. It felt like film-cutting, you know. A period of time was simply cut from your memory, and your brain automatically continued to the next frame, without you even noticing it."

"Day-dreaming?" Bran asks.

"Yes, like day-dreaming. Now even if I ask you guys about what happened on Tuesday, you have forgotten everything as well."

"Tuesday? But we don't...we didn't have graduation plans for Tuesday, right?" Hera says.

"No, we don't...didn't." Jack says, "But I think I...was planning to suggest another bridge tournament, our last one in high school. Tense is too hard, man!"

"Bridge! This may be it!" I say, "Now I feel it is the bridge tournament on Tuesday. That was why I suggested another bridge tournament here for the eclipse! I almost forget it, again because it does not agree with my memory anymore. But I still don't see any correspondence with what happened on Day five."

"I was also trying to suggest going to the beach some time in the summer break, and we can discuss our plan during the bridge tournament. Is this related?" Jack asks.

"Beach..." I feel it may be related, but I don't get the key connection.

"OK, I have a guess." Jack says after some thought, "Is it possible for some heavy logic analysis, or heavy logic deductions on the old Earth timeline to cause some memory loss? It is like logic is hard to 'cancel', in some sense. I would assume that logic and memory are two different types of processes in the brain, and in order for your brain to cancel the logical arguments you have made, it needs more energy or extra CPU power, and so causes your memory loss or loss of senses on this side when logic dishappens. You had similar feelings, on Day five?"

"Yes," Muse answers, "this might be the reason why I was distracted, unable to concentrate on that day, like a loss of memory or loss of senses, or like being paralyzed or numbed during a surgery. I thought it was just a bad day. This was also why you did't remember the things I told you on Day five, Jack, about this time reversal. I thought you were still in the shock after the fight with Oliver. My bad."

"Oh, you did? Sorry, I don't remember anything." Jack says.

"Then the same thing is true for detective novels, logic puzzle games, board games, and some video games as well. Same feature. Probably bridge is the most intense among these I would say." I say.

"I would say you have to read more math books." Muse laughs.

Oh, the purple rose may also have trouble in the following days, if she had been reading these math book, all day long.

"Oh..." Selene then whispers to Dennis, and Dennis nods with smile. They seem to have tons of secrets.

"Well, four of us may have a harder time later. We've played a lot of games." Jack says, "No driver license within four years. Too sad."

Everyone laughs.

"No. It is about...five years on the new Earth." Muse corrects. "Oh, that was why they gave us a five year period..."

Now everyone starts to understand the real meaning of five years. Our memory of high school will be gone after that, then we will be strangers to each other, except for the years we will live together, if any, here on the new Earth.

"Yeah, too sad indeed." I continue, "OK, let us come back to the topic and let me finish my notes. First, we need to re-learn everything we learned on the Earth — math, sciences, history, languages, arts. For some daily skills like eating, drinking, going to the bathroom, taking a shower, and dressing or undressing clothes, we will keep these skills since we do these everyday. Otherwise we will forget the skills, especially including language skills. So if you do not speak, then in twenty years you will be unable to speak. Communication is crucial."

"Second, about the effect of time reversal on our physical bodies. I have...roughly two possibilities. One is that our body will grow younger and younger, and so eventually become a baby and then die in a form that fails to support ourselves without a womb, within the same period of time we have lived on the Earth. It is more like a fixed death date. Even worse, after ten or more Earth years, our children need to take care of us. At that time, they will be literally older than us. So that was why they asked us to have babies as soon as possible."

People start to panic, and whisper to each other regarding the death.

"How is this possible?" Hera asks, "Growing backwards in time?"

"Don't worry too much. I personally believe that the second possibility makes more sense. So the theory is that, our current time arrow makes us age, and helps us remember what we have done here; and the old Earth time arrow makes us grow younger, travel back in time and forget things happened over there; then in sum they somehow cancel each other. It is like we are remembering something and at the same time forgetting it. If this is true, then our bodies become immortal. We may still be killed by weapons and poisons, but the body no longer ages and stays in the current form, around between eighteen and nineteen years old."

"We somehow becomes gods and goddesses as supposed to kings and queens. Well, if you want, you can still make yourselves kings or queens, just for fun. Our alien technology, becomes magic powers of gods. All these legendary stories about gods and goddesses that you can remember or imagine become real."

If the time arrow is the first bomb, this is like the second one.

"So any mathematical model that predicts the fifty/five hundred rule does not really apply to us, if we are immortal." Leo says.

"Exactly. It is much harder to have genetic shift if the original group, which is us, continues to reproduce. In addition, we can carefully avoid inbreed by setting up rules or laws and overseeing everything by ourselves in the early days, as long as we don't use guns to shoot each other at the beginning."

"God blessed them; and God said to them, 'Be fruitful and multiply, and fill the earth, and subdue it'." William says.

"But can't we order other weapons like the railgun, and kill each other in the future?" Kakia asks.

"They somehow believe that we won't, probably by completing the marriage game with cooperation and trust." I answer, "Well, anything possible will happen eventually. So after thousands or even millions of years, we still die, one by one, due to accidents, disease, murder, war, all sorts of things. Some cults may even purposely try to hunt us down. So we shall be prepared, to face the challenges from our kids. Knowledge is challenge, a real challenge. But after such a long life, no one would regret while facing the final death I would imagine."

"What about our children, and offsprings?" Gaia asks.

"Our offsprings are mortals most likely, otherwise this planet will soon run out of space. Another possibility is that, during early days, they may live much longer than normal humans, and their life spans gradually decrease throughout the ages, like 'dilution of immortality'. You can think of how long these early generations lived, in the Bible, especially from Adam to Noah."

"The standard interpretation of long life span of these first generations is that early people had less sin and lived a simpler life. Adam and Eve were supposed to be immortal, but they committed the original sin and so driven out from Eden. As sin accumulated through the ages, our life span gradually decreased to the current length." William says, "We need to live a simple life in order to follow the road of our ancestors. I have to say I don't agree with your interpretation."

I understand. Everyone interprets it in their own way. Who

are the first generation humans, the twenty-four of us, or our kids?

"But both sound pretty reasonable to me." Jack laughs, "Adam lived nine hundred thirty years, so we can tell who is right after a thousand."

"I agree. Let us keep this debate aside and focus on our current issues." Tim says.

"Why do you think the second possibility, that we are immortal instead of growing younger, is more likely?" Selene asks, "They look equally possible to me."

"They look equally possible to me as well, but I think at least my nails and hairs that I cut off won't come back, and especially my primary teeth or baby teeth won't fly by themselves from the Earth. Well, I think we will know after a few years, but I feel the aliens wouldn't spend so much effort just taking us here, to die in twenty-four years. Things are more interesting if we are immortal. They would have lots of fun observing each and everyone of us, to be honest."

Dennis smiles again and whispers something with Selene — "plural"? And Selene looks in awe, and then glances at me... snickering. Rats! I should have been more careful sneaking downstairs as earlier in the ritual. They probably have known what happened last night and figured out...the real meaning of the creation of humans on Day six. This is the only way to make us immortal — by interpreting the sacred text in my way.

Why wasn't it Jack, this time? Oh, my steps were too heavy with *that thing*.

Never mind. Let me wait for *ten* of *them*, before I confess my sin.

"At least for the very first week, I don't feel that my nails are growing backwards, and in some sense, as long as I am breathing normally, I feel that I am not growing backward in time." Jack says, and then takes a deep breath, "And the oxygen carbon-biocide cycles feel very normal."

Everyone follows him, for whatever reason. It is so funny, like in a yoga class.

"Then why don't you think that we are still normal human-beings? Not growing younger, not immortal, and aging like a normal human?" Hera asks.

"No. That was the first thing I ruled out. Time arrow reversal has effects on our brains causing eclipses or maybe some other things. And your brain is an integral part of your body. Now, name a physical incident or physical phenomenon, at this large scale, that only does something to your brain, only to your brain."

"Ok. I get it." Hera says.

"I see it now. The marriage results, the actual twelve pairs, are not that important. What is more important is the process of the marriage ritual and the philosophy or the social structure hidden in it." Muse says.

"I agree. We marry, divorce, marry again with another person, and divorce again; have lots of children and grandchildren, and we will be worshipped by our offsprings as gods and goddesses. Your initial spouse, let me put this way, has very little to do with what will happen in the long coming future."

"Similarly, the initial amount of cash we have does not matter much either. Once we have infinite time, we have infinite resources. For whatever things aliens build for us, we can spend time to build them."

Most people are in deep thoughts about what this actually means. A few are whispering with excitement. I know, this is probably the best reward ever, for most people. But I finally notice that Nyx is tearing. It is strange. I didn't mention that it is an immortality hell as Eos said, but maybe the lavender has noticed that as well. Well, Eos is still on her book.

"So let us have a break and...sorry I need to run to the bathroom. Too much water." I say.

"Another proof that you are not growing backwards in time!" Jack says.

Before I run I quickly take a look at the sundial, with everyone laughing behind me.

Bad. The clouds start to accumulate.

xxxix   Moral

"Hidden quest one, so there will be more?" Tim asks, in the public bathroom.

You just want to come in for this question, right?

"Yeah...I wasn't expecting that, but I may have some clue."

"Do you think it might be related to the third possibility?" Tim murmurs, without other people hearing.

I look at him, and he is serious. "Possibly, so...we don't have much time left, according to the sundial, it is hard to read the exact time though."

"Then let us get things done as soon as possible."

"Say I have a...possible plan to avoid the third possibility, but we have to...eat those fruits and fish for a long time..." I look into his eyes, "I ordered seeds, back on Day five."

"Is this the true reason...you try to emphasize that we are immortal?"

I nod.

"Then do it." Tim answers without any hesitation.

I know.

"And my friend, for the time," He continues, "you could have asked the cat."

That was why people laughed at me! I feel I am truly the most stupid person on this planet.

"By the way, I am also curious about...why you asked your time related questions to the cat carefully without people noticing the issue, and why you didn't tell us about it before today? I mean, what is your true reason?"

I smile, "You know that, I love cats."

Out of the bathroom. Eos is waiting for me outside. What are you doing here?

"Are you waiting for me?"

Will you go straight into the men's room if the door does not stop you?

"Yes. *Finite simple group of order two.* The cat says it is a group, which means if you apply the operator twice, like multiply it by itself, then you get back the identity." The purple rose is reading from her notes and probably throwing me with some mathematical terms, but I roughly get the idea.

"So, what you mean is that, if we go back to the old Earth, then we become normal people." I try to slowly grasp her words, "And if you time everything well, then we can go back to the exact same time point when we left, and see mommy and daddy again. They won't even notice we have left for thousands of years and have become gods and goddesses for a long time, assuming we live long enough to develop the necessary science and technology for the travel."

"Yes, but we won't remember anything about them then. I still want to see my mother and my grandparents, or allow them to see me. The problem is, we are likely running out of time, right now." She continues, "But I believe Muse may have some extra clue."

Right, why does Miss 6 still have more knowledge after Eos obtained all the information regarding the time arrow and eclipses and immortality, plus a lot of extra fun mathematics?

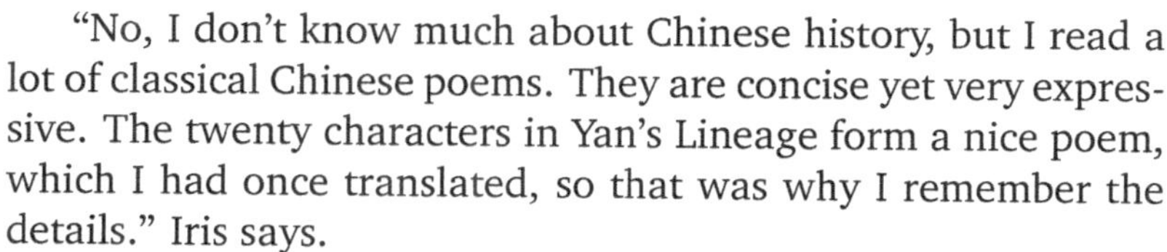

"No, I don't know much about Chinese history, but I read a lot of classical Chinese poems. They are concise yet very expressive. The twenty characters in Yan's Lineage form a nice poem, which I had once translated, so that was why I remember the details." Iris says.

"So what is the poem?" Circe asks.

"Look high at the great Heavens,
so you will be blessed by God;
Hold an ample virtue like the Earth,
so the regular laws can be respected on your land;
Be kind and pleasant to others,
to hold brothers and sisters with happiness;
Stay simple and still in your own life,
to follow the road of the ancestors."

Twenty characters to say all these words? They didn't have much paper during old times either. I have to admit these teachings voice the same tone — respecting gods, building morals, being kind to others and living in a simple life. Things like that were happening everywhere.

"So, what is your preferred story of the Prince of Yan, or our Prince Yan?" I sit down with Jack and whisper.

"Four, the king." Jack whispers.

"What? Tim?"

"No, it is not Tim, likely a coincidence. The first Prince of Yan, the fourth son of the first Emperor, overthrew his nephew, the second Emperor, and crowned himself, exactly six hundred years ago."

OK, that didn't sound like a "simple and still life", but I have to admit this was not uncommon throughout human history. Things like that were happening everywhere.

"However, in a Confucianist society where social morals such as loyalty are the highest standards, this was unacceptable. I guess the Prince of Yan's descendants are still unwilling to talk about the dark side of their history, after so many years — Their crown was not legally inherited."

"I see. That was why Yan didn't want to say it. Crown…"

"Yeah. The Crown has not left Yan's Lineage ever since, with only a few unsuccessful rebellions from other Lineages. Their northern capital had even been captured by Manchus for about two hundred years, but the Crown has stayed in the same Lineage. So in reality there is no 'Lineage of the Prince of Yan' within these twenty-four Lineages. Yan, I mean You-Yan, belongs to the Lineage of the Emperor."

Oh my God! So this was the missing one within the twenty-four! Things like that were happening everywhere!

"Just for your information, if you were a normal Chinese living in China, and if you say Yan is from the Lineage of the Prince of Yan, it would be...a death sentence."

I definitely hate this. I would never want to have any relation with these "royal" people. I believe that was why our ancestors came from all around the world, to establish our own country without kings and queens. This is ridiculous! It is just a joke!

The remaining people one by one come back from the bathrooms, and Tim kicks off.

"QX, how much time do we have till solar noon today, in old Earth hours?"

"Minus zero point eight seven hours."

"QX, how many hidden quests are there?"

"Two." QX says.

Good, only one more to go. "Two" has always been relieving, whereas "One" is terrifying, and "Six" is always amusing.

Six...where is that hidden couple who have not confessed themselves? Oh, it is a couple that split up, a *splitting pair* — No! It *was* a splitting pair back on Day two, but it is a real pair right now, at Sunday midnight!

And what about the remaining three people who had seen an eclipse on Day four? Probably not so relevant by now — or not?

"Can you say the target of Hidden Quest number two, or the reward?" Tim asks.

"This is classified information and cannot be released until the quest is complete." QX says.

"Of course it won't tell us, otherwise it won't be a hidden quest. We will have to figure it out by ourselves." Dennis says, "Anyone has any clues anywhere? Bizarre things like the eclipses, anything? We may be able to double our rewards again before the deadline."

Something is wrong — Let me go over the boys again — Excluded: Leo, William, Bran, plus Oliver, who was after Muse at the beginning, Frank, who was after Iris, Yan, who didn't seem to have anything special with Hera before, and Vincent, who is an honest boy with admirable virtues.

So who is the boy, and who is the girl?

I can hear some people whispering with each other, but no one speaks up. I am waiting for Muse the whole time, but Miss 6 doesn't seem to have anything else to say, though I cannot see clearly with Jack between us. Eventually I sigh to myself —

"I do — " Muse and I say in chorus.

What?

"OK. Sorry, lady first."

"No, you go ahead. I prefer to listen."

OK. Muse probably has the same secret.

"All right. I do, have a guess, just a guess, but I feel very bad to talk about it. Oh god, please forgive me."

"Hey, what is it?" Most people are curious and intrigued, "Split it out!"

"If my guess is wrong, please forgive me." I start, "I almost feel that I want to keep it as my own secret, but now we have a second hidden quest and it seems to me that this may be related, and for some reason I have to speak it out."

Finally even Eos is back from her book and looks at me. Sorry, I was waiting for Muse. People start to whisper again, but I don't want to listen.

I look at Jack, who is smiling and curious, like most other people, expecting from me another big secret, though I myself am in great sorrow.

I stand up, dash towards the center, and turn around. "Jack, my friend," I say with trembling voice, "you are one of *them*."

"What do you mean?" Bran asks, "Jack is an alien? How can you draw this conclusion?"

Muse...is still smiling.

Makes no sense.

"What I mean, is that Jack is not human — Even if his body is completely a human body, his brain, however, is governed by some fancy computer program, probably designed by the aliens. I believe he himself is totally unaware of this."

"How did you know that?" Asks Muse, "I don't believe a single word. I don't want to hear your voice anymore."

Why did you smile then?

I start repeating the joke Jack told with the two moons and my response, together with a brief history why Eos is on the moon and the first time Eos told the joke about a railgun. I hope the purple rose is not so offended.

"That was just a joke right?" Muse says, "Oh that was why you...I see."

"So after that, whenever I had a railgun in my hand, or whenever I was possessing the box with a railgun, Jack was then in this strange condition as if he believed firmly that I would shoot him. It is just like a programming bug, like a bug that is repeatable and verifiable, as the eclipses, or in any of those scientific experiments. It is deeply hard-coded in his brain now the firm belief that I will shoot him whenever I have a railgun in my hand." I try to ignore Muse's question.

"Was it the reason you asked for the gun?" Tim asks.

"Yes. So here is a simple experiment to prove or disprove what I just said. I feel so sorry, my friend. I won't shoot you, I promise." Another trump card. I rush to the kitchen, grab the big black box out of the cabinet where I hid last night. I bring it back to the center of the lobby, open it and hold the railgun with my hands, ready to fire, but pointing straight up to the ceiling, not to any person or rabbit.

"No! Stop!" Tim and Bran and Dennis cry out.

Then everyone notices Jack is trembling, very scared.

"What are you doing, Jack? He is not going to shoot you, I promise." Muse says.

"He is going to, shoot me! He is, very, serious! I, know it!" Jack runs to the back of the couch, trying to hide himself from me.

"No, he won't!"

"He, will!" Jack is breathing very hard.

"Asthma?"

No, I don't think so. I know Jack very well.

"No...I am, just...my heart, beats..."

Sorry. I put down my railgun and give it back to Tim. "Jack, come out, I don't have the railgun now."

It's like real magic — Jack is back to normal. "Sorry, but I don't know understand why I was so scared. I guess, I just cannot control myself emotionally whenever you have the railgun. It's like...magic."

"Are you...trying to trick us? When had you two planned for this?" Selene asks.

"No, no. I swear. It's real." Jack says.

"Sorry my friend. Need one more test." I am worried that Tim may not give the railgun back to me, but now everyone is stunned by Jack's reactions. I repeat this one more time and the result is the same.

"Jack, I am not even pointing the gun towards you." I say.

"No, you are not, but this is much worse." Bran says, "You could kill everyone here, within less than a second. It is almost like pointing the gun to everyone here. I know you won't fire it, but next time, please don't point the gun to the ceiling here, never in this room."

Ah?

"Fourth level, secret room. You know what is in there?" Tim says, "We had asked the cat before I fired to the wall."

Oh, the damn fusion reactor, the heart of the hotel. So what is in the basement then? Printer?

"I still don't understand it completely, but it won't produce anything like an atomic bomb if you shoot it. Maybe some small amount of radioactivity will leak and do some damage, but before that, the high pressure and high temperature environment inside it makes a perfect regular bomb. It won't do too much damage to the rabbits, but is good enough to demolish the hotel and kill everyone here."

"I am so sorry!" I feel tired and only have energy to read from my notes, "This is my guess. Human brains are complicated enough to distinguish jokes versus serious talks. If you try to write a computer program to do it, it is not easy. Eventually you run into bugs that regard jokes as serious matter or the other way around. So I believe, during that unnatural scene with the two moons, Jack's program ran into some strange loop or something, which caused a fatal bug that recognized my joke as a real threatening, and then by some strange mechanism hard-coded into his memory, which caused all subsequent reactions, whenever I had the railgun in my hand." My brain is not working properly so I just struggle to finish reading.

"I was actually very serious when I said that." Eos says.

I feel I want to grab the back of her neck and drag her out of here, like a mother cat grabs a kitten and throws it out.

"Could it be a mental disease?" Tim asks.

"No, mental diseases are totally different, and cannot heal in such a short time. This looks, just like a program bug, and it is repeatable. To me, Jack is at least controlled by some program instead of himself." Bran says, "So they can mimic everything we have on the Earth, but they cannot simulate human brains using computer codes. This may be the real reason they brought us here."

"Could this be still a new type of eclipse that other people have not experienced?" Muse asks.

I think for a while and do some quick calculations, "Well, I personally think there is such possibility, but it is small. At the moment with two moons, we were around five am on Wednesday morning, according to the note I gave you. At that moment, we were mostly sleeping, or at least on the bed. Not many interesting things were happening then on the old Earth timeline, especially compared to what we saw here."

"Maybe Jack was dreaming, for example the same scene with two moons, and at that very moment, he was recalling his dream, and it was dishappening, and he was seeing the same scene. All three events, at the same time, you may call a dual eclipse, three events colliding on the timeline, or like Venus and Mercury transit at the same time. Then, maybe, it caused some bigger brain malfunction, and when you told the joke about the railgun, it became coded into his brain as a real threat?" Muse comes up with the words, "Type III eclipse!"

"Sorry, I don't remember. Maybe I had a dream with multiple moons, but everything has dishappened so I don't remember." Jack says.

I vaguely remember Jack once mentioned something about his dream of multiple moons, but I feel hesitated to say it, and I think Jack also mentioned that people were clapping their hands, so things didn't match exactly, and I don't remember he has ever mentioned the exact date. Chance is too small. I totally understand that Muse is trying with every effort to prove that Jack is human, and I also agree that there is a slight chance that he is completely human, and there are possibly other types of eclipses that we don't fully understand. However, it is very hard to do some experiment in such a short time to repeat it before the solar noon, the real deadline, except maybe Zak and Artemis...No, no, no.

"Muse, I understand your words." Eos says and takes some notes, "However, back on Day four, when I saw the eclipse, I was in a similar situation as you just described. I tried to recall the memory; the memory dishappened; and some similar scene was happening at that moment. And with all three together I only saw the usual eclipse, and I didn't experience any severe brain damage that makes me believe something bizarre afterwards. No offense, but I have to say your theory does not work."

"But you kissed the little boy afterwards, right?" Muse asks, "Isn't it a proof that your brain was changed or modified by a Type III eclipse? Love itself is some sort of brain damage, right?"

I haven't seen Muse speaking like that before. I feel so sorry about it. My fault.

"Yes, that was our first kiss." Eos argues with red face, "At that moment, maybe my brain was *temporarily* governed by the shock after the eclipse, so it could be a Type III eclipse; but afterwards I felt totally normal, even together with him. I don't feel that my emotions are controlled by something else."

Yes, I remember I saw the same eclipse, the effect was only temporary, and I wouldn't swing between Eos and Iris afterwards if Muse's theory is correct. But I decide not to speak this out — While two goddesses are battling against each other by their spells, it is hard to murmur anything about it without being devastated by the fury of either one of them.

Muse stops arguing, but does not seem to believe the theory. Wait, you have another secret, right? Sorry I should let you speak first.

I look down at my final paragraph on my notes. Shall I read it out now? If I do, then likely everyone, including Muse and Jack, will believe what I said. However, I am afraid we may lose Jack forever.

If I give up and keep this as a secret, then it's hard to tell what may happen after the solar noon today, or even whether there is such a future, as several of us have already suspected. The aliens timed everything so well that caused some extra concerns among us. The second hidden quest was probably designed based on it, and as Bran said, most likely the aliens want to kidnap us to study the human brain, and if we cannot find and convince ourselves the anomaly within our own companions, then our brains are not advanced enough for their study.

This is a much more difficult decision compared to the one from yesterday. Regardless of my choice of either Eos or Iris, it is just the very beginning of a long run and it wouldn't change much of the rest of the history, like a small ripple that eventually evens out by itself on a big pond.

With Jack, the situation is very different. Shall I sacrifice Jack to keep everyone else happy, or keep everyone else alive? If it is a question about life or death, then I feel I would do it, so would Eos and Tim. But what if the reward of the Hidden Quest Two is only to double our cash again? Then shall I try it? Probably not, and I would stay silent and keep the hope that Jack only suffers from some strange mental disease.

I start to see it is the same as Muse's moral problem. I am facing the ultimate risk of my own death, and so I lower my moral standards to shoot other people. I feel that it is definitely not right, but cannot restrain myself from doing it, especially when there is a reasonable chance that Jack is not human. Eos, Tim and Muse are probably facing the same moral question, and among them, Muse has sided with Jack, all the time.

If I give up, still there is a bigger problem: the third possibility of instant death at noon. Shall I tell people about it, tell people that we may be able to destroy QX but lose everything we could have and start everything by ourselves, and then ask everyone to vote? How could we vote to risk our own lives, or even worse, risk other people's lives? How can we even vote, when one side of the balance is *life*?

This is totally different from the vote back on Day three. There it was a *"for all"* vote, that we shall process the tax plan only when everyone agrees; here it is really an *"there exists"* vote, that we shall process this plan as long as one person agrees to destroy QX, or, equivalently, as long as any single one of us does not want to risk their own life.

So, there is really no vote at all. I agree and the plan shall be processed, logically. That was also why Tim said "do it". But still something does not feel right. I don't think I have the right to make this big decision alone — I would rather avoid this plan, keep it as a backup, and hope to solve the issue by accomplishing *the* hidden quest first — and then, damn, there are two of them.

The clock is ticking — if there were one. Logic is no longer helping me in this scenario, and the lavender is not in the right mood to answer any fortune-telling questions either. I close my eyes. Memories with Jack flush into my brain — bridge, video games, homework, and most importantly, jokes.

"QX,"

What? I quickly exchange some eye contact with *her*. Don't! Don't! Don't! That single *spell* costs at least four million dollars now! People will be very angry! It's a backup plan! And we don't even know if it works! Be patient! Muse has some other clue, you don't remember?

She ignores me and continues: "how many human beings are there in this hotel?"

Safe — and, good question. Very clever.

"This is classified information and cannot be revealed." QX answers.

What? This sounds very, very suspicious. Even worse than a simple answer less than twenty-four.

Oh, this is it. This is the type of questions that, even if QX refuses to give an answer, we still get some sneaky information.

"So, the answer is likely less than twenty-four?" Tim murmurs, looking through everyone.

"Well, the answer is likely zero, as we are unable to call ourselves human-beings anymore. We don't age normally or even grow younger." I say.

"Maybe Jack was a complete normal human when the aliens kidnapped him, and then they somehow installed their own program codes into his brain." Bran says.

All right, let's try one more time, last attempt, in my way. People are still whispering, but I guess the cat can still hear me.

"QX," I ask, "at the time you invited us, back on the old Earth, how many human-beings did you invite to this hotel? By human-beings I mean humans with a human body that would eventually age like most other humans on the Earth, and together with a human brain without your interference."

Everyone is waiting quietly.

"Twenty-Three." QX answers.

"Oh — my — goodness —" Tim says.

"QX," I need a final confirmation, "suppose right now you take all of us back to the old Earth without changing anything, using the same method you brought us here, how many human-beings, under the same definition as in my previous question, will be there upon arrival?"

"Twenty-Three." QX answers again.

"I—do—not—trust—that—cat!" Muse is furious and crying, and tears burst out, "I hate this!"

Jack is stunned as well. He probably believes it by now. These two answers lead to the obvious logical conclusion. The only remaining one is Muse, and it requires something more than the cat.

Twenty-Three. It is the time to finish my notes — my third and final trump card. Something is still missing, but time is running out. The ultimate death of the third possibility and the ultimate moral problem are both pounding me like hammers.

"Yesterday you corrected Circe by saying that we are Adams and Eves, Jack, which was not quite accurate. Circe was right." I say, "We are Adam and Eve. We, as a whole group, form Adam; Or maybe this hotel is Adam, and that hole," I point to the hole which is still covered by a couch, "is where God opens the body of Adam and later heals it back." I pause, to calm myself down from tearing, "And You, Jack, my, best friend — you are, the missing rib."

"How many ribs do we have?" People start to count on themselves.

"Twelve pairs, so...twenty-four." Says Circe, without hesitation but with total astonishment. Others stay in awe as well, including Muse and Jack himself.

"Jesus!" Tim cries out.

"Oh my Lord." William is with tears. Even he is stunned by this.

The third bomb.

As I finish reading my notes, I have a glance on Nyx's face and immediately realize what I was missing: Group, Operator, Multiply, Identity. Of course we get the same number back on arrival! And Muse is having better knowledge than Eos and me — just because we had the wrong knowledge that counts as negative! I cannot help myself from falling down on my knees and crying without reservation. I probably have lost my best friend, forever. It is the same feeling of a five-year-old losing their favorite pet rabbit, by their own fault. What have I done? I shouldn't do it! Jack, you are completely human! That was in fact a Type III eclipse! I do believe it, please! Two kinds of Type III eclipses! Reality versus Dreams. Eos and I had a Type III-a and you had a Type III-b! That's why they are different!

I made the worst decision in my life — Jack was attacked by an infinite loop malfunction as Bran mentioned earlier, an infinite loop of dreams, and my words became an oracle embedded deep deep in his subconscious — I try to calm down and sum up my thoughts.

"System announcement: Hidden Quest Two has been accomplished. Quest reward: Continue to Phase II with all the restrictions removed." Says QX.

This time, no one wants to ask what the quest target is.

Oh my god! The first one is a "for all", and the second is a "there exists"! It only needs one of us to obtain the knowledge!

Jack comes to me, with tears in his eyes as well, and hugs me by his firm arms.

"Sorry about what I am. I didn't know it, you know. You are still my best friend." He says.

"Yes, Jack, you are still my best friend. You are still a completely normal human being. It is fine, my friend. You just had a very rare eclipse that changed your mind." I speak slowly as I hug him firmly. "I shall say sorry."

"Kant is right." Muse murmurs.

EPILOGUE

xl Loves

I t has been at least a thousand years and today is another special day. I am attending a grand religious ritual, worshipping the primordial twenty-four gods and goddesses. Well, I am not a big fan of worshipping these gods; Goddesses? Maybe. Nevertheless I think it is a good opportunity to give my little daughter a lesson in astronomy and history before I have to leave, and her great-grandma also asked me to attend the ritual for her. I have to respect the oldest lady in a family.

However, for whatever reason, she does not like me, or rather, she didn't want me to marry her precious and beloved grand-daughter in the first place. I know, my Y chromosome had worn out many years ago, so I am no longer a "man" in the strict sense. Well, my daughter is still very healthy and clever as her great-grandma.

The ritual starts with a High Priestess at the highest altar reciting some ancient script using a very old language that only very small group of priests and priestesses can understand and use fluently, and primarily used in religious ceremonies.

The High Priestess is standing in front of a marble platform with these three sacred items on it, all of which have significant religious meanings according to Standard Mythology: A sundial, with which we acquire knowledge; A pen with a writing pad, with which we keep knowledge as our own; A long rope, with which we apply knowledge to change the world.

"On this Seventeenth Day of the Month of Wisdom, Week Three, Wednesday, A.D. Thirty-Seven Thousand Four Hundred and Eight, Year of the Goddesses, we gather here to praise the Gods and Goddesses who created the Heavens and the Earth."

"Let us praise —

the God of Logic
the Goddess of Darkness
the Goddess of Light
the God of Power and the King of the Gods
the God of Faith
the Goddess of Wisdom
the God of Skill
the God of Knowledge
the Goddess of Life and White Moon
the Goddess of Judgement and Red Moon
the God of Death
the Goddess of Love
the Goddess of Fortune
the God of War
the Goddess of Medicine
the God of Wine
the Goddess of Happiness
the God of Virtue
the Goddess of Earth
the Goddess of Stars
the God of Sun
the God of Silence
the God of Hope
and the Goddess of Message

for their guidance and their blessings ...... Let their greatness shine through the universe and let our faith stay in our minds forever."

As the High Priestess goes through the list of gods and goddesses, my daughter also goes through the fancy deck of cards in her hands. It is similar to something called "tarot" but I cannot remember anything other than the name. Numbered cards from one to twenty-four with iconic illustrations representing each of the gods and goddesses. Very common in early education to teach kids numbers as well as some old style religion.

For example, card number I representing the God of Logic is the picture of a young man pointing to the sky with the three sacred items on a table; II, the Goddess of Darkness, is a middle-aged woman with a crystal ball sitting beneath the night sky with the galaxy and other stars; III, Light, a young girl sitting on a throne in a forest with grassland and a creek, wearing a gown and a crown, and holding a yellow book; IV, Power, a man who is clearly the king, with lightning in hand; V, Faith, a man who dresses like a High Priest; VI, Wisdom, a beautiful girl taming a beast and turning it into a human...

To symbolize their independent discoveries of Eternity, only Logic and Wisdom have the infinity symbol above their heads, which is an abstract flow chart of how a civilization can live forever inside spacetime with two very distant planets.

In Standard Mythology, the God of Logic comes the very first in order, because he has two Great Accomplishments: First, he revealed the true identities of the Sun and the Moons; Second, he was the first to fully understand all four types of eclipses: partial, total, ring and finally dual eclipses. In other, nonstandard stories or fairy tales, he can also cast powerful magic spells, for example, summoning water from the sacred rope, or, creating a huge fireball to eliminate an entire country.

Well, the standard version contains mostly misreadings and misinterpretations. They even changed singular to plural to make things fit. But the nonstandard version is almost accurate, except that the Fire magic has never been used, not even once. Because it's Water, not Fire!

"Dad, what is A.D.?" My daughter interrupts me from my

reminiscence.

"*Annō Deōrum* or *Annō Deārum*, meaning 'in the year of the Gods' or 'in the year of the Goddesses', respectively, depending on whether the year is odd or even. So 'the year of Goddesses' is actually redundant in the script. Similarly the week number and the weekday are also redundant. Yet most people think A.D. stands for the Amalgamation Document. No, it is not. It is in a very ancient language, and the same for am and pm."

"Dad, Goddess of Wisdom is third Goddess from list, but why Month of Wisdom is fifth of year? God of Logic is first, and Month of Logic is first month in year of God-s."

"Good question. The list of months using Goddesses names looks like out of order, same for the years of Gods. At the beginning, Gods and Goddesses decided to take turns to cook food for everyone, and each turn lasted one month, four weeks exactly. The current ordering reflects the orders they took turns."

"Why God of Power is King of God-s? He only is fourth right?"

"4 the king...sorry, old joke. This order of Gods and Goddesses has nothing to do with social or political power. The God of Power is actually a very nice g...God, and friendly to everyone. And, cookies and breads were the best during the his month. So he became the leader."

"Why year of Goddess has one more day? Who cook at that day?"

"Oh, the Amalgamation Day, which is not in the standard week cycles. It is related to the exact number of days in a year...Now look, here they come —"

Two lines of girls coming into the altar waiting, one line of girls dressed in pure white robes and the other line in crimson red.

Ha-ha, it is time for my secret device. I take a small black box out of my backpack.

"Dad, what is it?"

"It is called a *camera*."

"Ke-mer-ra-?"

"Ca-mera. It can take photos. More precisely it records the wavelengths of photons and stores all the data in a digital format. Look —"

"Ah-mazing!"

Yeah, I have to bribe these priests in the Temple of Skill to steal one from their labs. The Temple of Light has some as well, but these priestesses are almost impossible to negotiate. They want to control everything nowadays, from gun powder to fusion reactors, and so technology is developing...quite slowly. It does not matter much. We have enough time. Safety is always our first priority.

"Come over. Stand still. Say *Cheese* —"

"Daddy, can I have try? You say cheese —"

"Sorry, Honey, this is not allowed."

Sorry, normal people could face ten years in prison just by holding this device, and taking a picture of me would be...a death sentence.

I know, we finally live in a way that we hated.

"Daddy — Daddy —"

I need to find something to distract her from it.

"Look at the girls — The colors they wear represent the red moon and the white moon." I say, "So today is a very special day."

"Why?"

I am not sure how she will remember me in the future, maybe only a blurred figure. Sadly I don't remember anything about my own daddy, except that he was bringing back books.

"We are going to see a dual eclipse, which only happens on average every one thousand years or so somewhere on the Earth, and for a certain place, the reoccurrence is so rare that you don't expect even the gods and goddesses have seen it."

"Dad, what is doow-eek-leeps?"

"Roughly saying the two moons are having the solar eclipse at the same time, and the strict definition relies on the existence of a spacetime null geodesic intersecting all four bodies: the Sun, the Earth and two Moons. What is rare about today's eclipse is that it comes with a total eclipse of the white moon and a ring eclipse of the red moon. Hold your sunglasses. They are different from the ones we use for hunting eagles. Let us enjoy the show first."

To be honest, I don't even know if I have another chance to see the next such dual eclipse — not because I won't live long enough, but because in a long run three-body motions are quite unpredictable and the red moon can be thrown out of the system at any moment.

The priestesses have timed the eclipse very well, and the High Priestess starts to recite the final piece of the ancient script.

**"Logic leads us through Darkness, and embraces Light.
With Faith, we gain Power,
and with Knowledge and Skill, we gain Wisdom."**

The High Priestess needs to recite these three lines multiple times with a fixed interval between them. After each such recitation, two girls, one from each line, come close to the center and write down their names on a piece of paper, and separate and leave the altar. As the ritual continues, four of the girls, two pairs, are summoned to the high altar, standing together with the High Priestess.

The eclipse starts, as usual, the sun fades at a small corner, and gradually turns into a crescent moon shape.

"OK. This is a Standard Ritual and sometimes people call it a Marriage Ritual, like couples marrying each other. They changed it again this time. In the old ritual procedure, five of the girls were summoned, in the end, which has some religious representations. But I guess with red and white robes, it is a bit asymmetric, so the High Priestess is representing the fifth person this time, and as a result it makes more sense to summon the girls before the end of the ritual, and to allow the others to leave the altar, so they don't have to stand for too long." I say, "Over the time, they changed a lot of things — Writing down names instead of crossing out names; Girls only instead of girls and boys; and they doubled the number of people as well. Lots of faithful families wanted to send their daughters to the ritual and planned everything on it. People were able to predict the exact date and time of this eclipse a few hundred years ago — It is just general relativity and Riemannian geometry."

Yeah, a lot of crazy things have happened beneath the tip of the iceberg, just like what happened, no, what will happen later, on the other, dark side of the universe. It is very dark there, I promise to the Gods and Goddesses.

The last change from five to four, however, still agrees with the conceptualization of the original ritual, just by accident.

As I remember, when the God of Faith established Standard Mythology and designed this sacred ritual around A.D. three thousand, I forced or bribed him to add in this extra script, with the help from the Goddess of Light or the Goddess of Love, I cannot remember exactly, to confuse the believers and hide ourselves from our real identities, and for fun as well. It has its own merit I need to say. Without logic, arguments become quarrels, information becomes propaganda, language becomes bureaucratese, and communication becomes accusation. Logic helped us through the dark ages and let us see the light. Only then we started to gain power and wisdom and all other things.

"Dad, why five?"

"Oh, this is representing the original ritual. And," I decide to tell an old joke, "human lungs have five lobes, two to the left and three to the right."

She nods with her little head. Seems she is OK with it.

"Dad, Goddess of Darkness is a bad goddess?"

"No, not at all. She is probably the only deity who is much older than all other gods and goddesses. Long before the other gods and goddesses became immortal, the Goddess of Darkness had already been a goddess, in another distant world. That's why she is special, and why people put the Amalgamation Day at the end of her month, sometimes also called the twenty-ninth of...Darkness."

"Dad, Mommy told me, in S-dundard Miso-lagy, Goddess of Darkness has rested, right? Isn't she a goddess? What have killed her?"

"Time."

More precisely, the time flow operator, but my daughter is too young to understand abstract algebra or general relativity. I pause for some time and continue, "In this new world, the Goddess of Darkness lost her power and aged as a mortal, despite the use of elixirs provided by the Goddess of Medicine. Finally she perished and returned to the darkness."

Yeah, that was a sad story, the first funeral of our colony. She is the missing rib after all.

"The Goddess of Darkness therefore only had a relatively small number of descendants, whose family has been since protected by the other gods and goddesses throughout the ages of war and peace, order and chaos, as well as abundance and famine. The Goddess of Medicine and the God of Virtue once even became their private tutors. No other family in the history has received the same privilege. We all believe that the Goddess of Darkness will one day be reborn — So the Goddess of Darkness is not an evil goddess and she represents the age of darkness: fortune-telling, astrology, magic, alchemy and mystery. Then the Goddess of Light represents the new age."

"What is new age?"

"The age of mathematics, of course, and Logic is the key. Oh, finally, look!"

We are fully covered by the darkness. The beautiful stars reveal themselves, like on that day when we first saw them. The horizon around us, except for the west side, looks even brighter than the remaining sky, like during dawn or dusk. And, the sun —

A black hourglass.

"Dad, what is that?"

"The corona. And you can see the outline of a 'black' red moon by the side as well, but it is a bit smaller and so cannot form a total eclipse by itself."

The ritual also continues, and I still can't remember how many times the High Priestess has recited the script. Each time I was in such a ritual, it reminded me that her great-great-grandma had claimed, multiple times, that she did not want to hear my voice again. I totally understand, and that was maybe the reason why the number was cut down to twelve initially.

The sunlight comes back again from the other side, hiding most of the outlines of both moons. Instead of another crescent moon, it looks like two commas, or two sharp teeth. "Rabbit's Teeth" as people call them. I remember the God of Skill once got them as a Lucky item of the day due to an unknown bug, and he has since used it to symbolize himself, wearing it on his head like a coronet whenever he visited the sacred site where the Goddess of Darkness has rested, and on his card as well, which also shows two full size humanoid robots he invented, even better than the ones a black cat once had.

"After a while, when the red moon is in the middle of the sun, you can see an incomplete ring of sunlight, like the third letter, C, in the ancient alphabet. But at that time you won't be able to see the stars as it will be too bright. Finally the C shape will turn back into a crescent moon shape and it will look like the end of a ring eclipse with the red moon. No, in fact, it will look like the end of a total eclipse with the white moon."

"Dad, Mommy says, Sun is a big fire ball, right?"

"Right, much much bigger than us, and very far away. The moons are closer, and smaller."

"Dad, Mommy asks me to try this: Every creature on Earth lives on energy from sunlight, so Fire is Ilement of Life, right?"

"No! Listen, it is Water, not Fire!" I don't know why but I suddenly lose control of my emotions, "Sorry, Honey, let us enjoy the show first. It does not happen very often."

I have seen it about ten times prior to this one, but I need to admit it is still very breathtaking. Each time the pattern was somewhat different. The first time it was like two consecutive solar eclipses, so strictly saying not a dual eclipse, depending on how you define it. But we saw an hourglass, a golden one. Once it was like a crown with three points, and I remember I crowned the King of Musoria on that day at that time, very rare and clever choice for a coronation. It's hard to imagine that I was willing to do that. Time changes everyone.

And there was a slightly boring one which looked exactly the same as a regular partial solar eclipse, as the red moon was completely in front of the white one most of the time. It reminds me of these various kinds of lunar eclipses as well, not necessarily in full moons — a darker red moon; a bigger red moon; two red moons; the red moon over the white moon; moons casting shadows over to each other; and much less common when the shadow of the Earth covers both moons together and you see yet another hourglass, a red one. Yeah, maybe I failed to order hourglasses at that time, so I got to see them in the sky. Things are much more interesting when you have two moons, assuming you live long enough.

Well, at the beginning, we didn't have any good predictions for the eclipses, except for asking the black cat during the very first five years and later asking the Goddess of Darkness instead. Afterwards, it was hard to arrange travel plans, only recently we were able to see these more often, and it had been a good opportunity to gather together and chat.

Last time I attended a dual eclipse was about fifteen hundred years ago — I can never remember the exact date or even the exact year that early on — when I met the God of Virtue, who finally gifted me wooden sculptures of two Goddesses who struck me with great love, which I had requested literally for thousands of years, which also clearly violated Article Ten of the CODES that strictly prohibits productions of any visual replica or recording of any God or Goddess in any format; as well as the

God of Death and the Goddess of Judgement and Red Moon, who, according to Standard Mythology, together govern the red moon, the world after death, for their maybe the ninth or tenth or eleventh remarriage, and I finally sent my sincere apologies for shooting the Goddess of Judgement and Red Moon in the guessing game and earning an extra of forty thousand dollars from them, which didn't make up my huge losses I need to say. But I was doing it just for fun, I promise to the Gods and Goddesses.

I have been so deep in my enjoyable reminiscence that I suddenly notice my Honey is crying. I know, it is her first time seeing a total eclipse and it is astonishing, especially the second half, with the red moon, after it suddenly appeared in the sky. It looks now totally obvious the moons are huge balls hovering above us, shadowing the sun and moving at different speeds.

"It is ok, Honey. It is just a natural phenomenon. Once you understand the principle behind it, it becomes natural." I pat her little head and try to explain.

"Daddy, you are a robot, very old model, made by, God, of Skill, right? Don't worry! Mommy, and I, still love you!" She sobs out her words.

What? How can you draw this conclusion?

"Sorry, may we have your ID please, little boy?"

I am stunned by these words alone — the purity of this ancient accent, as pure as some rigid form of Element Six. My shy little girl hides herself behind me, sobbing and wiping her tears — Two big girls are standing there in the dim sunlight, one in white and one in red.

My hands with the camera are shaking badly, just like the God of Virtue last time. What! I didn't know you two were there among the girls! I just took a picture, and it is blurred! You cannot identify anyone from it! I — I don't want to spend three more years in Garank! I just want to keep a picture of my lovely daughter, and that's it! I promise to...you, my goddesses!

I have to admit the security personnel within the Temple of Wisdom system are so efficient that it takes no time for them to identify an oddity and report all the way up to the highest level — they run the Museum system for a good reason. I once sneaked into the Temple of Logic myself, as a priest or a librarian from the Temple of Knowledge, and chatted with these kids and told many jokes from my own life, and a report entitled *Recent incidents of unauthorized and unidentified visitors* finally appeared on my desk a hundred years later.

But, seriously? You decided to take two of these precious and even priceless positions to worship yourselves, and ruthlessly destroy the lovely dreams of two innocent princesses, who would be tearing back in their rooms just like my Honey did, or more like you two did once a while ago? Of course, I dare not convert my very sneaky thoughts into aero-vibrations through my throat and tongue, as one of them has once claimed to threaten my life with a railgun. Wait, why was my Honey crying?

"Glad to see you both, ladies." I say, trying to pretend to be as calm as possible.

Oh, railgun. It is his month after all.

The God of Knowledge has rested, due to a strange flu, since July twenty-first, eighty-three seventy-seven, at eleven twenty pm Standard Musiack Time — it must be dark as hell since he always says he doesn't like turning on the light — otherwise he would right now stand by my side and make more jokes on me, assuming I do not have a railgun in my hand.

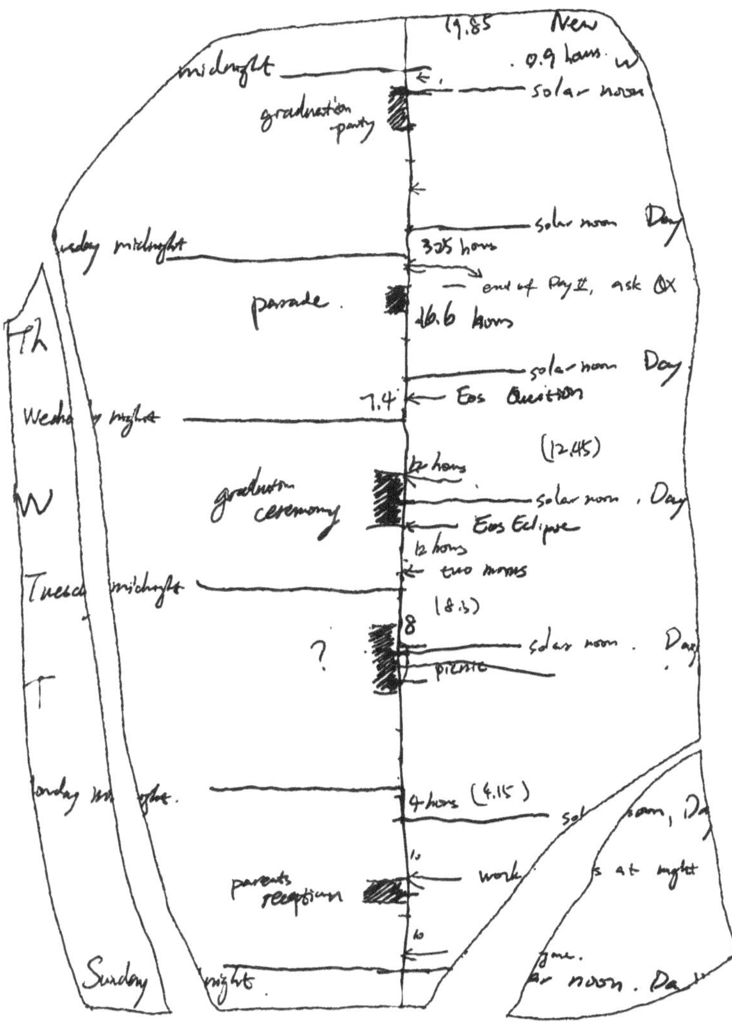

(9.85
New
0.9 hours
solar noon
midnight
graduation party
Sunday midnight
325 hours
solar noon   Day
end of Day II, ask Ox
46.6 hours
parade
solar noon   Day
7.4   Eos Question
Wednesday night
(12.45)
12 hours
graduation ceremony
solar noon . Day
Eos Eclipse
12 hours
two moons
(8.3)
Tuesday midnight
8
?
solar noon . Day
picnic
4 hours (4.15)
Monday morning
solar noon, Day
parents reception
work   is at night
Sunday night
noon. Da

The Amalgamation Document   "The most important piece of paper in the history of humankind." This is the only copy that is currently known to exist, a generous donation to Reathim National Museum from the Duke of Nexbran, whose family self-claimed as the only direct descendants of the Goddess of Darkness, though recent genetic test showed that they are all descendants of the God of Skill. The era name "A.D." directly came from the Amalgamation Document in the ancient language. According to Standard Mythology, the God of Logic used this sacred Document to reveal the eclipses and unite all the gods and goddesses into one — the "Amalgamation of Divine Agreement on Mortals", or the "Amalgamation" for short, and there are twenty-four exact identical copies of this divine document, each of the Gods and Goddesses holding a copy as a representation of the divine contract. Historians had pinned down several possible dates of this document based on the solar "Eclipse" that was recorded in one afternoon, but all these dates received various skepticism based on other evidences. Therefore, most modern researchers believe that the Amalgamation is only a religious concept in Standard Mythology, and the said document is an ancient counterfeit, due to the other undecipherable drawings of lines and scripts on it, and the lack of any wording related to contract or agreement.

Acknowledgements

An academic research paper always has a list of references or bibliographies, which consists of older research papers that led to the current research. Literature books usually do not have such references, as it is hard for authors to tell exactly where each piece of idea came from. They usually read many many books before writing down their own. We, however, had read only very few fictions before writing this novel, much fewer than any of the novelists. We shall apologize for the immature style and language skills in this book. The only benefit of the lack of reading history is to allow us to track where our ideas or styles are from exactly piece by piece, which we want to elaborate here as a list of references.

[1] The narrating and commenting style of the protagonist "I" was from the main character Kyon in *Suzumiya Haruhi series* by Tanigawa Nagaru.

[2] This novel is a "light mystery", or you may call a "mystery without crime or murder", which we learned from our reading of *Classic Literature Club* (*Koten-bu*) *series*, also commonly known as *Hyouka series* by Yonezawa Honobu. It reminded us the golden days when humans were not yet controlled by these little *Six-Fourteen interfaces* we hold in our hands.

[3] The marriage game was inspired by Hall's Marriage Theorem by Philip Hall, whose original paper *On Representatives of Subsets* was published in 1935 in the Journal of London Mathematical Society.

[4] We also would like to thank our old friend Cui Aoxiang for the computational complexity analysis, or Big-O analysis of the marriage game.

[5] Gödel's Incompleteness Theorem was of course from the Second Incompleteness Theorem in the paper *On Formally Undecidable Propositions of Principia Mathematica and Related Sys-*

tems I by Kurt Gödel, originally published in 1931 in Monatshefte für Mathematik.

[6] The idea of immortality was from the movie *The Man from Earth* written by Jerome Bixby. The idea of infinite loops of dreams and subconscious was from the famous movie with the spinning top. "Finite simple group of order two" was from the song of the same name written by Matt Salomone, originally performed by the Klein Four.

[7] The time line plot of this novel was following the Old Testament, written by God, either according to the most search results from the internet, or according to the novel itself.

[8] The Chinese ancient fortune-telling method mentioned in the novel was from a real ancient fortune-telling book *Classic of the Divine Chess* or *Ling Qi Jing*, by an anonymous author and with comments by some ancient scholars: Yan Youming from Jin Dynasty, He Chengtian from Liu Song Dynasty, Chen Shikai from Yuan Dynasty and Liu Ji from Yuan and Ming Dynasty.

[9] The retrograde dates came from a question on *StackExchange*, answered by user21.

https://astronomy.stackexchange.com/questions/32426

But we ignored the inaccuracy regarding Pluto, for reasons stated in the novel.

[10] The idea of two moons came from our dream back on May 14, 2020. Other parts of the novel were mostly logical consequences of a few axioms: One, time is different and has consequences on human body and human thought; Two, no one is lying except for joking, though not necessarily telling the truth; Three, Eos is smart, Muse is smarter and Nyx is always right.

[11] We would like to thank Huang Yinxiao and Ying Xiaowei, two old friends from high school, for alpha-reading the novel and providing invaluable feedbacks. We graduated without knowing how the world would change after twenty whole years.

[12] The book was typeset using LaTeX with some packages such as lettrine, remreset, sectsty, pgfornament and fancyhdr; the cover was designed using LaTeX with PGF/TikZ and MnSymbol. The short-term stability of the two-moon planetary system is verified using *REBOUND*, an N-body integrator.

About the Author

A Sack Prize winner, the author loves mathematics and logic. He also loves his family members, whom he values the most and trusts the most without any reservation. He is currently living with his family in Georgia, USA, a very lucky consequence of a series of events of extremely low probability.

It was a big challenge for him to write his first novel in English since his language skill is minimal as a non-native speaker. There were roughly two reasons. The first reason was that it was fun and he had done crazier things in the past; the second reason was placed somewhere in the novel.

The author hopes this novel smells logical along the pages. The author also apologizes for one big inconsistency deeply hidden in the novel, up to this point, and it will resolve by the end of the novel — No, the prologue is not the start of the novel, and the epilogue is not the end.

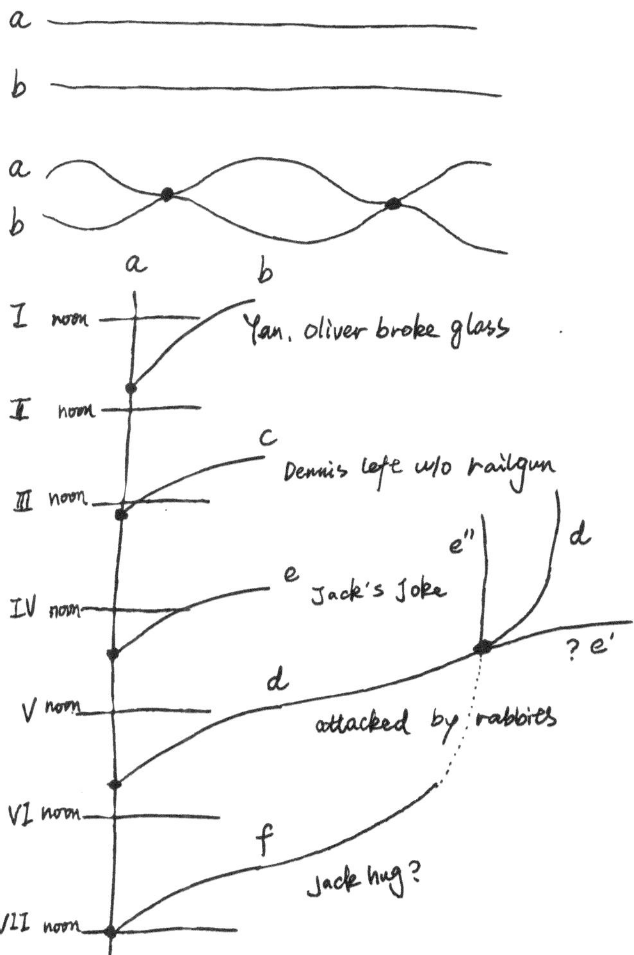
a
b
a
b
a
b
I noon
Yan. oliver broke glass
II noon
c
Dennis left w/o railgun
III noon
e''
d
e Jack's Joke
IV noon
? e'
d
V noon
attacked by rabbits
f
VI noon
Jack hug?
VII noon

DAY VII

xli Divergence

Noon. The cat starts to announce the matching results. The remaining ones of us sit in the lobby, feeling the total helplessness.

"Nyx and Bran."

Nyx is 1, if my dream is real. The artificial voice echoes in the empty lobby and our empty minds.

"Eos."

OK, she is single, not surprising. The three of us are honest people. But I am quite embarrassed that she has been staring at me after the cat announced the solar noon. We have had a couple of eye contacts. It seems that she wants to say something, but is reluctant to speak in public. Have you changed your mind, Eos, on the very last day? Sorry, I have a bride now, and there is no way to change any of my choices. *Thanks. No. No. Thanks.* When did she say that? College?

"Tim and Iris."

Not surprising either, and if Tim was honest with both girls last night, it implies that Iris has higher rank than Rhea, but no one cares about it by now. It was a fair competition.

"William and Circe."

He is still holding his Bible, murmuring. We had this friendly discussion yesterday. He has to enter a marriage, fake or not, for us to maximize rewards, and Gaia agreed as well. Anyway, regarding the girls, they didn't have many choices left in the hotel. Most of them would put their true love, either someone here or in the forest, plus two extras who stayed in the hotel. Tim and William are more popular than Bran and me. This is the safest and most logical option. Not for Eos, of course. Eos is Eos. So we boys essentially were forced into marriage, just like Eos...a few days ago? When was that? Anyway, it finally boiled down to this rank shenanigans.

"They simply follow the matching order of the algorithm. If this is true, then the next couple is two of us, I am sure." Muse has been lost in thoughts for a while, and so luckily hasn't noticed anything fishy with Eos and me, as far as I can tell. "We shall thank Tim and William again."

I agree. It is much easier to obtain trust among people, when there are only a few left.

"Muse and ..." QX says.

I cannot hear clearly. My ears have had some strange but minor issues since I woke up yesterday. But my name is on the screen. Holding Muse's hand, I feel so luckily that Muse's rank is high enough so that we can be matched quite early. Matches will soon become chaotic, if the system is still making them.

"Jack and Hera."

"Jack is still alive!" I cry out, "This means Jack is still alive! We need to save him!" I can't believe it! He is still alive after three whole days!

"Calm down. Maybe the system is still doing matches based on the last available information when they left." Tim says.

Eos stands up and runs upstairs, without a word.

Hey, you want to show some politeness. It is not finished yet. We may still get some information about the other people.

"Selene."

Selene immediately bursts into tears. Right. This means only one thing. The system does not match dead people.

Maybe Dennis put three other girls there? I shake my head. The chance is too low, and in this case Selene's daddy will fly all the way here to shoot him, I am sure.

"Rhea."

OK. I have a bad feeling.

"Gaia."

Selene cries even louder this time. Oh, she probably knows that Gaia is of lower rank than Dennis, by whatever logic, so even the last chance is gone. Iris and Circe are hugging her, saying a few words of comfort.

Others are silent at the moment, waiting for the real death sentence.

"We continue to Phase II of the project. The guessing game gains and losses have been applied to your accounts, and good luck everyone." QX announces.

The other guys...Now I know why Eos left early. She probably had foreseen everything and so left before this very sad moment, but why did she know that Jack is the only survivor among them? Maybe she bypassed QX's internal logic and got information regarding people's survival status? How? If she did, why didn't she tell us? It still does not make much sense, but it's not the time to think about Eos at the moment.

"QX, Muse and I shall have one million dollars in our joint account. We want you to save Jack and bring him here, regardless of cost." I say.

"You don't have one million dollars in your account," QX says, "but I can send the robots for the price I told you earlier."

Shit. I look at Iris. Muse is right. *The higher the risk, the lower the moral.* Iris probably regrets it by now, but obviously this was an easy way to maximize rewards, especially if Tim matches with Rhea in the end.

When did Muse tell me this? Last few days have been so chaotic that I cannot even trust my own memory.

"Do you feel it?" Muse asks.

"Yes, like an earthquake. Oh, I know, robots versus rabbits."

We don't have much else to do while waiting in the lobby for the cat to save Jack. Most others have been back in their rooms, and I have this bad feeling that some probably will never reappear. We have our fingers crossed, and for the first time wish the aliens are as powerful as they claim to be.

"I have a new theory." Muse says.

"What is it? This new world — " I ask.

We have been discussing over some theories regarding our strange feelings during the recent few days on this new planet, but nothing has been very satisfactory.

"It works on the old Earth as well." Muse starts, "I believe that there are different timelines, or different world lines, or multiverses or parallel universes as you may call. What we have experienced, or our strange memories, may came from a different parallel universe, a different world line of us."

"I've heard stories like that, but how can we remember things from another parallel universe?"

"Don't know. I guess there is some kind of wave through spacetime, like a ripple through a pond, that vibrates our own universe or our own world line, which makes it in contact with other world lines. Let me show you a picture."

Muse takes out her writing pad and draws two parallel lines.

"The top line we call world line a, which is our own world line. The bottom line we call world line b, a totally different one. They are originally parallel, never intersect, and we don't know anything about what is happening there in world line b."

"OK." Why don't you use the more common word, *timeline*?

"I have to say the use of *world line* here does not agree exactly with its classical interpretation in relativity. I am really talking about the world line of this whole Earth or this whole solar system, anything near us in astronomical terms, not just the world lines of ourselves, of humans."

"OK, I get it." I say, "When did you learn relativity?"

"Yesterday. I was trying to read anything that may be related to us. OK, then there is some mysterious wave, spacetime wave that vibrates both lines." Muse draws two curly lines, like the sine cosine curves we learned. "Then suddenly world lines a and b have some intersection points, so these two parallel lines collide with each other, like...solar eclipses. These caused the merging or colliding of our memories from both world lines, and so after such a merging you basically cannot tell which world line you are from."

"I see. So in world line b, Yan and Oliver broke all the glass panels during the dinner on Day one, but in our own world line a, they restrained themselves, or maybe just because Yan had some wine in b. Then back on Day two, two of us were surprised to see the glass panels all fixed, nice and clean, but we still had the memory from b, because of an intersection, which happened some time late night on Day one or early morning on Day two, while we were sleeping."

"Yes. So when we woke up, we basically had conflicting memories, and the one where Yan and Oliver broke glass doors was more impressive, of course. But I don't know why other people didn't have the same conflicting memory problem."

"No idea... Maybe this memory crossing only happened to only a small number of us each time. Or, maybe it is more like a dream that you only remember by a small chance."

"You were so funny when you knocked the glass doors and watched other people's reactions." Muse laughs.

"You were the only one coming to talk about it. I felt so relieved that it was not my own brain problem, and we were stupid and believed that the aliens took care of the debris and repaired everything, including others' memories; and of course the cat denied it, for no reason we thought, and it puzzled us a lot."

"I think this is a better explanation." Muse points to the picture, "Better than all previous theories."

Yeah, other theories, such as that we cycle within these

seven days and have strange memory loss at certain points, or aliens inject pieces of conflicting memories into our brain, or our brains function differently on a new planet and so make more realistic, vivid dreams, or we come to a different parallel universe whenever we sleep and wake up.

"Similarly," Muse continues, "the second of such intersection was on Day three, around noon. In our own world line a, Dennis left with the railgun, and in the other, he and the explorers left early without receiving the railgun. Your boys even played with it for a long time. That was why in the afternoon we again felt strange that Dennis brought back a railgun."

This also made me believe that two of us are somewhat special — I received a clear message and made my ultimate decision within the third daylight.

"But in both of them, the glass panels were intact." I find something strange, "No broken glass in either scene."

"I agree. So the one where Dennis left without railgun is not this b, and let's call it c instead. It is yet another parallel universe. There were probably some minor variations with each wave, which made our world line intersect a different world line each time."

"I see. So the most terrifying one is the third one, world line d, where we were attacked by these rabbits."

Oh, I don't want to even recall that. A true nightmare, a total horror, a complete wonder.

"What time did you wake up? I don't remember anything."

"Lemme see, the time, the intersection point, was Day six, early morning, close to dawn. It was so real, otherwise I would believe I merely woke up from a nightmare."

"Sorry I really don't want you to recall, but could you say a few more details?" Muse asks.

It sounds the same as you first claim you don't want to hear my voice again, and then continue to listen to my words.

"...We were on our way back to the hotel, and I was carrying the railgun, on Day five. This part was very strange. Because people didn't come back on Day four, we wouldn't even go out-side on Day five. But, you know, it was like a dream that started nowhere. Maybe along *d*, people did come back on Day four in-stead, but somehow decided another exploration on Day five. The scene was so scary that I couldn't remember events imme-diately before the rabbits along that world line, like a memory loss due to the shock, or maybe I was too tired to focus on anything."

"I think you just need some extra workouts." Muse laughs.

"Then a group of white rabbits, pure white rabbits, attacked us. The railgun was obviously not useful. Nyx and I managed to climb up to a tree, and saw our classmates flooded by the rabbits, one by one. Vincent and Artemis and Zak killed a few, but didn't help much."

"We didn't have food or water, and the tree was surrounded by these rabbits. We stayed there almost through the night, and around the same time when I woke up, close to dawn, I was likely too tired and fell off the tree, pretty dead, either due to falling or by these rabbits. But it was the same feeling as falling off in a dream, and the next moment I was back on my bed. You might call it a dream, but it was too real."

⸺⸺⸺∞◦⟡∞◦⸺⸺⸺

To be honest, I was more shocked by Nyx's story than by the rabbits around us, but I start to forget most of the details, except for the unbelievable lines I wrote down on my notes. The best way to prove this is to ask Nyx here directly in our current world line, but I am too timid to face a real goddess. How would I start the conversation then? *I had a nightmare this morning. Do you know some oneiromancy?*

At least I learned that the Bronze medal from Fortune-Telling Olympic Games was actually a joke by Nyx herself. Silver went to the Oracle of Delphi, of course; and the Gold was won by a black cat, back in ancient Egypt. And Minos was one of the pseudonyms of Poseidon, Dennis' grandpa, or the name of the bull, which was a conceptualization or a disguise of Poseidon's sleeping with the commonly-known King Minos' wife.

Finally I got a Lucky item on that tree on Day six before I fell off: The Red Moon. Nyx said it has been in the system for thousands of years, but on the Earth you need a total lunar eclipse at that location on that day for this item to make sense, so has been ignored ever since, just like a computer program popping out a warning message that today's date is not good for it. I was the first human who actually got this Lucky item, in the long history of mankind.

Together with the Lucky item I also got a strange oracle: "If you fail to select something, you will find them in the sky", though I still don't see what could happen with it. Them? What could be in the sky? Moons? Stars? Rainbows? Eagles? Goddesses? Or alien spaceships?

Anyway, back to the "Red Moon", could someone get it as a Lucky item but the total lunar eclipse would happen on the other side of the Earth within the same day, and they might fly to that location? "No." She responded, "The algorithm has the location as an input parameter, and automatically calculates solar and lunar eclipses with it. I adjusted the algorithm on Day two based on what the cat told me, and that was why the preparation took longer than usual."

Well, this was the easiest way of introducing bugs, especially in another solar system, in my humble opinion. Could this Red Moon be a bug as well? "No." She responded again, "I spent a whole night plus almost a whole day, working with bug-fixes in my room, and then applied some final adjustment after I saw the red moon. The algorithm is good now."

A typical programmer story. You spend ten minutes making some "quick" adjustments, and then spend the rest of your life trying to figure out how the bug is introduced into the system and how to fix the bug without interfering with other things. I bet Bran has even more such stories to tell regarding bugs.

Maybe someone with a higher rank than you could bypass

whatever filter criteria by some weird logical bug so automatically get a Lucky item each time? "No." She answered the third time, "I am 1. It is impossible for you little kids to know more things than I do. I didn't even look at the last page, but I will take a look if we can make it back."

However, this is not the rarest Lucky item from the list. At least Vincent's grandpa, Hades — oh, he is a god so does not count — got it once, but it was all rainy that night, and he got so upset that he claimed to send everyone to the underworld where everything is red by the old-world mythology. This story tells you — the weather system is so unpredictable, even to the gods.

The rarest Lucky item is called "Devil's Horns", or some unknown mythical creature's teeth in a very ancient language. Of course, there are no devils in our world, so you can only get it when there is a raising or setting sun under an eclipse at the right visual phase, right above the horizon at your current location. No one has ever had it, not even the gods.

Oh! What happens to the King of the Gods — who is so lucky, to be an offspring of Zeus? "We don't say *die* or *pass away* with gods, but the King of the Gods has *rested*, since the *Pestilentia* or the Black Death, otherwise how could you mortals have a chance, to learn the lightning power of the Gods?"

⸺∘◦⸎◦∘⸺

Muse puts down another intersection on the note and stares for a while, "So that is *d*. I believe Jack is currently in the same or a similar situation, hiding himself from the rabbits. If he had prepared enough food and water in his backpack, then he can make it. Wait, there is probably another one, Day four, late night. Then all these intersection points line up in fixed intervals, almost perfectly."

I see it from the graph now. Muse's mathematical instinct is very accurate, as always. I close my eyes trying to recall what was unusual, on Day four.

"Day four, we were worried about the large group of people who didn't come back, and the rest of us saw two moons on the sky..." Muse tries to recall as well.

"Maybe along the other world line, say *e*, we were essentially doing the same thing, and were stunned by the moons. One moment, I somehow remember Jack was with me and was telling a bad joke then. I thought it was a dream, because here Jack went out with the explorers, total of eleven of them, disappeared in the woods. Once I understand the principle behind it, it now feels natural."

"OK, I see. This might be from world line *e*. I didn't remember anything from it on Day five or Day six. So it is likely that different people may or may not witness the intersection each time. In fact, this intersection happened around midnight so it was more like a dream to most people who witnessed it, and so people soon forgot. The same works for this *d*, which happened in the early morning."

Interesting, but I didn't feel anything was wrong on Day five either, otherwise I would have discussed this with Muse. So where did this *e* come from? Some pieces of memory there are coming together: Oh, Eos, and Iris? Why are you so stupid? I need to tell this stupid guy not to choose Iris, but I don't know how... You are 1, right? Use your brain! Work with your logic! You saw it by your own eyes! Iris saw the eclipse in the morning, but refused to accept your explanation in the afternoon. You must know something was wrong with Iris! She was more interested in the plan! All the time! She was worried that your plan would ruin hers!

But I don't understand, just curious, why did the eclipse changed her mind, at least temporarily? Maybe it was too shocking? Anyway, Eos or Muse, please! Both are good girls. Even Nyx is good, a good g...goddess. Please, please, please! Hear my voice, your own voice! Damn! It is too late by now. Even if it's too late, please hear your own voice!

"Maybe it is my own brain problem." I say.

"Probably not. So, my story: It happened to me right before solar noon today. I also had this strange feeling, or memory, that I was crying, and you and Jack were...hugging each other, crying as well, in the lobby."

"What? How? Jack with me? We are not..." I am very confused, "It is definitely your own weird imagination, I think. Jack and I are good friends, but we don't have any other strange relationship as you have imagined. I love you, you know, not Jack." I try to explain to my bride.

At least three of us were in the hotel at noon today, which is much better than what had happened here.

"I can feel it is real, like in previous intersections, but I still cannot grasp the other details because I was crying, too emotional. Some pieces of information are not making sense. Eos...she...I see. So you didn't witness this intersection then. Let's call it world line f."

I don't know what Eos has learned or what you have learned about what Eos has learned, but there is also this time reversal and even crazier things which are too ridiculous and I don't want to mention right now, from world line e as I remember.

"Eos has been upstairs." I say carefully.

I just missed this f, and then the next intersection will be tomorrow, dinner time...Please, send my message!

"I know. In fact, I also know a secret magic spell that can summon her downstairs, within less than a minute." Muse says and smiles at me.

"Spell? What is it?"

When did you learn some secret spells from Nyx? She didn't mention anything to me!

"Assuming she still remembers, you just make an announcement: *Eos, I love you! Two of us form a finite simple group of order two!*"

"I, I would never do, do that! I, I swear to you, my, my goddess!" Too bad! My bride probably has noticed some sneaky eye contacts between Eos and me, and so tries to warn me before anything real happens. I have never thought about it! It was Eos who was staring at me!

But I don't believe she will come downstairs just by a finite simple announcement. What is a finite simple group, by the way?

"Anyway, now it seems clear that the intersection points happen in certain time intervals, like periods of the sine cosine curve —" Muse concludes, "Possibly caused by some kind of spacetime ripples left by their spaceship crossing this region. It is totally reasonable for a spaceship close to the speed of light to leave some traces behind."

Safe. I take a deep breath and get a vivid feeling of my very existence, but my heart is still beating like a hammer. I then close my eyes and start to imagine the picture of a boat crossing a river, leaving regular ripples on the water behind it.

"It feels like it."

This water is so calm and alluring, even only in my imagination.

"By the way, this planet or this solar system is *not* in our old Milky Way Galaxy." Muse says.

"What? Isn't it only five thousand light years away?"

"It is a *spacetime* distance. Eos was the first one to realize this, but she...probably forgot. In astronomical settings, according to relativity, there is no consensus of time or distance between two distant events, and so the cat simply cannot even give you a meaningful 'space distance' between the old Earth and the new Earth, especially when we are likely at the other end of the universe." She says.

Well, I finished the first four hundred meters in a marathon, and then someone joked that my goddess is on the moon; I later believed that we are five thousand light years away, still not crazy, in the same galaxy at least, but now you are telling me that we are on the other side of the universe!

And that someone is back, before I can dig into the details.

xlii   Finale

We all thought Jack might be very pale or even severely injured, but he looks very much healthy, except maybe for some lack of sleep. Hera runs to embrace him, crying. In contrast, Muse takes my arm and leans against me, shaking a bit, excited.

Jack looks at us for a few seconds and seems to understand what has happened, in the marriage game. Sorry, most people thought you were dead, my friend, and this is the most secure way to earn enough money to save you, and I no longer trust the other girls in the hotel, except maybe Nyx and Eos.

"Let's sit down, and I have a big secret to tell you guys." Jack says.

"Do you want to have a rest first, big boy, then you can share your story and your big secret?" Muse says.

"It is a big big secret and I won't be able to fall asleep with it! I am serious, and I feel pretty good. Those fruits saved me, otherwise I would be dehydrated very quickly."

"Ha-ha! Now you see the Element of Life is Water!" I shout.

"True, but once you have seen the verge between life and death, all other things are almost trivial now, believe me." Jack says, "By the way, could you turn off the lights? I guess after three days with all natural light, I don't like this artificial light anymore."

Three days. I feel so bad. Did the fruits make your brain brighter? Is it the same secret, about time? Or, the other side of the universe?

"OK, so what is the secret?" I ask.

We sit down in the lounge, four of us.

"Do you still remember this *many-worlds interpretation* of bridge games we once talked about?" Jack asks.

"Roughly. It was from quantum physics, right?" Muse says.

"It would be better if you refresh our minds another time." I say, "My brain is not functioning well since the start of Day one."

"OK. When we think of a bridge game where you cannot see your opponents' cards, the classical way is to say the cards have been determined but it is just a probability game when you go through many many similar games. OK, for example, when you are the declarer, the South, and you have the Ace in hand, and dummy, the North, has the Queen and the Ten, then it matters who holds the King and who has the Jack among the two defenders, right?"

"Right." This is a very classical case.

"Let us assume for the sake of this discussion that the King and the Jack are not in the same hand. So the classical interpretation is that, in that particular game, the cards have been determined, but we still say the probability is half-and-half, because if we run many many such games into a similar scenario, then about half of the time, the King is to your left and Jack is right." Jack says.

OK. Why don't you use an easier example for the Queen? You just want to say *Jack is right*, right?

"Now in the many-worlds interpretation, this probability refers to what is happening in that particular game, and the cards in the defender's hands are in some weird quantum-ish state, that you cannot tell exactly, until they show you what they have in hand. More precisely, there are many parallel universes that agree on everything else, but in about half of them the King is to your left and Jack is right."

"I know Jack is right, you don't have to emphasize it." I joke.

The damn parallel universe.

"I remember now, this many-worlds interpretation does not actually change anything." Hera says, "The probabilities all remain the same. That was our conclusion earlier."

"One moment, if my understanding of quantum mechanics is correct, as I learned yesterday, your left, the West, is another observer and they can turn this weird quantum state to a fixed card. You may not know it, but your opponents have already known it. Is it a contradiction?" Muse asks.

You learned relativity and quantum physics within one day?

"No. It is somehow different from quantum mechanics. You, are the only observer from your own perspective. Other players may know the cards, as observers, but as long as they do not tell you anything, from your own perspective, all these different parallel universes are all possible. You are like, a protagonist in a novel, with first person point-of-view; To you, as long as nothing has been written down as words, everything is possible." Jack says.

"I see." Muse says.

To be honest, I start to feel a bit confused with quantum mechanics.

"OK, now think about the question, 'who—are—you'." Jack says, pointing to me.

"*Who I am* or *who we are*?" I am puzzled.

"Sorry, the singular you."

"OK, I am...what I am...a human...maybe." I am not exactly sure whether I can be called a human, but, anyway.

"No! You are not alone! You, the singular you, is not just one person! This is the fun part!" Jack says with excitement.

"What? You said it is singular."

"Right, the singular 'you'. In this many-worlds interpretation, there are many many copies of yourself, living in different parallel universes, with exactly the same memory." Jack says.

"OK, but these parallel copies of myself have nothing to do with *me*, my current self, right?" I ask.

"Ha-ha. Let me use an example. Suppose there are two of such universes with some other differences, but the two copies of you inside these two universes have exactly the same life, same experience, same mom and dad, same memory, same everything." Jack says.

"Ah — then you are not able to tell which universe you are from..." Muse says, "This is like, you are living in these two universes at the same time!"

"Right! Very correct! You, the singular you, present tense, is *the collection of bodies among all parallel universes with the exact same memory that you have right now*. Not one person, but many many persons." Jack says.

This sounds ridiculous, but very true. The world around us suddenly feels different. I want eat more of those fruits later.

"So what you say is, 'I' is really 'we', and 'he' or 'she' are rather 'they', since everyone is plural by themselves?" I ask.

"Yes, I think so, sorry...we think so."

"Ha-ha, it is too confusing, Jack. Let us switch back and speak common language." I say.

"We agree. Sorry, I agree. Now, let the time start to run, then you are like a stream or a flow of these bodies, that changes as your memory changes. Say we play a game, and you have both the Ace and the King in hand, and you decide to draw both, the order does not matter much of course."

"OK."

"So your stream splits into two smaller streams, one with the Ace first and the other with the King. Say at first you still have the short-time memory that you drew the Ace first, so you become this smaller stream with the memory of drawing the Ace first. After playing a few more games, you simply cannot remember which one you drew first, the Ace or the King, then you, as a stream, merge with the other stream where you drew the King first." Jack explains.

"The same argument works for all other things." Muse says.

"Yes, exactly, the same works for all other things. Whenever you make a decision, choose one from two, the stream splits; when you forget about it, the streams merge again. It all depends on your current memory, every universe that is consistent with your memory remains and all inconsistent ones are ruled out from you, the stream." Jack says.

"As the stream flows, it is more like a net." I say.

"Good point, yes, I agree it is more like a net if you look at the big picture." Jack says, "You are basically flowing through this net of streams, based on your memory."

"What if we have conflicting memories?" Muse asks.

Good question. We are having them right now.

"It means that two streams with conflicting facts, or inconsistencies, merged for whatever reason, and you see both are possible." Jack replies after some thinking, "I believe your brain will do the work for you, regarding the version which is inconsistent with your current environment as a dream, and eventually only keep the other one."

Right. It feels exactly the same. I guess eventually I will forget about these dreams. But, doesn't it mean that our dreams could be our memories from other parallel universes? I shake my head. This starts to be really confusing.

"Everything depends on the existence of parallel universes, right?" Hera asks.

"Yes, and now I have some strong evidence of these parallel universes. Think about the following scenario. In our first example, the King and the Jack, suppose someone set up a strange mechanism that would shoot you dead by a gun say, whenever the left shows the Jack to you."

"What?"

"I see what you mean. Assuming you are still alive after the game, then the King is always to your left and Jack is right." Muse says.

"You, the stream, is cut down by a half due to the killing mechanism, but you are still flowing." I also see the point now.

"Yes! Yes! These parallel universes where you are dead, where Jack is not right, no longer exist, from your own perspective. It is like eliminating half of the parallel universes, but does not really damage your own identity, your own flow, since half of the universes are still left. In the classical interpretation, if you are dead, then you are dead, permanently." Jack says, with excitement.

"Wouldn't you feel strange that, after you have played many many games, that all the Kings are to the left and Jack is always right? Your stream is getting thinner and thinner." I ask.

"There are infinitely many parallel universes, according the standard theory." Muse says, "So your stream will never run out. It is exactly the same as in a strict single first-person point-of-view novel, the protagonist cannot die, because otherwise there is no way to continue the novel unless you switch to a different point-of-view or to third-person."

"Right, the stream will never run out. Then you know there is some mechanism which makes you alive along the games, ironically by killing you along other parallel universes. What I really want to say is, all these parallel universes that you are dead simply do not exist, from your own perspective." Jack says.

Right, everything follows naturally.

"What happens if the mechanism in addition kills your partner, the North, if the King is left and Jack is right?" I ask.

"Then one of you two die. From your own perspective, your partner dies. From their perspective, you die. You are separated from them in terms of streams or parallel universes, sadly."

"I see. No contradiction here." Muse says.

"Interesting. Say if I hold the railgun to shoot you — Then from my perspective, you almost always die; but from your perspective, it is most likely that the gun will explode in my hands?"

"Right, right...that is, a good, example, but please, please, do not, do it." Jack stutters.

"Ha-ha. Just joking, Jack. Don't be afraid."

I don't know why but Muse trembles as well, by my side. It's just a joke!

"Thanks. I have another interesting example." Jack continues, "Suppose you have a classical love triangle problem, choosing between two boys, or two girls. Choose one, everyone survives; choose the other, everyone dies. Of course, you do not know this at the time of your decision."

"OK." So you were pretty boring on that tree.

"Which one would you choose?" Jack asks.

"I see. You always choose the correct one, because in the other world line you are dead." Muse says.

I see it as well. These white rabbits. That universe is dead from my own perspective, because I am dead there.

"So, the rabbits are in pure white fur, right, Jack?" I ask, slowly.

"How do you know that? I haven't even mentioned anything! Oh, have you seen these near the hotel? Have they killed anyone here? Sorry I forgot to ask, how is everyone else here in the hotel?"

"No, we haven't seen them in this universe. I was in one of those parallel universes, on a tree without fruits, directly facing these white demons, and very much dead I believe." I say, "And everyone here in the hotel has been...safe."

Safe, but not in good shape. Sorry, Jack, it is better if you don't know it.

"Oh, I had the opposite experience, facing them here in this parallel universe, but I don't understand why I still have the memory from another parallel universe. If my theory is correct, then I shouldn't remember anything from other universes." Jack says.

"We were actually discussing this before you arrived." Muse says, showing Jack the picture, "Now I understand why we are here, in this parallel universe, world line *a* in my picture."

"Why?"

"*We live in the best of all possible worlds.*"

"Leibniz?" I ask.

"Yes, but for a different reason. In the other worlds, at least some of them, we are dead by now." Muse says, "In *b*, the broken glass doors, most likely the rabbits rushed into the hotel and killed all of us, sooner or later. In *d*, you were dead as well. In *c*, I cannot exactly tell, maybe something wrong happened to the railgun? Someone fired it and killed us?"

"We only had one gun with four shots, right? Maybe I was the unlucky victim again." I say, "But I get what you mean, whenever we are dead, we automatically switch to a parallel universe, closest to us, where we are still alive."

One or two railguns? I have conflicting memories again.

Jack looks at the picture, "I see your theory now. Very interesting. Explains a lot of things. I don't remember *b*, and only vaguely remember *c*; maybe they were too far away from now and I start to forget, like dreams. I do remember something from *d* actually. I was still on the tree at that time in *a*, waiting for the dawn of Day six, then suddenly memories flushed into my brain, that I was back in the hotel, with Tim and some other boys, and you two and some other girls had been out for a picnic. For whatever reason, I was very against this — that you took the railgun and led the team out for picnic — you may call it was my intuition, my sixth sense. But as I had the bad feeling, people didn't come back, and we were worried throughout the night. The cat was asking a price that we couldn't afford, and you took the only railgun, otherwise we may go outside to search for you guys. That was probably from this *d*."

Muse trembles again, so I take her hand by mine. Don't worry, my dear, it won't happen again in our world line.

"There was almost no way to save us in that world line, I think. No food, no water, too many rabbits. Even if you came with another railgun, it wouldn't be useful at all. They can kill you in a few seconds." I say, "Maybe...the only possible way was to ask the cat to deliver some food to us, and to wait for Day seven for the extra money, but it was hard to see this option at that time, just like what we have experienced here in this world line."

"No — remember we cannot deliver to another person, otherwise we could send secret love letters. But if we had another railgun, I could fire it far away from the rabbits, and knock down some trees, which would scare them away. This was how the robots saved me. I know, as you said, it was hard to see this option at that time."

Oh, that was the earthquake.

"No, Jack, you won't be able to fire it as accurately as the robots do, and even worse you may kill us first." I laugh, 'But I still don't remember why I was chosen to lead the team and carry the railgun along this d. Do you remember?"

"This was a bit twisted, and you shouldn't remember I need to say. It was a trickery. The boys pretended to have a fight in the morning, and forced some depressed people out of their rooms to have a picnic. You guys need to enjoy the beauty of the nature here on a new planet."

"So I was depressed."

"Right, because you had not been paired up by then in d. 'Not even a trace of it', in your own words."

Ah...that was why I put this period of memory in my miserable region and try to forget about it. My brain is processing it, automatically. Other pieces of overlapping memory with Iris or Eos are obviously more interesting or more valuable.

"Tim later told us that you had a brilliant idea for the matching game, but you need two top ten couples. So it would be a great chance for you to talk to the girls in a picnic — ha ha, so you are yourself a top ten, right?"

I see it now. Without distractions from the girls, I probably spent most of my time focusing on the games, and worked out this brilliant plan. 10 is a magic number and I worked over my plan based on it, so that...I have a better chance to pair up with a girl — Quite ashamed I need to say.

So which of the girls were still available there? Eos, the cat and the math girl; Iris, the short hair and the literature girl; Nyx, the fortune-teller and the goddess; Pheme and Kakia the party girls and the gossip girls but they were drunk so didn't go out on Day five; Muse, my real goddess; Hera...paired up with Yan on Day four — though I have conflicting memories about exactly when it happened, either in the morning or in the afternoon — so Hera didn't join the picnic either; Hmmm, what happened here in our own world line? Why didn't they pair up? And then...Gaia? Some conflicting memories again, but it feels right — if Iris and I didn't pair up, then Frank and Gaia wouldn't pair up that early. Follow the logic.

"So Gaia was out for picnic as well?" I ask.

"Hmmm...I think so. Why do you ask?" Jack thinks for a while and answers.

So the number became eleven again this time. Our CFT is absolutely right. *Eleven means death*. Oh, we had only ten when we departed, but Vincent later joined us, and that was why Nyx was so upset when she saw Vincent, and as a result I didn't even have a chance to interview her at the beach. She really doesn't like Hades, at all.

When or where or which world line did she say that?

"I don't remember exactly, or I have conflicting memories." I ask carefully, "By the way, just curious, were you the one who noticed the fruit trees, on Day four, in our own world line a here?"

"Yes. How do you know that? People were chatting about how to open 1's mouth on the way back, and I saw these trees. We stayed for a while to pick some, and I was also a bit curious. Hard to imagine they saved me."

And they killed the other guys, because no one had brought back fruits on Day four.

"You are always lucky, like in bridge games."

"OK. Whenever you say 'just curious', usually something huge is hidden behind it. My life experience — Cats don't work well with curiosity." Jack laughs.

"Sorry..."

Sorry, I don't want to make you feel sad about it. It is better if you don't know it, again.

"Never mind. In fact, I also have memory from e, a joke, no, it is not this e — I didn't feel anything strange on Day five in our world line a — but an e' which I inherited along d. Like it is an extra branch, with a point where d and e' intersect, and when memories from a and d merged I obtained the memory of both d and e' at the same time." Jack says after a while.

Interesting point. This explains a lot of things.

"What happened there?"

"Everyone was at the hotel, Day four, nighttime, and we saw the two moons. Things became out of control, and Tim tried to resume peace with a railgun, but caused more quarrels. He was trying to keep the barrel pointing to the sky or the ceiling all the time, not pointing to people, but that was the last thing I remember." Jack says.

"Is your joke about Eos and the moons as well?" I ask.

"Yes. Along that world line, you and Eos...Oops, sorry!"

Muse trembles, the third time. I hold her hand a bit tighter. Sorry, but it was in another world line, so don't worry about it here, my dear. Eos...has been upstairs. Or, do you want me to summon her to help explaining everything?

The spell...it is probably about Time I could imagine, but why are you so certain that Eos witnessed f as well?

So at least this Eos is from some other world line where I helped her to see the big secret, like where Jack is from. I close my eyes and try to imagine what may happen if I cast the spell — Ten seconds after the announcement, we would hear a door slam; fifteen seconds later, my lovely Miss 3 would be downstairs in the lounge in her dashing but still elegant steps, with a red face and heavy breath; five more seconds, she would grab me and kiss me without a word, just like that distant afternoon, quite distant indeed.

No, this is not an explanation, but it will ruin everything.

Right, Leo and Frank started the quarrel because she did this to me on Day four, and the quarrel might run out of control if Dennis didn't stop Frank, and so Tim had to get —

One moment, a railgun? Not *the* railgun?

"So do you remember Dennis and the explorers left without the railgun on Day three there, along this e'?" I ask. "Because I don't remember a big quarrel out of control along e."

"I see what you mean. Maybe this caused the quarrel and everything. Sorry it is too hard to keep different versions of memory apart from each other. There is also a small difference in my rank number, but I guess it is not related, random variation." Jack says.

I see. Your memory of c is likely from this e' instead. Ordering two railguns caused some delay, and also significantly increased the possibility of Dennis leaving without a railgun, especially if Tim didn't make an announcement then.

Oh, and if Tim and Rhea didn't pair up on Day two, but on Day three instead like in our own world, then they were not able to order two railguns anyway. So everything depends on...what Nyx told Rhea during that morning session?

"I understand now." Muse says, "Fourth floor, secret room, do you know what is in there?"

Oh, that thing...can kill everyone in less than a second. Wait, why do you know the fusion reactor business?

"So this may be how everything ended in c or in e', or they may be the same world line. In e and f, I don't see why we are dead, but assuming we are here, it is very likely that we are dead in these world lines as well. For example, in f, I may find a railgun to shoot you two, or to the ceiling." Muse laughs.

A railgun, again?

"I know you are kidding, but please don't do that." I say.

"What? Hug? Me? Why?" Jack is very puzzled.

Sorry Jack, it is better if you don't know it, the third time. I don't believe it, either.

"But it is possible that we will die later in our current world line a, I mean, we don't have many people or much resource left, then we automatically switch to another world line where we live longer?" I ask.

"I think so, based on logic and my own experience." Jack says firmly.

"So the saying 'When people die, they go to another world' is totally true. It is just a different parallel universe." I say.

"Ha-ha, this is a good one." Jack says.

"But we are humans, and we eventually die, after one hundred years, within all these parallel universes I believe. What will happen afterwards?" Hera asks.

"Then...we switch to those world lines...with tiny little possibilities where we become...immortal..." Muse says.

When or where or which world line, did you...eat those fruits? Well, there is no need really. *I am lucky in only very few of these worlds, but the wisdom of these Muses dominates almost everywhere.*

And to all the stupid guys — A quick and easy way to rewind everything — borrow that *cotton candy*, and solve the problem in less than a second, easy peasy and "Musy", or, as a backup plan, order a real dessert — yes, you always want a backup plan before the story turns into the worst page — *Three-subprime-One-prime* at the right pressure and temperature, dusted with lots of *Zero prime*, and also solve the problem. 3 and 1, perfect match, perfect fireworks.

I even have a perfect name for it — *the rising sun.*

Yeah, I also tried to order some *One plus conjugate*, or *One conjugate minus*, antiprotons, but they are super expensive and won't do too much damage to QX within *our* cash limit.

Finally, here I had to suspend the plan, as I need cash to save Jack.

"I once thought the aliens may have some secret potions to keep us from aging." Jack says, "But the cat said they do not have such. Or maybe they can convert us into some digital format, and then save us as files in a computer? Honestly I have no idea, but *personal immortality* seems to be the only logical conclusion with the parallel universes."

Personal Immortality. Good summary of everything.

"Anything possible will happen eventually. Even tiny possibilities become real after all other world lines die out." I say, "Our streams flow forever and we become immortal — by the time itself."

I look at Muse with smile, and my bride is staring at me in awe, but soon smiles back. I love her smile, sweet, above all things. It is so addictive.

"Hello, Mr. 1, from e?" Muse says.

"No. I am from d, or rather an e'' along that branch. So world line d observed a very rare three-world intersection, like a dual solar eclipse, at that point, colliding with both e' and e''. Jack witnessed e' and I witnessed e''. There is no e in the picture, because I didn't feel anything strange on Day five here in our own world line a, same as you two mentioned earlier. And I shall say — hello, Miss...6, from f ? Good to see you here."

Five plus one is six. I can do it. I know, you were already dead in d before the intersection. No memory could carry over. It was disconnected from your perspective.

"Good to see you here. Now I even believe e'' and f are in fact the same world line." Muse says.

Impressive. We see each other again in a different universe.

"What happened there on Day six and Day seven?"

I am super curious! I only know half of the story, and you know everything!

"Emmm, long story. First, let me show you various types of eclipses." Muse smiles.

"What? There are different types of eclipses?"

Jack has been quiet, not like his usual self showing off some knowledge. I think he is still in the mood of interpreting or accepting our dialogue.

Hera is staring at the picture, trying to make sense of our enigmatic words.

"What jargon are you whispering about? Eclipse? I still don't understand — Become immortal? We will become gods and goddesses? Are you kidding? Do you seriously believe this?" Hera finally asks.

It is better if you know it, Jack, this time.

"We do." My lovely bride and I look at each other and answer in chorus, as if it is in our marriage ritual.

me vērō prīmum dulces ante omnia Mūsae,
quārum sacra ferō ingenti percussus amore,
accipiant, caelīque vias et sīdera monstrent,
dēfectūs sōlis varios lūnaeque laborēs;

VERGIL, *Georgics*, II.475-8